# HEART'S DARKNESS

Book V of 'The Magician's Brother' Series

HDA Roberts

Cover by Warren Design

# CONTENTS

# CHAPTER 1

As was so often the case, this screw-up started as it meant to go on... badly.

It all began six weeks after my breakup with Cathy, six weeks which I would not be remembering fondly. After too long feeling sorry for myself, I decided that I needed a distraction and, fool that I was, I thought that trying for my Level Ten Magical Proficiency Certificate would be the way to go.

In my defence, it *did* distract me... even if it did absolutely *nothing* for my stress, and this at a time when I was anxiously waiting for my A-level results. All things considered, it was a miracle I made it through without suffering a minor stroke.

Other than the self-flagellation, my life had otherwise been quiet. I hadn't annoyed anyone, insulted any dignitaries, offended any god-like Entities, started any wars or blown anybody up. I was, essentially, minding my own damned business for a change, and yet trouble was *still* quite willing to swoop down and crap all over my head.

On the day it started, I was enjoying the fading August sunshine at a small park in Stonebridge, eating an ice cream and simply relaxing for what felt like the first time in months. It was a very peaceful moment; the tree I was sitting under was shady, the grass was green and the sky clear of clouds; I was surrounded by the happy babble of people having a good time.

I let out a sigh and closed my eyes for a moment, smiling as the cooling breeze washed over me and blew a few of my cares away, even if only for a little while. And then, just as

I was at the most peaceful I'd been in ages, *that's* when I felt the power start to flow. It was a dim thing at first, barely noticeable in the most Magical city in the world, but notable for the fact that it wasn't human, it was Fairy.

I'd barely had the chance to notice it before it was on me... and then *in* me, reaching deep into my chest, where it felt like a great hand had taken a hold of something important and yanked on it, *hard.*

As you might imagine, it hurt. A lot.

I clutched at the spot, right where my heart was, feeling for damage even as my mouth started to open in a scream, only to find that the pain had stolen my breath. I felt nothing wrong, and it didn't take me long to figure out that it wasn't a physical attack at all, it was something much worse. I felt another tug, and then an awful, almost horrifically *slow,* wrench, the pain increasing to something truly monstrous, until the Spell (for that was all it *could* be) finally managed to rip out two pieces of me, of my very soul, if I was any judge, and carry them away.

I finally managed to draw enough breath to scream; an awful sound that spoke of terrible loss and dreadful heartache. I could feel the gaping holes where those parts of me had been, where I'd been attached to something precious to me, something that was now gone...

My screams had drawn stares, and people were coming over to help, bless them. The last thing I saw before I collapsed into darkness were concerned faces and phones put to ears.

I woke up, after a fashion, into a very dark place, not that this was normally a problem for me; darkness and I were old friends. As I became more and more aware, it brightened up a little, revealing my library at Blackhold, the residence of the First Shadow, and my home. I was lying next to the fireplace, which was unlit.

It didn't take long to realise that this wasn't really *my* Blackhold. The place where I lived didn't usually have huge holes in the walls that looked out over a vista of eternal darkness.

"That's just disturbing," said a cheerful, familiar voice from behind me.

I tried to conceal a cringe. If I was where I thought I was, then he was the very *last* person I wanted to see.

"Dare I ask what you're doing in my head, Neil?" I asked as nonchalantly as I could, turning to look at the man who I was fairly certain was the Devil.

He was a stylishly dressed man, appearing to be in his late twenties, with dark hair and sparkling, nearly black, eyes. His face was finely chiselled, with classical features and a vaguely aquiline nose. As always, he was immaculately dressed in a dark suit, carrying a black cane topped with a silver snake's head.

"Sorry if I'm intruding," he said politely, taking a seat on the sofa next to me, "Open goal, and all that."

I rolled my eyes and shifted myself off the floor and into an armchair.

"What happened to me?" I asked.

"Immense damage to your soul," he replied with a smile, pointing his cane at the hole in the wall, which stretched to the floors above and below, "Just be thankful it didn't hit the more delicate parts of your psyche, or you'd never have woken up."

"What did it?" I asked, though I had a fairly good idea. My memories were starting to come back, though they were still a little fuzzy around... whatever had happened to drop me into this state.

"Oh, I couldn't possibly comment," Neil replied smugly, "I'd imagine you'll figure that out on your own, anyway."

"You still haven't told me why you're wondering around inside my head."

"Angels exist to shepherd lost souls, didn't you know? And you are a *very* lost soul."

I gave him a look, which made him smile.

"Fine, I'm here to see if I can prod you over a moral cliff while you're too weak to do anything to stop me, are you happy?"

"Not especially."

He chuckled, "No, I wouldn't be either. You have had a rough run of things lately, haven't you? Demons landing on your head, ancient horrors trying to eat you, that delectable bit of blond goodness giving you the boot..."

"Gloating is a terrible trait in an immortal being."

"That explains why *you* have so many enemies," he replied.

Ouch. He had a point, but still...

"Well, all that's over now. New school, new opportunities. New chances," I said brightly.

The smile on his face turned positively evil, and that is *not* a good look on the bloody *Devil.*

"What?" I asked, perhaps sounding a little exasperated.

"Nothing," he replied, looking away, still smirking.

"Just spill it."

"I am but a poor Angel-"

"Archangel," I interrupted, he pretended not to notice.

"-just a mere servant of the cosmos. What could I possibly know about your upcoming trial against the darkness?"

I gave him a very dry look this time, "Isn't that a touch melodramatic?"

"You're going to lecture *me* about melodrama? With your track record?"

"Do you have to be such a prick about this?"

"I'm the Devil, and you really might consider not being quite so rude to me," he replied, his eyes narrowing.

"Seeing as how you'll likely arrange for unpleasant temptations and calamities whether I kiss your arse or not, I see no particular downside to it."

He laughed again, "Oh, I do like you, Graves. You're quite straightforward for such a fantastic liar."

The Devil liked me... oh dear. As if being kissed (and

groped) by the odd Demon wasn't already enough to explain to St Peter (and that didn't begin to cover the rest of the sinning I enjoyed. My record on Sloth *alone* was going to take some fast talking).

"Hey, I have cut down on the lying!"

He waggled his hand back and forth. I rolled my eyes.

"So... how are you feeling?" he asked, looking right at me.

"That seems like a loaded question."

"And so it is. The damage ripped out some important parts of your emotional core. I can't imagine you'll be entirely stable. Any homicidal urges?"

"One or two," I replied, giving him a glare, "And souls heal."

"Not quickly. You've already begun sliding down a very interesting slope, young Shadow."

"Seriously, *melodrama*."

He harrumphed (yes, I'd made the Devil harrumph), but he didn't look any less amused.

"Deny it all you want, but I'm really going to enjoy this. It's so much fun watching the *really* righteous ones fall to their Demons."

"Oh, is Gabby around?" I asked innocently, looking behind me.

Gabrielle was the Succubus Neil had appointed as his 'liaison' to me, which was really just a euphemism for 'walking temptation'. No doubt he saw the success Tethys had at wrapping me around her little finger and figured *that* was the way to go. If my enemies ever figured out that all they needed to do to get me on side was to send a pretty girl to ask me nicely, I was so screwed...

"You know very well what I mean, stop ruining this for me!"

I chuckled and looked out of the hole in my 'wall'. It was dark out there, but in a familiar way, swirling with dark purples and blues, undulating gently. It was quite relaxing, actually.

"In all seriousness, Graves," he said, his tone taking on a more human note, which brought my attention back with a vengeance, "I owe you for what you did for my Gabrielle. What's coming will be... unpleasant. Try not to die before you've fallen."

His tone was almost... parental.

"I don't suppose you'd like to give me a *clearer* warning?"

He lifted a very expressive eyebrow. I rolled my eyes in reply.

"No, I suppose you really can't."

"Clever boy, you're learning!"

He opened his mouth to say something else, but stopped, cocking his head.

"Ah, good, the damage has healed enough for you to wake up! I leave you with this final thought: if Demonic doesn't always mean 'evil', then can Angelic always mean good?"

"Just what the hell is that supposed to me-" I started, but then everything went a sudden, blinding white, and the world disappeared.

My real eyes snapped open, and I sat up with a start, only to find myself tangled with tubes, catheters and cannulae. I was wearing a hospital gown, which left me feeling exposed. Alarms bleeped madly from a monitor next to the bed...

My bed?

I was a bit groggy, but I recognised my bedroom in Blackhold (the real one, this time). The walls were covered in dark wood panelling, which also made up various shelves full of books, DVDs and electronics. There was an open door opposite the bed, which led to the bathroom and a closed one to my left, which led to the rest of the house.

The conversation with Neil was fading like a bad dream, and I desperately tried to hang onto the details even as I was panicking slightly from the jarring transitions. I did my best to slow my breathing, as I'd been taught, but before I could really get started, the door to the corridor burst open and a complete stranger came rushing in.

She was dressed all in white, middle aged with steel-grey hair and beefy arms. She had a nurse's watch pinned to her lapel and a phone in her hand, which seemed to be beeping in time to the alarms next to my bed.

"Stop that, you'll tear your tubes out!" she snapped, shoving me back down, which hurt and served to further fray some badly jangled nerves.

I noticed a pain in my chest that only seemed to intensify as I became more and more aware of it. It was hard to describe, almost like a physical manifestation of loss, of *grief*. It was horrible, and it was making me more anxious with each passing moment. I wanted to run, to move, to *scream*, and I didn't appreciate this behemoth of a woman shoving me around like a slab of meat.

"Get off me!" I shouted, still disoriented, still groggy, and now veering towards panic.

She didn't listen; in fact, she shoved even harder on my torso, right where that aching wound was. That turned the pain up to eleven and really was the last straw.

Entirely on instinct, reacting to the sudden pain, a tendril of hardened Shadow came out from under the bed and swatted her like a fly. She flew through the doorway and into the wall opposite, where she fell to the ground in a heap. She was already stirring to come at me again (I hadn't hit her too hard, thank God), and I didn't like the look in her eyes.

I threw together a quick Sleep Hex and put her down properly before she could break my neck (it was *that* sort of look she had on her face).

Before anything else could come at me, I started yanking the tubes and monitoring things off (and out) of me. The ones in my plumbing were the most painful, but I wanted out of that bed. I was functioning on some sort of fear response, even though, objectively, there was nothing to be afraid of. I was in Blackhold, the safest place in the country for me to be. I could feel the power of the place, the active defences that meant destruction for anything or anyone meaning me harm, and yet I was still practically on the verge of hysteria. I felt almost like a cornered animal.

And there was *still* that pain in my chest, driving those emotions, making them worse.

It *was* grief, I could understand that much, but couldn't begin to reason why I felt that way. Nobody I knew had died, to my knowledge. It was confusing me, driving me to distraction; I suddenly felt tears in my eyes that had nothing to do with pulling a tube out of my bits (though that hadn't been pleasant...).

I finished freeing myself and tried to stand, only to discover that my legs weren't working properly. I fell to the carpet, the tears in my eyes flowing freely as I gathered my Shadows to me and they propped me up. An effort of Magically-infused Will got me moving towards the door. I had to find Tethys, or Cassandra. They'd know what was going on.

I staggered into the corridor, checking for more nurses who might be lurking. Wait... nurse? I looked her over, and the details I'd noticed earlier began to crystallise at last. That left me feeling terribly ashamed of myself. My household had obviously arranged for this woman to come in and take care of my needs while I was healing... and I'd knocked her out.

I would have to make that right somehow, but not this minute. I needed answers.

I cast Mage Sight and looked around. I relaxed slightly as I saw that people were coming, likely attracted by the noise (or by the sentient book running the house's defences telling someone to come help me before I did something stupid). I still almost conjured my shields, I was that amped up, almost paranoid.

"Matty!" I turned to see Tethys sprinting for me, and I relaxed a little more. She almost leapt into my arms, wrapping her own around me and squeezing me tightly to her.

Tethys was the kind of beautiful that has started wars in times gone by. She was tall and statuesque, pale skinned, with a soft, heart-shaped face, full, kissable lips and deep violet eyes framed by long and slightly curly ebony hair. Her normally elegant wardrobe had been replaced by jeans and a cotton shirt, with no jewellery except for my signet ring on her left pinkie. She radiated sensuality in the way only a Succubus can, but it had been a long time since I'd learned to look past that and to the wonderful friend that lived underneath. She and I were very close, closer than I was to anyone, in fact, especially in those days.

"What happened?" I whispered, barely containing my tears, keeping the strain from my voice by sheer stubborn willpower, "I feel like I lost someone, but I can't remember who..."

"Hush, Matty, it's alright, I'll explain everything, just breathe. Relax, calm," she said. She kissed my cheek and stroked my hair, "And easy with those Shadows, they're coming up on some very intimate places!"

"Sorry," I said, noticing that my constructs had wrapped themselves around us to the waist. I concentrated, but they didn't budge, "Damn, my focus is all messed up."

I gritted my teeth and they slowly slithered away, back into the recesses, except for the ones that were keeping my legs and back straight.

"Better," she said, cupping my face before taking me by the hand, leading me back towards my bedroom on my shaky legs.

She settled me on a sofa and gestured at the woman on the floor.

"Why'd you swat the nurse?" she asked with a grin.

"She startled me, tried to hold me down, I didn't mean to," I said softly, "She's only sleeping, not hurt."

I started to shiver. Tethys brought me a blanket and wrapped it around me, rubbing my shoulders.

"Okay," she said, "first, you've been out for two weeks,

this is day fifteen."

I blinked. That would explain why I felt so weak. But... two weeks? My parents must be a wreck by now.

Before she could continue, Demise and Cassandra came barrelling in, both of them were carrying weapons, a pair of pistols for Cassandra and a black rod for Demise. Their faces drained of tension when they saw me conscious.

Cassandra Vallaincourt was my Warden Commander, sort of my chief bodyguard. She was a tall woman with black hair and classically beautiful features, built like a gymnast, but stronger than an ox. She wore a conservative suit, black with a white blouse, very neat and tidy. She was like the sister I never had, the one who kept me humble and grounded, my rock in many ways.

The other, Demise, was also a Warden, a Death Mage of whopping skill and power. She was a little shorter than Cassandra, but more severely beautiful, with dark brown hair and eyes. She was whipcord thin and looked deadly, even at rest. Trust me when I say that the 'look' badly understated what that woman could do if she was angry.

The pair darted for me, almost tripping each other over in their haste.

"Thank God," Cassandra said, kneeling next to me. She gave me a hug before gently punching my arm, "Never do that to me again, you bastard!"

"Sorry," I said, smiling at her.

"You said that the last time," Demise added, touching my cheek gently. She wasn't given to public displays of affection; for her, that was almost a loss of control.

"What do you remember?" Cassandra asked.

"Pain then passing out. Hopefully without peeing myself," I said.

"Nope, sorry," Cassandra said, "and drool."

"Crap," I said with a sigh.

"That too," Cassandra replied, with a little too much relish.

"Oh, come on!"

"Just kidding, just kidding. Wake up, you've had two weeks napping, you should be more alert than this!" Cassandra teased.

"I hate you," I said.

She thumped me again, just as gently.

"What hit me?" I asked.

They looked at each other pointedly, as if trying to get one another to tell me what had happened.

"Just one of you spill it," I said, "I'm not going to keel over... again."

"Lady Palmyra figured it out. It was the Fairies, Matty," Tethys said, "After you collapsed, they sealed themselves off, blocking all the ways in and out of their Realms, which meant that the princesses couldn't visit you any longer."

Tethys' eyes took on a furious look for a moment before she continued.

"As you know, those princesses were bound to you. If they couldn't be with you, it was likely they would eventually go insane, or wither away, so the Queens... they carved off enough of you that the princesses would be able to survive without you. They essentially ripped the links out of you, root and branch."

"It's like they died," I said quietly, "It feels like I lost them."

Cassandra sighed before gently laying a hand on mine, "You *did*, Matty. They're gone. When the Fae cut themselves off like this... it's not a frivolous act. The last separation lasted two hundred years."

I looked down. Damn, but it hurt. And it was so much worse now that I knew what I was missing. I wrapped my arms around my chest, feeling exposed and miserable. It seemed that everyone I cared for was being taken away from me, one precious person at a time.

And then an even worse thought hit me.

"The Grotto!" I said, darting to my feet, before falling

right back into my seat again.

"It's okay, they're still there, they're *all* still there," Cassandra said, "the Pixies have been sleeping in with you at night; they all send their best."

I was truly grateful for that, I didn't know what I'd have done if I'd lost them too.

"They're okay with that? Being cut off from their home?" I asked, worried for them.

"They wanted to be there," Tethys explained, "Don't worry about them. And just so you know, the population has rather increased since you were last there. It's now sort of an exiles' stronghold."

I rubbed my eyes again.

I was saved from any further response when Tethys' phone rang. She pressed the ignore key, and then it buzzed to indicate a text. She scoffed and picked it up. Her eyes went wide.

"What?" I asked.

"I don't know yet," Tethys said, she looked like she'd return the call there and then, but took a look at me and stood, heading for the door.

"Dee, go eavesdrop, will you?" I asked, worried. Knowing Tethys like I did, she'd left because there was a problem I would normally deal with, but which she felt I was too battered to handle at the moment.

"Don't you dare!" Cassandra said as Demise stood up.

"Either she goes or I go," I said, but Tethys came back before the argument could be resolved.

"The Red Carpet's under attack," she said, her face was white, her expression afraid.

Now? More or less the *second* I'd woken up? That was just the tiniest bit suspicious...

Of course, that was far from the most important thought of the moment.

"Who would dare?" I asked, getting unsteadily to my feet. They were under *my* protection; a fact that had been firmly hammered into the few idiots who'd had a problem with them settling in Stonebridge (once using an *actual* hammer).

"Sit back down, Matty," Cassandra said, "I'll deal with this."

And she was out the door before I could argue.

"Who's attacking?" I asked, unwilling to just leave it at that.

"That's the bad news, Matty. As far as I can tell from Price's rather panicked warbling, it's the Champions."

Oh dear...

"Dee, stop Cassandra right now, sit on her if you have to!" I said to Demise, who nodded and was through the door just as quickly as Cassandra. I wrapped myself in Shadows so I could stand again, and used my Will to pull a set of clothes towards me. I quickly dressed in tracksuit bottoms, t-shirt, hooded sweater and trainers while Tethys watched, glaring.

"Matty, look at me," she said.

I turned.

"Let your Wardens go. You've been awake for less than an hour; you can barely *stand.* Don't go," she said, her voice very quiet.

"I gave them my word, Tethys. They're my people. Karina's there, and Crystal."

Karina was Tethys' sister. It said something about how worried she was about my condition that she wanted me to sit this one out.

"They can take care of themselves," she said, a little doubtfully.

"Against anything else, I might agree, but we're talking about the *Champions*, Tethys. Nobody wins against the Champions. They're relentless. If they've come for Price, even her Fortress Shield isn't going to keep them out for long."

"And you think *you* can stop them?" Tethys asked, "Them?!"

"I'm in that sort of mood. And... and it seems a bit too

much of a coincidence that I woke up at just the right time to intervene in this. I think someone's playing silly buggers again."

That idea was *really* worrying me. Perhaps I was just being paranoid, but better safe than sorry when the Devil was poking around inside your head.

I applied a little Will and the blinds closed, filling the room with soothing darkness. My Magic was a lot closer to the surface now, easier to get to, easier to use, like there was a thinner barrier between me and my Well. It was exhilarating, but also a little worrying. It was almost more of an effort to do things *without* Magic. I should probably keep an eye on that...

"Call Hopkins for me?" I asked.

"Sure Matty, be careful?" Tethys replied.

"Always," I said with a smile.

I looked for a deep patch of Shadow and opened at Gateway into the Shadow Realm.

I loved it in there; it was peaceful and so quiet. It was a reflection of the entire world, almost a negative image, where every non-living object had a mirror, and every Shadow in our world could be seen as mist. In there, I could go anywhere, listen to any conversation within hearing of a Shadow and call on its inhabitants when I was in need of a helping hand.

Quite a few of those inhabitants were nearby, as a matter of fact, floating gently in the dark, at once part of it and separate from it, taking the forms of various aquatic creatures when summoned to the Newtonian World. In their natural environment, they were simply deeper patches of contented darkness. I would have chatted with them (in as much as I could, they weren't especially chatty beings), but I had to get to the Red Carpet.

I focussed intently on its location and drew it to me.

The *original* Red Carpet had been a... well, let's call a spade a spade, it was a brothel. One run and staffed by supernatural creatures, mostly Vampires, but also Lycanthropes,

Shapeshifters and Ghouls (everyone has their thing, I guess). The proprietor, a Vampire by the name of Vivian Price, was an ally of mine, and one of her girls was a very good friend.

When Gardenia (also known as Gomorrah) fell (which *wasn't* my fault, in spite of what some Wardens keep insisting), Price had decided to relocate, which was sensible of her, and had chosen Stonebridge as her destination, where she had friends in high places (me) to help smooth her way. Now, Stonebridge wasn't the sort of place where you go could get away with simply opening a brothel, but then, Price wasn't an idiot. Within a month, the Red Carpet Hotel and Casino had opened, and Price quickly established it as the city's premier playground for the rich and powerful.

Knowing Price, I doubted very much that she'd abandoned her old business model, which had been very profitable for her, in information as well as in terms of simple money, but she kept that side of the business *very* quiet, delegating it to Karina (as far as I could tell from the various hints and double entendres thrown my way).

As a result of all this, Price was now vastly rich, and gaining both power and influence. She already had some rather influential people in her debt, and the information she was getting made her an important player in Stonebridge as well as an important ally, whose information network operated hand-in-glove with my own. It was difficult for Tethys to determine where one ended and the other began, these days. As a result, the Red Carpet's value was incalculable.

But that wasn't why I was tearing over there in such a hurry. They were useful, true, but even if they weren't, I'd still be going. Weird or not, sleazy or not, I was fond of Price and her people. And I'd never forgive myself if anything happened to Crystal.

I found a patch of Shadow inside the building and opened a Gate, stepping out into the lobby. The building had once been a swanky, upmarket hotel on the outskirts of

Stonebridge, perched atop a small hill with a nice view of the city centre. It had been closed for a number of years, and Price hadn't told me how she'd come by it; but then, I hadn't asked.

It was twenty floors of hedonism, with vice of some kind available on every one of them. Again, I hadn't asked for specifics. As long as nobody got hurt who didn't want to be, it was none of my business...

The lobby was full of white marble, exotic plants and expensive furniture in front of a set of wide stone stairs, ornately carved with images of country life, and no doubt impressively expensive. Everything was pristine and normally calm, but now there was a babble of scared voices, and a gathering of Vampires at the front door.

The entire building, and the grounds, had been Enchanted to keep the harmful effects of the sun off the girls and their boss, not that the sun was too harmful to a Saphyron Vampire, it just made them weak and lethargic. They could also get horrific sunburn if it was too bright, but they wouldn't burst into flames or anything (unlike some other varieties of Vampire).

I could feel Price's Fortress Shield up and running. That was just about the most powerful defence a Magician could conjure. Somehow Price had managed to get one bound to the building, which she could switch on and off at the touch of an Enchanted button (I was really rather jealous of that, but I digress). The point was that the shield could easily hold out against anything short of a very high-end Sorcerer for quite some time.

But it hadn't been designed with the Champions in mind.

Price was at the open front door, looking out at five figures standing on the other side of the shield, one of whom had his hand on it. Ripples of energy expanded from the point of contact, distorting the view.

Some of Price's customers were wandering around, looking worried, but they mustn't have had much of an idea what was trying to get in at them, or there would have been more panic, and I wouldn't have blamed them.

The Champions were not given to New Testament tolerance and mercy; quite the opposite. When they were mentioned, it was generally in connection with acts that could only be likened to Old Testament *wrath*. They would view everyone in that building as guilty of something; lust, greed, pride... take your pick.

Hell, they might even bring the whole place down, if they were feeling particularly puritan.

"Dare I ask what you did to attract *this* sort of attention?" I asked, coming up behind Price.

She turned to look at me, relief flooding her features. But before she had the chance to say anything, there was a distinct squeak from my left, and I barely caught Crystal as she jumped into my arms (with my Shadows, just FYI, I could barely lift *me* at that point, much less six feet of gorgeous, blonde, leggy Vampire).

She planted a whole bunch of little kisses on every exposed part of my face, rendering me down into a blushing wreck.

"Thank God! We thought you were dying," she said between pecks, which left me grinning broadly. She wore a very attractive, and tight, white ensemble complete with corset and miniskirt, fishnet stockings and knee-length boots. It was impressive (and just wonderful to have pressed up against me, bearing in mind the contents).

I smiled at her, and she just kept on kissing me.

"Down Crystal, don't monopolise Mister Graves," Price said with a smile of her own.

"Aw," Crystal said, hopping out of my arms, but remaining close, looking me over, "You don't look so good, Matty, are you alright?"

"Only woke up an hour ago, still not in the best of health," I said, trying to remain alert. Truth be told, I still felt awful. I wasn't up for this by any stretch of the imagination, but what else could I do?

"Then you shouldn't go out there, Mathew," Price said, her face creasing with concern.

I waved her off, "I can feel that shield, and it's coming down. I don't know how quickly help can get here, but if it was readily available, it would be here already. Did they say anything?"

"That we were abominations and a stain on the soul of the city," Price said, "You know, the old favourites that monster hunters like to spew."

I snorted and took a deep breath.

"Let me see if I can diffuse this, then," I said, walking towards the door.

"Mathew," Price said, putting a hand on my shoulder; I stopped, "You don't need to do this. You can't go up against the Champions. We can evacuate."

"That's the thing about zealots, Vivian, they aren't going to stop just because you ran. If they want you, they'll find you, especially these dicks."

Price smiled and Crystal planted another kiss on my lips before they let me go.

I pulled my hood up over my head. Hopefully I'd be able to avoid retaliation, if they couldn't recognise me. I took a breath and started walking.

Oh, this was such a bad idea...

# CHAPTER 2

I wasted no time with anything fancy, and simply walked down the main steps towards the Champions. It struck me then just how on-the-ball Price's security must have been in order to alert her in time to get that shield up; that spoke of some good training and some considerable expense, at the least. But then, this was Price... she wasn't one to skimp on things that might improve her survivability. I worked much the same way.

The front drive was set into the top of the hill, a wide gravelled area with a decorative fountain at the centre, leading to a curving tarmac road that snaked a serpentine path down the hill to the nearby main road.

The Shield covered the property to the edge of the gravel in a perfect, shimmering blue sphere that extended underground, providing total coverage. That wasn't necessarily the wisest idea on a hill, as the shield essentially sliced its way through the rock, but the mound was big enough that there shouldn't be any shifting problems (I hoped).

I wasn't going to risk stepping through the Magic they were using to breach the shield, so I angled myself to the left a bit. I made sure to cast a set of regenerating shields and Mage Sight while I was safe.

Then I took a breath, and stepped through the shield, my heart pounding in my chest. Thankfully, the shield was mono-directional (one could get *out*, but not *in*), or that would have been embarrassing; I really should have checked that with Price before leaving the hotel...

So... the Champions.

I knew a little bit about them, but the most important thing I'd been taught was that if you see them, don't *walk* away, RUN! They called described themselves as guardians of humanity, protectors of the innocent, but their idea of 'innocent' was... skewed. They were well known as being the most intolerant bunch of fire-breathing, fanatical bigots you could hope to find in this day and age. They hated *everyone* who didn't hate the same things that they did.

It really was a shame, because they hadn't started out that way. They'd once been rather the go-to thing in heroes, almost like the medieval A-Team, way back in the day. But that was several incarnations ago.

The Champions had their origins in an order of Errant Mage-Knights; a bunch of rather good eggs wandering the German countryside, trying to do good deeds. They righted wrongs, rescued princesses, fought monsters, all that good stuff. But somewhere along the line, things changed. The membership became more hard-nosed, less tolerant, less about justice and more about vengeance, and then pre-emptive action... getting worse and worse until we ended up with *this* mess. If we could use a political analogy, they'd started out as liberal centrist and ended up slightly to the right of Tomás de Torquemada (known as the fellow who took the Spanish Inquisition *mainstream*).

Once an order of dozens, *hundreds* at its height, it had now been whittled down to five militant nutcases, following the teachings of a charismatic, but extremist, leader, determined to purge the world of evil. Now, this was not the worst goal to aspire to, but the problem comes with how you *define* evil. Personally, I defined it as things involving guts, gore and screaming. *These* people tended to include everything up to and including not looking both ways before crossing the street (I exaggerate, but only a *little*, that's the terrifying thing).

And, as you might imagine, they didn't tend to treat the people they considered 'evil' very well once they'd caught them.

So, there may only have been five of them left after years of growing hatred and the continued shedding of blood, but they were the most hardened five; three men and two women willing to do what was necessary to fight what they considered to be the 'good fight'. I didn't know too much about the current roster, so I made sure to take a good long look with my Mage Sight, hoping for insights that would help in what was about to happen. I had a little hope for talking my way out of this... but not much. I doubted that someone like me made it onto their 'good guy' list.

The leader of the group was a half breed, like Tethys, but from the other side of the eternal fence, a half-angel... or so he claimed. I'd *Seen* Angels, and I was fairly sure that he was half-*Cherub* if he was anything *remotely* like that. He had power, yes, but nowhere near enough for an actual Angel-spawn. He was tall and strong, muscular and handsome, dressed all in white, suit, tie and even shoes (which was a little on the nose for someone like him, if you ask me). He carried a sword in a scabbard over his shoulder, its outline shimmering slightly with Enchantment and Power. His eyes matched his suit, completely white, and yet somehow still piercing.

He turned to look at me as I approached.

He stood with his hands on the shield, the other four behind him, two facing forwards, two facing back, the formation defensive and professional even to my layman's eyes.

The closest man was simply huge, a Vampire of some sort (goodness knew how he got past the screening (or was that screaming?) process), one of the varieties that could stand sunlight without too many deficits (which was more than half of the active bloodlines, so I wasn't getting much of a warning there). He was seven feet tall and very broad; hell, his *muscles* had muscles. He had dark hair and darker eyes, the pupils dilated and staring so that his irises appeared completely black. His fangs were two inches long and looked sharp; his meaty hands held machine guns like they were pistols. He too wore a suit, but his was charcoal and bulged with even more weapons.

One of the women was short and blonde, a little stocky, but attractive in a tough sort of way. She was built like a gymnast, but was wider at the shoulders. She was a Lycanthrope, though I couldn't say what sort. She didn't wear much, presumably so she could change quickly, just a tracksuit and sweatshirt, but she was coiled and ready to leap on someone.

The last man was young, about my age, short and a little rotund, with astonishingly dark skin, almost midnight-black, with startlingly white hair and cold, grey eyes. He reeked of Magic, but not in a good way; there was something distinctly *off* about him. I took a closer look at his Aura; he was a Sorcerer-level practitioner, that much was obvious, but his powers looked... wrong, twisted and... violent. I grimaced and nearly recoiled.

I knew what he was. I'd read about people like him; Warlocks. I'd never met one before, but they were Magicians who knew nothing but Battle Magic, who lived to kill with it. His Aura dripped with death, with murder and violence. My lips twisted in revulsion. I hated the very *idea* of Warlocks, they were abhorrent to me, and this one looked especially nasty. It was all I could do not to swat him on the spot, but it wasn't the time for that... yet. There was still a chance I could talk my way out of this.

The last woman was... very different. She and the half-cherub were the ones I'd been told about; *warned* about. Vampires, Were-creatures and even Warlocks could be dangerous, but rarely to an Archon. The other two were the problems.

The woman... she was unlike just about everything else I'd ever seen. The term Valkyrie sprung to mind. She was every inch the warrior woman, tall, athletic and strong, with just enough femininity to make those features beautiful rather than striking. She had long blonde hair, with red eyes (slightly worrying), and was wearing fitted, black, leather armour, almost like thicker motorcycle leathers. She carried a whole plethora of weapons about her person; guns, knives and swords.

I had real trouble getting any sort of handle on her Aura. There was *some* Magic in there, wisps of Space, some flashes of Fire and Flesh, but something beyond that. Hopkins *had* mentioned that there was some Demigod in her ancestry, but I was damned if I could begin to understand how that all fit together in the woman standing in front of me.

Yes, apparently Demigods were a *thing*, now. There was even a sort of breeding program somewhere in the Mediterranean, trying to get enough 'divine' blood back into a human line to rekindle the ancient pantheons (a cosmically powerful monster *ate* the originals). Sure, it wasn't working, but that didn't stop them trying, and producing some truly powerful individuals as a result. Cassandra was from something of an... offshoot family, and had more than a little touch of the bloodlines herself. She didn't like to talk about it, though.

The Champions turned towards me as I approached. I decided to start off politely. I didn't need to start yet *another* conflict with a group of powerful monsters that I couldn't kill off.

"I'm going to have to ask you to stop that, please," I said.

See? I added a 'please'. Normally I'd start with Shadow Tendrils and it generally got nastier from there.

The half-cherub (and that was still funny, by the way), whose name was... Barney? Barabas? Crap, I should have been paying more attention when Hopkins told me about them, but I never thought I'd actually *meet* them, much less have to contemplate beating the snot out of them. Let's go with Mr White for the moment. Anyway, White cocked his head, turning those odd eyes of his on me, trying to look inscrutable and intimidating. It would have been more effective if he wasn't dressed like Colonel Sanders (and as a result, all I could think about was fried chicken. I was *starving* after a two week coma!).

"We're here to dispense justice, Mortal," White said, his

voice deep and booming.

I couldn't help but snort; he'd said it with such dramatic flair! He glared at me; he was likely unused to that sort of reaction.

The silence stretched for a long moment.

"On who?" I asked. I wanted to move the process along, I was already tired, and I could practically hear the siren call of my nice warm bed.

"Everyone in here," he said acidly, his tone ugly... and *too* eager. It snapped all of my concentration back to the matter at hand.

"Meaning?" I asked, my eyes narrowing, "And what form is this justice of yours to take?"

"Each man or woman is to be judged. We will brand the fornicators and geld the whores," he said.

"Geld?!" I asked, "You can't geld a woman, you lunatic!"

He smiled again. It had to be the nastiest smile I'd ever seen, and it reminded me of what Neil had said, "-if Demonic doesn't always mean 'evil', then can Angelic always mean good?"

And suddenly the Colonel was much less funny.

"We'll see," he said, that ugly smile widening. Now that I was close up, I could actually *see* the madness in his eyes. They were full of hatred, though goodness only knew what of, since he was actively working with a vampire, a murderer and a Were-thing. But then hypocrisy often walked hand in hand with fanaticism.

I knew this, though; he was not a good man. Which was nice, it meant I could do terrible things to him without feeling guilty about it later...

I'd started this encounter moderately pissed-off, but that had rather rapidly graduated to furious. I was (and still am) somewhat... old fashioned. I didn't like it when people hurt women. I didn't even like it when people talked about it around me. When it's women I knew, women I cared about... I didn't necessarily act rationally.

"Question," I said in a very cold voice that made all but the Demigod take a heavy step back, "when you call me 'mortal', does that mean you're not?"

"Of course!" White said, quickly recovering his nerve and resuming his glare.

"So... you can't actually *die* then?"

He sneered, "No. Even if you banished me, I'll just come back!"

I could believe it, he radiated divine power, and I think I remembered something about this topic from when Palmyra had told me about Angels and their various sub-species. If he was damaged enough to 'die', he would simply vanish, regenerate, and return at some point in the future.

"Excellent," I replied.

And then I tore him in half.

It was actually rather a simple bit of Shadow Magic. You'd be amazed how much dark, empty space there is *inside* the human body. In the stomach, in the lungs, throat, sinuses; you get the idea. He wasn't undefended; I could even feel those protections, and there were a lot of them, bound to his very nature and what passed for a Well, but they were all inactive. The arrogant prick hadn't considered me a threat. Oops for him...

He screamed once, horribly, and then vanished, body, blood, mess and horrible suit, all into some sort of cosmic holding zone, or such; it wasn't really my area of expertise. He'd be back eventually, but I could just chop him up again.

"So," I said to the remaining quartet, who were staring at me in shock, "has my point been made, or do I need to knock down another pin?"

Valkyrie's reply was a scream.

Right at me, she screamed, but there was far more to it than simple sound. It was Will and power and raw *hatred.* I felt that horrible sound sear into my mind, if not my soul, a form of energy I'd never experienced before and wasn't prepared to defend against.

I felt as if my brain was being flooded with terror, banishing reason and will into a maelstrom of emotion. It was like every higher function just juddered to a halt for a long moment.

And then that energy just... stopped.

The terror had been drowning me, filling me up until I was ready to burst with it. But then it reached the parts of me that were damaged, broken by what had been taken away, and the woman's strange power was like salt in the psychic wound.

If I'd been a normal, healthy human being, it's likely I would have died right there, bulldozed by Vampire, Warlock and Demigod. But, being somewhat damaged, the energy that was supposed to incapacitate me instead soaked into the exposed parts of my mind, picking and slicing at already raw emotions, making them worse, causing them to build upon one another until I felt as if I was drowning under an ocean of emotional pain.

And through it all, running through a tide of misery, loss, fear, hate and panic, there was something darker. A rage. An utter, dreadful, horrible *rage* that burned through me, banishing thought and reason until there was nothing else left. I hadn't known that I was capable of fury like that. It was as all-consuming as the terror had been, almost as if my fight-or-flight switch had been firmly slammed in the angry direction and then subjected to a power surge.

At least it was more useful that cowering in a heap, waiting to die, if somewhat less pleasant for my long-term mental health.

To Valkyrie's scream, I returned one of my own, and she quickly recognised that it wasn't quite the sort she was hoping for. She looked right at me, and she must have seen something rather terrible in my eyes, because she drew a sword, stepping back.

Yes, she had guns, but drew a sword... I'll never understand some people.

My Shadows came as my rage reached its crescendo, flooding in from every nook and cranny, a black wave that went right for that little clutch of monsters. The Warlock looked like he was going to try something to stop me, gathering heat, but the Lycanthrope girl took one look at what was surging towards them and thought better of the whole situation. She wasted no time, simply slung the Warlock over her shoulder, and legged it down the hill.

Clever girl. I would have killed him first.

The Vampire charged forwards at the same instant Valkyrie did, but he got slightly ahead of her and drew my attention. My Shadows were operating at an instinctual level, responding to my subconscious as much as to my Will. They lashed out at him, the tendrils razor-sharp, harder than rock.

They simply tore him open, connecting with enough force that he went spinning into a decorative tree, spilling blood and viscera in a grotesque pattern that would leave me feeling quite ill when I remembered it later (once I wasn't feeling quite so... murdery). I knew that it wasn't enough to kill him, but that it would keep him out of my way for a *long* while.

That left the woman. She really was something well beyond human. Divine blood had been greatly watered down over the generations since the last pantheon had been destroyed, but she seemed to be as close to a true demigod as it was possible to be (not that my experience in this arena was extensive).

The impact of my Shadows knocked her away like a bowling pin, bouncing her off the fortress shield and down the hill a bit. The force of the strike should have broken her body from head to toe, but it hadn't. She was back up in a second, like some grotesque, martial whack-a-mole.

My thinking was fragmented; actually, *shattered* was more accurate. All I could feel was bloodlust and sheer loathing. It was like the most important parts of me were stuck in a loop of hatred and rage. I wanted to kill this thing in front of me, the one who'd come for my people. I wanted to cause pain and suffering. I wanted it to hurt as it was going to make my friends hurt.

But, mangled though my thinking was, some part of my reasoning was intact enough to recognise that this was a *horrifically* dangerous woman. Anyone powerful enough to shrug off a hit like that, and keep coming, was someone who could turn me into paste if she could land even a glancing blow.

So I cast a Spell.

It was normally very complex, but in that moment, it seemed *so* simple. I did it on instinct, and in seconds, Spell-work that should have taken at least a minute. My Shadows coalesced onto me, moulding around and around my limbs, head and chest into a suit of form-hugging black armour.

Even monsters paused at the sight of that armour. But she just *smiled*, spat blood (it would seem my swipe wasn't as ineffective as I'd thought, which was somewhat reassuring. Invulnerable enemies could be a pain), and came at me again. She was quick, much quicker than any mere muscle and nerve speed I could have managed, but I still had my Will, tied to my rage-addled mind, and that was even faster than she was.

She smacked into a plane of Will and bounced off. Her eyes opened in shock, and she froze for an instant, an instant in which I leapt for her and grabbed her sword arm with my armoured fist, though she was fast enough to wrench herself out of the way of my other hand. With only one firm grasp on her, I did the only thing I could.

With all the power at my command, I squeezed.

Her bones were harder than steel, stronger than titanium, but I wasn't some hedge-wizard shaking a stick with chicken bones tied to the top. I was an Archon, the First Shadow, Lord of the Deep.

There was a wet crunch. She didn't even cry out, only grunted, that was the only indication of her discomfort. Once I'd finally got my wits back, I would be impressed by that. When *my* bones broke, I tended to make distinctly un-manly sounds.

She dropped her sword, though; there was enough damage to ensure that. But her other hand came up and she started emptying projectile weapons into my armoured face, one after the other. Within seconds, she blasted away with four pistols, two submachine guns, and even a sawn-off shotgun (which I had no idea where she was hiding), until there was a small heap of guns at our feet.

All of this, by the way, before I'd had the chance to do more than collect myself after making the grab. Damn, but she was dangerous! If Cassandra found out the specifics of this fight, she'd never let me out of her sight again.

When the guns failed, she drew knives and short-swords, many of which were enchanted in one way or another, and tried to stab me. Finding that each in turn had no effect, she dropped them to join the guns. Finally, she came up with a knife wreathed in Dispel. It likely wouldn't have worked, but she did manage to wedge it under the helmet section of the Spell. But, in that moment, there was a fraction of a second where she was off balance, and I was able to swat the weapon away and grab her by the throat.

Once again, I started to squeeze.

Her face went white, and she started to die. In that moment of triumph, deep under all that ugly armour, I was smiling; smiling about the fact that I was slowly throttling a person, a living, breathing human being, to death. Later, much later, I would realise that it wasn't me, it was Valkyrie's Magic, but that was small comfort.

In that moment, I fully intended to kill her, and that would leave me feeling horribly ashamed.

But then she managed to get her fingers in among mine, and twist our combined digits just enough to wheeze out two words.

"I surrender!" she gasped. Then she put her free hand out of the way, raised up.

I paused, neither releasing nor squeezing harder. It was like my brain was trying to turn over like a badly tuned engine, desperately trying to restart and understand what was happening.

Unarmed, surrendering. Harmless. Her Aura was right there for me to see, I hadn't shut down Mage Sight and it had remained active, somehow.

Unlike the other Champions, there were no telltale streaks of black or red in her Aura. She hadn't murdered an innocent. She was no monster.

But she worked with them...

*She should die,* a nasty part of me said. *She was going to hurt our friends.*

*Magic isn't for that,* said something else, something from deeper inside me, something which cut through the rage and the hatred that I knew wasn't entirely my own, to get through to the better parts of me, the parts that were asleep, half smothered.

I breathed slowly, and with great concentration, released my grips on her.

She didn't fall as I let her go. She just stood up, tall and proud, like she was the winner of our little contest.

"What did you do to me?" I asked, that anger threatening to erupt again, my voice sounding hard and cold through the armour.

"I... I don't know. That shouldn't have happened," she said, her voice was surprisingly gentle, high and... girly. It was incongruous.

"What's your name?" I asked.

"Margaret."

"I'll remember you, Margaret. If you should threaten my people again, I shall not be this nice."

She nodded.

"Tell the same to your partners, and take the Vampire with you when you leave, he's stinking up the place."

She nodded again and walked slowly over to the tree, backing away so as not to appear threatening or dismissive. She acted as if she were dealing with a dangerous animal, which was probably a good idea. I was just waiting for an excuse to make a mess.

After some work, she pulled the Vampire out of the tree, shovelling as much of him back inside as she could before wrapping his torso up in his jacket.

Her arm seemed perfectly fine already.

She looked me over very carefully.

"We'll meet again, Warrior," she said.

"You'd better hope not."

She smiled her predatory smile and darted away, running down the hill, the half-dead Vampire over her shoulder, his head bouncing against her shoulder blades, blood flowing from his nose and mouth.

Now that my brain was working again, I recast my shields and dismantled the Shade Armour. The rage was passing quickly, but I was still shaky and paranoid enough not to take safety for granted.

Seriously, what the hell *was* that? What had she done to me? I'd nearly... *very* nearly...

I shuddered and looked back towards the hotel, where a small crowd had gathered. They were all cheering and clapping, not that I could hear them through the shield.

I nodded to Price, and she tapped something in her hand, which made the barrier drop. I actually sagged, my legs feeling loose. Crystal came to my side, and I let her through my shields so she could help keep me upright.

"That was amazing," she whispered in my ear as Price dispersed the crowd with promises of discounts and free rounds at the various tables.

"I need to sit down," I said wearily, feeling a little dizzy, actually.

"Sure you wouldn't prefer a nice warm bed? I have one in my room," Crystal said, her breath hot on my ear.

"I'm afraid that after all that, I'm not going to be of much use to man or beast for a while. I think I overdid it a bit."

She kissed my cheek anyway and helped to settle me

down on a bench.

"My sister should be here in a minute; do you have a phone I can borrow?" I asked. Now that the adrenaline was fading, I was having trouble keeping my eyes open. I would have gone home, but I knew that I had at least one Warden on the way, as well as Hopkins, neither of whom would be much amused at having to come all that way and then turn right around without an explanation. So I settled down for a wait.

"Sorry," Crystal said, gesturing at her outfit, which couldn't conceal a *feather*, much less a phone.

"S'okay," I said, lowering my shields at last, "I'll just rest my eyes for a sec..."

I closed my eyes, leaning against the Vampire.

And woke up with my sister shouting in my face.

"Mathew Graves!" Jennifer Hopkins (the Starborn Lady, Archon of Space, my former English teacher, one of my best friends, and frequent scolder) shouted, jolting me awake.

"What?" I asked, suddenly alert again. Cassandra and Demise were with her, both looking slightly ruffled (no doubt from Demise's aborted attempt to keep Cassandra from attacking the Champions on her own).

"What do you think you're doing?" Hopkins said, looking me over for injuries (with a little too much poking), "You were in a bloody coma! You should not be wondering about!"

"Sorry," I said with a wide yawn, I couldn't help myself.

Hopkins sighed, rubbing her eyes. She sat down next to me, dislodging the Vampire, who looked a little disgruntled, but she took it in stride.

"Are you alright?" Hopkins said, a little softer this time.

"Fine," I said, trying for a smile, though from the look on her face, it didn't quite come out that way.

"Yes, that was convincing," she said dryly.

My smile was a bit more realistic this time.

*It hurts*, I sent to her, mind to mind, *like my heart's being squeezed.*

*I know, I know*, she said back, taking my hand.

*How did this happen? And why? Couldn't they have talked to us first?*

She pulled me into a hug, which helped hide the tears I was trying not to shed. Now that I was just... sitting, with nothing to do but think and feel what was missing (if that makes sense), it was getting harder and harder to hold back the pain I'd been trying so hard to ignore.

Cassandra discreetly led the Vampire and Demise out of the way so I could be alone with my sister.

"We don't really know what happened or why," Hopkins said, "One day, the ambassadors from both sides simply showed up and told us they were pulling out; severing all ties. Within an hour they'd cast the Spell which supposedly freed the princesses of you, without warning anyone, I might add. Seconds later the barriers went up, and that was that. They'd sealed themselves off from us."

I sighed, miserable, "I miss them. I didn't know how much I'd cared until they'd gone, and now I can't tell them."

"I know. I'm sorry."

"How long? Cassie said something about it being a while, but, is there any chance...?"

"I don't think so, Matty," Hopkins said gently, "these aren't the sorts of spells you cast for a weekend away. It could be decades, or even centuries."

I nodded sadly, "They could have asked me to go with them."

"Would you have gone?" Hopkins asked, a little nervously.

"I... I don't know. I guess I never will now."

She sighed, "You and your women, Mathew," she said in a long-suffering way.

I couldn't really blame her for that one, much as I'd have liked to. My relationships had all ended... badly, to say the least.

I managed a glare, which made her smile.

"Give it time, you'll be alright," she said, patting my hand.

"I know. I always am, eventually."

"Well, at least you managed to avoid the Champions, there's that."

I coughed a little and looked away. Normally I lied like Mozart used to compose, but not so much to Hopkins, something about her cracked my poker face and always had.

"Oh, what did you do?" she asked.

"It was self-defence," I said, getting my defensive fire in early, "sort of."

"And in that 'sort of' lies the source of all my stomach ulcers," she said with a frown.

I told her what had happened and why. Her face turned grim.

"Geld?" she asked in a rasp, her face actually turning red with fury (rarely a good sign in an Archon), "That's what he said?"

I nodded.

"*All* of them?"

"I assume."

She snarled.

"What does that mean?" I asked.

"Something very ugly that hasn't been done in five hundred years, as far as I know. It's a metaphor, really, like castrating a horse, only for supernatural creatures. It's ripping their essences away, their energy, power and nature, leaving them as human as they can be with what's little is left of them. It's an abhorrent practice, as close to evil as you can get without using the Black. When he resurrects, I think I'll kill again him myself on general principles!"

I chuckled.

"Any idea about what the hell that Margaret woman did to me?"

"That, I don't know. She has quite a few powers we don't understand. That War Cry of hers should have left you near powerless and catatonic with terror, that's what it does. That you went the other way is... interesting."

"There's something else," I said, looking around to make sure that Cassandra was still out of earshot, "I feel... thinner; stretched, since I came out of the coma, like there's less between me and the Black than there used to be. I'm scared, Jen."

She looked at me for a long moment, her dark eyes boring into me.

"What you've lost will come back in time. But who you are is who you are, and *that* has not changed, little brother. You are the man who stands in front of legends and dares them to come past you to the people you care for. Angry, scared, happy, sad, grieving, with the Black or without it, you are the man you've chosen to be. And so will you continue," she said, very quietly, very seriously.

"You really think so?"

"Of course. If there's one thing you've proven, it's that you're far too stubborn to be anything other than exactly what you want to be. And speaking as one of the people who's been in your head, that's not such a bad person. Try not to be too hard on yourself. That's my job."

I laughed, feeling a bit lighter.

"That's better," she said, "keep the faith, Mathew. It'll be alright."

I nodded and shakily rose to my feet.

"You know Palmyra raves about this place?" Hopkins said, "Comes here every Saturday."

"I know," I said with a shudder, "My deal with Price ensures that all records of her visits get *very* effectively destroyed."

She snorted, "Good to know. Wait, does that mean she keeps *other* records?"

I nodded, "You wouldn't believe half the things that crop up in the files Price sends me from time to time."

"You pretend to be all sweet and naive, but you're an evil little genius, aren't you?"

"We live in the information age, Jen. The man with the biggest file cabinet wins. And my file cabinet is your file cabinet, so everyone wins in the end. Well, everyone I'm fond of, anyway."

"If I didn't know you so well, I'd be a little worried."

"But you do, and you know I'd only use information like this in the cause of mischief, not malevolence or megalomania. Just, for example, Price has gathered a whole plethora of interesting titbits on a certain Primus of our acquaintance; the one who really doesn't like me? Well, I've had all this stuff for months, and haven't done a thing. I should get points for *that*!"

"No!" Hopkins said, practically dancing with glee, "But he's such a straight arrow. Doesn't even drink!"

"Not according to his housekeeper," I said with a smile (an ever so slightly *evil* smile).

"Oh, tell me!" she said.

I whispered the secrets in her ear and she blushed from her chin to her crown.

"Oh, that sanctimonious little bastard! I can't wait to drop that into conversation!" she said happily. If there was one thing a Magician loved more than a good argument, it was a good secret (and a good gossip).

"It is a good one, isn't it?"

Hopkins grinned, "You need a Portal home?"

"No, thanks, I need to smooth things over with Price and maybe find out what drew those pricks here."

"I think I'll make my way to the poker tables," Hopkins said, "since I'm here."

"Careful, don't cheat, they're watching."

"They caught *you*?" she asked, aghast.

"Of course not, but I'm smarter than you," I said with a grin that earned me a flicked ear.

"See you later Mathew, I'll come by tomorrow?"

"I'd like that."

She walked off and Cassandra came back with Demise,

Price and Crystal.

"It seems I owe you a favour, Milord," Price said.

"How many does that make now?"

"I've offered to pay off my debts in trade, but alas..." she said sadly.

"You don't owe me a thing, Vivian. If it wasn't for you and your information, I'd likely be dead right now, along with a lot of other people. So, kindly stop keeping score, alright?"

"Yes, Milord," she said with a sarcastic little curtsey. You wouldn't think it was possible to make a curtsey sarcastic, but there it was...

"And stop doing that, will you? It's just odd. And I have begged you not to call me that."

"Maybe I enjoy it," Price said, moving in close so she could tangle a finger in the cloth of my jacket, "both respecting and defying you all at the same time. Women are complex creatures, Mathew, I'd get used to it, if I were you."

"Oh, I know, believe me, I know. There are days when I think that your whole gender exists just to *be* complicated!"

Price just smiled.

# CHAPTER 3

So, all things considered... not the best start.

Coma, then a new enemy, then a nearly cataclysmic loss of control.

It was half an hour before I was able to disentangle myself from Crystal and make my way home in a cab (I was too tired to try anything Magically clever). I had trouble staying awake on the ride back, and barely made it into my bed before collapsing into a deep (and thankfully dreamless) sleep. Someone had been decent enough to clear out all the hospital gear and lay on nice clean sheets for me, which felt amazing.

I didn't wake for hours, and when I did, I actually felt a bit recovered, a little more vital. I also awoke with three Pixies curled up at my side and a redhead wrapped around my back... which helped even more!

The Pixies were just under a foot tall, and not as light as you'd think. They were all of a kind, delicate features, pointed ears and blonde hair. They were called Meadow, Jewel and Melody, and I was really rather taken with them. The girl at my back was Kandi, Tethys' girlfriend of the moment and 'assistant'. She was beautiful, friendly and always cheerful, even first thing in the morning (in spite of my offers to Hex her if she didn't cut it out, at *least* before I'd had my breakfast).

I would have been in love with Kandi if her relationship preferences weren't quite so... esoteric. In short, she liked to have fun, and for her that meant... well she was Tethys' girlfriend, you can probably guess what that meant. Their relationship defied easy description, but I knew there was love there, even if it was non-traditional and tended to involve more participants than I would be able to manage without some sort of indexing system.

Kandi and I had been growing closer lately, forming a deeper bond of friendship and trust that I found very soothing, even if it seemed to be making her a little more bossy (and quite a bit more handsy). She spent a solid chunk of her leisure time with me, generally lying with some part of her on my person while we watched TV, played chess or just chatted. She was an immensely comforting presence, like having a little piece of humanity's better nature cuddled up with me.

When I woke, the Pixies did too, yawning adorably, dressed in the little cashmere onesies my mother had made for them. I smiled at them; just the sight of them made me feel miles better. But if Kandi was overly active first thing in the morning, those three were only a little less than an adorable *nightmare.*

They immediately jumped on me, hugging me tight with their tiny arms, all talking at once, which woke Kandi, causing her to stretch in a very interesting fashion, exposing a long length of toned midriff. Her head slid up, her cheek leaning on mine as she took in the scene.

"And you complain about my morning activity," she said during a break in the excited babble, before kissing my cheek, "I'm glad you're out of the coma, there's only so much fun I can have with you when you're unconscious."

"There once was a time when the mere mention of a Shadowborn would strike fear into the hearts of young ladies... I miss those times."

"I've seen your Spiderman pyjamas, Matty, you could try for a hundred years and not scare me after *that.*"

The Pixies started talking again before I could reply.

"We missed you!" Melody said.

"Very much," chimed in Jewel.

"Don't do that again," said Meadow.

"No, don't do that again," Jewel agreed.

"We were very worried," Melody said.

"Very, very worried!" Jewel added.

"I'm sorry," I said, enveloping their tiny backs in a hug, "I didn't mean to."

"We know," Meadow said, "but we're still mad at you!"

"I'll make it up to you," I said with a smile, "and I'm sorry about what happened to your home."

"What happened to the Grotto?" Melody asked, looking confused.

"I mean Seelie, it's blocked," I replied.

"That's not home, Silly," Jewel said, "This is home."

I felt my eyes watering a little and bit on a lip that was trembling slightly. Don't tell anyone.

"I'm very happy you're still here," I said in a whisper.

"Where else would we be?" Meadow asked with an impish grin.

They snuggled in closer, and I felt... a little lighter again, better than I had in weeks. Then my stomach rumbled, ruining the moment; the Pixies giggled.

"Breakfast bell!" Meadow squeaked happily, jumping up and down, "we'll tell your cook. We love her, by the way."

"She makes us pudding whenever we want," Jewel added.

I laughed and they flew away, butterfly wings appearing on their backs as they darted up, flickering with Magic as they slid *through* the wall.

I started to sit up and was pulled back down by Kandi.

"Ten more minutes... and then you need a shower."

I turned towards her and she tucked herself in under my chin, her arm around my chest.

"And a shave, and a haircut, and feeding up," she continued.

"Anything else while I'm at it?" I asked, stroking her back in that way she liked.

"I'll make a list," she said, shivering a little, her leg twitching.

Ten minutes became thirty, and then forty, at which point the Pixies came back and stomped up and down on my head until I agreed to get up. Kandi giggled as I obeyed the tiny creatures, heading for the bathroom. I ran the shower and shaved while it was warming up.

I made quite a sight in the mirror. I'd been pale before, but 'corpse-like' was now a better descriptor; my skin almost deathly white, and my damaged eyes didn't help; they were a dark, blotchy red where there should have been white, with black irises. My face looked a little gaunt, which made the shaky scars in the shape of a pentacle on my left cheek more prominent. I'd had an appointment to get those scars seen to by a plastic surgeon... last week, damn it! And now there wasn't enough time to see to it before university started.

I looked the rest of myself over, and tried not to wince. The skin on my body matched that on my head, grey and pale. I'd lost muscle mass as well as fat, leaving me looking a little gaunt. Before the coma, I'd been recovering from the effects of Demonic poisoning, which had very nearly killed me and left me very weak. Kandi had taken it as a personal mission to feed me up and get me healthy again, and all her hard work had started to pay off. I'd almost been able to pass for vaguely human (in a bad light, and if you didn't look too closely). And now it was all undone! And only a little over two weeks before I was due to start at Stonebridge University, so there was no fixing it now. And that was assuming I'd even gotten in...

Come to think of it, I should have had my A-level results by now...

And now that I was thinking properly again, where were my parents? They should have been at Blackhold, doing their nuts, or at least *one* of them should.

I showered thoroughly, getting the stench of two weeks' immobility off me before dressing in comfortable clothes and heading down to breakfast. It was just after nine in the morning on a warm August day, and the house was bustling. I exchanged good-mornings with the valets and Wardens before having a quick word with Mister Webb, the Butler. He was the kindly, middle aged man who ran the more mundane parts of the house; he always had a kind word and a smile on his face. He reassured me that all was well, and that nothing had burned down while I was out.

He went back to his duties, and I continued on my way, across the great hall, past the open door to the large garden at the centre of the hollow square that comprised the main structure of the house. I could feel the gentle hum of Fairy Magic coming from the large oak tree at the centre of it, connected to the larger source at the Grotto; it made me feel calmer, safer.

I opened the door to the breakfast room and found Kandi, Cassandra, Demise and Tethys *inhaling* food (not that Tethys needed the nutrition, she got her energy in *other* ways, but she could still enjoy it). They said good morning distractedly, not that I could blame them, Blackhold's chef was a marvel. The little Pixies were slumped in a heap inside a large fruit bowl, peelings and pips everywhere, deep into their usual post-breakfast nap.

The breakfast room was small and cosy, with a round wooden table in the centre, always covered with a pristine white cloth (well, pristine before Kandi got at it; she ate... enthusiastically). I sat and was soon tucking into a plate of bacon and eggs while the others picked at the last of their meals and chatted amongst themselves.

"Oh, where are my parents by the way?" I asked once I was half-done, hunger at least partially sated, and thus willing surrender a little brainpower to curiosity, "I'd have assumed at least one of them would be here bossing someone around."

They all immediately looked away, except for Demise, who didn't really do shame very well.

"What?" I asked.

"Um," Kandi said, looking to Tethys.

"It's... that is to say..." Tethys said, looking at Cassandra.

"We decided not to tell them," Demise said, cutting to the chase.

"What?" I asked, "Why?"

"Well, after their... difficulties the last time you did yourself a mischief, we thought it might be best if... well, we didn't want them coming in here, it's as simple as that," Demise said.

"I video-call them three times a week, how did you deal with *that*?"

"You shouldn't have taught Demise Illusion Magic," Cassandra said with a smirk.

Demise concentrated, and her upper half suddenly looked like me.

I scowled and rubbed my forehead. If I argued, they'd just gang up on me. And I suppose they had a point. My mother hadn't been dealing with Magic and Magical injuries very well since I'd been poisoned. If she'd had to sit around with me in a coma...

"Okay," I said finally, "I suppose that was a pretty good idea."

Four sets of eyes narrowed.

"That was too easy," Tethys said, "He doesn't let things go this quickly."

"I was expecting a good dose of some sort of discipline," Kandi said with a pout.

I reached over and tickled her ear, making her squeal and bat me away.

"I trust you all, and it saved me an unpleasant conversation, so thanks," I said, attending to the rest of my breakfast.

Everyone seemed to relax, and went back to their conversations.

Tethys handed me a pair of envelopes when I was finished.

"These came when you were... out," she said, "I believe they were the letters you were waiting for?"

I said thank you and wiped my hands on my napkin before picking up the first. A-Levels; the big ones, the rite of passage, the barometer for the future... alright, I was just stalling. The paper crackled as I tore through the flap. I pulled out the letter and read it quickly.

I smiled.

"Thank goodness for that," I said, dropping the piece of paper on the table so I could open the next letter.

Kandi snatched up the sheet.

"Son of a bitch, you did better than I did!" she said with a growl. Tethys grabbed the paper and grinned.

"Not bad, Matty," she said.

Cassandra snatched it, and then Demise, they all looked pleased and proud. The attention made me blush.

Next was the results for the Level Ten Magical Proficiency Test. Compared to the A-level mess, a slam dunk...

Only it wasn't, apparently.

"Huh?" I managed.

*Failed*?! I read the letter through twice more. It didn't change with the re-reading.

"What is it?" Tethys said, no doubt recognising the slightly miffed look on my face.

"I failed my Level Ten!" I said, handing the letter over, "Which is impossible! My theory answers were word-perfect, and my Spellwork was a thing of beauty!"

"Let me see that," Cassandra said.

Tethys handed it over, and my Warden read it through. Her eyes narrowed dangerously.

"What is it?" I asked.

"Under 'Notes' the examiner put 'Lacks necessary maturity and societal focus'," Cassandra said, "I acted as an examiner a few times. That's the kind of crap I put when a Shadowborn crossed my path. The bastard failed you because of your Affinity."

"Are you sure?" I asked.

She nodded angrily, "There's sort of an unwritten rule; no Shadowborn gets past Level Five. Certain clubs, societies and resources are only available to people of a certain skill level and once you get past five, you're considered a Journeyman Magician and allowed to join a lot of them. Level Eleven, and you'd have the same standing in our society as a Master Magician. Nobody wants a Shadowborn to get *that* high, they get access to too much."

"Like what?" I asked, my interest overcoming my irritation, for the moment.

"Certain clubs, some organisations, more levels at the Archive, naturally. Also, the qualification gives respectability, and that can be dangerous."

"Why didn't you mention this before?" I asked.

"How was I to know someone would be stupid enough to fail the First Shadow?" Cassandra asked.

"They didn't know I was the First Shadow."

There was a long moment of silence where I could almost feel them try not to roll their eyes. Demise failed.

"Ah," Cassandra said, "That would explain it. Look, the way these things are supposed to work is that a Magician seeks out a mentor, whether as part of a school, or independently, who introduces him or her to Magical Society, attending to your education in history, ethics and Magical theory. Now, if you've completed your training to your teacher's satisfaction, then they act as a reference when you're getting your qualifications, a way of confirming that you're ready for greater responsibility, as judged by the one that trained you."

"Nowhere in any of the sodding manuals or books is that even *mentioned*!" I complained.

"That's because it's not a legal requirement," Cassandra explained, "it's just the understood way of doing business; a check against kids with more power than sense, I suppose. But that shouldn't have applied to *you*. You're a Level-Nine; that makes you a Practicing Magician in your own right. You had every right to apply for a Level Ten, and you should have got it, too. But some examiners would view a lack of references as a warning sign, though that may have been overlooked, if you *weren't* a Shadowborn."

I closed my eyes, rubbing my forehead.

"Perfect," I said, "just bloody perfect. If my Affinity doesn't get me blocked, my lack of a qualified teacher will, wonderful!"

I was fuming, which was odd. I didn't normally sweat things like that. Since I'd woken up from the coma, my temper had been much shorter, which worried me (that War Cry thing hadn't helped).

"Not having a piece of paper doesn't make you any less a Magician," Cassandra said, "You know more than any fifty Mages your age, *combined*, generally not even a really good Sorcerer would get past Level Five before they're twenty. Few ever get to Nine at all, certainly not in their first century."

I was barely listening. Mostly, I was brooding, nasty possibilities floating through my head as Cassandra tried to make me feel better. I was thinking along the lines of having Tethys track the examiners down so I could pay them personal visits; that would be satisfying...

I shook my head, trying to clear it. What was wrong with me? That wasn't who I was. I didn't do things like that. I wouldn't.

So I took a breath.

"How do I fix this?" I asked.

"You already are. You go to University, you do things the traditional way. You're still a Level Nine, that means you'll be able to take specialist courses; Demise and I have been leafing through Stonebridge's prospectus and have a few suggestions for you," Cassandra said, which made me smile, returning my equilibrium a little.

"The Magicians there will act as your teachers and eventual referees, many of them even administer the tests, so let them get to know you and they'll soon realise what you're worth."

"Okay," I said, rubbing my eyes.

I was tired again. How long was *that* going to last?

"Come on, Matty," Tethys said, standing up. She offered me her hand and I took it, "We have a few more things to sort out before you start your day."

I nodded and let her lead me into the garden. We sat on my favourite bench, across from the small pond and the oak tree. I loved that tree...

"I saw that in there," she said, "You got angry, actually *angry*. What's wrong?"

"Oh, it's nothing to worry about. Spiritual damage has some side effects, that's all. I'll settle down in a while," I said tiredly.

"I don't like this look on you, Mathew. You look... wounded, dangerous, like a cornered bear. You have that desperate look in your eye. It frightens me."

I turned to look in her lovely eyes, a little hurt by that.

"I would die before I ever did you harm. I thought you'd know that."

"I'm not afraid *of* you, you idiot! I'm afraid *for* you!" she said, squeezing my hand, "Despite what you try to put on for the others, I know when you're hurt, and I've never seen you this bad before."

I sighed, taking a moment.

"It just seems that whenever I get close to someone...," I started, but had to pause, as my voice stopped working.

Tethys wrapped her arms around me and leaned her head on my shoulder.

"One by one, they leave or they go insane, or their lunatic mothers rip them away from me. How long until it's one of you? I'm on a ragged edge, Tethys, I don't know if I can take another loss and stay sane."

"I'm not going anywhere, and neither are the others. We can all take care of ourselves and you know that we take care of each other as well. Even Kandi doesn't go out without a guard these days. You know Lacy, that new girl? Kandi takes her everywhere; it's why they take twice as long, the little hedonists."

I chuckled at that.

"Nobody will take any of us away. And you're stuck with *me* until your toes curl up, you know that."

"I do, I know. I'm just tired, that's all. I'll get over all this in time. I'm just not healed yet," I said, "Sorry I'm like this, I hate it."

"You have nothing to apologise for, Mathew Graves. This was done to you, and when those Fairies come back, I'm administering one firm kick up each of their snatches just on general principles," she said. She kissed my cheek and held me tightly.

"Thank you. I mean that."

"Any time, you idiot."

Lady Lucille Palmyra, Archon of Life, came by that afternoon to take a look at me. She was one of the most decent people I knew, and by leaps and bounds the very best healer, as you might expect. She was petite and blond, with bright eyes and a perpetual look of mischief about her, wearing a bright blue summer dress.

She smacked me over the back of the head for walloping her nurse (which I *absolutely* deserved. I'd already asked Tethys to find out the lady's contact details so I could send her every flower I could lay my hands on), but pronounced me as fit and healthy as I could expect to be. Even so, she still laid out an excruciating regime of diet and exercise that Kandi promised to inflict on me. She stayed for lunch, and we chatted for a good while about what I'd missed over the last couple of weeks (not much, as it turned out). She commiserated about the test and advised that I show up with my signet ring and Demise next time, which made me laugh.

Though I'd be lying if I said I didn't at least *consider* it. The stigma attached to Shadowborn didn't really apply to the First Shadow, as far as I'd been able to tell, but I was happy(-ish) in my anonymity, and I had enough people calling me 'My Lord' as it was. That, and I was simply too stubborn to take a win just because of who I was. I'd *earned* my Level Ten Certificate fair and square, damn it, and I wasn't going to cheat (I might Hex someone if that sort of rejection happened again, but I wasn't going to cheat).

The days went by quietly, and I started to recover. It was hard going at first, but having Tethys and Kandi there helped a lot, especially with the... non-physical damage. I spent my time recovering my strength and stamina... and being force-fed almost to the point of internal damage.

I went to the Grotto and caught up with the various Fairies living there; now more than seventy of them, by the way. Lunson, the boss up there, introduced me to the new arrivals, which included a new clan of gnomes, the Treelent, a quartet of Earth Trolls, called Slom, Agnor, Kretin and Mossley, who were very friendly and quite lethargic, not at all like a River Troll (of bridge-toll, Billy-goat gruff fame; nasty creatures, they would happily eat everything and every*one* in sight). There was also a small clan of Wood Elves, who'd already moved into the tall trees (which they'd made even taller with their own brand of Magic), they were quite stereotypically Elfish actually, tall, elegant and graceful, pointed ears, the whole thing. There were twelve of them, three men, five women, four children; three extended families, in fact.

They were all of them from the Seelie Realm (the good one), gentle people. The original populations of Nymphs, Otters, Sprites and Centaurs had also expanded. I met them all, and made sure that they had everything they needed, which they did. Lunson had already expanded the range of my Place of Power so that everyone had enough space to live. He'd also filled the forest with game and growing consumables so that they'd never starve. There were also some new, and rather subtle, enchantments encouraging people to keep away, and some less subtle enchantments for anyone that came in anyway (some of them involved wasps... I think that's all I need to say).

Next to Blackhold, the Grotto was the most heavily

defended location in the country; a confluence of Fairy and Human Magic that would do a thorough mischief to anyone stupid enough to make trouble there. Even Kron didn't have the foggiest idea how it worked, but work it certainly did, which meant that I didn't have to worry about *them*, at least.

The Pixies spent just about every waking moment (and most of the sleeping ones) with me, knowing that I'd be 'going away' for a while, even though I promised I'd visit (and it wasn't like I was going very far!). Tethys helped me wade through all the University paperwork, and even made a few calls to make sure that I'd get a good room in the Halls of Residence, which I didn't really need because... palace, but I wanted to at least *try* and have a normal university experience.

And also, with any luck at all, I'll meet people, hopefully make friends, and it would be easier to keep the whole 'First Shadow' thing under wraps if I was seen to have a normal room at Uni. Magicians, especially, got very peculiar about the Archon thing, and I wanted to avoid that, or, even worse, making friends off the back of it (though my feelings on the ethics of meeting *women* that way changed depending on the time of day, I was still eighteen, after all, with all the hormonal issues that brought).

Speaking of age, my nineteenth birthday was a week before the start of term, and that was a *wonderful* day. Kandi woke me with a rather charming rendition of happy birthday. Charming because she was half naked, lying on me and crooning sweetly into my ear; this was followed by a spectacular breakfast, calls from my parents (safely in Mexico, where nothing could abduct, eat, or otherwise bother them) and the few of my friends I was still in contact with. Tethys took me to the theatre that night, and we all had a quiet dinner at home, with a sixteen layer chocolate cake that even Cassandra was baulked by (which didn't stop her from eating most of it, I hasten to add). Hopkins and Palmyra came and celebrated with us. Lucille did her best to help Cassandra in her quest to demolish the cake, but even she dropped out of the race eventually.

That was a *very* good night.

When dinner was over, I rescued some cake and placed it in a Tupperware box before borrowing my signet back from Tethys and dressing in a hood that covered my features. I told Cassandra I was heading out for a bit, and she was so stuffed that she didn't even raise a token protest (something to remember for the future!). I quickly hopped into a Shadow before she could change her mind.

Getting to the Magicians' Prison, commonly known as 'the Farm', was not particularly hard. There were secured entrances in four major cities, Stonebridge, London, Manchester and Edinburgh. The Stonebridge one was inside of the local SCA headquarters about a quarter of a mile from the Conclave building.

I walked out of a nearby shadow and up to the front door, box in hand. The building was a modern, concrete mess of a place, with enchanted bars over the safety-glass windows, wedged between two much nicer constructions of glass and steel. I opened the heavy wooden doors and walked up to the front desk.

"Can I help you, Sir?" said an irate looking older man in a grey shirt and trousers, which was the undress uniform of the SCA rank and file.

I showed him my signet ring, which caused the officer to dart to his feet and stiffen to attention. The rings could *always* be recognised. Any Magician who saw them would instantly know that they were dealing with an Archon (even if they couldn't see said Archon's face). Even those who'd never even *heard* of an Archon would recognise the bearer as someone in Authority. It smoothed the going in situations like this.

"Good evening Lord Shadow, how may I serve?" he said, suddenly seeming much less irate.

"I need to visit the Farm, please, the Criminally Insane

Wing, is that possible?"

"Is it urgent, Lord Shadow? Only it's very late, and visiting hours are long since over."

He'd seen the box of cake.

"Not urgent, but time sensitive," I replied, "I'd consider it a favour."

"Of course, Lord. He shouted out a name and another officer came in, dressed much the same, but taller and younger, radiating competence (and Magic), "Take Lord Shadow where he wants to go, Pimin."

"With pleasure, Sir," he said before nodding to me.

I told him where I wanted to go, and thanked the desk officer. Pimin led me through a side door and down a set of concrete stairs. The Portal was a simple marble archway with a heavy stone covering it. Pimin spoke to one of the six guards, and one of them placed his hand to the stone. There was a small pulse of Magic, and the Enchantments of the stone activated, causing it to slide into the floor, revealing a wide concrete room with barred gates on either side, a caged reception desk opposite me. A little shimmer around the edge of the archway was the only clue that space was being bent.

I headed for the desk, which was safely behind heavy bars and safety glass. There were Wards and Enchantments everywhere; even I would have had trouble using Magic at the Farm. My signet *could* have protected me from those effects, but the other signets told her not to (the last First Shadow was a bit of a prick, and nobody was taking any chances).

Pimin stayed long enough to hand me over to the Farm's receptionist and then beat a hasty retreat (no Magician enjoyed being under the Wards of the Farm). I told the young man at the desk where I wanted to go, and he summoned a guard to take me.

The Farm was built deep underground, in a colossal cavern which had no natural entrances or exits, the sides hardened and impossible to dig through. I knew there to be several wings, each dedicated to a particular sort of criminal, and more for non-human prisoners. I couldn't see much of the complex, but it was mostly made of reinforced concrete, with heavy chain-link fences topped with barbed wire separating the various precincts.

My destination was a white-painted building, with a square base, just a few minutes' walk from the entrance building. It was three stories high, fifty metres to a side, with tiny windows, too small to squeeze through. A black psi symbol on the front marked this building out as the Mental Hospital, both informing visitors, and warning them, of what lay within.

My guide handed me over at the front doors to someone in charge, this new fellow dressed in a suit under a white coat. He introduced himself as Doctor Watkins, and took me the rest of the way.

"He's been quieter lately, Sir, more stable," said Watkins. He was tall and thin with dark brown skin and bright blue eyes. He spoke quietly but intelligently, and he projected a calm confidence that was very reassuring.

"Still expressing his desire to eat people?" I asked.

"Not for a while, but don't be fooled, Sir, he's still *very* dangerous. We don't turn our back on him for any reason. He'll be bound and chained for your interview, but as you requested, you'll be alone."

"Thank you."

Watkins gave me a brief safety lecture and inspected the cake box before leaving me alone while he went in to complete the arrangements for my meeting, it didn't take him long.

The interrogation room was padded, floor, walls and ceiling, the table too, all in a dirty white that smelled faintly of urine, desperation and bleach. The light was dim and unpleasant, the table and chairs bolted to the floor.

*He* was chained by his feet to the floor and his hands to a loop on the table. His normally golden-blonde hair was lank and dirty, his eyes sunken, surrounded by dark circles.

His skin, so healthy when I'd last seen it, was waxy and grey, though he still looked strong, like he could run a marathon if only he could be trusted not to murder the other participants.

He looked at me as I came in, his eyes never leaving my face as the door shut behind me. I pulled my hood down and placed the box on the table in front of him.

"Happy Birthday, Des," I said to my brother.

Palmyra had done a lot to repair the damage Black Magic had done to Desmond's body, but while the various psychics had done what they could with his mind, it wasn't much in the grand scheme of things. They'd carved off some of the raw edges, sanded away some of the insanity, but that was really the best that they could do.

His eyes looked like mine used to, one blue, one brown, though his blue was right, and mine used to be left. His stare seemed to bore into me as he reached for the box and pulled the lid off. He sniffed the cake and closed his eyes, his expression peaceful for a long moment.

"Come to gloat, at last?" he asked, his eyes snapping open to glare at me, his tone gravelly and unpleasant. He put the cake to one side, but didn't throw it away, "Does it feel good to see me like this? It make you happy?"

"Do I look happy to you?" I asked, my voice taking on that nasty tone that made monsters run.

He flinched but didn't take his eyes away from mine.

"No, I suppose not," he said after a moment. He pulled the cake towards him and started eating it slowly, savouring every bite. He had to use his fingers; they wouldn't let me give him the plastic fork I'd brought with me.

"How'd you get in here?" he asked.

"Can't tell you that. Suffice to say, I did, and let's leave it at that."

"Who would I tell?"

"Everyone, you've rather proven that my secrets can't be entrusted to you."

He'd been the one who outed me way back when, in a fit of pique.

"Touché," he said sardonically, "so, why are you here?"

"I missed you today. I wished you were home with me."

"Then maybe you shouldn't have put me in here!" he spat.

I stared him down, "You know very well how you ended up in here. And while I bear some responsibility, it wasn't intentional, and the only way I could have prevented it would have been suicide. Literally."

"That would have worked for me," he said with an evil smile.

"You are here because when you were given a choice between love and hate, you chose the latter, and you included cruelty for good measure. Don't lay this entirely on me."

"Is that what you tell yourself, late at night? That it wasn't your fault?" he asked with a sneer, "That you have no blame in this?"

"What happened to you was *not* my fault. I was the cause, but it wasn't my *fault*. My Magic resonated with yours and made you insane, but that was it. I could no more control it than I could breathing."

"How's Jocelyn?" he asked nastily, licking frosting off his fingers. I froze.

Jocelyn had been my girlfriend, the youngest scion of the Faust dynasty, beautiful, smart and sweet. I'd loved her, an adolescent love, but it felt all too real to me at the time. It had allowed me to move on from what I thought was unrequited love for Cathy.

At the time, I was planning to use a bit of Black Magic to sever me from Des, and hopefully prevent him going crackers. Hopkins found out, and persuaded Jocelyn to make me believe that she and Des were cheating on me, thus convincing me that Des was already too far gone, and that using the Spell (which would have hurt me terribly) was no longer worth it.

I know, it was a complicated mess, but the whole story

need not concern us here. Suffice to say, not fond of her, not fond of Des, and occasionally still mad at Hopkins about it.

Des smiled at me again, "What? Did I strike a nerve?"

I electrocuted him a little. It took all my Magic to do it, too. It took that much to cast a spell in places like the Farm; pretty much only an Archon could do it.

"No," I said after he'd stopped twitching; I smelt pee and it made me smile, "*That's* striking a nerve."

I stood and picked up the empty box while he stared at me, an ugly look on his face.

"I'll get you for that," he rasped.

"You wouldn't be the first to try, and I sincerely doubt you'll be the last," I replied.

I walked out and left him there. I knew it was a mistake to go visit him, I knew he wasn't the boy I'd grown up with. But I'd so wanted to see him; I missed him so much. I should have known he'd lash out, and I was ashamed that I'd lashed right back, and nastily, too.

I'd never claimed to be a saint, but I thought I was better than *that*. Apparently I was wrong.

# CHAPTER 4

The site that would one day become known as the City of Stonebridge had been a place of learning for Magicians thousands of years before there was so much as a mud hut in the area, much less a city. Back then, there was just the river and the forest; a place where ancient Sorcerers imparted terrible secrets to their apprentices in groves dedicated to dark gods. Not the most civilised of times, or places, but Kron told me that their... oh, let's call them 'co-ed rituals' could be rather interesting, if you catch my drift.

The community began as a simple meeting place, where the various Magicians living in the area could gather in safety, to learn, to teach, to talk (and argue!), but this eventually became permanent, with Magicians putting down roots, attracting farmers and other craftsmen as time went on. Eventually, villages would be built, then towns, growing and merging until they became the city I knew and loved. And always, Magicians were there, teaching, learning, living amongst the Pureborn and eventually governing.

The university itself was about six hundred years old, founded by a group of very crafty Sorcerers who buried a Magical college in amongst a number of more traditional ones. In the days before Magicians came out of hiding, this provided their apprentices not only with a Magical education, but also experience and contact with Pureborn, which helped them prosper (and keep their powers hidden). As word spread, Stonebridge University, and the 'exclusive' colleges grew in fame and popularity (and size!), and soon most, if not all, of the great Magical families were sending their children there.

These days, it was a bit less exclusive. Once Magicians were out in the open, the other great institutions wanted in on the act and started their own Magical schools. Cambridge's, in particular, had a very good reputation, and Oxford's wasn't far behind. But, for me, there could be only one choice. Stonebridge, for all the heartache I'd suffered there, was my home. The Conclave was there, as was Blackhold; I wouldn't have wanted to be anywhere else.

The university had begun as a cluster of privately purchased buildings in Stonebridge's older boroughs, but had long since expanded into the city's more modern areas. The heart of the grounds remained with the most ancient buildings, practically steeped in history, but there were also new and amazing complexes for the sciences, arts and student housing. It was a complicated architectural and logistical hodgepodge, but it was essentially laid out with the various 'Schools' towards the centre, near the older administrative buildings, and the various halls of residence and more exclusive colleges spread out around the periphery, the more prestigious ones to the east (near the old quarter) and the more modern and accessible ones to the west.

Registration was in the Great Hall. The building predated the university, being more than a thousand years old, a gothic masterpiece, with gargoyles, cornices and spiky protrusions. My introductory paperwork told me that it was the centre of the university's administration, as well as the site of the main dining hall, big enough to accommodate a couple of thousand students with room to spare. I noted, to some joy, that the introductory pamphlet said it was just one of a couple of *dozen* places within the University grounds where one could eat.

The Great Hall also contained the Dean's office, the chancellery, the post office and a variety of smaller spaces for administration and logistics, laid out in a vague cross shape, with offices and reception rooms in each of the four arms, and the hall itself at the centre, and occupying the majority of an enlarged southern arm.

The Hall was packed full of registering students, hundreds of them, the place was abuzz with conversation and the energy of pure anticipation. I was dressed simply, in grey trousers, striped shirt and jumper; I also had a minor Illusion in place concealing my scars and red eyes. I felt that there was no need to scare the villagers too early in the process (that, and my distinguishing features were well known enough that identifying me would be pretty easy for anybody with a bone to pick).

I was at the back of a long line, a satchel in hand containing my paperwork, waiting as it inched slowly forward. The interior of the building was wood-panelled and interesting, covered in carvings, with paintings on the walls, which kept me occupied while I waited.

But that wasn't all that interested me.

Most Magicians could sense Magic around them to a greater or lesser extent. I was particularly sensitive, even compared to the other Archons, which meant that I could detect even the barest whisper of Magic.

And there was quite a lot of it.

As much as a tenth of the crowd were Magicians of some sort, mostly Acolytes (the lowest end of the magical spectrum) but there were all sorts, including one or two Sorcerers (thankfully I'd long since mastered drawing my Magic inward so I couldn't be detected this way).

Everyone seemed excited; many seemed to have made friends already.

That made me sigh softly, I missed my friends very much in that moment. Not as they were at *that* point, but as they were before everything turned to crap. I didn't even know where a couple of them were, now. Cathy was at Oxford, and so was Bill. I hadn't spoken to Belle in a while, but I knew she was busy.

So, there I was, alone. Bill and Cathy should have been with me.

I was so *angry* about that. But then, I was angry about a lot of things in those days.

The line took an hour to get where it was going, but I finally got my paperwork and my room assignment along with a timetable, and a very detailed map, from a friendly older lady behind a fold-up desk.

I thanked her and made my way to Naiad Hall, my halls of residence, which was a ten minute walk from the Chemistry School, where I'd be spending a lot of my time. I'd decided that I wanted to explore the whole Magic-Physics-Chemistry relationship when I graduated, so I'd registered for Physical Chemistry. I was also signed up to three advanced Magic classes, which would eat up a lot of time.

Finding the room was easy enough, moving my things in wasn't a problem, either, Magic solved most problems, after all (well, except for the really important ones...).

I made the bed, set up my laptop and put away my clothes and books. The room was small, but comfortable, a single bed on one side and a desk built into the wall opposite, next to a cupboard. There was even a small bathroom containing a shower, sink and loo. It was on the third floor of a relatively new building, on a corridor with ten more just like it along with a communal kitchen.

It didn't take me long to sort myself out, and I was left staring out the window into a small park across from the School of Magic, which was a large, wide building resembling a palace. I could see protective Wards and Enchantments all over the thing, designed to keep students from breaking the place while learning to control themselves.

It was the Sunday of the second week in September, classes were supposed to start the next day. My first, the general orientation for Advanced Magicians, was at ten in the morning in a lecture hall across the way from me.

I frowned as I stared. I thought it would feel different, being at university. I'd been expecting purposefulness, a sense of... I don't know, belonging? But I just felt empty.

And alone.

That hadn't been a problem before I'd been with Cathy. I'd always been quite content to be by myself. I just needed to get back to that equilibrium, then I'd be fine... probably. It was just after midday. There were supposed to be Freshman mixers later on, but I had almost no interest in anything of the sort. I hadn't been great with strangers *before* they started trying to kill me, and besides, drinking was out of the question (mind-altering chemicals + Magician = colossal cock-up).

I sighed (again), put my jumper back on and decided to go out for a walk, maybe get the lay of the land a little. I stepped out into the corridor, which had a couple of people wandering around, girls and boys. I walked carefully around them and towards the door leading to the stairs and the lift... which slammed open and hit me square in the face, cutting my lip and making me swear.

"Oh, God, sorry!" said a young and very earnest voice. I turned to see a boy, about my age, I thought. He was tall and handsome, with a straight back, elegantly styled blonde hair and blue eyes. He wore an Armani suit complete with platinum tie clip and signet ring, and carried a pair of crocodile-leather suitcases. Already the women on the corridor were eyeing him up like my dog looked at an unattended T-bone. Lucky bastard.

"Don't worry about it," I muttered, pulling my hand away from my cut lip. Not much damage, ten minutes work with a Healing Spell and it would be back to normal.

"No, I should have watched where I was going," he said. His accent was very upper class, and I recognised the crest on his signet ring as belonging to a very old house I couldn't quite place, one of the various Hannover offshoots, I thought; I didn't really care enough to search my memory.

"It's alright, my fault I'm sure," I said, sliding past him while I could, the girls were already moving in. He tried to protest, quite a nice gesture actually. He seemed pleasant enough, but my face hurt, and it didn't combine well with my mood, I could feel my Shadows close at hand, ready to swat something.

So I made my way down and into the square. It was mostly grass, bordered and crossed by paving slabs, trees offering shade, and dark wooden benches in strategic positions. I made my way over to one and sat with my map in hand, getting orientated.

The University was simply huge, I could walk the rest of the day and not see a fraction of the thing, so I settled for a walk to the buildings were I'd have my classes, just so I'd know how long it took, and where they were (I got lost at the drop of a hat, it was ridiculous enough that I did my best to minimise it as much as possible). That used up about an hour, but only because I made it drag on; I wasn't in a rush. I stopped at a relatively quiet sandwich place, which made your meal to order from ingredients in a counter. I made a note of that; their meat feast was a thing of beauty...

I explored the Student Union, which was already half full of students getting plastered, the shopping district, the laundrette, the six book shops, the theatre (which doubled as a cinema), the auditorium, the Magic shop, which too restrictive to be really useful, but at least I knew where it was.

With nothing else to do, I went to the movies. I already knew quite a bit of Stonebridge, though my knowledge was mostly confined to the Old Quarter and the shopping districts. When I came out of some piece of B-Movie nonsense that was a waste of time I should have spent reading, it was dark and I was in an even worse mood. I walked back towards Naiad Hall and picked up another sandwich on my way. It was after six, and the sun had already set. I'd wasted my whole day, but I was too proud (and stupid) to go home and face questions.

I took the scenic route and came upon a small square near one of the university's more exclusive clubs, the Harrington Club (not exclusive as in Magic, exclusive as in *money*).

It was quite well appointed, with marble benches and a

small water feature, there was a Willow tree at the centre, its branches drooping and it leaves on the turn.

"What do you want?" said a scared male voice from under that tree.

The voice sounded familiar. I cast Mage Sight and nearly swore.

There were two Magicians under the tree, along with a young man; the kid who'd hit me in the chops with the door. He was backed up against the tree trunk flanked by the two women, his escape cut off. He was still wearing the suit, but his tie was at half mast.

The Magicians were young women, about nineteen, tall and thin. I did notice that there was something rather peculiar about their Wells, though; almost like the energy wasn't entirely theirs, if that makes sense. Very odd, but Magic was Magic. They were Adepts, which were not especially powerful on their best day, and laughably weak compared to a Sorcerer, much less me. But against a regular person, they could be lethal if they chose. Both were dark haired, wearing a lot of black, with silver piercings in ears and noses. One wore fishnets, the other a long skirt, both had black nails.

"Why you, of course, Sweetie," replied the girl on the left, her voice a throaty chuckle, "noble blood is a rare commodity, and the rest of you isn't so bad either."

She was flickering with power; Air Magic. I saw electricity coiling around her hands. The other was quiet, but her eyes were sinister and haunted; she was eyeing up the guy in a way that was not pleasant.

"I have an appointment," the young man said, his voice breaking into a squeak as he took a step forward. A gust of air blew him back against the tree and his lips began to tremble.

"Now, now, don't be so hasty, it's not going to hurt too much... the first time," Electric Girl said.

Oh, crap. Why couldn't I ever walk in on fun things? It's always got to be stuff like *this*...

"Is there a problem here?" I asked quietly, pushing

through the branches of the tree, a set of shields cast and ready.

The girls spun quickly, I felt the other prepare Flesh Magic.

"Oh, thank God," the boy said, relaxing a little.

"Push off," Electric Girl snapped at me, "We're busy."

"Hardly my problem," I said, staring them down, "Now, I ask again, do we have a problem?"

"Oh yes," Electric Girl said, "I rather think we do."

She threw lightning. Not a lot, it would have been enough to knock me on my arse and render me unconscious, but it wouldn't have done any permanent damage. Naturally the attack just smacked into my shields, without even taking off a layer.

"Not your evening, girls," I said politely.

"Come on Patty, we can take hi-" the Flesh-Adept started to say... before I tossed a Sleep-Hex into her and she dropped like a sack of Goth-potatoes.

"Final warning," I said.

Patty swallowed hard and let go of her accumulated energy.

"We were just messing around," she said, a note of fear in her voice.

"That sort of messing around is why Pureborn burned us at the stake," I replied coldly, Patty started trembling.

I really had to watch my tone; I was terrifying people almost by default. Tethys said it was my body language combined with a kind of quiet menace, particularly when I was angry. She said she found it attractive, but then she *was* peculiar.

"It goes without saying that if I should find you doing anything like this again, there will be consequences?" I continued.

She nodded, unwilling to meet my eyes.

"Good. Then take your friend and go. Before I change my mind."

Patty nodded and gestured, her first attempt to call her

Will failed and she had to try again before she could float the other girl away. I made sure they were out of sight before turning back to their victim.

"You alright?" I asked, making an effort to lighten my tone.

"Yeah, yes, fine," he said, wiping sweat off his forehead with a silk handkerchief, "Thank you, I was a little scared there."

"No problem. I'd steer clear of that lot if I were you. Intimidation only works until the threat's out of sight."

"Don't need to tell me twice!" he said with a grin. He stepped forward and offered his hand, "Tom Watford."

"Mathew Graves," I said, shaking it.

"I take it you're a Magician?" he asked politely.

I nodded.

"A good one, apparently, you handled those two like they were nothing!"

I shrugged off the compliment.

"They're just kids," I said, "I doubt they'd actually have done you harm, if that's any comfort. Might have messed with you a little."

"What makes you say that?" he asked; he seemed genuinely curious.

"If they were the harming sort, the one with the lightning would have hit me harder; she threw an attack hard enough to knock me out, and no more, like a Taser shot."

"Can *you* do that?" he asked.

"Sure. But it's a bit flashy for my taste. Come on, those outfits looked almost uniform-like, and I'd hate to think they have a coven within shouting distance."

"Coven?" he asked, gulping audibly, "Should I be worried?"

"I don't think so. I think they're probably a bit scared now, they'll probably behave."

"Shame they were a bit psycho, they were so fit."

I snorted, "And coral snakes are pretty, but that doesn't

mean you should let one nibble on you."

He barked out a laugh and clapped me on the back (which hurt. He wasn't a weakling, that was for sure...).

"So, what are you in for?" he asked, "I assume some sort of witchy-thing?"

I gave him a glare, which affected him not at all, and answered his question before asking him much the same thing. It turned out that he was in the business school and already had a very pleasant job lined up at his father's company. He was supposed to be going to Cambridge, but his father bribed the wrong fellow, and now he was stuck in Stonebridge.

"Stonebridge isn't so bad," I offered.

"If you're a Magician. This isn't even day one, and I've already been accosted!"

"Fair enough. Next time, just run. The element of surprise is far more effective that you think, and Magicians don't tend to be overly physical creatures-"

"Oh, I don't know, some of you seem to get by," said a familiar girly voice from behind us.

I spun, calling Shadows. My heart started hammering immediately, even as my brain tried to tell me that if *she'd* wanted a fight, she'd already have broken my fool neck.

"Get behind me," I hissed at Tom, and he darted to obey, stepping over my Shadows very carefully as I stared down Margaret, the Demigoddess.

She was leaning casually up against a tree, dressed in jeans and a jacket. She looked entirely unruffled and wasn't obviously armed, but that meant nothing. After what I'd seen her do, I was confident that if she decided to do me an injury, her hands would do just fine, if I was unprepared.

"Friend of yours?" Tom asked.

"Recently banished her boyfriend. So, unlikely."

"Banished?"

"Later," I said, "What do you want, Margaret?"

"Maggie, please, all my lovers call me Maggie."

That made me pause, as you might imagine.

"Care to run that one by me again?"

She smiled, it wasn't a look that made me feel secure, "We fought, Warlock, you and I. Strength against strength, Will against Will, giving our all to the battle, tell me there's not something intimate about that? Something that draws us together, almost like an embrace."

"First, don't call me Warlock, it's offensive. Second, I wasn't giving it my all. If I had, you'd be dead and in tiny little pieces all over the side of that hill. You weren't an effort for me. I gave you less attention than I'd give to a particularly large spider. Just be thankful I wasn't in the mood to start pulling off legs."

All crap, just so you know. I may not be fond of spiders, but I don't pull limbs off things. I was just going for enough intimidation to get her away from me.

She laughed.

It wasn't the reaction I was going for.

"You think I came here without looking into you? Besides, I can *see* you, right down to your core. There isn't so much as a drop of blood on you anywhere. You haven't taken a life, not one. You talk a good game, but you are a gentle man. Don't worry, I'll help you get over that."

"Don't confuse not killing with gentility," I said dangerously, "I don't kill because my enemies can't suffer if they're dead."

Not entirely untrue, but also a terrible lie. I will not kill. Not ever, not for anything. I didn't have the *right*.

She just kept smiling.

"Whatever you say, Milord," she said. Damn, she knew that, too?

"You're a lord?" Tom asked.

"*That's* your takeaway from all of that?"

"No, I have other questions," he said reasonably, "That was just the one that stuck."

"Quiet, Mortal, higher beings are talking," Maggie said

to Tom.

He subsided, cowering behind me, actually. Not that I could blame him. If there was a convenient back, I'd have done the same.

"What are you after?" I asked her.

"Why you, of course. You won me, after all. You accepted my surrender."

"You're not quite sane, are you?" I replied.

"Easy, Graves, she looks dangerous!" Tom hissed from behind me.

"Oh, she very definitely is. Just not to me."

"Oh, the arrogance of the Archon," Maggie said with a chuckle.

"What's that now?" Tom said.

"Oh, thanks very much," I said to the woman with a glare, "I was keeping that to myself!"

"I won't tell anyone, if that helps," Tom offered quietly.

"That's decent of you."

"Least I can do really," he replied.

"And it's not arrogance if it's true, then it's just pride," I said to Maggie, damn but carrying on two conversations like that was getting to be a strain.

"Pride goeth before a fall, Warlock."

"I'll give you one more warning about the Warlock thing, and then I'm taking things personally," I said with a glare.

"I was forged of blood and iron, *Warlock*, your little stares don't intimidate me."

"I don't doubt that," I replied, "but my Shadows should give you a *little* pause."

She smiled again, looking me over.

"Let me see your eyes, your true eyes," she said.

"No."

"Why? Why shouldn't I see them?"

"I'm going to save you a lot of pain, alright? I am in a foul mood, I find the very idea of the organisation you represent abhorrent, and I have found that my temper is not as well controlled as it used to be. Adding that information to the whole 'Archon' thing, how much further would you like to push your luck tonight?"

"All the way," she whispered, her eyes dancing with interest.

"If that's what you want..."

"Oh, yes it is," she said, moving towards me.

And then she fell to the ground, out like a light.

The Illusion of me standing in front of Tom vanished and I stepped out from behind my glamour. I'd gotten in behind her while we were chatting and dropped a Sleep Hex into her head as she advanced.

"What just happened?" Tom asked, a little shocked.

"My favourite trick," I said with a smirk, "See what I mean about surprise?"

"Oh yes," he said, looking down at the girl, "She's not... I mean you didn't..."

He mimed slitting a throat.

"What?" I asked, "Oh! No, she's sleeping, not dead!"

I called my Will and shoved her up into the lower branches of the tree she'd been leaning against, where she'd be out for an hour or so.

"So, you're an Archon?" he said, "Shadow, I'm guessing?"

I nodded.

"Are you just going to leave her there?"

"Have to. Technically speaking, I committed a Magical assault. And I suppose she does deserve this one pass. I did blow up her boyfriend."

"Won't she just track you down again?"

"Maybe. Cross that bridge, I guess."

"I would have expected an Archon to be taller," he said as we carried on our way.

"Sorry."

"Not your fault, I suppose," he said magnanimously, "Does that happen often? Women dropping out of the sky and offering themselves to you?"

"Not what she was offering."

"Sure sounded like it was," he said, nudging my ribs.

I concentrated and an image of the half-breed Cherub appeared in front of us, making Tom jump.

"This was her ex. Still think she's inclined to trade that in for me?"

He snorted and shrugged. We carried on.

"Girls are crazy, you never know," he said, smirking.

We made it back to Naiad, and as he hit the corridor, I kid you not, girls appeared. And not just from our floor, *all* of them, as far as I could tell. I grinned and left him to it. The walk back had been filled with his questions about Magic and Archons. I'd answered them, and he didn't seem terrified at the end. He really did seem like a decent sort; he even reminded me of Des before he went insane, nice but a little lacking in higher thinking. Not exactly dim, just absent of deep thought.

I slid into my room and sat on my bed, kicking my shoes into the corner.

I should have known that crazy woman would be back eventually. Maybe I should have put an Asimov in her head while I had the chance? I could have, I normally *would* have, but I had trouble shaking the idea that she wasn't evil. There wasn't a drop of blood in her aura... nothing to make me think that she'd done something nasty. But then she'd been with the Champions at the Red Carpet; she would certainly have helped the others when they stormed the place. *That* made her my enemy.

I sighed. I wasn't solving that problem today. I slapped a movie on my laptop and settled in with my sandwich, leafing through a textbook between bites. The sounds from outside had increased for the last hour, and soon music started blaring.

I frowned and cast a Muffling Spell, which cut it out nicely.

Still heard the door get knocked on two hours later,

though.

"Yep?" I said, the door opened and Tom staggered in.

"You have to hide me, those women are *animals*!" he said, slamming the door behind him.

I laughed, taking in his appearance. There was lipstick on his collar, neck, cheeks and shirt, which was pulled open to his navel. His jacket was torn and his belt wouldn't hold up his trousers. He was missing one shoe, and he didn't have socks on.

"What the hell happened to you?" I asked, barely containing another laugh. He looked like he'd been mauled by a tigress (or two... or six).

"Well, one of them, Harriet, I think her name was, asked me back to her room, and I thought fine, why not? She's attractive! But when I got there, there were four more of them, and then there was touching and everyone was naked, and now I have some bites and pulls in some places where I shouldn't have either, and the rest heard, and now they want in too, and they won't take no for an answer!"

"You poor thing," I said without sympathy.

"I don't know what to do! I can't physically carry on, Graves! The first lot nearly killed me! I didn't even take part in most of it!"

"Do you want this stopped permanently, or just for tonight?" I asked, trying to resist the urge to throttle him for complaining about having too *much* female attention...

"Just tonight," he said after a minute, blushing terribly.

"Then all you need to do is tell any girl you come across that you're tired, and you want to be your best for her. Then just set an appointment."

"Oh, that's good!" he said, darting out the door again.

Lucky bastard. Nice fellow, but I rather *had* to hate him for that, just a little bit...

# CHAPTER 5

And, naturally, I couldn't get rid of him after that. He woke me up at *seven* the following morning with suggestions of breakfast. I responded with creative swearing that would have frightened a smarter man, but which only seemed to make him even more chipper. In the end I got up so I wouldn't have to Curse him (it was a close-run thing).

"I heard about this great breakfast spot ten minutes from campus," he said as we walked down the stairs, ahead of any pursuing women, "I heard they do wonders with tofu."

*Mustn't punch him, mustn't punch him...*

"If you're dragging me out of my nice warm bed at this ungodly hour, then we're going to *my* breakfast place," I said, pulling my jacket a bit tighter about my person.

"Are they organic?" he asked dubiously.

I turned a glare on him and he grinned.

Maccaby's Diner was one of those businesses Tethys had her fingers in. And as far as I knew, there wasn't a single healthy thing on the menu (except maybe the lettuce they put in the burgers). I once heard a tourist ask if there was a house salad, and all the regular customers laughed so hard, he started to cry.

The space was long and thin, with booths along one side, opposite a counter, with windows on the bottom end, facing Wallingford Park, not too far from the University's Western border.

"My God," Tom said as he perused the menu, "I feel like I'm getting artery plaque just reading this."

"One more comment like that, and I'll revoke your Man-

Card," I replied.

He snorted and kept reading, nodding appreciatively.

"My mother never let me eat in places like this," he said conspiratorially, "I always had to eat healthy."

"Live a little. That's what university's for, isn't it? Look who I'm talking to, you've already made good use of your time."

"My everything hurts after that," he muttered.

"I would hit you if you weren't so much stronger than me."

He smirked and put down his menu, "So, what's there to do in Stonebridge? I know nothing about this town."

"There's a bit of everything. What are you into?"

"Girls, mostly, and drinking, and did I mention girls?" he asked, with a bit of a leer at the waitress.

The kid was nothing if not a credit to our gender.

"Anything else?"

"Sports, I'll play anything, or watch anything. Games of chance are always fun, preferably high stakes."

My God, he was like the anti-me...

I went through what little I knew that could be pertinent, not that it was much. Meanwhile. he ordered something with bacon, butter, bread and cheese that would give even *me* pause, while I ordered scrambled eggs (my stomach was bothering me). Tom quickly overcame his attachment to healthy living, and ordered three more things off the menu before we settled up and left, with me almost having to prop the twit up.

"Best breakfast ever," he said as he staggered back towards Naiad, "Oh, I'm going to have to run for a month to work that off.

I smiled. If nothing else, I could make him fat; that would do the trick...

Damn, that was evil, even for *me*.

It was just before nine when we turned the corner into a bustling plaza near the centre of the campus. Students with early morning classes were out and about, most seeming bright and eager. I was actually starting to feel a bit better about the place. Tom may have been something of a twit, but he was good company; he had dirty jokes and stories that would make a sailor blush, and he had a genuine interest in Magic that kept me thinking.

As we were approaching the Great Hall, a small clutch of girls appeared, books and pads in hand as they laughed and joked. They were freshmen, like us, all of them attractive and dressed fashionably (and just a little bit provocatively, even in spite of the cold weather). I moved to steer us clear, while taking a surreptitious look.

And then I stopped dead, the blood draining from my face as my mouth dropped open. Tom noticed and turned to see what was wrong.

"Wha-"he started before I darted to put his bulk between me and the girls, where I cowered.

I was hyperventilating, trying not to panic... what was *she* doing here?!

"What is it?" he asked, his voice slightly panicked, "Are we in danger?"

"My ex-girlfriend is right behind you," I whispered.

He took a subtle look at the group.

"Which one?" he muttered.

"Redhead on the left!"

Bloody Jocelyn Faust! This was just not sodding fair! Though quite predictable if I'd given it even the tiniest bit of thought. Damn it!

She looked good, though. Long copper hair in a headband, falling in a sheet down her back, her blue eyes dazzling as she smiled and laughed with her friends. Her lips were full and red, her face heart shaped and lovely. She wore a cotton shirt, blue cashmere cardigan and silk skirt over knee length socks and patent leather shoes.

My appreciation came to a screaming halt as the image of her and Des sprang into my head and I gritted my teeth against remembered pain.

"I take it this isn't a happy reunion?" Tom said sympathetically.

"Cheated on me with my brother, nearly got me eaten by Ogres, it's a long and complicated story."

"Nothing's simple with you, is it?"

I ignored him, and kept peering around his body until they'd rounded a corner.

Finally, I relaxed, letting out a breath.

"Not as such, no," I finally answered.

I led the way back towards Naiad Hall, my equilibrium ruined, and my mood along with it. I made my way back to my room. I still had an hour to go until my lecture, and I didn't want to spend it out in the open (or near Tom while he was pawed by the Naiad ladies).

What the hell was I going to do now? I didn't want to have to deal with Jocelyn. The emotions were too complicated, and still too raw, even after all this time. In the end, there was no way to avoid her forever; I was fairly certain she went to the Magic School, so we almost had to run into each other eventually...

I would just have to take things as they came. Maybe luck would be with me for the next three years, and I'd never run into her at all?

Don't look at me like that; denial was all I had to work with!

The hall where I'd have my first lecture was easy enough to find, located in one of the sub-levels beneath the Magic School. There was enough space for about two hundred, the seats in ascending rows, covered in cracking brown leather. There was a projector in the ceiling; a podium and wide table on a stage at the front.

I was the youngest student there by quite a margin, which I should have expected. It was an introductory class for advanced students, after all, which meant level seven and above (not something one generally managed before the age of forty or fifty, unless you were a prodigy or an Archon). About fifty men and women filled the seats towards the front of the room. Most *looked* young, but they were all Wizards and Sorcerers, so that was misleading.

I'd discovered that I could get a general feeling of someone's age from looking at their Aura with Mage Sight. Experience accumulated as complexity in the shapes and colours, and from that I made a guess that nobody else in the room was less than fifty years old, and a couple were over three hundred. This was quite a normal sampling for an advanced class; education was an ongoing thing for Magicians, with many continuing to attend classes and seminars throughout their lives.

I noticed that the other students seemed to know one another already, or knew someone who could introduce them to those they didn't know. One or two introduced themselves to me, but it was out of simple politeness rather than as a genuine desire to include me in their conversations.

Already there were cliques, and I wasn't a part of them...

At ten on the dot, the professor came in. He was tall and thin, wearing tweed under an academic gown. His face was lined and craggy and his eyes were bright and incisive under short-cropped receding white hair; a short white beard covered the lower half of his face.

I recognised him immediately as the head examiner of my Level Ten test, and current number one on my shit-list. He had introduced himself as Professor Martin Aldwich. I hadn't known he was a professor at Stonebridge when I'd taken my test, which was idiotic, now I thought about it. The test had been held at the bloody university, after all. My eyes narrowed, and my temper flared dangerously at the very sight of the bigoted prick.

"Good morning everyone, it's good to see so many familiar faces. Most of you know the drill by now, but the rules say I have to give the talk, and I believe that we do have a new face or two, so we'll do the introduction properly," he said with a smile as he took in the familiar crowd.

"Firstly, before we carry on, Concealing-Magic is dishonest. Someone in here is using it, and I invite him to stop immediately."

That was odd, and worrying. I hadn't seen anything with my Mage Sight, and that Spell was supposed to be able to see through just about any Illusion or Concealment Magic. I looked around for the culprit more carefully.

"We can do this the easy way, or the hard way," Aldwich said, "makes no difference to me."

I still couldn't see the culprit; maybe this fellow did have some things to teach me after all?

"Alright, have it your way, Mister Graves. Would you come to the front, please?"

My eyes narrowed in suspicion. What could he possibly be playing at?

"Now," the professor said, his eyes boring into me.

I did what I was told. I stood and walked down the aisle and stepped onto the small stage.

"You were given a chance to be honest with your classmates, the people you sit among as your peers. You lost that chance, and now you will stop what you are doing, or you will leave."

"What?" I asked, aghast and annoyed at the accusation. I wasn't doing anything... oh! The Illusion covering my scars and eyes!

"My Illusions are doing no harm, and they make me feel better," I said after a moment's thought (and a couple of *very* deep breaths).

"This is a place of knowledge; fact, not deception. If you are not willing to be who you are, then you have no place here. Now, shut down the Illusions, or leave."

I was fuming mad and grinding my teeth, but again, I did as I was told. My eyes turned back to their normal colour and the scars reappeared on my face. The other students gasped, one woman actually squeaked. Aldwich looked satisfied.

"You are a cruel man, Sir," I said softly before turning on my heel and walking back towards my seat.

"We're not done yet, Graves. You will now apologise to me and your classmates for your deception," he said.

There was angry muttering from the other students. Magicians stuck together, and that kind of humiliation was not to our taste. Aldwich didn't care; he was so determined on my debasement that he didn't realise that there were now fifty powerful and experienced Magicians looking over their shoulders for the day when he might do something like this to *them*.

Not that any of them spoke up for me.

"I offer my apologies," I said to the others, "I merely wanted to spare myself a little humiliation. I can't imagine why I thought that would be an issue."

I turned to look Aldwich in the eyes, and something in mine made him flinch, "Will that do, Sir? Perhaps you'd prefer it if I gave it another try on my knees?"

"Don't talk back to me, Shadowborn. You're only here on sufferance."

He'd said it like that so that the others would know what I was, and would be less likely to sympathise. A few did look scared, but the rest didn't seem particularly bothered. Most had figured out what I was already; the scars on my face were very well known, about a dozen people had been given them a while back by the same group of Shadowborn-hunting fanatics. It was meant to say, 'Here's a Shadowborn! Feel free to aim the rotten fruit at this point'.

I had to say, though, this was a new record for me, only ten minutes into day one before my first public humiliation... wonderful.

"You are straying dangerously close to a complaint for discrimination, Professor Aldwich," I said softly.

And also a Shadow Lance to the face.

"You don't intimidate me here, Graves," he replied, sneering.

"More fool you," I said, now starting to get *really* angry.

"Was that a threat?"

"More a comment on your intelligence."

"You think you can stand there, a duellist and a monster, and speak to me like that in my own lecture hall? And get away with it?!"

"Yes, and I'll tell you why. Three reasons: one, you are in the wrong, two, you are in the wrong in the most stupid possible way, and most importantly three, I've been recording this conversation," I said, pulling my phone out of my pocket for him to see.

There were some appreciative mutterings from the others.

"Start being civil right this second or this goes to the Dean by close of business."

Even if he did as I asked, it was *still* going to the Dean. I was that mad.

"You may return to your seat, Mister Graves," he said in a snarl.

"Thank you," I said, slipping my phone back into its pocket.

"I'll take that now, please," he said, pointing at a sign on the wall:

*No Mobile Phones.*

He held out a box and I turned my phone off before placing it inside. He smiled at his small victory and turned away with it. I thought I felt a bit of Magic, but if I had, then it was nothing, barely a flicker of a flicker. Probably just anger on his part; no teacher liked to be shown up in front of their students.

I don't remember much of what he said after that; though I retained some little bits and pieces of orientation. It was mostly warnings about using Magic outside of the School building and other things like that. But as long as I used some version of common sense, then I shouldn't have any problems. Finally, he was done and everyone filed out, some eyes lingering on me as I remained sat down, staring at the Professor.

"What do you want?" he asked with a glare.

"To provide you with food for thought," I said.

I stood and walked slowly down towards him.

"If you're wrong about me, if I'm not the monster you think I am, and I find a way to live quietly, without using the Black, then you've just been unnecessarily cruel to a good man just trying to live in peace."

He snorted his disdain at that idea.

"And if you're *right*," I said, my voice a menacing whisper that made his eyes go wide in fear, "then you've just seriously annoyed the next Master of the Black. Tell me, *Professor* Aldwich, which of those scenarios makes you look like a genius?"

He gulped audibly and took a step away from me.

I picked my phone out of the box.

"Like I said, food for thought," I said, stepping back, "I'm willing to let today go. Damage done. I won't report you; all I ask is to be treated like anyone else, and not like a second class citizen because of my powers."

His face remained a snarl, I doubted I was getting through.

"Or, we can just do this until you piss me off so much that I call you out. And it seems to me that you can guess how that would go."

"I wouldn't demean myself by fighting the likes of you!" he spat.

"You say that like you'd have a choice," I said, turning on my heel and walking away, "Think on the benefits of civility, Professor."

Well... that was a pain.

I started stomping towards the exit, barely looking where I was going, I was that upset. I thought briefly of re-casting my Illusions, but what would be the point? Even if I covered up, people would still point and stare at the Shadow-born. It wouldn't be too long after that before they realised that I wasn't just *any* Shadowborn, either. Aldwich had used my name, and I was relatively well known in my own right, First Shadow stuff aside.

As far as Magical Society was aware, I was a Shadowborn Sorcerer, and there hadn't been one yet that hadn't gone *cataclysmically* bad, and taken significant chunks of a population with them. I already had something of a reputation in that direction; I'd beaten up Conclave Hunters as well as Councillors, I'd assaulted the nobility, caused scandals...

It wasn't all bad; I had a little *good* press. That Agrammel thing, for example, I'd saved a hospital; oh, the Crooked House, that was common knowledge, saved some Fairies.

Even so, very little of what I was known for made me look warm and cuddly. Generally speaking, people were scared of Mathew Graves, Shadowborn Sorcerer, and I couldn't blame them. On paper, at least, I was rather an unsavoury fellow.

I emerged into sunshine, and found a few people were already pointing and staring, though they were taking the trouble to at least *try* and be subtle. I scowled, which actually sent a couple running, and walked away from the building. I had my first Advanced Flesh-crafting Class in an hour, which would then last two, but in the meantime I intended to hide in my room until I had my temper under better control...

"Mathew?" said a gentle voice from behind me.

Oh, balls. Not her, not now...

I stopped.

"Jocelyn," I said turning around, "I'd heard you were here."

"Me too, about you, I mean," she said, a little nervously, I thought.

The crowd was being less surreptitious about their staring, one woman in particular, who stood out. She looked young, but not *that* young. There was something in her eyes that spoke of experience, and she wore clothes baggy enough to conceal weapons. She watched our interaction very carefully. I met her eyes and she actually blanched a bit. I deliberately looked at her hand, which was inside her jacket, and she twitched it back to her side, flushing slightly.

"Your bodyguard, I assume?" I asked.

Jocelyn turned to look and went red herself.

"Nobody's supposed to know. She's supposed to be discreet," Jocelyn said, a tiny expression of annoyance crossing her features, which crinkled her nose in a rather adorable fashion.

"Don't feel bad, paranoia is a habit I've had to form. Well, good catching up with you."

I turned away; I didn't need her sort of stress...

"Matty, wait, please?"

I winced, but like an idiot, I turned back.

"Did you talk to Lady Hopkins?" she asked softly, "Did she tell you what *really* happened?"

The last time we'd met, I'd been unaware of Hopkins' involvement in the Jocelyn-Des drama. Jocelyn had told me, and Hopkins had later admitted her role as mastermind, leading to a colossal falling out that took an assassination attempt to resolve. Like I said... complicated.

"She did," I said neutrally.

"Then... then why didn't you call?" she asked in a tiny voice.

"Because it didn't help," I said, with a sigh, "I loved you, and you broke me. I was a zombie for a solid week. I still think of that as the worst day of my life, and there have been some *bad* ones since then."

I exaggerated a bit for effect, but it *was* a bad day...

"I'm sorry, I'll always be sorry! When are you going to forgive me? You know I only did what I did for you. It disgusted me, I felt dirty after. I was miserable too! You're the only boy I ever met who saw *me*, not a Faust. Do you know what it was like to lose that? It broke me too, Matty!"

I rubbed my eyes, feeling frustrated and guilty.

"What do you want, Jocelyn?" I asked, my voice very

tired.

"Can we start over? I don't expect... I'm not rushing anything, just talk? Maybe we can both find a little peace?" she said, her eyes starting to glisten.

I had to fold. I couldn't deal with crying girls, especially if I was the cause. Something in me panicked and drove me to do anything, no matter how stupid or expensive, trying to get them to stop (that was how the Pixies got their way all the time).

"Alright. I have class at twelve till one, I can meet you then?"

She nodded, "See you here?"

"Okay."

She beamed at me and bounced off, the tears gone, and the bodyguard following at a discreet distance, giving me the evil eye. Unwise of her; mine were scarier. She looked away first.

Advanced Flesh Crafting was held in a small laboratory in the west end of the Magic School. It was a relatively small space with three rows of benches, shelves around the walls and fridges set into a small alcove. I was one of four students, two other men and one woman. I recognised them from the introductory lecture, and they obviously recognised *me*, as none of them would sit anywhere near me.

The Professor came in, a bright, young-looking woman with blonde hair, brown, soulful eyes and a wide smile. She wore a business suit under robes and carried a thick textbook under her arm.

"Good morning, I'm Professor Hadleigh, and welcome to- Eeek!"

Saw my eyes. I didn't normally get this strong a reaction from other Magicians; she must have been startled. After the screech, she just stood there, staring at me. Like a deer caught in headlights, she couldn't look away. Her face had even gone white with mounting terror. I sighed and recast my Illusion, which seemed to snap her out of it, just a little. It also caused her to go bright red and become even more incoherent.

"Um...," she said, "I was just saying..."

She mumbled on for another five minutes, not taking her eyes off me. In the end, mostly out of simple pity, I just made myself invisible; she looked around in fear for a bit longer but managed to get herself back together.

"Welcome to Advanced Flesh Crafting," she said, starting again, "this is where you learn all about advanced medical Magic, and the principles under which it is employed."

She talked for about half an hour, outlining a course that was as much anatomy and physiology as it was Magic, covering the basics of Magical diagnosis and treatment. Even her brief introduction was enough to show me just how brutish and energy-intensive my use of Flesh Magic had been.

The Professor, for all her initial panic, managed to take a topic I was already interested in and make it truly fascinating. Her module would teach the basics (well, advanced basics) of gross repairs and excisions, basic cures and treatments. A true healer would need to dedicate at least five years to courses just like hers, something which I seriously considered. I had the time.

She spoke like an artist in love with her medium, describing a skill based on knowledge, technique and focus; I could imagine Michelangelo speaking that way about marble, or Mozart of music. I felt it would be a privilege to learn from her, she sounded like she *really* knew her stuff. If I could learn even a fraction of what she was offering, I could vastly improve my ability to heal myself and others, something which was, unfortunately, essential in my life.

For the rest of the hour she directed us to several texts on physiology and gave us a primer on infection as it related to Magical cures. It was very interesting stuff, at least to me. I could already see how I'd been doing things the hard way.

Finally the class wrapped up and the others filed out. I dropped my Illusion and walked towards Hadleigh.

She swallowed hard, her eyes darting and afraid.

"Are you quite alright, Professor?" I asked as nicely as I could.

"Um... yes... yes, Mister Graves, of course. What can I do for you?" she asked, her voice trembled a little.

"Have I done something, Ma'am? You'll forgive me, but you seem more startled than my appearance usually accounts for."

"No, no, of course not... I'm just... you're...," she began but then subsided into embarrassed silence.

"You shouldn't believe everything you hear. I'm really not that bad."

"Oh, yes, I'm sure!" she said unconvincingly.

"You're even now wondering if you can outrun me to the door, aren't you?"

The ghost of a smile crossed her features.

"Window," she replied in a whisper, still looking down.

"Look, if I'm making you uncomfortable, I'll drop the class," I said; her head darted up, a mortified look on her face, "Nobody should feel uncomfortable in their workplace. I just... I liked the outline, and it looked interesting."

"That's not necessary, Mister Graves! I should know better than to judge a man on hearsay. I was just a little startled... I wasn't expecting someone so..."

Silence again.

"You weren't expecting the monster to look like one?" I offered affably.

"Something like that," she said, and then clapped her hands over her mouth.

"It's alright, I'm getting used to it. I'll see you next time, then?"

She nodded and I walked out, making sure to give her plenty of space.

I sighed when I was out of earshot.

God, day one and I already *hated* that place...

And now, as if that wasn't enough for one day, it was time to present myself for the rectal exam that was Jocelyn.

I met her outside the Magic School and she smiled shyly, tucking a stray lock of her hair behind her ear as she watched me. There was no fear in her eyes, no wariness, which I appreciated. But then she knew me for the coward I really was.

"Hi," she said, coming over to kiss my cheek.

I tried not to wince, we weren't there yet.

"Hi," I replied.

"Want to grab a coffee?"

*No, I want to go find someplace dark and scream...*

"Sure," I said instead.

She took my hand and led me off.

"I heard about your first class, I'm sorry."

Word travelled *way* too fast in that hell-hole...

"It's nothing new, I'm sorry to say-"

"Hey!" said a loud, deep voice from behind us, "Stay away from my girlfriend, freak!"

"Damn it Gerald! I've told you before; I am not your girlfriend!" Jocelyn said, and then to me, "I went out with him *once* as a favour to his sister, and now he's obsessed."

He was tall, dark haired and slim. He wore a designer jacket, jeans and t-shirt along with heavy walking boots. Handsome guy, too, classically so, with an aquiline nose, high cheekbones, good chin, the whole nine. The good looks were somewhat ruined by the look of jealous hatred plastered on his face.

And then he saw my eyes and his look of hate became one of disgust.

Then he laughed. It was a very loud, very obnoxious sound that grated dangerously against my temper. It went on for far too long, and, just like that, I was quite thoroughly *done*. At the end of my bloody rope. I was so sick and tired of it, all of it!

"Sorry, don't know why I was worried!" he said as he

looked me over, "What a mess!"

*Oh, you want to see a mess?!*

I raised my hand...

Time stopped.

I blinked. Hard.

Then *she* was there, appearing out of nowhere right in front of me. Rose; one of my Liaisons, the Angel. She was a tall, lovely woman with dark copper hair that shimmered in the September sun, her bright blue eyes were shining and narrowed, staring straight at me. She wore a white dress down to mid calf, her hands and feet bare.

"Think very carefully on what you choose to do now, Mathew Graves," she said, her eyes narrowing further, into a glare.

# CHAPTER 6

I lowered my hand with a sigh.

"Sorry," I said. It was the only thing I could think to say.

"Oh, it's not really your fault, Mathew," she said, walking forward so that she was standing close to me. She touched my cheek gently, her eyes locking with mine, "Well, it is in a way, in as much as your choices led here... let's say it's not *entirely* your fault."

"Hey!" said another familiar voice from off to the side, "That is cheating!"

I turned to see Gabrielle, my Liaison from the other side of the fence; she was as tall as Rose, with black hair and scarlet eyes, milk-white skin and a *spectacular* figure. If Rose was beauty, then Gabrielle was sensuality; the perfect contrasts to one another. The Demon wore black, everything tight, leaving her arms and midriff bare. It was like her very *being* chipped at a crack in my defences, drawing me to her, to temptation and darkness.

"Hardly," Rose replied, "it's a conversation."

"No, it's *cheating*. He was about to do something very naughty, and now you've ruined it!" the Demon said with a pout (a very interesting pout...).

"Hi Gabby, how's the family?" I asked, interrupting them before they could start shouting (or blasting things).

"Call me that infernal nickname one more time and I'll come upon you while you're sleeping and post what I do on the internet where your mother can see it!"

I smiled at that little outburst. She was a very peculiar Demon. And she'd gotten worse since she and I'd had our little... moment.

"Bearing in mind the sources of your names, surely your *full* name would be the infernal one, whereas the one I'm giving is really more accurately described as Magical?" I said in a very even tone that made Rose giggle.

Suddenly the Demon was hard up against me, her eyes inches from mine. I met her gaze, unafraid. There were rules.

"It's unwise to taunt a Demon, Graves," she said. Her breath was warm on my lips, smelling faintly of copper. Her perfume was heady, the scent thick in my nostrils.

"Really? Seems fun to me."

She growled a little, low in her throat. I saw horns appear on her head, four of them, curling and ridged, as her concentration slipped and her glamour vanished. Her true skin colour was dark red, a match for her eyes. Her tail was wrapped firmly around my waist, her arms on my shirt as she opened her mouth to reveal sharp canines.

"I could kill you right here," she whispered, moving her head around to nip my neck with her teeth, just enough to let me feel the points, not enough to break the skin.

"Is she always this aggressive?" I asked Rose, while trying to concentrate on something less interesting.

"Generally she's more subtle, but you seem to be able to get a rise out of her, somehow," the Angel replied, shaking her head.

"Annoying people is rather my thing. And I wasn't going to *hurt* that idiot."

"What *were* you going to do, then?" Rose asked, lifting an eyebrow.

"I don't really want to tell you," I replied, "it was a *little* naughty."

Simultaneous soiling and vomiting; a favourite trick of mine for people who'd *really* annoyed me, but hadn't done enough to justify a Magical neutering or some sort of immolation.

Gabrielle snorted, and seeing as how she'd just started

nosing at my neck, her breath caused all sorts of misfires in my nineteen year old brain...

She'd wrapped her arms around my neck, and I found myself returning the embrace. I found her attentions simultaneously relaxing and exciting, which wasn't doing anything good for my blood pressure. I shook my head to clear the confusion, but it didn't work very well. Pureblood Succubae were meant to be 'confusing', I didn't really stand a chance.

"Can't you do something about this? It's breaking my brain," I asked Rose, who rolled her eyes.

"She can't help you, Magician. Besides, she *likes* to watch," Gabrielle whispered into my ear.

"What's that, now?" I asked.

"Nothing!" Rose protested, glaring at the Demon, who chuckled naughtily and sent more goose bumps up my neck.

"Oh, I think he likes it," the Demon whispered, moving gently up against me.

I shook my head again, counting in prime numbers, which seemed to clear out some of the cobwebs. I set my Will against whatever she was doing... only to find that there was nothing there to fight. There was no Demonic Magic, she wasn't beguiling me with tricks; this was simple attraction and lots of it.

I can't really be blamed for that, she was meant to be the most physically attractive woman you'd ever see.

Bit of a blow to the old ego, though. I'd thought I was made of more reasonable, mature stuff than that, but it turned out that I was just as much a victim of a pretty face and a saucy smile as every other man my age (I know, you're shocked).

Rose sidled up and took one of my hands from Gabrielle's back, moving it up so we stood palm to palm, fingers interlocked. I think she was trying to help, but she triggered a sort of confusing melange of the natural affection I felt for her and the rampant attraction I felt for the Demon.

Gabrielle laughed a little.

"Doesn't work. There's a teeny piece of me in you now.

Even your pretty friend can't save you from *that*," she whispered.

"Gabby, that's not nice," I complained.

"Really? Are you sure? Because I think you like it. I think you like it a lot..."

"You know the rules! He may have let you in, but you may *not* exploit it! He's the balance, you idiot. Break him this way and you might break us all!"

Gabrielle rolled her eyes, but she gave my backside a final grope (making me jump) and stepped away.

"There, happy?"

"No! You take that part of you out of him, and you take it out *now*!"

"No can do. He chose it of his own free will... and all because of an act of compassion, isn't that beautiful? An act born from the inspiration of an Angel has brought a good man closer to the Devil-"

"Just you say that again!" Rose snarled.

You see what I mean about those two? I was fairly certain that they loved each other quite a bit, but in the manner of siblings who also couldn't stand each other for more than ten minutes at a stretch. I sighed and shaped a bit of Shadow into a chair to sit on while they had their domestic moment. They seemed to have forgotten that I was even there, which was a shame. I'd rather been enjoying the cuddle.

"Yes, just think of it!" Gabrielle continued, "A piece of Hell's finest seducer, lodged deep within the First Shadow, darkness incarnate, influencing him, making him darker still, pushing him further and further towards evil and the Black, and it's all because of *you*!"

"So that's your plan?" Rose hissed, her form suddenly bright with solid light.

For heaven's sake, anyone could see that she was just winding the Angel up. I was about to say so (and avoid the collateral damage) when another voice spoke up, and made the situation ten times more complicated.

"Well, I think that's all I needed to hear," said the voice, making me jump.

"Damn it, now what?" I said with a sigh as Neil walked around my seat and glared at his daughter.

"Father?" Gabrielle said, sudden fear in her eyes and stance.

"You've been very bad, Gabrielle," he said coldly, cruelly, in fact "Apologies for this, Mathew, family matter."

I nodded, thinking hard, standing so as to be ready for trouble.

This was... odd. He rather gave the impression that his relationship with his daughter was far more cordial than this. But then... Devil.

"I only took an opportunity," Gabrielle protested.

"You dare speak to me of opportunity? The souls of the Archons are not for you to amuse yourself with!" he said, energy seemed to flicker around his form, "They are off limits, you know that!"

Rose moved up to stand with Gabrielle.

"And you," Neil said to Rose, "you were supposed to be the best of your limited breed. I'm tempted to send you back to the Host in pieces! You instigated this whole mess!"

"Father please don't send me home!" Gabrielle begged, now on her knees, "I don't want to go, please!"

"You have nothing to bargain with, child," Neil said, "and I think it's time you were away."

He raised his hands and fire flickered on a patch of ground, until a black opening in the universe appeared, surrounded by white hot flames. There was nothing but darkness on the other side.

Gabrielle retreated, backing all the way up to me, wrapping her arms around my legs and weeping pitifully while Rose put herself between us and Neil.

"This isn't your business, child!" Neil snapped at Rose.

His form burst into flames, a match for the ones on the ground. His eyes were bright with white energy, wings of fire sprouted from his back, spreading out a dozen feet.

Rose braced herself, backing away, clearly terrified. I sniffed, looking at Neil, and then down at Gabrielle, who was still snivelling away. I caught her looking up at me, and our eyes met. I raised an eyebrow.

"This isn't even slightly fooling you, is it?" she asked.

"Nope, sorry," I said, "Points for effort, though."

"Shit," she said, standing up before leaning against my side, "Sorry Daddy."

Neil sighed, but the fires went out, the light in his eyes vanished, and he grinned as the 'Portal' vanished.

"What's happening?" Rose asked, a very worried look on her face.

"Neil's playing silly buggers. Unfortunately he forgot that the Devil's in the *details*," I said completely deadpan.

Gabrielle stifled a laugh and buried her head in my shoulder.

"Oh, very droll," Neil said, rolling his eyes, "What gave us away?"

"Gabby doesn't snivel. And as much as I may dislike your methods, you love your daughter too much to frighten her. And *that* wasn't a Portal."

Rose had come to stand by us. Neil grinned.

"Clever boy," he said, "I do so like it when they're clever. Very annoying, though."

"I presume that the idea was for me to barter for her freedom? At great cost, no doubt?"

"Can't blame me for trying."

"Sure I can," I said coldly, his smile went even wider.

"That sounds rather... definitive," he said, "almost threatening, in fact. Are you sure that's wise?"

"Can you open a portal to the Shadow Realm, Neil?" I asked evenly.

His eyes went wide, "You little bastard," he said angrily.

"Thought not. Do anything like this again, and I'll feed you to the Leviathans. Even you'll have trouble fighting them on their own ground."

"They don't call me Lightbringer for nothing, Boy," he snarled.

"Nor do they call me a monster for no good reason. I'm guessing your energy isn't infinite, even less so in *there*. And it just occurred to me that you're only arguing with me right now because that's exactly what you want," I said, realising my own stupidity.

What the hell was wrong with me? I was threatening the cosmic being in charge of eternal punishment! Well, I knew what was wrong with me, there was a hole in my soul putting me into a perpetual bad mood and making me spoil for a fight, but this was just ridiculous...

"Oh, do be a sport, Graves!" Neil said, "I put effort into these plans, you know!"

"How much effort? It seemed like this one needed a second pass."

"Well, you're really more of a side-project. I'm currently working this delightful little deal down in Rome. You should read about it in six months or so. Oh, it's going to be fun! I came because my girl was making good progress, and I like to support her. She'd have had you, too, if you weren't quite so on the ball..."

I sighed heavily, but he was gone before I had a chance to hit back with a snappy rejoinder.

"Stop that, I'm not happy with you," I said as Gabrielle started nuzzling again.

"Neither am I!" Rose said as she came forwards.

"Oh, relax, it's not like it came to anything," the Demon said.

"And if it had?" Rose asked icily.

"Then my week would have been much more fun!"

Rose slapped her. Hard.

Gabrielle reeled back, her hand going to her cheek in shock.

"You know what he did for you, what he *gave* for you,

and willingly. And you'd do *this*?" Rose hissed.

"Don't you play the high and mighty with me!" Gabrielle snarled back, her form flickering with black fire, "I've seen you, I've heard you whisper in his ear, and it's not all on the approved script, now, is it?!"

"I have discretion to speak to my charge as I see fit!" Rose replied, her form glowing with energy as her wings and halo flashed into being.

"Hey!" I shouted, both women jumped before turning to look at me a little sheepishly, "Would someone kindly explain to me what's going on? Because I'm not cleaning up the collateral damage if you two face off in the middle of a crowd!"

The Angel and the Demon looked at each other and seemed to silently agree to settle down.

"Simply put," Rose said, "When the Fae tore those chunks of soul out of you, it did a colossal amount of damage. Because there's a piece of *her* inside of you, your natural inclinations are more easily swayed towards... darker impulses as a result. So I try to use my influence to... shift the balance back, when I can."

"Which is just as interfering as what I'm doing, if not worse, because he doesn't have the chance to resist *you*, does he, Feathers?!"

"Oh shut up, will you?!" Rose practically screeched. She really was having a day... Angels weren't supposed to screech.

"And it doesn't work, does it? He's just getting darker! He was going to peel that kid open!"

"No I wasn't, just for the record," I chimed in.

"You're right," Rose whispered.

"And another- what?" Gabrielle said.

"You're right. And I have to fix this." Rose said, her eyes turning hard.

"What?" Gabrielle replied, "I was just being facetious, don't you bloody da-"

The Demon froze too.

"You can do that to *her*?" I asked.

"Sure," Rose replied, "Time doesn't discriminate."

She walked closer to me, taking my hands in hers.

"She is right, your actions brought a piece of her, a piece of Hell into you. Surely you've felt it by now? Especially since you woke up from the coma? It's harder to rest, easier to get angry, to lose control. Easier to lash out."

I nodded, reluctantly.

"I can't actually fix this, Mathew. It's not in my power to remove something from you, or repair the damage to your soul. But I can offer a little... peace. Think about those you care about, all those people you can't live without. Picture them, feel them in your heart."

She put her arms around my neck and leant her head on my shoulder.

I did as I was told, and she planted a little kiss on my cheek.

And, oh my...

You might say it was a revelation. If Gabrielle's touch had made me feel wanted, needed and masculine, Rose's made me feel loved, adored even, simply and wonderfully. I instant broke out in tears and she held me as I cried, whispering soothingly in my ear as I let myself grieve properly, at long last. For Des, Jocelyn, Cathy; for Gwendolyn and Evelina, for myself... for the things I'd lost and the pain I suffered.

Finally I felt the darker parts of me settle, just a little bit. They hadn't gone, they were still a part of me, but they weren't grating against me anymore. It was like some parts of me had been out of alignment, and now they were once again part of the whole, the ragged edges smoothed out. I felt more like me again. I was still angry, but it was just that bit easier to bear, enough that I could control myself properly.

"Oh, thank you," I gasped.

"That's alright, Mathew," she said, taking my hand, "it was the least I could do. I was the reason she got her hooks into you, after all."

"How did you fix me?"

"You know I can't tell you much, and nor could I do that much. I was able to do just enough to counter what she did. I balanced things out, only. No more, no less. You would have gotten there on your own eventually, as the part that is *her* integrated with you more fully, but you're vulnerable right now, and I wanted to make sure that you weren't unduly influenced."

"You're not going to explain that, are you?" I asked with a smile.

She smiled back.

"I figured," I said, and then gestured at Gabrielle, "Why was she carping on like that? It's like she wanted you to lash out at her."

"You're not the only one she likes to tempt. Technically speaking, she won today. Though she may see it differently; she liked having an open goal in your soul."

"She still does," I confessed, "The crack in my defences is still there, I can feel her when she's close. You too, now that I think about it."

"Don't worry about it too much. You have shown a remarkable ability to Will your way past temptation."

"Really? I live with two of the women who've tempted me, love them both and would chop my own arm off if either of them asked. Well, providing they had a good enough reason."

Rose snorted, "That's not quite the same. That Tethys of yours set out to make you her foot soldier, her muscle. And now she belongs to you. She'd burn this world down to the ground for you. Cassandra too, by the way, all your immediate friends and family would. You have a way about you Mathew, something that draws people. It's a quiet thing, a gentle thing. You make people feel protected and valued. That's a rare gift."

I waved off the compliment and blushed while Rose unfroze Gabrielle.

"-are," Gabrielle finished. Her eyes narrowed almost immediately as she quickly realised that we weren't standing where we had been a few minutes ago. The Demon looked me over for a long moment and then she let out a *stream* of invective that made me blush even harder.

"Oh, you bitch! He was perfect, and now look at him!" Gabrielle finally barked, glaring at Rose.

"You practically dared me to," Rose said with a smirk.

Gabrielle let out a most un-ladylike sound and vanished in a puff of smoke.

"I'd better get after her, the last time you annoyed her this much, she went into a convent and converted everyone *back* to sin," she said.

Yes, it's always *my* fault...

Rose pulled me into a warm hug that made me feel terrific, putting me back into place next to Jocelyn.

"Oh! I forgot. Keep an eye on things here. There are events in motion that could be... problematic for you. That's why I came."

"You don't say?" I said ironically.

She kissed my cheek and smiled.

"Be good."

"No promises."

She vanished and time resumed its normal flow.

I heard laughter and remembered that I still had an idiot to deal with. I'd been so angry before, so willing to do harm, but now... the sun was shining just that little bit more brightly, the grass was just that bit greener; Jocelyn was fuming, but her eyes sparkled, and my own eyes were drawn to the angry set of her beautiful face. Everything seemed much more amusing than it had when this all started.

I smiled, then chuckled, and Gerald's eyes narrow dangerously. Jocelyn looked at me with a frown on her face, no doubt confused by the sudden change of atmosphere.

"Oh, sorry, something funny I saw on TV last night," I lied, stretching my back, "Now, what was your problem again?"

"Are you insane?" he asked.

"Little bit. Shadow Magic, you know, makes you a bit crazy," I said with wide and staring eyes (doubly sinister when taking into account what mine looked like).

"Come on Jocelyn, get away from this nut-job," he said, reaching for her.

I crafted a little memory enhancer and released it gently into his head. He blinked, froze... and simply started laughing; blasting out great guffaws and big, bellowing belly-laughs, his face wide in a happy grin. He laughed so hard he fell on his backside and squealed, almost like a hyena.

"What the hell?" Jocelyn asked.

"He's just remembering all his favourite jokes," I said with a smile, gesturing for her to move onwards.

"Not what I was expecting from you," she said cautiously.

"I've mellowed."

"Evidently," she said with a smile.

"Hold it right there!"

Oh, now what?

Two men in light blue uniforms were approaching, both wore Spelleater amulets; both were a little on the heavy side, but neither looked weak. They carried batons in their hands and had tasers on their belts.

"Hello," I said cheerfully.

"Did you just use Magic on that kid?" the taller one asked, glaring at me.

"No, of course not," I lied glibly.

One pulled a crystal from his pocket and it glowed faintly, flaring to form a dim line of white light between Gerald and I. Gerald had stopped laughing by this point and was lying on the ground with a big smile on his face. Not really the sort of thing that should have drawn a pair of uniformed types... I smelt skulduggery (or, more likely, Aldwich).

"I think you're going to have to come with us," the one with the crystal said, brandishing his baton.

"Are you police?" I asked.

"What?" the shorter one said, "No."

"Then no," I said.

"That wasn't a request," the taller one said.

"Oh please," I said, "Please make me."

Okay, so my anger wasn't *completely* gone. And neither was my contempt for overbearing authority.

They sneered and came forwards. I raised my hand and their Spelleaters darted away from their necks in a shower of steel links, landing in my palm, where I crushed them with my Will. Spelleaters were powered by their user's Living Energy. No host, no function.

They paled and stared for a long moment before good sense got the better of them, and they nearly fell over each other running away.

"They were something official, weren't they?" I asked, dropping the mangled amulets.

"Campus security, I think," Jocelyn said with a giggle.

"Oh, then who cares?" I said, letting her lead the way.

"I didn't know you could do that," she said, eyeing up the Spelleaters with an amused eye.

"I'm versatile."

That encounter *did* have ramifications, as it turned out, but nothing a little bribery couldn't fix. A little enquiry revealed that it had indeed been Aldwich who'd 'mentioned' me to Campus Security (and well in advance of that first lecture, too). Unfortunately for him, he didn't have the budget for a sustained campaign against me, whereas my 'peace and quiet fund' more than stretched to the long-term greasing of the Security Chief's palm.

That actually ended up working out pretty well for me. Having Security in my pocket made my occasional... problems much easier to sweep under the rug.

We eventually ended up at a small cafe near the Great Hall. It was student run and, judging by the truly hideous artwork on the wall, student decorated as well. It had a cheerful atmosphere and smiling staff who served tiny artisanal drinks made from things that I wouldn't willingly allow past my lips, but which seemed to be rather popular, somehow.

Jocelyn and I picked a table near the window and sat across from one another while her bodyguard leaned against the far wall and glared at me. The small crowd of patrons largely ignored us once it became obvious that the red-eyed monster wasn't going to do anything interesting.

I sipped at a hot chocolate while Jocelyn drank one of those designer monstrosities; they'd called it coffee, but somehow, they'd made it purple.

The silence stretched a little awkwardly.

"So," she said, "You seeing anyone?"

Wow, right to the hard stuff...

"I was," I said, looking down, "It didn't end well."

"Oh. Sorry."

"You?"

"A couple of dates. Like I said, they mostly come for Faust, not Jocelyn."

"Sorry to hear that."

Damn, this was just painful...

"I heard about the attack," she said, touching her cheek as she looked at mine, "I wanted to gut those people."

"I beat you to that," I said a little icily, it wasn't a pleasant memory.

"Good."

"So, what are you studying?" I asked, desperate to steer the conversation into more pleasant areas.

Her course was much like mine, half Magic, half 'normal', though she was studying law with an eye towards business, and her Magic classes were at the introductory level. She was still living in the Faust ancestral home, which was only four streets over from Blackhold (too close for my comfort), and was otherwise enjoying herself since she got out from under her grandfather's thumb.

She filled me in on some news from her extended family and glanced at the clock as time went on, looking a little agitated.

"Somewhere to be?" I asked.

"I'm a bit concerned, actually. My grandfather had some legal stuff happening today. I was waiting for news."

I winced. I was not a fan of the elder Faust.

She noticed, "It's okay, I'm glad he's gone. He's been controlling my life ever since my parents died. The only good parts of my childhood were the ones when he was away."

"He's not getting out, or anything?"

"God no. They threw away the key."

I smiled at that and took a sip of my drink. This was actually nice. Jocelyn was good company, even if there was tension. She was easy with a smile and quite beautiful; lovely enough that even my jaded heart started to beat a bit faster.

But people outside the cafe started shrieking, and the moment ended. I turned quickly to see a Portal open outside the coffee shop, out of which sprang Cassandra and Demise, surprising me no end, I can tell you. They looked around and I stood, waving to them. They darted in, scattering students.

"Mathew, where have you been? We've been calling and texting for an hour!" Cassandra said.

I pulled out my phone, which was on, but it wasn't showing a signal, which was odd, Stonebridge's mobile cover was damn near perfect. A nasty thought came over me and I cast Mage Sight.

It was a miniscule thing, very, *very* subtle. It's no wonder I didn't sense it, it was barely even a *spark* of Magic, below even my detection threshold. It was just enough to disrupt a tiny circuit in my phone. It would take someone with impressive skill to cast that spell and get it past me.

I nearly swore as I remembered the *one* time my phone had been out of my hands that I could remember; that morning, in fact. Bloody Aldwich!

"What's the matter?" I asked

"Lord Faust, Matty," Cassandra said, "They just overturned his conviction."

# CHAPTER 7

I turned slowly to look at Jocelyn. She went pale.

Now, someone with my paranoid disposition might think that her being with me just as all this had happened was a little *too* convenient to be coincidence, but the look on Jocelyn's face... I knew this had nothing to do with her. That left Aldwich; was he working for Faust, or was this simple opportunistic spite?

"No," Jocelyn whispered, distracting me from thoughts of lightning-related revenge. She looked down, tears in her eyes, a look of pure shock on her face, "Not again!"

My heart went out to her. She was clearly more than a little horrified.

"Jocelyn, don't worry, I'll go and have a word with a few people, see what I can do. It's going to be alright, I promise."

"You don't know that!"

I moved my chair next to hers and, against my better judgement, I took her hand, "Yes I do," I said firmly.

She met my eyes and looked at them for quite a while before nodding and letting me go. I stood and turned to my Wardens.

"Where?" I asked.

"Houses of Justice," Cassandra said.

"I don't know where that is, can you Portal me, Dee?"

She nodded and led the way out of the cafe. I didn't look back, not wanting to see Jocelyn cry.

This... wasn't terrific. Faust was dangerous not because he was especially powerful (though he was an exceptional, and *very* dangerous Telepath), but because he understood the value of information, and he was a master at gathering the right people into the right place at the correct time to do the most damage to the people he hated.

By that reasoning, alone, I probably should have anticipated his getting out of the Farm sooner than expected, but I'd trusted the justice system to be incorruptible; it usually was, damn it!

I had to do something *now*, before he got any momentum going, because if he did... I knew where his first blow was going to land - right on my head.

Faust and I had a very troubled history. The man was a minor megalomaniac who'd gathered an army of Shadow monsters called Shaadre. He'd been determined to add me to it, and that hadn't turned out well for him. I'd beaten him at his own game and in such a way that he ended up at the Farm, where I was assured he wasn't getting out for a *very* long time.

"Mathew, we're too late," Cassandra said before we'd gotten too far, "They called for objections, and nobody was there. He's almost certainly gone by now."

I slowed to a halt and just stood there, fuming for a long moment, thinking hard. Well, if the legal system couldn't be relied upon, it wasn't like I was without options... or resources.

I took a breath. There was no use going off half-cocked. I needed information, and there really was only one good place for that.

"Let's go home, Dee, you can tell me what happened," I said after another moment calming myself down.

Cassandra blinked for a second and looked at me strangely while Demise concentrated on making another Portal.

"What?" I asked.

"You seem different," Cassandra replied, "a little calmer. More... you, I guess. You haven't been yourself lately; it was starting to worry me."

"Sorry," I said with a yawn and a stretch.

"Don't apologise to me, Mathew. You have every right to be angry after what's been happening these last few months."

"Wait until you hear about this pile," I said, gesturing around me.

"I can guess," she replied, looking at the hostile eyes and angry postures surrounding us, "Would you like me to stomp on one or two for you?"

"Have at it, far better you than me, I might actually hurt someone," I said slyly.

She turned to look at me and saw the evil grin on my face. She burst out laughing, which startled a couple of on-lookers.

"I hate you, you know that?" she said, punching my shoulder.

"And yet you stay, do I detect a hint of masochism?" I replied, massaging the (now bruised) shoulder.

"It goes well with the sadistic streak I'm about to demonstrate," she said in a menacing growl as she cocked her hand back.

"If you two are quite finished with the foreplay, your Portal is ready," Demise said sardonically.

"Don't even joke about that!" Cassandra said, walking through the Portal, "Just yuk!"

"Was there no other way you could have put that?" I asked, following her through as Demise brought up the rear, shaking her head.

"Such as?" Cassandra asked as we emerged in front of Blackhold's gates.

"I don't know, anything other than 'yuk', there were girls there!"

"How about 'bleuch'? Or would you prefer 'eek'?"

"With a Warden like you, who needs assassins?" I asked, which earned me another thwack for my trouble.

We walked through the front doors and I said hello to the Wardens on duty and Webb, who went off to see to a light lunch for us while we made for the library. I spotted a very attractive young businesswoman coming down the stairs as we walked up. She wore a conservative, and perfectly cut business suit in dark green, with a white blouse, elegant tights and matching high heel shoes. She wore her red hair up in a severe bun that showed off her pretty- wait a minute...

"Kandi?!" I nearly spluttered.

She grinned widely at me, giving me a twirl, "You like? I'm off to a meeting with some of Tethys' investors."

"S'nice," I said, trying not to drool.

Kandi giggled and came over to give me a hug and a kiss on the cheek.

"You like the librarian look, huh?" she asked in a sultry little whisper.

"You're the only girl I met who pulled it off quite this well," I replied honestly.

She snorted and stepped back, "Watch this," she said mischievously.

She pulled the pin out of her bun and slowly shook her head to release her hair into a cascade around her face and down her back.

"Oh, my," I said, grinning stupidly.

Kandi smiled and moved in close, "So, how long are you home for?"

"I seem to have rather forgotten... everything."

"Good grief, show him a redhead, I'll show you a gibbering idiot," Cassandra said, nudging me on my way.

"Hey!" Kandi protested, following us up, "I was playing with that!"

"What's going on out he-" Tethys said, coming out of the study, "Oh, good you found him!"

"Too late," Cassandra said.

They'd actually been searching for a while before Demise caught a whiff of my Magical Signature, allowing her to home in on me.

"Damn it," Tethys replied, following us into my library and onto my favourite furniture set, it was one of several sets in the large room, covered with shelves full of books, aside from a wide nook where my entertainment centre was located.

I sat on a small sofa while Tethys and Cassandra took another and Demise dropped into an armchair. Kandi took her usual spot on my lap.

"Not sure I can call you Kandi while you look so... grownup," I said with a smile.

She snorted, "I go to these meetings as Carol Thornsby, if you must know," she said, leaning her head against my shoulder.

That was her real name; I thought that Carol rather suited her, actually...

"We found him with the Faust girl," Cassandra said, "She looked honestly mortified, but I'm not sure that we can trust that; she may have been there to distract him."

"Jocelyn may be many things, but she's not duplicitous like that," I said.

Cassandra gave me a long, level look, "See what I mean about him and redheads?" she muttered to Demise, who nodded.

"Hey!" I protested.

"Really?" Cassandra said, looking pointedly at Kandi, whose back I was even now rubbing gently, which made her sigh contentedly and nuzzle into my neck.

Tethys snorted, smiling widely, wearing her very best 'all according to plan' look.

"Kandi, Honey, don't you have a meeting to get to?" Tethys asked.

Kandi shook her head and grabbed my spare hand.

"Kandi, don't make me put you over my knee," Tethys threatened.

Kandi made a tiny little distressed sound and hid her eyes in my hair.

"Mathew, do something with her, will you?" Tethys said.

Before I could answer, Kandi turned those big eyes of hers on me, "You wouldn't make me go, would you, Matty?" she said in a small, trembling voice, batting her eyes.

"I've got to fold here, Tethys, the Pixies have been training her."

Tethys shook her head and came over to glare down at Kandi, who quailed and drew herself up into a little ball that I had to support. I knew it was an act, but that didn't make it any less adorable (or effective).

Tethys responded by sitting next to us and reaching her hands around to Kandi's sides. She then proceeded to tickle the little redhead mercilessly until she emitted a final squeak and rolled off.

"Oh! That's not fair!" Kandi said, glaring at Tethys, who had made sure Kandi couldn't retake her former position by the simple expedient of taking it herself.

"Don't blame me, he taught me that trick," Tethys said, stroking my cheek possessively.

"But at least he has the decency to make it dirty," Kandi protested.

"What's that?" I said, a little distracted by the Succubus sitting on my lap.

"You know," Kandi said meaningfully.

"No I don't!"

Tethys looked at me with a raised eyebrow.

"Really!" I said, Tethys just smirked.

"Not to interrupt this scintillating repartee, but we do have the slight hiccough of Lord Faust to deal with!" Cassandra said.

"Oh, that's not a problem," I said, smiling broadly.

"Really?" Cassandra said doubtfully, "How is that 'not a problem'?"

I smiled even wider, "Oh, I'm sure he and I will come to an... arrangement."

"Mathew, please don't start another war," Cassandra begged.

"I didn't start the last one, and I think that 'war' is a bit of a stretch."

"Mm hm," Demise said with a raised eyebrow.

"If you make him cry, record it, I think I'd enjoy listening to that," Tethys purred into my ear.

"I'll see what I can do."

"You still going to be here when I'm back from my meeting?" Kandi asked.

I nodded.

"Okay," she said, bouncy again as she retied her hair into the bun. She kissed my lips, glaring half-heartedly at Tethys all the while, and then walked out.

"Do I even want to know what's going on between you two?" I asked.

"What do you mean?" Tethys said with a wide and evil smile.

"You two seem to be... I don't know, butting heads?"

"Just a matter of queen bees, Matty. Kandi's coming into her own, and she's discovering that she rather likes the woman she's turning into. And I certainly do, as well... it's just that she's taking *your* example rather than mine, and that can lead to... problems."

"I don't understand that at all."

Tethys rolled her eyes.

"She's inclined to be decent," Tethys explained, "and while I'm willing to do that from time to time, and if it doesn't cost too much, I generally prefer a more direct approach to business. She's too *nice*, and it's all your fault."

"What isn't these days? But how, exactly?"

"Before you came along with your high-minded nonsense, she was a delightfully perverted, flighty, promiscuous, *cut-throat*, little darling... I mean, she's still delightfully perverted and promiscuous, but now she's *serious* about certain things, and that can make it difficult to gouge people."

"Well, I think that we could probably leave before we have to listen to any more of this..." Cassandra said, standing up and gesturing for Demise to follow her out.

"I think I could stand to hear some more," Demise said in mild protest as Cassandra shuffled her away.

"You're worried about her?" I asked once they'd gone.

"A little. We deal with dangerous people, and I worry that her way of doing things will mark her out as weak. I want to keep her safe."

"She has a Warden," I reminded her.

"I know that, but Kandi's *family*, Matty, I can't lose her."

"I understand," I said, taking her hand, interlocking our fingers, "We'll keep her safe."

She kissed me then, a gentle, affectionate thing, and I returned it, holding her close.

"As long as you're around, I don't worry too much. Kandi will never go too far from you. She wants to impress you."

"She already does, just being her, and you can tell her I said that."

"You are the most girly human being I've ever known, you realise that?" she said, cuddling in tighter.

"I just use that to get women to let their guards down. I'm a wolf in sheep's clothing."

"Yes, you're quite the player," Tethys replied, deadpan.

I laughed and so did she. She leaned more comfortably against me, and I relaxed a little.

"You feel like telling me what made you so suddenly mellow?"

I smiled, and told her about Rose and Gabrielle. Tethys was the one I told about that kind of stuff.

"That explains a lot," she said, "and I'm glad, *very* glad, that you're back to being you."

"Me too. I'm not all the way there, yet, but it's... better. I hated feeling that out of control; that close to the edge."

She shivered a little and held on tighter.

"Meet any girls yet?" she asked mischievously.

"It's my first day," I said, "and already I met two girls who I had to scare off, another who's so terrified she can't look at me, and let's not forget Jocelyn, who I don't know what to do with, quite frankly, and then there's Maggie knocking around somewhere..."

"Well, I'll admit it's not the best start," Tethys said with a grin, "but I've seen worse!"

I rolled my eyes.

"I really don't know why I'd bother. I've had two serious girlfriends, both were *disasters*."

"Maybe the problem is in the 'serious' part of the equation. Sow some oats, embrace casual for a while. You never know, you might like it."

"I'm a nineteen year old male, of course I'd like it, but you know that's not me."

"Why?"

I had to think for a second.

"Um..."

"Go on, give me a reason, I'll wait," she said with a snigger.

"Because I was raised with certa-"

"Crap," she said, looking me in the eye, "try again."

"I don't like the idea of-"

"Nope, you know your reason, spill it."

I sighed, "I like having someone. I loved how I felt with Cathy, and even with Jocelyn way back. Simple physical pleasure would be hollow after that, I think."

"How do you know?" she asked, "Just because it's not deep doesn't mean it can't be intimate. Does Kandi seem unhappy with me?"

"No."

"Well, we are certainly not deep. I love that girl, but we're not 'in love'. I frequently fill this place with women and turn it into a palace of the senses, at which time I enjoy the kind of fun that would make the uninitiated keel over. Kandi will enthusiastically get herself thoroughly involved with everything on offer; I didn't even see her at the last one."

"Please make sure I know when you're planning things

like that so I can make sure to be elsewhere," I begged.

She snorted.

"My point is that you don't have to be in love to have fun and friends and all sorts of carnal delights. You're nineteen, Mathew, don't assume that you've got everything figured out yet. You're *supposed* to screw up your first couple of relationships, that's how you learn."

"I suppose. I just don't see why it has to be such a bloody minefield."

"It's a minefield because you always pick the same girl, cute, pretty, smart, serious, it's a type you're not compatible with."

"What would you recommend?" I asked jokingly.

"Fun. Someone light-hearted, funny, maybe a little mischievous," she said with a very pointed look, "Of course it would have to be someone close by, someone easily persuaded as to your good intentions."

She licked her lips very slowly.

"You are the most sneaky, manipulative woman I've met in my life," I said, going for her sides, only to be intercepted and quickly tossed to the carpet, where she held me down one handed and proceeded to dose me with my own medicine.

"Okay! Okay, you win!" I said, bright red and dishevelled.

"Don't I always?" she asked before lowering herself gently onto my chest, resting her head under my chin.

"Yes," I said, wrapping my arms around her back.

"And who's the boss of you?"

"You are," I said with a snort.

"And don't you forget it."

"No, Ma'am."

She shuddered.

"Careful with that tone, Mathew, you'll set me off," she crooned.

"Don't tempt me."

"Fish gotta swim, bird gotta fly..."

We laid there like that for quite a while, the warmth of her disinclining me to go about my business. We chatted idly, comfortably. Eventually we made it back to the sofa (my leg had fallen asleep).

"So, how do you like school, aside from the lack of unterrified women?"

"Hate it. Hate everything about it. It was bad enough before Jocelyn turned up and twisted my head around again."

"You and your redheads."

"Please don't start that bollocks again!"

She laughed.

After a while, Tethys had to go back to work, and I headed to my bedroom to change into a dark suit and tie. I decided not to take the signet with me; Faust was a Graves problem, not a First Shadow one. I checked my appearance, and I didn't look too bad. The dark cloth set off my eyes to good effect, enhancing the more fearful aspects of my looks, which was the idea.

From there, I went into the central garden and started making my preparations. I asked Cassandra to make sure I had the place to myself as I needed to do some rather delicate Spellwork. Faust may not have been my match in sheer power, but he was still very dangerous, and I was going to do my level best to make sure that I was ready in the (likely) event that he refused to be reasonable. It took an hour, and I had a headache afterwards, but I was as prepared as I could reasonably be.

I walked out of my front door just after three o'clock in the afternoon, managing (mostly by begging) to leave my Wardens behind. I told them that all I wanted was a little chat with my old enemy, and that had mostly done the trick (Cassandra was still not very happy with me, but it turned out I'd gotten rather good at begging).

I decided to take a cab, which I hailed from the front gates. This let me get a better lay of the land between my house and Faust's. I had a feeling I would need to know the route in the future.

The Old Quarter of Stonebridge moved almost lazily past the window. There was a millennium of architecture there, with nothing younger than two hundred years old. There was a little of everything, from turn-of-the-millennium blocky, through gothic grandeur to Edwardian formal, some white, some brown, a few black or grey. The streets were thin enough that many of them had been made one-way to speed traffic along a little, and the pavements were broken by trees, with small parks nestled in among the various mansions and housing blocks. It was a very nice, very *expensive* area to have a home.

I hoped I wouldn't have to burn any of it down...

The Faust Mansion was located deep in the district, closer to the newer parts of town than my place, though. Clarion Hall was ten stories of white-stoned gothic splendour, riddled with Wards and Enchantments, though these were not as extensive as Blackhold's. The front doors were wide and black, sunk deep into the light red stonework of the arch. I paid the cabbie and hopped out, walking easily up to the door, where I pressed the button for the bell.

It took a while for someone to arrive and open up for me, but it *was* a big house. One of the double doors creaked open a little, revealing a middle aged woman in a maid's outfit.

"Can I help you?" she asked politely.

"I'm here to see Faust," I said cheerfully, "it's Mathew Graves."

At the sound of my name, her face twisted into a snarl. It was obvious that I was not well liked in the Faust family, can't imagine why...

"His lordship isn't receiving visitors today," she said, and then she slammed the door in my face.

I sighed and looked around me. I'd expected something like this. Getting in the hard way was fine with me, too.

And more fun, anyway.

There was a set of stairs leading down towards a basement loading area. The doors were closed up tight, but it was dark enough down there for my purposes. I walked down the ramp and opened a gateway into the Shadow Realm.

It was easy to hop up into the house proper from there, and simple enough to find a large enough patch of shadow to let me back through into the real world. I emerged into a downstairs loo and opened the door into the front hall, where the maid was glaring through a window at the ramp I'd just walked down.

I coughed and she turned, emitted a strange 'meep' and ran off, I assumed to get help.

I wandered past a magnificent carved staircase, and into the main reception hall. It was full of the kind of Magical esoterica that I would have happily spent days poring over. There were ornate scrolls from dead civilisations, puzzle boxes that needed to be solved in four dimensions, weapons from before the age of Chivalry, wands from Camelot... it was a collector's dream.

I found a comfortable wing chair under an arch and settled myself down to wait, leafing through an antique edition of Macbeth, which was actually quite impressive in its own right; more than three hundred years old and still pristine.

I wasn't waiting long before there was a great bustle and three burly men came in, all dressed in black suits with white shirts, they carried hunting rifles and looked ready to use them. One even had a Spelleater amulet. I took it from him and cast Sensory Overload, dropping all three to the ground, *very* unconscious.

It was a nasty little Spell. It projected a simultaneous burst of light and sound, conjured to a particular frequency, one that would cause immediate unconsciousness in the people around you, in addition to a few other side effects, if you were feeling particularly sadistic. I wasn't right then.

I smiled and went back to my leafing, twirling the mangled Spelleater around my fingers until Faust himself *finally* showed up.

He was an older man, appearing to be in his sixties or so, his black hair greying at the temples. He wore a charcoal suit with a waistcoat, a dark tie (fixed with a white-gold clip), gold signet ring on his left pinkie and a diamond-encrusted Rolex on his wrist. His blue eyes sparkled with menace and hatred, but he kept a smile on his finely-boned face. He was a Sorcerer-level practitioner, about mid-range, but his rare Telepathic affinity made him far more dangerous than that would indicate.

"Mister Graves," he said cheerfully, "so good to see you again."

I rose and placed the book carefully back on its table before we exchanged grips. He motioned for me to resume my seat.

"So, what brings you by?" he asked, "I'm afraid I'm still somewhat at an end, having only just returned home today."

"Apologies for bothering you so soon," I said, keeping my expression neutral, "But I felt that we should have a little chat before you resume your activities."

"Oh? And what would this 'chat' be regarding?" he asked, leaning back in his chair, utterly relaxed, confident in his surroundings.

"Your intentions towards me and mine."

"Oh, I expect that you'll all be quite dead or dying within the next month," he said cheerfully.

My careful expression froze. That had degenerated a *lot* faster than I'd thought it would.

"Really?" I said, my voice now low and ugly, if he noticed, he didn't show it.

"Oh yes. After I'm done with you here, I'm going to track down that whore Tethys and I'm going to skin her alive. Very slowly, in fact. I'll find all those school friends of yours and do worse to them. The SCA bastards will be next, I'll take their jobs and then their families, that'll be fun. Your parents, certainly something must be arranged for them. I have a whole feast of delights waiting for everyone you love, Graves."

"You wouldn't dare," I hissed back, "You don't have the pull to get away with that!"

"Really?" he said, standing up with an awful grin on his face, "I haven't been idle in the Farm all this time. I've been planning, carefully and thoroughly, for this day. I was expecting to have to find you, but I'm glad it happened like this. Maybe I'll make Jocelyn finish you off. She has been very disappointing of late; time I fixed that, I think."

He called his powers, created a Telepathic probe of awesome power, and slammed it into my mind.

Well... he tried, anyway.

You see, I hadn't been idle these years, either. I'd been preparing for this day, as well. And that hour I'd spent in my garden was the result.

The Spells were subtle, as they had to be for Faust; a trap of rather *delicious* cunning, though I say so myself, one designed into the very cracks of my mental landscape, hidden where Faust couldn't spot them. And he didn't, not until he was *far* too late to do anything about it. There were three elements; the first was a sort of mental bear trap that locked his probe in place. The second part froze it in a kind of Magical stasis while the third component, the actual attack spell, darted up his *own* probe and into his brain.

Technically, the attack was known as a Neural Shredder, and it was a very ugly weapon. They were to mental architecture what a wood-chipper is to pudding.

My trap ripped right into the parts of his mind containing his Magical knowledge and control, and tore them all to pieces. Hundreds of years of knowledge and experience vanished in an instant. He gurgled briefly, blood flowing from his nose, and then he slid gently to the ground.

He just knelt there for a long moment before he started making this low, keening, mewling sound, like a wounded animal. No doubt he was reaching for things that simply weren't there anymore, his mind so scrambled by the sudden loss that it couldn't cope, not yet.

It took him a while to recover something resembling coherent thought, and I didn't waste that time, carefully crafting another Spell that I dropped into his head as he was starting to come out of his fugue. He was weeping by that point, tears streaming down his face and soaking his shirt along with the blood. I might have felt a little guilty if it weren't for the threats he'd just made. Instead, I was just vindictively satisfied. Besides, I'd only set the trap, he'd walked into it while trying to do something similar to me, let's not forget.

"What did you do to me?!" he shrieked, a most unmanly sound. At least he could talk again, I'd been a little worried about that. Shredders could do incidental damage on their way to their targets. I'd tried to be selective, but minds were convoluted, tricky things, and mistakes were possible.

"Well, not to be pedantic, but if you hadn't tried to attack me, nothing would have happened at all, so really you did it to yourself," I said smugly, crossing my legs; I hadn't even bothered to leave my seat thought all of that. I called my Shadows and yanked him back into his chair, none too gently, either, making him moan.

He sat there, glaring at me, his eyes wide with fear and loathing.

"So, Faust, as you've no doubt surmised, I've taken your Magical knowledge, you'll have to start all over again, not that it matters, because I've also installed a pair of mental blocks."

He fumed, his face going red and enraged, but he realised the precarious nature of his position and stayed quiet.

"The first will cause you quite a whopping amount of pain if you use your Magic. I invite you to confirm that at your leisure, if you can figure out a way to use it. The second is called an Asimov. It ensures that you will not be able to harm a sentient creature, or allow harm to come to one."

"How dare yo-"

"Quiet," I said icily. He looked like he was about to keep

talking anyway, but something he saw in my eyes shut him up.

"I intend for this to be the end of things between us. After so many years abusing your powers on man and woman alike, I'd imagine this fate to be something of a personal hell for you, and that's enough for me."

I leaned forward, letting my eyes bore into his.

"However, I must caution you, that if you should find some oblique way to harm me and mine, then I shall come back. What happened today was the result of an hour's planning. Imagine what I could do with two, or a day," I said calmly.

He let out an incomprehensible sound of defeated anguish. Two more guards came in, presumably summoned by the noise, and both had Spelleaters this time. I dropped them both without even looking, something which terrified Faust even further. Powerless and defeated, he dropped to the ground again and cowered, shaking in fear and loss, rocking back and forth.

Served him right. The man had abused his powers and hundreds of people for centuries. This was a *small* piece of comeuppance, and less than he deserved.

"Oh, and if anything should happen to Jocelyn while she's under your care, the same applies, do I make myself clear?"

He shook his head.

"I'll need a verbal response," I said evenly.

"I understand," he whispered, his arms wrapped around his body, his expression horrible and exhausted.

He looked suicidal. That was funny because he came under the heading of 'sentient being', and he'd find ending his own life just as impossible as ending someone else's, I'd made sure of that.

"Good," I said before slapping his shoulder, "cheer up, old sport. It could have been worse. You're still rich, and no doubt you still have some political power. I'd use both of those things wisely if I were you, we wouldn't want me to have to come and speak to you again, would we? No? No."

He started crying again.

I walked away, happy as a clam.

Later I would worry that what I'd done had hardly been the work of a good person. I'd tortured a man, ripped his mind apart, and imposed my will over his, denying him even the release of a swift death.

But what really worried me, what made me concerned for just who I was starting to become, was the fact that I didn't even *slightly* regret it.

# CHAPTER 8

I popped out of a Shadow in my downstairs loo and whistled a happy tune as I walked into the front hall, where I found Tethys chatting with Cassandra.

"Well?" Tethys asked, looking me over, "What happened?"

I reached into my breast pocket and pulled out a silver coloured Dictaphone.

"For you," I said, handing it to her, "pour some wine, find a comfy spot and enjoy."

She licked her lips, "What is it?" she asked in a whisper.

"I wouldn't want to spoil the surprise."

"I'm using your room," she said and darted into the kitchen, emerging a few minutes later with a dark bottle, a box of chocolates and Kandi, who gave me a wave as Tethys jogged along with the little redhead over her shoulder.

I smiled and turned to Cassandra, who looked... 'miffed' isn't a strong enough word.

"What did you do?" she asked with her arms crossed.

"A little bit of personal catharsis that will keep me chuckling for years to come," I said with a grin. We made our way to the library, where I told her what I'd done.

"So... breaking and entering, Magical and Telepathic assault, and on nobility, no less, have I missed anything?" she asked, rubbing her eyes.

"It was really, really fun?" I replied.

"God damn it, Matty! I told you not to start a war!"

"Did you hear the whole 'kill everyone I love' part of my story?"

She subsided, muttering, but seemed to relax. And then she grinned.

"Well, I suppose that it's not *so* bad. What did you give Tethys?"

"I've taken to recording important conversations lately," I said, with a smile.

"Where is he?!" I heard Tethys shout to someone. I heard a muttered reply and the door burst open.

She'd gone full Succubus, except that she wasn't showing her wings; her skin was ivory-white, her forearms and calves black with bone-hard flesh, her horns and tail in evidence. She was stripped to her bright red underwear, and that was in disarray. She was sweaty and breathing hard, growling low in her throat, her normally violet eyes were black and locked on mine.

"You magnificent man... Cassie, you don't want to see this," Tethys rasped, which provided Cassandra with barely a second's warning before the Succubus was on me and had tossed me onto the biggest sofa in the room. She hopped on, straddling my hips.

I wasn't really sure what to expect. She was hot to the touch and trembling, her canines were longer and sharp. She grabbed my hands and shoved them over my head before her head came down and she fastened her lips to mine.

"Bloody hell, I *really* don't need to see that!" Cassandra said, darting for the door and shutting it behind her.

The kiss lengthened and deepened, Tethys' whole body pressed up against mine. She let go of my hands and let her own wander over my head and chest. Mine went for her back and hair.

She sat back a little, her eyes looking deep into mine. She smiled and kissed me again, gentler this time. Her eyes shifted back to lovely violet and I saw tears in them as she cupped my face.

"You keep impressing me, Love," she whispered.

"I do my best."

We just laid there like that for a long moment, looking at each other. And in that moment, something... shifted. A gentle thing, really, just a little poke, where lust started to turn into something deeper, something far better. We'd loved one another for a long time, but it was separate to things like this, something more akin to a familial bond. But in that moment, something else started to happen between us.

Naturally, Tethys being Tethys, she panicked.

It only occurred to me much later, but the simple problem was that Tethys had a few... problems with intimacy. In fact, if you opened a dictionary, and looked up 'Abandonment and Intimacy Issues', you'd see a little picture of Tethys right next to the text. She had fallen in love exactly *once* in her long life. A Sorceress, naturally (Tethys did rather have a type), and she'd died, leaving my friend so hurt that she'd spent the next two hundred years trying to hump the pain away.

Naturally, when she felt herself start to go that way again, she tensed up and bolted for the door like a chicken with a firecracker attached to its tail-feathers, leaving me in rather a confused, randy heap.

When I went after her, I found her door locked and a stern, "Go away," as the only reply to my knock.

I didn't know what else to do, so I did as I was asked. I didn't go back to University, though. There was no way in hell I was leaving before this was sorted, education be *damned.*

I woke up early the next morning when Tethys dropped into bed next to me. I was tired, not having slept very well, but I woke up quickly once I realised who it was. She wore her silk pyjamas, and her hair was in a loose tail. It was a good look for her, relaxed and genuine.

"Morning," I said, not wanting to scare her off again.

"Morning," she muttered, shuffling in a little closer to me, tucking herself in under my arm.

"Want to talk about it?"

"No."

"Okay."

"Okay?"

"Since when have I ever been pushy?"

She chuckled and wrapped an arm around my chest.

"Sorry," she said, "I... I'm sorry."

"Good grief, what for?"

"For... for just running off like that. It was rude, you must be thinking that I hate you or something."

"Yes, because yesterday was the day my brain fell out. Give me a little credit, Tethys."

She looked up at me again and smiled sweetly.

"It just hit me so hard, is all. I hadn't looked at anyone like that since... since my Lucy died. It felt... wonderful, and then I felt confused and so guilty because I was thinking about *her* when I was with you, and I was with you when I was supposed to be with her..."

"You're very complicated, aren't you?"

She snorted and nuzzled herself in under my chin.

"I can't do it Matty. I can't go through that again, I'm sorry."

I kissed the top of her head very gently.

"Why are you still apologising? Do you really think I'd hold anything like *this* against you? I love you, dummy; do you think I'd ever want you to do anything that hurt you this much?"

A tear trickled from her eye and she cuffed it away.

"I love you too."

"Well, that's more than enough for me, Tethys. I've never said otherwise."

She sobbed and squeezed me so tightly I started to worry about my bones.

"Air! Air!" I gasped, which made her laugh.

She leaned up and kissed my lips, taking her time about it, too.

"Alright, now you're just sending mixed messages," I complained, once my brain started working again.

"Like you said, I'm complicated."

She settled her head back down on my chest.

"Just because I'm not ready now, doesn't mean I won't be."

"I know."

"We're still going to end up together. Remember that I had a fifty year plan, you moved things up on me!"

"Oh, this is *my* fault? And wasn't it a seventy-year plan?"

"See? Moved things up!"

"That makes even less sense than usual."

"Not if you think about it."

"I *am* thinking about it, and you're *still* insane."

"I'm a woman; you're not supposed to understand me completely."

"Playing the W-card, eh? That's hardly fair."

She kissed me again.

"How's that?"

"Wonderful, but still *very* confusing!"

She laughed, which made me happy. I was glad that she was herself again. She wasn't telling me anything that I hadn't figured out while staring at my bedroom ceiling, but it did make me a bit sad. There were few people in the world I got on with as well as Tethys. We were compatible in a very deep way. We never argued, we never even exchanged a harsh word. This had been the closest thing we'd ever had to a fight, and it wasn't even that close!

We loved each other; that much I knew. But as long as Tethys was afraid of losing me, or being hurt, we would never be anything other than best friends. I wasn't going to complain; she was precious to me, and I didn't want to risk that any more than she did. And, if there was one thing I knew, it was that romantic relationships tended to end badly.

Perhaps I was just as damaged as she was, in my own way.

"Besides, you couldn't have handled what I'd have done to you," she said, settling down again.

"Of that, I have no doubt."

"Are you going to be completely reasonable about this? Where's the manly chest-thumping? The complaints about an insult to your manhood? The demands for sexual compensation?"

"What sorts of men have you been sleeping with?"

"Come on, give me something to work with! At least pretend to be devastated that I deprived you of heaven!"

Ah, there it is...

I swear, all the women are just out to see if they can make my brain come oozing out of my skull.

"There's nothing I can say that won't make this worse, so I'm shutting up."

"Oh, go on, be a sport!"

"No."

"I'll sic Kandi on you," she threatened.

"Oh, the horror," I said dryly.

"Oh! So it's like that is it? You won't speak to me, but you'll welcome my younger assistant? You are such a cliché!"

"You are quite insane; I just want that on the record."

"But you love me anyway."

"Not 'anyway', I love your brand of crazy just how it is, thank you."

"Good answer," she said, kissing me *again*.

She settled back down, cuddling in, making herself comfortable.

"So we're okay?" she said softly.

"Always."

She nodded and I started to doze off. I always slept better with her in the bed, always drifted off faster.

So peaceful was I that when I eventually awoke again, I discovered that I had less than ten minutes to get to class, which amused Tethys no end when I tried to explain my situation. By the time I'd persuaded her to disentangle herself (which had resulted in quite a bit more groping on her part than one might have expected), I had less than five minutes to go, which resulted in a less than professional look for a brand new class...

Said class was Advanced Telepathy, which I'd really been looking forward to... before I'd met Professor Hadleigh, now I didn't know what to expect. There were four other students; again, ones I recognised from the orientation. As in Flesh Crafting, they were sitting as far away from me as possible. It was actually starting to get a little depressing.

The lecture hall was more of a sitting room, with a number of chairs around the walls and some brightly coloured cushions on the floor; there was also a wide set of windows looking over the square, and an empty fireplace in the corner.

The professor was a good ten minutes late and barrelled through the door at a great rate of knots. I liked her on sight. She was a little shorter than me, with a mass of curly brown hair, big brown eyes and a gentle face with a frazzled expression on it; her gown was askew over her shocking-pink, calf-length dress. She tripped over the carpet on her way in, and her pile of books went flying as she fell head-first into the room. I managed to catch both her and the stack with my Will before they could hit the ground.

I set her back on her feet and reassembled the stack before returning it to her hands. She blushed scarlet from chin to crown, it was actually rather cute.

"Thank you," she said a little sheepishly, straightening her outfit, "Good reflexes!"

I grinned back and waved off the compliment. She looked me over, and saw my eyes. She didn't recoil, though, which made a nice change.

"Ooh! You're Graves, aren't you? My cousin, Vanessa Knowles commended you to me, it's a pleasure to meet you!" she said, taking my hand and shaking it very vigorously.

Vanessa Knowles worked for the SCA, I had a lot of time for her. It seemed that Telepathy ran in her family.

"How's she doing?" I asked, "I haven't seen her in a few

months."

"Oh, very well, she got a raise, she's chuffed. Oh! I forgot, Amy Porter," she said, offering her hand again, which I took, and she shook just as vigorously, "Your professor, I suppose!"

I really liked this woman. She was so obviously enthusiastic that her energy was practically contagious. And her rather ditzy personality was quite adorable, reminding me of a hyperactive puppy.

She introduced herself to the others and set her books down on the one desk in the room. She outlined the course, which was to be about improving on basic Telepathic skills, firstly with an eye to improved mental defence, followed up with a series of psychology classes that would allow selective manipulation of a subject's mind (in a healing way, not a 'You obey *me*, now!' sort of way... I hoped). It all sounded very interesting. Again, I'd been doing a lot of this stuff the hard way, relying on power and creativity to compensate for a lack of proper training (though my mental shields were quite well made, I'd been told).

"Okay, any questions?"

There weren't any.

"Good! Alright, let's everyone partner up," she said, "and we'll run through basic defence strategies."

Naturally, I was the odd one out and Porter came over with a wry grin on her face.

"Vanessa told me you weren't much for playing with others," she said, dropping onto the floor next to me, and dragging me off the chair with her.

"Okay, nice and simple first lesson, mental defences and their weaknesses," she said, "I trust you wouldn't mind volunteering, Mister Graves?"

"You say that like I have some sort of choice," I said with a raised eyebrow that drew another grin from her.

She pulled a small round object out of a pocket and settled it on the floor between us. She directed me to place my hand on it and erect whatever defences I felt appropriate. I shrugged and did as I was told.

An image of my mental defences appeared above the class. They were based loosely on the Lonely Mountain from 'The Hobbit', only bigger, and with a far more complex interior. The mountain made up my innermost defence, and was surrounded by a massively complex maze and a chasm that dropped deep into the imaginary earth.

"Wow, Van wasn't kidding when she said you knew what you were doing," Porter said.

"I get by."

She smirked.

"Okay, everyone, I was intending to tell you all about weaknesses in Mental defence, but I think that might be a bit tricky with this much detail. Still, we'll give it a bash! Now, every mental defence is based on certain rules, determined by the defender. Generally speaking, it's a three dimensional world with gravity, because that's the easiest thing to picture."

"Now, your average intruder will have to follow those rules themselves, which puts them at a disadvantage on a defender's home ground. But your more *competent* Telepath will know better, and will *change* those rules on you. I'll ask you not to actively defend, alright, Mister Graves? This is just a demonstration."

I nodded, and suddenly a mental probe dropped straight out of the 'sky' and right onto the top of my mountain, completely bypassing the maze and the outer defences! I blinked, rather impressed, actually. I didn't know one could do that...

"See? Gravity is a construct of the defender, but your *trained* opponent can attack from any direction she chooses," she said, her probe beginning to burrow.

"Yikes, you build to last, don't you?" she asked after a few minutes of futile digging.

"I try," I replied.

"Okay, I'm going to push a little harder, don't take it personally, alright?"

I nodded again.

She retreated a bit and added a solid chunk of power to her probe. Her construct expanded and multiplied before attacking from multiple angles, each probe was about ten times as powerful as her first, and they went ploughing into my mountain like lightning, making me wince a little.

"Easy, that's my brain you're poking!"

She giggled and lost concentration. Two of her probes vanished and she scolded me for my interruption. She eventually made it through the outer slopes of my mountain and into the corridors, where she spread out, trying to find the spark of my mind.

"Um, Mister Graves, would you mind pointing me in the right direction?" she asked sheepishly.

"Down. Very far down. And there are no stairs on your level."

"Bollocks. Alright, you get the idea," she said, pulling out and letting the image vanish, "the point is that an attack can come from any angle, and a good defence must take that into account. I'd like you all to take a few minutes to adjust your mental architecture, and then we'll practice."

She left me for a while and handed out more of those little round projectors to the students before circling the room, watching the other in actions. I went to work, carefully adjusting the image of my shields, using the mnemonic device I'd learnt for this express purpose.

The other students' defences were quite impressive, I have to say (which I should have expected from practiced Telepaths in an advanced class). One had a massive floating sphere suspended over a rushing river, another's was a colossal monolith protected by row upon row of razor wire, a third looked like his spark was constantly moving about the inside of a pinball machine; impossible to nail down.

Impressive though they were, Porter demolished them one by one, taking her time and showing each person what they were doing wrong, giving them pointers and helping them come up with better strategies. She was patient and good-natured; I don't think anyone felt patronised or put out.

She came back to me.

"You ready, Mister Graves?" she asked, settling back onto the carpet.

I nodded and erected my adjusted shields.

She dove in from above again and squeaked as she hit the mist around my mountain.

"Oh, damn, Graves, that's hardly sporting!" she said as a weight of sticky mess adhered to her probe, compressing it and slowing it down. She split again, and her other probes hit the same problem, the whole mass of fog squeezing in on the intruders.

She darted and ducked into easier paths through the murk, only to get hopelessly turned around, by design. Two probes collided and she grunted as they cancelled each other out. Two more flew out in the wrong direction and the last one was simply squeezed to a stop.

"Okay," she said, rubbing her forehead, "it appears that you've understood the principles I was getting at."

Sotto voce, she muttered something about braining her cousin for not warning her adequately.

I smiled at the praise and shut down my shields.

She looked at the clock, and I was surprised to see that the whole hour had passed already, and I must say that I was quite sorry about that. This was the first class where I didn't feel like a complete outsider.

Porter dismissed us, but held up a hand for me before I could leave.

"Vanessa said you really pissed her off when she first met you," she said with a smile once the others were gone, "I'm starting to see why."

"Sorry," I offered with a smile of my own.

"Oh, don't be. It's nice to meet a student who can grasp my lessons without a constant struggle. Where'd you learn your Telepathy, by the way?"

"Mostly I'm self taught. I had an unpleasant Uncle I used as a guinea pig."

"She also said that she never knows when you're joking or not. She said that when I'm hoping you are, you're usually not."

My smile became an open grin.

"She seems to have mentioned me quite a bit."

"Don't tell her I told you this, but she's had a little crush on you since that whole Arianna Hellstrom duel. SCA types like a man who can take care of himself," she said in a sly whisper.

"She would stab me in the face if she thought I knew that," I said, which made her laugh. But then her face took on a more serious expression.

"I hear that you've not been getting on too well with the other professors. Don't worry about Hadleigh, she's just a little jittery, but she'll come around. Nothing we can do about Aldwich, I'm afraid, he's a mean old bastard and hates Shadowborn. Your other Professor is Mark Law. He's a good egg, but a little gruff and impatient. You and he will probably get along fine, and I'll put in a good word."

"That's very decent of you. I appreciate it."

"You saved my favourite cousin's life," she said with a shrug, "and even if you hadn't, I don't like prejudice. We'll do what we can, I promise."

"Thank you," I said genuinely.

Day Two... not really so bad at all, as it turned out. Woke up well, good first lecture, and now that Porter had promised to put in a good word for me, I could actually look forward to the High Magic introduction that afternoon. So, it was actually turning out to be a damned good day and- oh, crap there's Jocelyn Faust again...

She was standing outside the front doors of the Magic School, looking distinctly ruffled. It was actually a cute look on her. Her normally perfect hair was in disarray, her clothes were rumpled and she was wearing mismatched socks. I couldn't help but grin a little.

"What did you do?" she asked, trembling a bit, "He... he just sits there, wailing and spitting, mumbling about 'the monster'. We had to bring in nurses to start feeding him!"

"Oh nothing much, we just had a little chat, nothing strenuous."

"Nothing strenuous? You terrorised him!"

"And this is a problem because...?"

"Because it's wrong, Mathew! You can't just invade someone's house and assault them!"

"How much do you want to bet that I won't even spend one day in jail over this?"

She glared at me, "How are you this confident? He's a Faust. He has contacts *everywhere*. He has dirt on everyone, from the Conclave's janitor to the *Primus inter Pares*!"

That's the Magicians' version of the Prime Minister, by the way.

"I'm not without the odd contact of my own, don't worry."

She glared at me, hard. Say what you like about Jocelyn Faust, and I could say quite a few things, that girl was nobody's idiot.

"What aren't you telling me? You lived in mortal terror of the SCA; what's changed?"

"Maybe I've already gone bad, and have nothing to fear anymore?"

She burst out laughing, which made me frown.

She continued laughing as she walked away, saying that she'd see me later.

Okay, she probably knew that I wouldn't hurt a fly (unless it grew to the size of truck and tried to eat me), but she didn't need to laugh *quite* that hard.

# CHAPTER 9

I won't bore you with the specifics of High Magic theory. Suffice to say it was complicated. Simply, casting High Magic Spells required at least a limited ability to feel the energy in question; I couldn't make a Portal without being able to 'see' Space Magic, for example. That meant that the course was, by necessity, mostly about learning to harness those energies, initially through meditation (which I was terrible at. I had immense trouble even staying awake; when I relaxed, closed my eyes and started breathing regularly, it was because I was ready to sleep!)

The professor was decent enough, though, didn't even scream once.

The rest of my day passed quietly enough. I caught up with Tom, who was now thoroughly down in the dumps because the Naiad girls had stopped making engagements with him, for reasons he wouldn't go into (and went bright red over). Given his professed fondness for alcohol, I decided that a trip to the Student Union might be just the ticket, and he did perk up while he drowned his sorrows. Well, he *tried* to drown his sorrows. He was such a lightweight that I doubt he even got his sorrows' feet wet before he passed out.

The Union was quite a large space, long and not too thin, with faux-leather covered benches along one long wall, the bar against the other, with large windows and doors at either end, and tables throughout. At half past one, it was maybe a quarter full, mostly with the robust, sporty type of student, like my snoozing friend, who I was thinking about waking up.

I'd never been the biggest fan of pubs. My more evil

grandmother always took Des and I to one of them during our days out, and never wasted the opportunity to compare and contrast her grandsons (to my cost and Des' gain). As a result, even the smell of the places triggered my flight or flight response, and the ambiance of boisterousness, addled by booze, only made it worse.

I started preparing the Spell that would wake up my idiot friend when a loud voice barked in my direction.

"Hey! It's that Magician!" said a strong-looking young man, dressed in a heavy jacket, sweater and dark trousers. He strode over to our table, looking down with some amusement at my snoozing comrade, who might have actually had the social skills to deal with our current predicament without starting an argument...

"Is it true you killed a Demon?" he said, looming over me, his expression saying how likely he thought that would be.

Incidentally, where were people getting this information?

"No," I said with a smile.

He grinned in an 'I thought so' way; the two girls with him already looked bored.

"You can't kill a Demon up here, you can only banish them back where they came from," I explained.

He had been turning away, but he stopped and looked back at me.

"And how would you know?" he sneered.

"I read a lot."

I'd decided to abandon my Illusions, but had taken up wearing sunglasses in places where I might meet strangers (no need to cause too much terror-induced screaming unless I had to), as a result, my new acquaintance couldn't see the mischief in my eyes.

He frowned, and seemed to realise that I was being evasive; he wasn't the only one.

"Are they scary?" one of the girls asked, moving past the

guy to sit next to Tom, staring at me intently. She was pretty, tall with sharp features and nice lips. Her black hair fell in a curly wave over her shoulders, reminding me of Tethys.

"I wouldn't recommend them," I said with a wince at the memory of the last lot of Demons I'd met face to face (not counting Gabrielle). I'd nearly died. Horribly.

"What did they look like?" the other girl asked, a pretty young thing, maybe a little older than I, dressed in tight and revealing clothes.

"Depends on the type, I guess. But nasty is a pretty common trait," I said with a smile, not wanting to scare anyone. I could have told them stories that would have kept them awake for a month.

"Does that mean there's a heaven?" the first girl asked.

"I hope so."

"Come on girls, we're going to be late," the guy said, sounding miffed, tapping his foot irately, no doubt realising that his initial attempt at looking superior for the ladies was backfiring rather spectacularly.

"You mustn't mind Laurence," the blonde said, "we talk to any guy who's not him, and just like that he's jealous, even though he hasn't even managed to ask one of us out yet."

Laurence spluttered, his face going red. The blonde grinned alarmingly. It didn't take a genius to figure out that I was being used as a prop to annoy her potential boyfriend.

"And you are?" I asked.

"Missy, and this is Mila, my sister," the blonde said.

"Mathew," I replied, "and this is Tom."

Tom snored a bit louder.

"So, Mathew, you have a girlfriend?" Missy asked, batting her eyes at me while Laurence went an interesting shade of vermillion.

"Laurence, for heaven's sake, ask one of them out before this one goads you into fighting for the privilege. That's what she's after, you know, I've met the type before," I said.

Several girls at Windward fell under this category; one

recognised them by their boyfriends' bruises.

"What?" Laurence managed.

"She wants you to ask her out, and she wants you to fight for her amusement, not necessarily in that order. I'd point out that this particular type of bunny-boiler is bad for you, but I doubt it would make a difference."

Mila looked like she was desperately trying to hold in a smirk, and was failing dismally. Missy had gone white with rage.

"You going to let him talk about me like that?" Missy said, turning to Laurence.

"Um... no?" he said, taking a hesitant step forward. Poor fellow, too many ideas had jammed his brain...

I slowly and very deliberately pushed my sunglasses down my nose a bit before looking right into Laurence's green eyes. He stopped and stared for a long moment before backing away, white as a sheet, his hands up in a gesture of surrender. Missy squeaked and Mila looked a little curious, but otherwise unworried.

I pushed my glasses back up and put a smile back on my face.

"Careful what you set up as bait, Missy," I said cheerfully, "not everything long and slithery is a worm."

Missy opened and closed her mouth a couple of times in mortification and then simply darted away, taking a flummoxed Laurence with her. Mila stayed behind.

"I *love* you," she said with a wide grin, "Nobody has ever called her on her bullshit before."

"It's a hobby of mine," I said with a genuine smile.

We chatted for quite a while. She was an English Literature student, her sister was in Art and we both had a good laugh at that. She was funny, clever and insightful; I rather liked her. I explained Tom, and she had a very long laugh.

"Oh! I've heard of him, everyone has. Talks a big game, but was a little short on... stamina, if you know what I mean?"

"Don't know, don't *want* to know!" I said, aghast. She

smiled again; I liked her smile.

"So, what are you doing tonight?" she asked, her eyes shining.

"No plans."

"Do you know Centaur Hall? Just across the thoroughfare?"

"I think so."

"Big party there tonight," she replied, "You should come. It'll be fun."

"Sure! Can I bring Tom? I think the poor fellow needs a pick me up."

"The more the merrier, just... don't tell him to expect much."

I sniggered, and she left.

Huh. Maybe this place wasn't so bad after all?

I cast a rapid-detox spell on Tom and told him about our invitation. He seemed distinctly unenthusiastic, but agreed to come along.

Centaur Hall was about three times the size of Naiad, wider and taller, but newer. It was built of white stone, barely stained, with a dark grey roof. There were wide doors in every wall and large windows over much of the surface. It was bright and cheerful and was already full to bursting when we turned up at about nine.

There was loud music blaring from half a dozen sources, intermingling into a cacophony that gave me an almost instant headache. And good grief, there were a lot of people. It made me a little nervous; my interactions with crowds had largely been in the form of angry mobs and small armies...

Tom led the way in and straight for a wide drinks table set up in the front hall. It was covered in a variety of horrors that would play merry havoc with my concentration if I ever introduced them to my bloodstream. Naturally Tom picked up a cup of something foul smelling and downed it in one.

"Easy, I can't cast too many Detox Spells on you without it making you sick," I said.

"You see how these girls are laughing at me? I need a drink!" he said before picking up another and staggering off.

I couldn't say I'd noticed any girls even *looking* at him, but you can't argue with a persecution complex, I speak from experience. I wondered off, looking for Mila. The place was full and loud, already there was rubbish and passed-out people everywhere. Rooms were open and being used for... never you mind.

After about an hour searching, and no sign of Mila, I was seriously thinking about leaving. In fact, I was heading for the door when I heard things that made me want to punch someone.

"And that's when I threw him down and hit him with the lightning!" said a deep and preening voice from a nearby room.

I peered through the doorway to see a student, tall and handsome, with slick-backed hair and a tiny goatee, wearing a dark suit without a tie, and highly polished shoes. I also saw that he was wearing the lapel pin of the Stonebridge Duelling Team. He was relaxing in a heavy recliner, a girl on either arm. He held a large cup in his hand as he bragged to about twenty other kids.

There were 'ooh' and 'aah' sounds from the audience, a couple of who clapped enthusiastically.

Mage Sight quickly revealed a Wizard-level Magician with an Air affinity. Unimpressive.

Wow, was I becoming a Magical snob? Well, maybe a little. I didn't tend to think too much of duellists at the best of times, and even less of the braggarts... like this tool.

"Hey, did you hear about that new guy?" one of the watchers asked, "You know, the one who won all those fights? There was that one against a Councillor, or something, right? He's in school now, isn't he?"

"Pfft, that guy? Arianna Hellstrom is a housewife, what

does she know about duelling?"

"More than you ever will," some idiot muttered.

Oh, right. Me. That idiot.

Arianna Hellstrom was a... well, bitch was too mild a word, but every questionable thing she'd done to me was for her children, to keep them safe. She remained a thoroughly honourable woman. I respected her a hell of a lot, even if she'd nearly killed me a couple of times.

The entire group, suddenly hostile, all turned to glare at me.

"Oh yeah?" said the guy, standing up, weaving slightly.

"Yes, but then that's hardly difficult, as most molluscs know more about Magic than duellists."

Wait, I hadn't meant to say that!

Why was I suddenly so combative?

"You want to take this outside?" he slurred.

"I doubt you could spell the word 'outside', right now, much less walk there," I pointed out.

He glared and took a deliberate step forward... and simply fell over. It wasn't all him, I helped it along with a tiny jolt of Will. I also dropped a little Sleep Spell into his head that would keep him out for an hour or so. I felt like a bit of a prick, really. He was just a drunken idiot; he didn't deserve to be knocked out in front of his friends.

What had made me so suddenly angry? It was gone now.

I shook my head and backed away as the audience moved in to help out their hero, nobody noticed I'd left (apparently drunken nonsense was common enough that his collapse went largely uncommented, that should have been a warning sign right there). I walked deeper into the house, avoiding the scenes that I didn't need to see. Couples and... larger groups were barely concealed behind doors and screens, loud and amorous. I saw Tom amidst a crowd of women, smiling and flirting; they seemed to be heading towards an empty room as well and I figured that my duty was more or less done. I headed towards the back door, thinking to get some air and probably head back to Naiad. This sort of party had never been my scene, just leaving me feeling even lonelier.

There was a small patch of grass behind the house, lit up with light spilled from the windows and doors. I walked down and onto the lawn, the grass soft under my shoes. I rubbed my eyes and head.

That confrontation still bothered me. I thought I had my temper under control, or at least *better* control than that! What had set me off? And so suddenly? It was just like I'd suddenly been in the mood for a fight.

Before I had any more time to think, strong arms were suddenly around my chest and neck, and a swift strike took my knees out from under me. There was hot breath at my left ear and the feel of a female body at my back. The grips were firm, but not dangerous.

I knew who it was almost instantly, but that didn't stop a distinctly girly squeak from coming out of my mouth.

"What do you want now, Maggie?" I asked after a moment calming down.

"Maybe I'm here to kill you," she whispered in my ear.

"If you were planning to do that, giving me this much warning would have prevented it. So it's not that. Why don't you tell me what you're really after?"

"Men aren't as fun when they're smart," she said, releasing me and walking around to stand in front of me.

"Well, not to toot my own horn, but I'm just about as smart as it gets. So I guess there's no further need for you to turn up and scare the crap out of me?"

In response, she plucked the sunglasses off my face. Damn, she was fast...

She smiled, "I like your eyes," she said, tracing her fingertips along my scarred cheek.

"You're a very strange woman," I replied, and then my eyes narrowed as I realised something, "And you just used your powers to make me angry, didn't you?!"

She grinned again, "And if I did?"

I sighed, "What did you want, again?" I asked, keeping my frustration under control only by great effort.

"The Champions are disbanded. Gone forever. The Vampire protested and has been dispatched. For you, my Lord."

"You're not telling me you killed a man for me, are you?!"

"No, I killed a Vampire because he wasn't being co-operative, and I wouldn't weep for him if I were you. He murdered for centuries and enjoyed it, before my former master... reformed him. Now, where's my reward for my good service?" she asked, her voice becoming a little coquettish towards the end, which just confused me.

"Reward?" I asked, still trying to catch up with the whole 'Champions are gone, and it's my fault' thing. They may have lost their way, but they had done a lot of good in their time, dealing with Demons and feral monsters all over the world. And now they were gone because of a stray comment I'd made to this lunatic.

"Yes, I don't work for free," she said, moving in close to me.

"I did not authorise anything you did!" I said, but that didn't do any good, she simply yanked me in close and planted a deep kiss on my lips. And she was not shy about it, either, the kiss was hard and toothy and a little desperate.

I didn't really have the necessary social skills to deal with situations like that. Generally my experience with crazy women involves throwing Shadows at them. Also, I was not a fan of the sort of woman who liked you because you were a good fighter. I *especially* wasn't attracted to the sort who started dating you because you beat up (or blew up, I suppose) their boyfriend. That was *not* a good basis for long-term happiness.

It was a nice kiss, though. Well, it started that way. Her arms snaked around my neck, and then there was a leg around my waist... then I was on the grass with her on top. It started to get a little uncomfortable as the pressure started to mount. I thought that she was forgetting her own strength...

Crack!

A loud, nasty, wet one, accompanied by searing pain.

Yes... broken collar bone.

I yelped, and she leapt away, her face white with sudden anger as she looked down at me. I was shaking in pain, damn, but that hurt!

Thankfully I was well practiced enough at Numbing Spells by then to get one cast. I groaned as the pain dimmed, and then vanished.

"So fragile," she whispered, kneeling next to me, before looking at my shoulder "Broken."

"Thank you, I'm quite aware!" I snapped. I called a little Magic and started casting the spell that would set the bone. My Mage Sight informed me that the break was clean, which meant easily fixed, but my shoulder would ache like a bitch for days after this...

"Solomon wasn't fragile," she whispered again, looking away.

"Solomon is a half-breed Celestial Being! I'm just a human with a few tricks up his sleeve," I said as I cast the spell, and the Flesh Magic went to work.

She laid her hand very gently on my other arm... and then wrenched it horribly around to break it too.

I screamed that time.

In pain, and rage and betrayal.

My Shadows came as she was lifting her hand to do something equally horrible to my leg. They arrived as a massive coil that tossed her off and away, smashing her through a nearby tree, out the other side and through a wooden wall into an empty lecture theatre. I knew that it wouldn't actually hurt the lunatic. Certainly it wouldn't break any of *her* bones.

I expanded my numbing spell and stood on shaky legs, glaring at the hole in the building. She pulled herself out, staggering a little, bleeding from a light head-wound.

She laughed, a high and nasty sound.

"Yes! Punish me, hurt me as I hurt you!"

"What is *wrong* with you?!" I asked, confused and hurt, and very angry.

"I can't belong to the weak, I'd rather die!" she said, charging at me.

My Shadows intercepted her long before she got anywhere near me, flinging her back as gently as I could manage.

"Stop it, you don't belong to anyone!"

"You accepted my surrender!" she said, "You claimed me, you let me touch you just now. I won't have it!"

"Then walk away!"

"I can't! I have to defeat you! I can't bear the shame!"

See what I mean about the warrior types? Utterly bloody bonkers. The Demigod thing didn't help. They were big into all that 'code of honour', 'surrender is death' crap. Personally, I viewed surrender as a means of getting my enemy to turn his back long enough for me to do something unpleasant to him, but then I was a... oh, what's the polite word for 'complete bastard'? Crafty! I was crafty.

"You can't win like this. And you don't even want to!" I said, thinking quickly, "If you wanted me dead you would have broken my neck, not my arm. Just stop, please!"

"Never!" she snarled, running forward again, but she wasn't doing it with her all. She wanted me to hurt her, maybe even kill her.

I couldn't think what else to do...

So I released my Shadows and dropped to my knees, "I surrender!" I shouted, putting my one (mostly mended) arm out, cradling the other against my chest.

She skidded to a halt right next to me, looking down.

"What?" she asked, glaring at me.

"I surrender," I repeated, casting the Spell that would repair the damage to my forearm.

"It's a trick," she said, grabbing my chin, forcing my head up, I winced at the vice-like grip.

"No trick. I can't be hurting any more people, Maggie, I've had enough. My pride isn't worth it," I said, looking in her eyes.

She stared at me for what felt like a long time, but she eventually let my face go and backed away.

"This isn't over," she hissed before darting away.

I sagged to the ground, cradling my damaged limbs.

Can't even go to a *party* without something bad happening to me. I swear, there are some days when it's just not worth getting out of bed!

People were coming out to look at the commotion. I made myself invisible and staggered over to a patch of Shadow. I needed bed rest... lots of same, and maybe a transfer to a quieter school far, *far* away... I hear Outer Mongolia's nice this time of year.

# CHAPTER 10

I woke the next morning feeling battered and bruised. I'd called Tethys before going to bed and she'd laughed her arse off for a solid ten minutes, the cow. She thought the idea of the first girl I'd kissed at University being a psycho who'd broken three of my bones was hilarious.

I cast a few soothing Spells before going about my day, not that it helped much.

My week was roughly divided between two courses. Monday through Wednesday was Magic, Thursday and Friday was for Physical Chemistry. As the weeks went on, the time would be more usefully booked, but the first week was light and introductory.

That morning (Thursday), I went to my first 'normal' classes, which was full of very serious students, none of whom seemed inclined towards small talk, and more than a few who looked incapable of even basic human interaction.

I wore sunglasses, but needn't have bothered. When those people saw my eyes and scars, they didn't seem to care at all; I found it quite refreshing, really. I must say I rather enjoyed the empirical normality of it all. It felt good.

Thursday and Friday were very pleasant. I spent them studying for the sake of knowledge, not survival, which was a nice change. I went to the Union with Tom, got to know the school and started discovering all the good places to eat and relax.

It was so wonderfully *normal*; I was wondering why I was even bothering with the painful Magic stuff when just being a regular student was so nice.

I emerged from an Advanced Physics tutorial just after three in the afternoon on Friday, enjoying the afternoon sunlight as I walked back towards Naiad Hall, whistling happily, if tunelessly. The campus was quiet, if not empty, and I leafed through my notes as I made my way along the path.

I was surprised to find a friend of mine standing outside the front doors of the Hall, looking grim.

Agent Jeremy Braak of the SCA was tall and muscular, with dark hair and eyes; a solid, reliable man with a good sense of humour and a ready smile. He and I had fought together once. He hadn't exactly covered himself in glory, but he'd provided a useful decoy. He wore a heavy, loose jacket, black over dark trousers and combat boots. If I had to wager, I would have said that there was armour under that jacket.

"Agent Braak!" I said with a smile, approaching from the side. He jumped and turned to look towards me, his expression bleak, which made me instantly wary.

"What's wrong?" I asked.

"Mathew," he said, turning to offer his hand, which I shook, "I'm sorry to just show up like this. I've got to take you in for questioning."

"Regarding?"

"Like you don't know? Faust."

I smiled evilly, he shook his head.

"It was self defence. Mostly."

"And in that 'mostly' lies the arrest warrant," he said, pulling out the piece of paper for me to read.

"Have you spoken to Agent Kraab about this?"

Kraab was the senior SCA Agent in Stonebridge; he knew I was an Archon, and thus quite immune to prosecution.

"He's deep in an investigation, incommunicado; so is Knowles," who didn't know, "I have to bring you in."

"If Kraab's out of town, who gave the order?"

"The Primus himself," Braak said uncomfortably.

"Faust has been busy. And are those other guys with

you? Four Wizards and a Sorcerer over my left shoulder?"

"Conclave Hunter Team."

"I have a Chemistry class now, I'll come by the station house afterwards," I said, handing the paper back.

He coughed, "Mathew, it isn't that sort of warrant. I have to bring you with me now; and if I don't, they will."

"Well, they'll try."

"Yeah, and I'll have to help. It's my duty, Mathew, I swore an oath. Please don't force me into a position where you have to do me a mischief."

I harrumphed, "You don't play fair."

"I learned from the best," he replied with a grin.

"Okay. But the station is as far as I go. If you try to send me to the Farm, I'm leaving, agreed?"

"Sure, Mathew," he said, with a released breath.

"And I'm going to call someone first, alright?"

"Um, I was told no calls," he said, looking shifty.

"And that wasn't suspicious to you?"

He swallowed, unzipping his jacket, "Orders, Matty."

He was indeed wearing armour, and there was a short stave across his chest, which he pulled out of its holster.

"I'm making my call first," I said, conjuring shields, which snapped into place within seconds.

"Don't do this, Matty."

"All I'm asking is two minutes to place a call. That is hardly unreasonable. In fact, I believe that I have the *right* to do so."

At least I thought I did. My knowledge of arrest procedure was based on what I'd seen on TV, and American shows, at that. I may have been rather wrong, but I still wasn't going anywhere without making that call.

"I can't let you do that," he said, raising his stave.

"You can if I order it," I said, my eyes narrow, my voice cold, "Who's your oath to, Agent?"

He paused in his movement, his eyes on me.

"Oh, you're kidding!" he said, lowering his rod.

"No, and be cool, will you? I'm incognito!" I said in a hiss.

"Prove it! Right now!" he said, his hand twitching.

I focussed and my signet appeared on my finger, I lifted my left hand surreptitiously for him to see. He swallowed.

"God, I'm sorry, Matty- I mean Lord Shadow," he said, hastily holstering his stave.

"Not so loud! Look, Faust isn't getting any relief from me, and the others aren't going to argue. I'm going to call Lady Hopkins and get her to call your boss, get this sorted. In the meantime, I'll come with you, if you can just keep this *quiet.*"

"Of course, my lord," he said, bowing slightly.

"Oh, don't start that bollocks!" I said, which made him start, and then laugh.

"Sorry, never knew an Archon before they were terrifying. But then you always were a little scary, this does rather explain that," he said with a grin.

I called Hopkins, but got her voicemail. I shrugged and sent a text instead; she was rarely more than a minute away from her phone; I shouldn't have to wait long before she dealt with all of this.

*>Slight cock-up, did something bad to Faust, not entirely my fault, please bail me out. Braak's arresting me.*

"You dick, she'll kill me!" Braak said.

"If you were worried about that, then you shouldn't have arrested her little brother," I said with an evil grin as I sent the text off.

"Oh, I just knew this was going to end badly," he muttered.

So I ended up in an interrogation room, with all my stuff taken away. Thankfully I was still dressed...

They'd slapped on a set of Spelleater manacles, though, for all the good they'd do.

After being left in there for about an hour, Braak came in with a rather thick file which had my name on it.

"Been in here a while, you know," I complained.

"Sorry. Paperwork."

"Agent Braak, you're looking nervous."

"No, it's just that I'm under pressure here."

"Why?"

"I told you that the Primus gave the orders!"

"Alright, alright, keep your pants on," I said, smirking.

"Okay, why don't you tell me what happened between you and Lord Faust?"

"Never met the man," I replied glibly, figuring I may as well get some amusement out of this mess.

He sighed. I checked my watch; Hopkins should have been here by now, where was she?

"Can I see my phone?" I asked.

"Why?" he asked worriedly.

"Because I've had troubles lately with people messing with it. I just want to make sure my text got through."

He scratched at the back of his head, looking away. He should *never* go undercover...

"You bastard," I commented.

"Not me, support team," he said, going pale.

"Leaving now."

"At least answer my questions first! I'm in serious trouble if you don't!"

I grumbled, but stayed in my seat.

"Alright, but make it quick, I'm now getting rather annoyed," I said, leaning back and rattling the manacles, "And kindly remove these, they're chafing."

"Sorry, regulations," he said, opening the file.

"Shouldn't I have a lawyer?"

"You don't need one, it's just an interview," he said, looking away *again*.

"What's going on, Jeremy? You know I'm not an idiot."

He looked meaningfully at the recorder on the desk between us.

Ah, we were being closely monitored.

"I'm afraid I must insist on representation. That's my

right, and I'm exercising it."

"Those are rights for Pureborn, not Magicians."

"I'm fairly certain that those rights are universal. And if they aren't, then what are my rights? That should have been something you mentioned when you arrested me, surely?"

"The laws are different when the case involves an act of Magical Terrorism," he said; his eyes downcast.

My mouth fell open, "What?"

"You're being detained under the Magical Clause of the Terrorism Act."

Well, that killed whatever amusement I might have been feeling stone dead. That *really* wasn't good. This was the sort of interview that ended with the subject stuffed into a deep, dark hole somewhere.

"I'm going to count to ten," I said softly, "and if I'm not convinced that there's a lawyer on the way before I reach five, then I'm gone before I reach nine, understand? One."

"Mathew, be reasonable, you can't just leave!"

"Two."

"Look, just answer some questions, get your side of the story on the record-"

"Three."

"What do you think you're going to do, fight your way out of an SCA station?!"

"Nope. Four."

"There's a full squadron of Battle Magicians in this building, you going to fight them all?!"

"There are two Magicians in this building of any strength at all, including you, let's not be dramatic. Oh, four more now, coming this way. Five."

"Alright! I'll get your lawyer," he said, darting away.

"And that's ten," I said as the door shut.

I applied my Will and the manacles broke, dropping to the table with a clatter. I sent my Shadows into the light fixtures, and the room was plunged into darkness. I chuckled and opened a gate into the Shadow Realm. I almost made it when the door slammed open, and the room filled with Magical Light. The Gate closed.

"Oh, crap, *this* close," I muttered.

Two Magicians darted through the open door, running for me. Both were men, taller than me and fit. Neither looked friendly, their expressions hateful and nasty. I wasn't inclined to let them get their hands on me.

I called Will and tossed one back into the far wall. The other one called his own Magic and deflected my attack while I conjured a bank of shadows between us. I had my shields up and Force assembling for an attack while he was still trying to tear his way through.

I cast a Force Lance, and it ploughed through his minimal defences like they weren't there, flinging him back, screaming as his newly broken shoulder hit the wall next to his comrade. Another Mage came in, a woman, just as tough looking, with a white scar running down the left side of her face. She threw lightning right at me. My shields took the hit, barely flexing, and I snorted as I retaliated, another wave of kinetic energy tearing her shields down before a Sleeping Spell dropped her to the ground.

The door had clicked shut behind the woman, so I gestured and it was blasted outwards, slamming into the far wall of the corridor. I walked out to see Braak and Faust standing together along with another Magician, a Sorcerer this time. He was the one generating the light, which had somehow cut through all the walls in the building , banishing every potential way into the Shadow Realm.

"Could you turn the light out? I'm trying to nap in here," I said.

The trio gaped in shock; horror in Faust's case. The latter probably wasn't helped by the sounds of pain coming from the room behind me.

"Subdue the suspect!" Braak ordered.

"Really?" I asked as the Sorcerer ran towards me, light flaring around his form. Faust was already sprinting for the door, sensible fellow.

I dropped my Shadows. Against a Light Mage, they would be worse than useless. I cast Mage Sight and closed my eyes as he started concentrating all that energy down into a beam that would have cut me in half, were it not for my shields.

He took a couple of layers away, and I retaliated with more force, which he caught neatly on a Light Shield. I replied with Dispels, which blasted apart a couple of his constructs. A follow up Force Lance tore the rest down completely.

The building was on fire by this point, from splash damage caused by his Light attacks. I gathered up all that heat, which neatly put out the flames, and hurled it back at him as a condensed ball of fire that exploded against his hasty Will barrier. The defence was flimsy enough that the impact still flung him back and into Braak, propelling them both further down the corridor in a tangle of limbs and not a few bellows of harsh language.

The Light Magician was down for the count, but Braak was back on his feet in an instant, sucking in vast amounts of gravitational energy, to the point that the building was starting to shake.

"Jeremy, stop it. You're only awake right now because you know where my stuff is."

"I can't let you go, Mathew."

"Do I need to show you the ring again?"

"Go back into the interrogation room," he said, his hands glowing orange.

"How long have you been working for Faust, Agent Braak?"

"Thirty-five years. Back in the room. Now."

"On the side? Or is it a matter of an inside man type thing?"

"Both. Last warning."

"Quite right, Agent Braak. *Your* last warning. Faust's a paper tiger now, he's harmless, I made sure of that, ripped his

Magic right out of his skull. I, however, am very definitely *not* harmless. And neither are my very protective brother, sisters and Wardens. So, even if you do get me back in there, you're going to have to pay for it. With interest. Give it up."

"Nobody knows you're here, Mathew. Just undo what you did to Faust, and this can all be over."

"He said he'd kill everyone I loved," I replied softly, "even if I thought you *could* kill me, I still wouldn't fix him. Now get my things, and get the hell out of my way, that's a command from your Archon."

He cast his spell. I was ready for it, a Dispel neutralised it, but the ground cracked and the walls split as all the gravitational energy tore at the fabric of the building. I sent Shadows, and he put power into his shields, which didn't help much, I was coming at him from too many angles.

He called a bust of light that threw my Shadows off, and lashed out with gravity again, a ball of it tore three of my shield layers clean off, and the ground around my defences buckled under the sudden pressure of increased gravity.

A bit of roof concrete fell on the top of my shields, and I used my Will to toss it at Braak with a great deal of force, along with a Shadow Lance that tore his shields down, leaving him vulnerable.

But Braak was no slouch, he had a Will shield in place, and deflected my Force before it could knock him down. I followed up with more Shadows, and they slammed into his Will-dome, draining him horribly. I heard him shout in defiance as his Well finally drained down to nothing and my Shadows yanked him off his feet to sprawl in front of me, sweating and exhausted.

He gasped as he slowly rolled over, gulping as he met my eyes.

"Just kidding?" he offered.

Twenty minutes later, I staggered up the steps to Blackhold, tired, hungry and in need of a change of clothes (that station hadn't smelt nice). It was just after six, and I was working myself up into a particularly mood. Braak was a bad guy now? And on top of that, they'd hacked my bloody phone! That was just...wrong. Magicians were not supposed to have *that* card up their sleeve! Braak told me that he'd removed the virus, but I was hardly going to trust that two-faced son of a Slime-Toad...

Anyway, I got through to Hopkins as soon as I was clear, who promised Wrath, with a deliberate capital W for Braak... and a solid chunk for me as well on account of that whole Faust brain-blender thing. Apparently I wasn't supposed to attack powerful, politically connected noblemen in their own homes without provocation, who knew?

I walked through my front doors, nodding to the Wardens on duty before making my way towards Tethys' study, which was empty. Since Cassandra and Demise weren't in immediate evidence either, I headed to my room, thinking to change and shower.

I'd barely finished before Tethys came in wearing a silk robe that barely covered her wonderful thighs and left an expanse of leg interestingly exposed.

"Felt you," she said by way of an explanation, moving in close to me.

"I came home to return your ring," I said with a smile, "You wouldn't believe the afternoon I've had."

She wrapped her arms around my neck and held me very close and very gently.

"Missed you," she said quietly.

"I was here a couple of days ago," I said, running my hands gently up and down her back.

"Too long," she said, "You won't believe the things I had to do to Kandi and that new Warden to distract myself."

I chuckled, just enjoying her closeness. Something had definitely changed between us since that day. You'd think it would have created a bit of a rift, but the opposite was true, if anything. Knowing exactly where we stood with one another had taken a lot of the mystery away, but had revealed a better sort of closeness that I found myself treasuring far more than any physical encounter. She pulled back a little, her eyes meeting mine. She smiled that naughty little smile of hers I liked so much.

"Hey!" Kandi said, suddenly appearing at the door, "That's just not on!"

"Oh! Sorry, Sweetie," Tethys said, colouring slightly.

Not that I really noticed, I'd had to avert my eyes to the ceiling on account of the fact that Kandi was stark naked and her hair was dishevelled from whatever activity Tethys had... left unfinished.

"Hi Kandi," I said.

"Hi Matty. Now kindly get back to what you were doing, it's hardly fair to just drop everything because he's back in the general area, you know!"

Tethys sighed and giggled as she took in the direction of my eye-line.

"Alright, I'm coming," she said.

"So was I," Kandi muttered as she left, "bloody men, interfering in a perfectly nice evening..."

"And now she's mad at *me*," I said, looking down at Tethys once I was sure Kandi was gone.

Tethys snorted, "Sorry. I'd better get back to it, or she'll pout for a week."

"See you later," I said, after I took her left hand and slipped my signet back onto her pinkie, which made her smile, "and tell Kandi I'm sorry for disrupting her evening."

"No doubt she'll be in later to express her displeasure," she said, kissing me once, lingeringly on the cheek before leaving.

I sighed and finished dressing.

Evening found me dozing in front of my colossal television after having eaten myself into something of a coma. God bless my cook, that woman was a genius...

Kandi flopped onto the sofa next to me and dropped her

head onto my lap without preamble, perhaps a little harder than usual. *That* woke me up quickly.

"Sorry about that," I said.

"Hardly your fault," she replied.

I stroked her hair, back and shoulders and she relaxed by inches until she was sighing happily.

"She hasn't left me alone in days, and then you show up and she drops me mid- you know- it makes a girl feel second string."

"What can I do to make it up to you?"

"Help me make her jealous?" she asked with a smile.

"Any time you like," I said, tickling her ear.

She giggled and slid herself up a bit, settling her head in the crook of my arm, wrapping her arms around my torso and curling up her legs.

"You know she loves you, right?" I said.

"Sure," she replied.

"But...?"

"But what's the future there? I mean, I love the fun we have, it's wonderful. But one day, I'm going to get old, and I want someone I can grow fat with."

I laughed at that; it was more or less how I felt about the ideal long-term relationship.

"Tethys will always be as beautiful as she is now. In another ten years, she won't be interested in me anymore. You see any old girls hanging around her?"

"Well, that's just dumb. First things first, the amount of time you've spent around me, and in this house, has likely slowed your physical aging to a crawl, you've got decades before anything even *remotely* starts to sag. Secondly, there aren't any old women around Tethys because she gets them married. She told me all about it; every girl she's loved finds someone, she sees to it; so, don't be ridiculous there, either. As for growing old and fat, have at it, I'll ride that grizzly train straight to a coronary with you, and fix you up when we get there."

She laughed and smiled wonderfully up at me.

"Really?" she asked.

"Yes to all of the above."

"Well, then I suppose I shouldn't worry *too* much," she said, nuzzling against my chest.

"No, you shouldn't. Seriously, I thought it was blondes that were supposed to be du- Ow, Ow!" I squawked as she bit some rather sensitive things.

"What was that you were saying?" she asked sweetly.

"Nothing, nothing at all," I said, rubbing at the tooth marks on my chest.

"That's right," she said with a grin.

We sat like that for a while, watching the TV, chatting a bit.

"You know I'm very fond of *you*, too, right?" she asked.

"Of course. Likewise. I don't know what I'd do without you."

"Well, I'm not going anywhere."

"Good."

Tethys came in a bit later, after Kandi had fallen asleep, and sat on my other side, dressed in a set of white silk pyjamas. She put her arm around my shoulders and leant her head against mine.

"I think I've been rather hard on her since *that* day," she whispered, "I've been... I've felt a bit odd, since."

"Are you okay?"

"Oh, it's nothing *bad*. Just stupid memories I'd gone to the trouble of burying digging their way to the surface. I blame you."

"Sounds about right."

"You just had to give me *that* look, didn't you? You couldn't just let me be naughty, you had to spray your girly feelings all over it."

"Are we still talking about the same thing?"

She bit by ear affectionately, making me smile.

"My point, is that you've made me *think* about things,

how dare you?!"

I smiled and squeezed her hand.

"You've stirred up a mess in my head, and it's making things very hard on poor Kandi, have you no shame?"

"Not especially, that's how you get away with so much."

She giggled, but her expression turned serious afterwards.

"I'm sorry that I messed things up; that I made things... intense."

I gave her a look, "Please stop apologising, will you? How fragile do you think my ego is?"

She looked up and away.

"That's not nice."

She looked back at me and kissed my cheek very gently.

"Okay; that's the end of it. I'm not mentioning it again. Things are back to normal as of now," she declared.

"Thank God!"

She swatted my ear, which made me jump, which woke Kandi, who glared up at the pair of us.

"Sorry, Honey," Tethys said, leaning down to kiss her girlfriend.

Bearing in mind her position, I couldn't help but go a bit red, which amused them both no end.

Eventually we all tumbled into bed, with Kandi in the middle; 'to prevent any funny business' was her justification. She slept curled around me, with Tethys curled around her, it was actually rather nice.

Naturally the pair of them ruined my good night's sleep with their amorous antics, waking me up not once, but *twice* (and in a very interesting fashion), but you can't have everything...

# CHAPTER 11

And that was my weekend, more or less. Hopkins came around to provide the scolding I very much deserved, but she was a little half-hearted about it, if you ask me. Didn't she care enough to yell properly, anymore?

Wow, my issues might be getting worse...

Moving on.

Hopkins told me that Braak was in the doghouse, but that there wasn't much to be done about any of it. If anything, I was more likely to be in trouble for breaking SCA property (and SCA persons) if we pushed it, so I agreed to let her sweep it under the rug until such a time as the incident might be useful for some greater purpose. That annoyed me, but what else could I do? As long as I insisted on leading a double life, things were going to be complicated.

I spent my time watching movies with Tethys or playing chess with Demise and Kandi. The Pixies turned up on Saturday morning, and I spent the whole time with them on or about some part of me, which made me happy; they always did.

So, when Monday rolled around, and I had to go back to Uni, I was actually in a pretty good mood. Tethys had hugged me goodbye in a way that left me tingling, but things had gotten more or less back on an even keel between us, which reassured me no end.

That week marked the real start of my courses, and was a lot more intensive than the one before. Ten until five, Monday to Friday, with an hour's break for lunch, in no way a mellow schedule. I actually rather liked it.

The Magic days were scheduled with lectures between ten and one, and then practical labs between three and five. Professor Hadleigh's class was the most interesting. We started working with slabs of meat, reanimating and repairing the tissue, it was astonishingly delicate and *really* fun, in a macabre sort of way. I *loved* it. It rather appealed to both my nit-picky, detail-oriented *and* ghoulish sides all at the same time.

If Hadleigh's class was the most interesting, then Porter's was the most fun. She decided that the other students could work on their defences while we mentally violated each other (her words, not mine). She taught me a huge amount about Telepathic attack and defence, pushing me to think in brand new and exciting ways.

She truly was an amazing teacher. Her mental constructs were complex and elegant; we took the trouble to create new mindscapes each lesson, for the other to try their luck against. Her favourite was a colossal baroque fortress I'd designed, set in a desolate crater, protected by traps and an army of machines. In reply she created a moon-fortress filled with attractive (and scantily clad) guardswomen. They distracted me *very* effectively; I got so repeatedly lost that I had to concede the bout.

It was terrific fun, and Porter was great company. As time went on, we linked our minds and created mental variants of board games we knew, but on a huge scale. So, Monopoly with actual hotels, Chess with our mental avatars sitting atop kings the size of skyscrapers, Risk with armies in the tens of thousands...

It was the most fun I'd had in years. Truth be told, I think we both rather forgot about the other students, and I don't think they liked it very much.

If I had a frustration, it was with High Magic. I was terrible at it, which was a monumental pain. As I mentioned, in order to use a High Magic you weren't born to, you had to be able to channel the energy. To do that, you need to sense it, and to do *that*, you needed to open up and quiet your mind; something I was having real trouble with. My mind just wouldn't shut up (much like the rest of me). The professor was decent about it, though, and I was comforted by the fact that the other students weren't making much more progress than I was.

Tom and I developed something of a friendship; I think it was mostly because I was the only idiot who would put up with him for more than ten minutes at a stretch. His reputation for... rapid fire seemed to have spread, which mortified him. I sympathised, which was probably why he kept coming back to me. I was quite impressed by how stoic he was about that; in his place, I would probably have been chewing the walls in sheer embarrassment. He was also a good conversationalist; surprisingly knowledgeable about the economy and public relations. He could even make intelligent conversation, providing there wasn't a well-filled bit of female clothing within leering distance, not that I was one to talk...

I spent my weekends at Blackhold with the Pixies and Tethys, and naturally Kandi, who'd become even more clingy, if that's possible, not that I was complaining.

People grew less afraid of me; life started getting easier. I hadn't heard anything about Faust, either one, and Tethys was keeping a close eye on the Conclave, all was well...

Yes, I know that sort of thing couldn't last.

But I could hope!

It was the end of my fourth week, and I was in one of the smaller squares, bundled up against the oncoming cold. It was just after eight on the Friday, and I was chatting with Mila (found her eventually). She wore a heavy jacket and tight trousers, along with a bright red ribbon in her dark hair. We had hot chocolates, bought against the chill, and I was laughing at a ghastly joke she'd told. She really was a nice girl, funny, smart, and with a sharp wit that I found very attractive...

"Hello Matty," Jocelyn said from behind me just as I was

about to reply to Mila.

I held back a sigh with *great* effort.

Typical. I knew something like this would happen; I just bloody knew it. Every time I made *any* progress with a girl, the universe conspires to ruin it. And nothing ruins a budding romance like the sudden appearance of an ex-girlfriend.

Especially *that* one.

"Jocelyn, how are you today?" I asked, turning to look at her. She looked nice... her hair was set in curls, framing her face, which bore a trace of makeup and some glistening lipstick. Her clothes were tight and revealing; madness in the cold, but she was a Magician...

"Mad. At you."

"What did I do this time?"

Mila turned to look, her smile disappearing, "Who's this?" she asked.

"Old friend."

"You broke the old man, that's what you did! And now I have to deal with *all* of his affairs. Do you have any idea what a pain that is?" Jocelyn said, as if Mila wasn't there.

She plonked herself down next to me, a little too close, really. Mila noticed and frowned.

"Could we talk about this later?" I asked; well, pleaded is more accurate.

"Oh no. You come into my ancestral home, break my grandfather, leave me with a mess to clean up; we'll speak *now*."

She was smirking. Evilly; her eyes darting to Mila.

"And he won't even tell me what I need to know!" Jocelyn complained, "He knows things about the family affairs, the accounts... I'm hamstrung, and I blame you!"

She didn't really seem that annoyed. Predatory was a better descriptor. I wouldn't have put it past her to have waited until the most inconvenient moment to have this conversation; when it would cause the most mischief.

"Then ask him to tell you what you need to know," I suggested, just to get her moving. If I could get rid of her quickly enough, I might be able to salvage my date...

She frowned, "What do you mean?"

"Just what I said. Get him alone and ask him to do a specific thing. I'm sure you'll find him... receptive."

"What did you do?"

"Have you directly asked him for anything? Anything at all? 'Would you tell me where the keys are?', that sort of thing?"

"Well... no. It was really more of a general 'help!'."

"Try," I suggested, smiling.

She looked at me, confused and wary.

"Just... ask him?"

I nodded.

"And... and what if I want something he can't give me?" she asked, looking down.

"I'm not a miracle worker, Jocelyn, just how many brains did you want me to scramble?" I asked.

"Maybe you could stop messing with other people and sort out your own stupid head!" she said, turning on her heel and stomping off. I got the distinct impression that I'd just missed important subtext...

"I swear that girl is trying to drive me mad!" I complained.

"What did you do to her grandfather?" Mila asked, her face a mask, part fear, part loathing; thank you Jocelyn...

"It's not what you think, and he started it," I said, beginning the process that would see me trying to justify mental mutilation, like an idiot...

"You hurt an old man?" she asked, her expression hurt, her tone deeply disappointed.

"Firstly, he's a Magician, so not old by our standards; secondly, he tried to have me killed, and that was *after* he tried to have me enslaved, but before he got bored of sending middle men and gave it the ol' try on his own. Anything that happened to him was entirely... mostly justified. May have stepped a pinkie-toe over the line with the most recent round of justice, but karmically I think I'm still ahead."

*So far, but try to keep the vengeance to a minimum, okay, Sweetie?*

I blinked, looking around, her voice had popped right into my head. She did that from time to time, but this was a little... unusual.

*Rose? Did you just call me Sweetie?* I thought.

There was a long pause.

*No...* she replied at last.

*Did so.*

*Did not!*

"What did you do?" Mila asked, now looking at me like I was a lunatic.

"Oh, reprogrammed his brain so he couldn't hurt me, himself or anyone I love. And threw in a little caveat that gives Jocelyn anything she wants for the asking," I said, still looking around.

***Trying to get in her pants, huh? Anything I can do to help with that?***

*Gabby?! How did you get this number? I mean head. I mean how are you in my head?!*

***Firstly, it's Gabrielle if you ever again want a quiet moment, and I'm piggybacking on our little feathered friend.***

*Why?*

***My own amusement, mostly.***

"That's monstrous!" Mila said.

"Sorry, lost the thread, what's that?"

"You're a psycho!" she said, dropping her hot chocolate and making a break for it. She was away and through a door before I could even... well, probably make it worse.

"Ooh, a swing and a miss!" Gabrielle said from right beside me, making me jump.

"That's not very nice."

"I'm a Demon, Graves. 'Not nice' is rather in the job description."

I glared hard, but it just bounced off.

"Besides," she continued airily, "she was all wrong for you."

"Wh- Jus- Who- I really liked her!" I said, going bright red.

"Really?" she said, smiling at me, "You know she was celibate, right?"

I made a highly frustrated sound that turned her grin evil.

"Aw, is the little Magician all pent up? It's true what they say... once you go Succubus you... well you can't stop till you die, there's not really a witty way to say that."

"Not witty, who'd have guessed?" I muttered.

She shoved me over.

Rose caught me before I could hit the grass, dropping me back onto my feet.

"Thank you," I said, rubbing the offended shoulder.

"No problem," Rose said sweetly.

"What brings you two by?" I asked as Gabrielle approached.

"We were in the area," Rose said evasively, "We thought we'd check in."

"And just in time, too, that was smooth," Gabrielle said, looking in my eyes as she slid past me.

"I was doing just fine! Right up until Jocelyn turned up."

Gabrielle smirked. Rose patted my shoulder reassuringly.

"So why were you in the area?" I asked Rose.

"I'm not sure, we were just told to come; we came," the Angel replied.

"Some of us do as we're told," Gabrielle said from right behind me, raising the hairs on my neck. I wished she'd stop circling like a bloody vulture. My heart wasn't built for this sort of stimulation.

"Are you alright, Mathew? You eating enough? You look peaked," Rose said, giving me a very hard look that reminded me of my mother when she thought I wasn't taking care of myself.

"Oh, I'm fine," I said, going with the safe response.

She was about to say something else when the man appeared. He stepped out of a dark patch and onto the square, the figure tall and forbidding, dressed all in black. I knew him the moment I saw his face.

"Oh balls," I managed as the half-cherub Solomon walked towards us (I'd finally got around to learning his name. My initial guess wasn't even close, as it turned out).

"That's not right..." Rose said, "He shouldn't have resurrected for years."

"My, my, Daddy, what have you been up to?" Gabrielle whispered, looking at the half-breed.

I sighed, bringing up my shields.

I cast Mage Sight, and had to swallow hard, because something was *very* wrong with him. His entire form was saturated with Black Magic. And he wasn't in full control of it, either, the grass around his feet was turning Grotesque, mutating into carnivorous horrors before my eyes. Green turned brown, and then barbed and sharp, splitting to reveal what looked an awful lot like thorny teeth; almost like razor-wire with mouths.

I shuddered as I felt it, something about it resonating deep in my soul, crying out to me to take it, to use it... and it would be so easy...

"That's it, take what's yours- Ow!" Gabrielle started to coo before Rose swatted her upside the head.

"This is hardly the time!" Rose said.

"This is exactly the time, he's right in the face of temptation, and he wants it so bad, don't you, Matty?" the Demon whispered.

"No," I said weakly.

"Liar," Gabrielle replied.

I started weaving anti-Black shields into my defences. Planes of hardened Shadows, bound by Will, separate from my core, so the Black couldn't seep in and infect me.

"Easy, Mathew," Rose said, sliding right through my shields like they weren't there so she could put a hand on my shoulder, "Be strong."

"No, no, she means *give in*," Gabrielle said, coming up to my other side, also ignoring my bloody shields, by the way...

"We're your liaisons," Rose said by way of explanation when I looked askance, "And no Black Magic! It's bad for you."

I took a breath, watching Solomon, he hadn't moved a muscle.

"Where is she?" he asked finally, his voice an awful gurgle, like his throat was full of blood.

"Who?" I asked, pulling in Heat, Force and Light.

"Margaret!" he snarled, "The whore who left me for my murderer!"

"How can you claim I'm your murderer... when you're alive?" I asked sardonically.

"Bring her to me. Now."

"Get stuffed," really seemed like the only sensible response.

He smiled, an awful, cruel smile, "I was hoping you'd say that."

He pressed a button on his cuff, and reality bent as Portals opened *everywhere.*

Monsters started pouring through, horrific things born of a fevered imagination and horrific amounts of Flesh Magic. They were made from the corpses of men and animals, combining the strongest, most dangerous parts of each into a nastier whole, reanimated by magic, bound to the control of even more grotesque creatures made from the bodies of Magicians.

I saw men with the heads of bulls and the claws of komodo dragons, women with the heads of poisonous snakes where their hands should have been, ogres with the arms of what looked distinctly like a lesser drake. I saw the same monster's head on the body of a polar bear... hundreds of different combinations of man, beast and mythical creature, each more loathsome than the last.

They were the Hyde. Their very existence was an abomination. Monsters for hire, made from the bodies of living things, generally against their will. It was a constant source of annoyance to Kron and Killian that they couldn't find who was making the damned things.

They looked, and even felt, wrong, but that was *nothing* compared to the smell. They were made from a very crude form of Necromancy; the dirty kind, with no Death or Spirit Magic at all; and that meant that, no matter how good the Spellwork, they would continue to rot.

And stink.

And there sure were an awful, *awful* lot of them.

"Oh... just shit," I said.

"Bring me the Magician alive. I don't care how many pieces he's in as long as he can talk," Solomon said.

There was no response from the Hyde, but then they weren't big talkers, as a rule. But they *were* obedient.

And, just like that, they charged me.

I fired the first shot, combining my stored Force, Heat and Light into a Chaos Lance which I swept across the front rank, tearing a dozen of the creatures apart and leaving their pieces in a smouldering heap.

Rose and Gabrielle vanished, which put a *real* damper on my plan of hiding behind the two of them. That forced me to really concentrate on what I was doing, because the real threat wasn't the Hyde, not at all.

No, they were simply cannon fodder, a distraction, something to soak up my Spells so that Solomon could finish the job. He threw Black Magic around like it was going out of style, and it was all I could do to shift it into the surrounding Hyde without getting any on me, and that was a close-run thing.

The things it did to them, though... I still have nightmares about that.

The Black was, at its heart, a force of Creation, the dark

side of it; the ugly side. For every flamingo, there's a goblin shark; for every phoenix, there's a labyrinth spider. Beauty and death, light and dark. White and Black.

It was an almost direct conduit between the mind of the user and the world around him, with reality itself warping to accommodate it. He could have used that power to raise monsters from my very nightmares, brought forth Demons from the darkest parts of hell, created an army of stone monsters with souls forged from his power... if he knew what he was doing.

Instead, he was using it to try and peel my limbs off.

I knew that because the Spells I redirected did *that* (and worse) to the Hyde. They were torn to pieces, arms and legs ripped away; some were skinned alive, or had their eyes and ears pulled off, some were simply gutted... it was hideous and utterly brutal.

Thank God he was too limited in imagination to realise what he was playing with, and what it was *really* capable of. On the other hand, he may simply have been incapable of realising the true potential of the Black. It took a very specific sort of soul to use it at all, without going mad, and it likely took a Magician's to do what my Grimoire had described.

Again, thank God! A true master of the Black was not a problem I could deal with on my own, not without going bad myself. It was fairly obvious that the idiot didn't know who he was dealing with. If he did, there's no way he'd risk using the Black on me. If it ever got into me, I could peel him like a ripe grape and barely realise I'd done it.

And then, likely everything else on the face of the Earth shortly afterwards...

It clicked!

Oh, that son of a bitch!

Bloody Neil, he *planned* this!

He was setting me up, and using this monster to do it. Oh, I was going to have *words* the next time I saw him...

That was assuming I survived this with my soul intact.

If I didn't, I'd likely be thanking him.

Thankfully, Solomon was blasting as many Hyde as I was, his attacks almost indiscriminate. That gave me enough breathing room to let rip with a blistering combination of Light, Force and Heat that blew more than a dozen Hyde into messy pieces, but which got nowhere near Solomon, unfortunately.

I started moving towards him, calling my Shadows to smash at the Hyde pressing towards me, swatting and crushing as they advanced, but there were so many of them! I could only imagine the sheer amount of money he'd have been forced to fork over to secure the services of so many.

There was *one* good thing about fighting the Hyde, though; I didn't have to hold back. I called a clump of Shadow to me, enchanted it and threw a shower of Shadow Lances, each of which lodged in a different monster before exploding, taking out the smaller constructs next to them as well. Some shards peppered an ogre-bull-lion monster and did no more than slightly annoy it, so I pulled heat from the air and sank it all into the creature's head, burning its brain from the inside.

The smell of that *alone*... yikes.

And the Hyde weren't the only things being damaged. The square was torn up and wrecked, the surrounding buildings were scorched, some broken badly. To top it off, I wasn't taking enough of them down, and their basic attacks were starting to damage my shields. They may not have been that strong, or Magical, but there were a bloody *lot* of them.

So, I cast a variation of Rending Fog just to see if it would help, and a dozen of the Hyde fell, their faces torn up, eyes, ears and mouths mangled so badly that they lashed out without being able to see what they were hitting. That helped, so I threw up a whole bank of it, which quickly caused the carefully managed attack to dissolve into chaos. That meant that there was no Prime in the vicinity, it could have directed them with its own eyes and mind. The sheer confusion likely meant that Solomon's funds hadn't stretched to the loan of a control creature... or perhaps Solomon was just too arrogant to assume that he needed one.

And suddenly the way to Solomon was clear! I raised my hand, and a beam of white light smashed into his shields, rocking him back with a grunt, but doing very little damage! He was a lot stronger than before.

This was not good. I was expecting him to have the same basic capacity as he'd had the last time we'd fought, which was still a lot, but manageable. As he was now, though...

Well, I still had a trick or two up my sleeve.

I called in other forms of energy, leeching it out of everything, Chemical energy from the grass, Gravitational energy from the very earth, Atomic energy from the heavier elements around me. I combined it with the energy I was already stockpiling, and just let him have it.

And the bastard, who'd standing in that *one place* since this had started, dodged easily out of the way of the attack... which brought down a small (and thankfully empty) cafe instead. He jumped high, great black wings unfurling from his back to flap and dart him towards me. I felt his Magic pulse, and a lance of Black Magic, seared towards my face.

I swear that, for one long, indescribably painful moment, I nearly let it through. But instead, I pulled my Shadow-shields in tight, and they bent under the strain of the attack. Solomon just kept flying at me, putting more power into his Spell. I didn't think he wanted me alive anymore. He was too furious... but that made him stupid.

I threw another Chaos lance, and he didn't dodge that one, so intent was he on his strike. It tore his left wing apart, and he fell to the ground with a scream of pain and fury. His small army surrounded him, and absorbed a second Lance that should have taken off his head and sent him right back where he came from.

The bastard was up again in seconds, throwing gouts of Black Magic at me, tearing his own army to pieces now, ripping the flesh from their bones, crushing their bodies; some just exploded into towers of blood and bone. I barely got a defence in the way of the energy that found its way through to me, and I was shaking with the effort of not taking that power and using it. It was right there... there for the using, there for the *enjoyment*.

It called to me, taunted me, teasing and seductive, all that power, not meant for him at all, forced down his gullet like a breathing tube. It belonged to *me*, all of it, I could feel it resonate deep in my very soul, calling to me in a voice filled with the promise of every ugly desire to ever flash through my mind.

*I could have anything I wanted...*

***No,*** said a dim voice of reason, quiet, but getting louder.

*Anything I'd ever dreamed of, it could all be mine...*

***No! Not at that cost.***

*What cost? It would be so easy, and it's right there...*

***No.***

*Just a little taste...*

"NO!" I screamed, pouring Magic into my Shadows, forming the strongest, densest Shadow Lance I'd ever made. It tore through twelve Hyde, detonating each one before it hit Solomon's shields... and still only gave him a glancing hit!

Still lost his right wing, right arm and a solid chunk of skull, though. Shadow Lances made messes even with glancing blows.

He was thrown hard by the explosion, sending him to the ground with enough force to render two Hyde goat-men things into paste before slamming straight into the side of a building and through the wall, making me wince. I hoped that the school's insurance was paid up, because I was making a *mess*!

I started after him, but a pile of medium-sized Hyde dropped on me; crocodile teeth snapped at my shields while eagle talons slashed and rhinoceros feet stomped. My defences held easily enough, but it cost me valuable time to dismantle my attackers, and by then Solomon was gone, the bastard having tumbled through a Portal while I was fighting.

And then the Hyde just mobbed me! Almost in a frenzy, they threw themselves at me. That actually made things easier. I filled the air around me with shadows, tearing and crushing with barbs and sharpened tendrils that ripped them to pieces.

It seemed to take forever, as they just kept getting up or dragging themselves towards me.

But finally, it was done, they were gone, leaving smelly piles of rapidly decomposing remains behind (those that I hadn't managed to burn, anyway).

I just stood there for a while, breathing hard, feeling the euphoria of survival. I started incinerating remains, but had to take a break as the adrenaline started to fade, and my limbs began to shake.

I staggered over to lean against a tree, almost completely exhausted.

Rose and Gabrielle reappeared.

"Oh, *now* you show yourselves?" I gasped.

"Rules, Mathew, you know that," Rose said, looking very upset. I sometimes forgot that their rules of conduct could be just as onerous for the watcher as the subject.

"Sorry," I said, not wanting to make her any more miserable.

"Well, that certainly *was* interesting," Gabrielle said, looking around at the devastation.

"Too interesting. And what was that you said about your father?" I asked, looking for confirmation.

Gabrielle grinned at me.

"It looks to me like Solomon made a rather interesting deal with my father to get back here sooner. The other side doesn't expedite their resurrections. You do make the very best enemies, don't you?"

I glared as Rose checked me over for damage, biting her lip in worry at something only she could see.

But I was having trouble paying attention to them.

Something was grating at the edge of my perception, something dreadful... and powerful. I looked around and saw little wisps of Black Magic swirling around, tiny things, really, barely there, hardly noticeable; residue from the fight.

One or two students were coming into the square, no doubt attracted by the noise (sensible people would have heard explosions and gone the *other* way...); they were looking around, camera phones in hand, taking in the damage. That drew my attention for a moment. I conjured an Invisibility Illusion around the three of us before they could get any closer. I also concealed the few remaining piles of Hyde parts before applying heat, turning them to ash. The students recoiled in surprise when things vanished, which bought me enough time to prevent them being scarred for life by stepping on people bits (thankfully it was dark enough that the piles weren't easily identifiable).

But the bulk of my attention was on the Magic, sliding sinuously around, the little coils binding together into larger shapes, moving in a vague circle around me, still slowly, guided by something I couldn't identify.

It was right there...

So close.

I licked my lips involuntarily.

And then there were blue eyes in front of mine and a pair of warm hands on my cheeks.

"Look at me and only me," Rose said.

I swallowed, obeying, but it was still there, I could feel it.

"You're calling to it," Rose said, "something in you isn't letting it dissolve. Let it go, Mathew."

"I don't know how," I whispered, trembling slightly.

"Then don't," Gabrielle said in my ear, "it's yours if you want it. You can have anything you want. All you have to do is take what's yours."

I breathed carefully. It took a minute to calm down.

"It's not mine," I said firmly, "I don't want it."

"Liar," Gabrielle repeated in a throaty whisper, "Take it while you can!"

Rose said nothing. She hadn't moved, simply watching me, looking me in my eyes. She'd done all she could. This *had* to be my choice, or there was no point. I focussed very hard, right down to the deepest, hidden parts of me, the parts that were calling to the Black, and with a great effort of Will, I silenced them.

The Black faded away; I felt the Magic sustaining it flicker and fail. I could breathe again.

Gabrielle made another very annoyed sound and stomped her foot on the ground.

Rose smiled at me, and it was a beautiful thing, a smile of faith rewarded, of peace and joy. I can't really describe how wonderful it felt...

Rose pulled back at last, her eyes glistening.

"I'm so proud of you," Rose whispered, cuffing a tear away.

"I'm not! On a platter, you bastard, what's it going to take?" Gabrielle said with a pout.

"Namia Sutton, according to the terror stains in my favourite underwear," I replied in a mutter.

"What was that?" Gabrielle asked with a glare.

"Nothing."

"And you!" she said, rounding on Rose, "Don't think I didn't see that stare of yours! You helped him!"

"I am an Angel; I needed do nothing more than have faith in my charge," Rose replied airily, "Besides, you do far worse!"

"I'm a Demon! I'm supposed to cheat, what's your excuse?!"

"It wasn't cheating!"

"Oh really? Shall we ask the Celestial Court what they think of *that* technicality?!"

I coughed politely, which made the pair jump and turn back to me a little sheepishly. They may well have forgotten I was there.

"What's your father up to?" I asked Gabrielle before the conversation could be diverted again.

"How should I know?" she asked, averting her eyes.

"You used to have a better poker face," I said.

"I know!" she said, kicking a clump of earth, which sailed through the air and smacked an unaware student in the chops, "You just... I hate you!"

"What did I do?!" I asked.

"You chose *her*!" Gabrielle said, her lip trembling a little,

Wait, how did the conversation get to *this* point?

"Huh?" I managed.

"She's baiting you, Matty," Rose said, "I can already see the crocodile tears forming."

"You are *not* supposed to tell him that!"

Rose smirked.

"Moving back to what I was asking you, what is Neil after?"

"Oh, no doubt he made a deal for Solomon's soul," Gabrielle said, conceding the bout to her feathered counterpart with a nod of her head, "So, strictly speaking, seeing as how you were the reason for it, you're technically responsible for sending one of the good guys to Hell. Congratulations!"

"If he was a good guy, then I'm a horse's arse!" I replied acidly.

"So you're willing to be judge and jury, are you? What progress!" Gabrielle said with a wide grin, "This wasn't such a wasted day!"

"The man is an animal," I replied, "and the sooner he goes back to Hell, the better."

"One thing," Gabrielle said, "Resurrection isn't one of the powers my side offers. You blow him up again, he *stays* blown up. Loved that, by the way, so deliciously vicious."

I sighed, "Balls."

Oh well, there was always-

"That won't work either. You won't be able to get past

his defences this time, even his mental ones," Gabrielle said with a grin.

"At least let me lay out the plan before you pooh-pooh it!"

"I'm sorry, go ahead," Gabrielle said.

"Never mind, I'll think of something," I grumbled, "At least we know why you two were here."

I'd been presented with a Choice. They would have been there for that.

"And, I also know the consequences of making any sort of deal with your father," I said, "You end up as an evil infused monster."

Rose giggled, looking away, Gabrielle scowled.

"Don't you get it?" the Demon asked, "He's saying that he's on *your* side! He made a profit on his end, and made sure that you'd be protected on yours. Solomon couldn't have harmed you if he used every scrap of power in his body!"

"Oh yes he could!" I replied, "I have to have a soul attached to a body for the Black to sink into. Some of those Spells he was throwing towards the end there would have left me a greasy smear!"

Gabrielle just smiled, "Are you sure about that?" she asked, "Do you really think the Black would have done that to you?"

I ignored her, "And don't get me started on how he knew where I'd be, when I'd be there and who I was. Those aren't pieces of information one comes by without help. I wonder where he could have come by them?"

Gabrielle scowled even harder.

"Figured that out, did you?" she asked.

"Worry when I don't. Because it means I'm too angry to think, which would be bad for everyone."

Gabrielle shivered, biting her lip, "I love it when you talk like that."

"Oh no, you're not distracting me that way-"

I stopped because Portals were opening, and SCA

people had arrived.

"Crap," I said, "I have to go before they spot me."

Rose concentrated and time slowed to a halt.

"That would have been useful a few minutes ago!" I complained.

"Doesn't interact well with offensive Magic, might have caused an explosion," Rose explained.

I muttered again before realising that, all things considered, things could have gone a lot worse.

I turned to thank them both for being there, only to find that they'd vanished... again.

"I still hate it when you do that!"

They didn't reply.

# CHAPTER 12

I used the moment of Time-manipulation to jump into the Shadow Realm and head home. The last thing I needed was another entanglement with the SCA, and there was every hope that I hadn't been identified, this time. I could only thank God that Solomon had attacked when the park was quiet, or... well, the alternative didn't bear thinking about. That was normally a rather busy thoroughfare.

I emerged into my usual downstairs bathroom. If you were wondering why I seemed to appear in lavatories so often, it was because they were *dark* when not in use, not because I was a pervert (something which had been suggested more than once by one of my less charitable Wardens; you guess which one). I opened the door with a stifled yawn. Using that much Magic took it out of me, and I wanted to rest in a safe place as soon as I'd put the warning out to everyone about Solomon.

"You hear about Tethys and the First Shadow?" said a female voice from around the corner in the front hall.

I walked a little slower.

"No, what?" said another woman, who I think was Jillian, one of the Wardens.

"I heard it from one of the housekeepers that she jumped him and was seen sprinting out of the room seconds later, face even paler than usual. Makes you wonder what she saw down there than made her run away like that!"

I immediately reddened, moving a bit quicker.

"Well, you know what they say about Archons, all that power must be compensating for something," said Jillian with a giggle that the other one joined in with.

Naturally that stopped when I came into view. The other one was Bethany, both went white as a sheet as their mouths shut with distinct clacks. I looked at them both for a long moment, my expression neutral. Neither met my eyes, simply staring at their shoes.

I walked on, making my way up the stairs, embarrassed and resentful.

Well... so what else is new? People talked about me behind my back before, why should things be any different now?

I stuck my head into Tethys' study, but it was empty. So I found Cassandra and warned her about Solomon. She said she'd increase the guard, not that it mattered. Even the half-breed couldn't do any harm in Blackhold. But she did say that she would make sure that nobody went anywhere alone until the crisis was resolved.

She suggested dinner, but I begged off and went to bed instead, tired and angry and thoroughly in a bad mood.

I woke up with the Pixies curled up beside me, no sign of Tethys or Kandi, which was unusual. The little Fairies hugged me hello in their usual sweet way, and I dressed before carrying them down to breakfast on my shoulders and head.

Cassandra and Demise were there, eating porridge of all things. I dropped the Pixies off in their fruit bowl and sat in my usual spot.

"Bacon is available, and you're eating grains?" I asked as one of the valets placed a proper, meat-based, breakfast in front of me.

"Some of us take care of ourselves," Cassandra said, pinching a sausage off my plate.

"Hey!" I complained.

"It doesn't count if it's stolen," she said, chewing happily.

I opened my mouth to protest, but the door to the breakfast room thumped open and Kandi fell in, dressed in her

'Carol' outfit and darted to me.

"Matty!" she said, excited and a little shaky.

"What is it?" I asked, standing to look at her, alert for danger.

"Big business deal about to go down the tubes. It's my father, we need him to sign on the dotted, but he'll only talk to the 'man in charge', the chauvinist pisshead. Come help? Oh, and you're also my fiancée. And put an Illusion over the scars and the eyes?"

I barely had time to comply with her instructions before I was dragged away from my breakfast (which the two 'dieting' vultures were already reaching for) and into the front hall. I was dressed in tracksuit bottoms and a baggy t-shirt under a light zipped up cardigan, hardly impressive. I made that point to Kandi, but she just snorted and led me to the drawing room door. She looked me over with a critical eye and moved her head up to kiss my unscarred cheek (she knew not to disrupt the illusion over the other side through contact).

"You'll do fine. This *needs* to happen, Matty. Just keep him happy and get him to sign, no matter what he says, okay? Just agree with it. Channel Faust's personality, that's what we need here."

I frowned, but nodded. I didn't *like* it, but I nodded. She'd mentioned chauvinism rather pointedly; couple that with Faust, and I could figure out the role she needed me to play. I didn't like the idea at all. If my mother ever found out...

But it was for Kandi, so I'd play the slime.

All I knew about Kandi's father was that he hit his wife (and occasionally his kids), and that he was a mean drunk. If I'd met him in any other context, I'd have done him a line of mischief that would make Lord Faust feel better about his lot in life.

Kandi opened the door and we found Tethys pouring coffee for a middle aged man wearing a grey silk suit, pink shirt and tie. He was a handsome enough man, with a distinguished air and salt and pepper hair. I didn't see much resemblance to Kandi, but I was willing to accept that he was the man I'd be introducing to Neil one day.

"Mister Thornsby," I said, extending my hand, "Mathew Graves."

"Ah!" he said, standing and offering a firm handshake, "A pleasure to finally meet the *man* I've really been negotiating with. Very clever, working through proxies, and such attractive ones, too."

He gave Tethys a good leer. I nearly removed his bladder control out of spite.

I smiled instead.

"Ah, well, I'm a busy man," I said, "My partners ensure that I only spend my time on worthwhile projects."

He chuckled.

"Well, Mister Graves-"

"Lord Graves, actually, but let's not rest on formality," I said, sitting down on the sofa next to Tethys, where Kandi joined me, placing her hand on my thigh.

"A Lord!" he said, "Well done, Carol. Strange that you never sought me out. It used to be that young men asked permission of fathers before marrying daughters."

"Why would I ask for something that already belongs to me?" I asked, placing a possessive hand on the back of Kandi's neck. She shivered under the touch, and I felt Tethys tense slightly next to me. She wasn't offended, though; the weirdo was blushing!

I still felt sick talking like that, but Kandi wanted this done, so done it would be.

The bastard grinned widely, settling back with his coffee cup.

"I like your style, Graves, though I have to say you're not what I expected one of my daughters to go for. All that hippie crap their mother spouted, I would have expected a less driven man," he said, winking at Kandi.

"Carol knows a good deal when she sees it," I replied,

"Now, what can I do for you? I'm told that you're having reservations."

"Not really. I just felt that I should meet the man I'm going into business with. You can't trust representatives."

I shrugged, "Well, now you've met me."

"I have. And, frankly, you seem a tad young to go into business with. Why should I trust my investment to a kid?"

"Has Carol told you about my situation?" I asked.

"Not much. She mentioned that you're a Magician. Made me wonder if you'd bewitched her or something."

He was half serious, but not disapproving, the animal.

I smiled nastily, an expression he returned, looking over Tethys as well. Let him assume, it only made our position stronger.

"Let's just say I get what I set my eyes on," I said, "but what you may not be aware of is that Magicians don't age at the same rate as the rest of the population. A person could look like me, and if he's strong enough, may be more than say, one hundred and thirty-two years old."

He nodded sagely.

"And further, such a man may have the resources to ensure that his records show nothing more than a modest nineteen, so as to propagate the idea that he's nothing more than an inexperienced boy, and thus no threat. In theory," I said, nibbling on a custard cream.

He smiled widely before laughing boisterously.

"Well! That certainly explains a few things!" he said loudly, clapping his hands together, "That's a clever wheeze, indeed!"

I nodded at the compliment.

"I have to say, I was half way convinced to drop this whole thing. After all, the recommendation came from Carol, who hasn't ever really been much a judge of *men*, if you know what I mean," he said with a sneer.

"Know and appreciate," I said, matching his expression with one of my own, nodding towards Tethys.

He laughed again, thoroughly enjoying himself. It was getting harder and harder not to do something nasty to him.

"Oh, I think we'll get on just fine," he said, "and of course, welcome to the family."

He nodded to me, saluting with his cup.

I nodded back, feeling dirty after that charade.

"Milord, you have that appointment in fifteen minutes," Tethys whispered.

"Hm?" I said, affecting disinterest.

Tethys tapped her watch.

"Oh, not those idiots again?" I said in a growl that made Thornsby lean back, "Apologies Mister Thornsby. A charity I was dealing with are annoyed because they were unknowingly providing silk for a golden parachute."

He laughed again; I think he loved me a little bit. It was creeping me out something vicious.

"I'll leave you in the hands of my partners," I said.

*While I go throw up...*

I stood up, and he did as well. We shook hands and I left them to it, not bothering to look back at them.

As soon as I was out of earshot, I ran to the shower to scrub the dirt off me. I felt unclean after playing that role. After that, I went to the nearest flower shop and bought a huge bunch each of Kandi's favourite lilies and Tethys' red roses. I felt a distinct need to apologise, even though they made me do it!

It was another hour before they were done and had seen that man out of my house. They came into my library looking for me.

"I'm really, really so-" I started before Kandi jumped onto me and bowled me over onto a sofa, where she started kissing me fiercely all over my face.

"You," kisses.

"Wonderful," more kisses.

"Man," even more kisses.

I patted her back and just went with it. It was rather nice...

After a few wonderful moments of this, she focussed more and more on my lips until the pretence was completely abandoned and we simply laid there, kissing intently, our arms around each other.

Like I said, I could very easily fall for Kandi, and allowing that self-indulgence was not good for my long-term mental health. But damn if it wasn't wonderful. Kandi was a spectacular kisser. I felt her go for her shirt, and I didn't stop her. But Tethys took the opportunity to interrupt (the cow), pulling Kandi's head up to plant a deep kiss on her lips, which snapped me out of my fantasy.

Quite right. Tethys' girl, bad form on my part, letting it go on for as long as it had.

Kandi stayed perched on my waist and was making some interesting noises as Tethys went about her business.

"Oh, you bitch," Kandi said without heat as Tethys finished her ministrations.

"Sweetie, don't play with toys you can't appreciate," Tethys said, jerking her head in a distinctly 'off' direction.

"What the hell is *that* supposed to mean?!" Kandi asked, glaring at her mentor.

"Are you planning to marry him? Settle down, have his kids? He wants kids, Kandi, lots of them. Why do you think he lives in this Brobdingnagian monstrosity?" Tethys asked.

Well, it was the official residence, but she had a point. I did want a big family one day.

Kandi went bright red. And good grief, did they have to have this conversation while I was in the room? Or *under* one of them...

"Maybe," Kandi said finally, Tethys blinked.

"He's monogamous, Kandi. Are you?" Tethys said finally, "And if you don't know, don't try it out on the one man you can't bear to hurt. That neither of us can bear to hurt. Why do you think I *stopped*?"

Kandi let out a frustrated sound, but slid off me and to the far end of the sofa, letting me sit up. I coughed and shook my head, now rather confused myself.

"Fine," Kandi said at last, "Sorry I did that, Matty."

"Well, I'm not. I mostly sorry that you stopped," I said, which made them both laugh.

Kandi gave me a hug and kissed my cheek, a little more conservatively this time, and settled back into her usual spot over my lap, her head in the crook of my arm.

"Got you going there a little, did I?" she asked, nudging a sensitive spot.

I tickled her ear and she subsided.

"Thank you for helping," she said after a minute.

"You did spectacularly well," Tethys agreed, "just the right combination of sleaze and chauvinism. Perfect."

She kissed the top of my head and dropped onto the sofa, lifting Kandi's legs onto her lap, stroking them while I did the little redhead's back.

"Oh, that's nice," Kandi purred.

"This isn't normal, is it?" I asked Tethys gesturing at Kandi.

"Shh, don't ruin it," Kandi whispered.

Tethys and I chatted idly while Kandi drifted off, nuzzled happily into my chest.

"So, you feel like telling me what all that was about? I showered twice and still don't feel like I'm clean," I said.

Tethys smiled, sliding in closer so she could lean her head on my shoulder.

"That was the last phase in Kandi's little revenge plan," she replied, "It's all very complex, but, essentially, he just signed away control of the company he spent thirty years building."

"Nice. How much did it cost?"

"We'll make a profit in the end..." she said evasively.

"That much, huh?"

She shrugged.

"If you wanted him broken, I could have done the job with a fraction of the effort."

"Kandi wanted to do it, and it was her right to do so."

I sighed, "Fair enough."

"You played that very well, I have to say. I didn't think you had it in you, it was a little... hot, actually."

"Agreed," Kandi said, not quite as asleep as we thought, "Hence my inappropriate oopsie."

"You two can't be serious! You have to be the most pro-feminist women I've ever met, I'm surprised you can even *look* at me after that!"

"It's sort of a power fantasy," Kandi said, "Try not to over-think it."

"Your entire gender is insane."

"Ooh, now say it in a firm, authoritative tone and maybe pinch me a little bit," Kandi said.

Tethys sniggered.

# CHAPTER 13

When I got back to Naiad Hall on Monday morning, things were a little odd.

Namely, it had been covered in pink lavatory paper, well not covered, but there was enough to wipe the bottoms of an entire regiment of Amazons.

And when I got within three steps of the place, eggs descended on me from a great height. I didn't even notice until I'd taken three to the head and one to the chest (out of a volley of twenty-plus; terrible accuracy, but enough to annoy me considerably just the same).

"Girl power!" someone screeched from one of the upper windows, a cry that was taken up by the whole building, from what I could see.

My first impressions were of confusion.

Was that even a thing, now? As far as I was concerned the battle of the sexes had ended in a rather stunning victory for the lady's team quite some time ago. Goodness knows I was as whipped as an unmarried man could be.

They threw more eggs. They splattered against my Will shield as I approached the front door, which was barricaded shut.

"Stay away from here, oppressor!" said a girl's voice from the other side of the barrier.

"But my stuff's in there, and I have a class in fifteen minutes," I said reasonably, "and now I also need to shower, thanks a bunch, by the way."

"Well you can't, this is a house of the Goddess now!"

"Look, either open this door, or I'll do it a mischief!"

"You wouldn't dare!"

I sighed, "More than a third of the people who live here are male, where are they?" I asked.

"Some are still in here, prisoners of the movement!" she said triumphantly.

"They are there voluntarily, right? This isn't something the police have to deal with, is it?" I asked, a little worried. I hadn't had much experience with university activism, who knows what they might get up to?

"No! Just... just be cool!" the voice spluttered, "We're trying to do a whole women's rights thing, here!"

"Well, can you do it while letting me get to my room so I can wash the egg off myself?" I asked.

There was an intense discussion on the other side of the door before the spokesperson spoke again.

"No."

"Oh for heaven's sake," I said, turning around.

My shields took more hits as I wrapped my Shadows around myself and flew towards my bedroom window. I took more hits to my defences after a moment's stunned surprise, but nothing actually got to me, and then I was safely inside.

I cast a simple spell to get the egg off my clothes and hair before gathering up my things and walking to the window again (I didn't actually *need* to shower; I just thought they might show a little compassion for an eggy person).

There was a pounding on my door as I got my foot over the sill.

"Open in the name of Gaia!" said a high voice from the other side.

"Oh dear," I said, darting back to my door and nicking my thumb on a Shadow so I could spread a little blood and enchant it against opening. It should last about a day or so. I hated enchantment, and I was awful at it. I was barely capable of this quick and cheap stuff, good thing it wasn't in the Magic tests. It was considered a form of crafting, and thus was examined under a different skill set (which I didn't have).

I jumped out the window as they started kicking, and best of luck to them, the poor idiots...

When I came back at five, they were still there, and music was blaring, loud and horrible. I sighed as I approached, taking in the various feminine banners, and some rather unpleasant slogans including suggestions involving shears and male genitalia; such a lovely group...

It was getting dark, and nobody challenged me as I flew into my room. I texted Tom, who'd been uncharacteristically quiet all day, and when he didn't reply for an hour, I went to look for him.

I found him tied to his bed, stark naked but for a small face flannel in a strategic location, he didn't look happy.

"Don't ask, just get me out of here before they come back!" he hissed.

I gestured and the ropes parted, not that they were especially tight, but he still rubbed his wrists and ankles before dressing quickly.

"Why'd they have you tied up?" I asked, suppressing a grin.

"They said I was disrespectful to women," he muttered, "and that I was treating them as interchangeable."

"And for that they tied you up?" I asked, "And you *let* them?"

"They said they were doing it for different reasons when they were actually doing it," he muttered, going bright red.

"Oh."

"Want to go to the Union?" he asked hopefully, "I don't feel too safe in here."

Oh, I really didn't want to do that...

But the poor bugger looked so wretched... at first glance. Taking a closer look at his expression, I quickly came to the conclusion that he just wanted to brag.

"Fine," I said with a sigh, he really was my only friend in that dump.

He grinned and pulled on a jacket before following me downstairs.

"Men!" said a loud, shrieky voice as we walked down the stairs, "Men walking around free!"

I looked up to see one of the girls from our floor. Mary, I think her name was. She was tall and skinny, wearing a flowery outfit, loose and baggy, but still nice to look at, with flowers painted on her face and a glittery headband keeping her red hair off her face.

A very pretty girl, actually...

"One of us is a Sorcerer," I said calmly.

"The one that lives on three?" she asked.

"Which answer gets us out of here faster?"

"Um, neither, really."

"And we're running," I said to Tom, darting down the stairs with a grin on my face.

"Jailbreak!" Mary bellowed and girls started appearing at the floor entrances, some stumbling in the grips of some sort of chemical influence, which caused enough confusion for us to get to the ground floor.

I led us off to the left, down a corridor, casting Mage Sight as I went, looking for an unlocked and empty room.

"The front door's that way!" Tom pointed out.

"It's also blocked and guarded... there!" I said, pushing through a door and walking to the window, which I unlocked and opened, swinging my legs out before dropping to the grass. Tom followed, and we were soon running across the square.

"They're getting away!" Mary said from an upstairs window.

"We live here!" I replied over my shoulder.

"Oh, so you'll be back, then?" she asked as we stopped out of egg range, and I bent over, gasping for breath (running was *not* my thing).

"Of course," I said between gasps.

"Huh, well, then we'll get you later, I guess. Can you

bring back snacks? We're running low."

"You tie me to my own bed, and you want me to feed you?!" Tom asked.

"Tell you what," I said, interrupting the jilted Adonis, "we'll trade you safe passage for snacks."

She tapped her lip for a moment, "Fine," she said, "but they'd better be good snacks, none of that home brand crap."

"Agreed."

"Seriously?" Tom hissed.

"The way to a woman's heart is through her stomach," I whispered back.

He muttered but stayed quiet as I took a list of requirements from Mary, ably assisted by additional shouts from other windows. By the time we were off, I had a much longer shopping list, and Tom was looking at his watch.

"Okay, we'll be back in a couple of hours," I said, and we walked off.

"Yeah!" said another girl, "Do our shopping, Bitches!"

I turned, "Was that the girl who asked for Jaffa Cakes?"

She immediately darted back below her window sill.

"That's what I thought."

I had to leave Tom in the pub while I went shopping. Thank goodness I could use Magic for things like this, they wanted a *lot* of stuff, and carrying Tom back after I'd fetched him wasn't exactly easy, either. In the end, I just floated the whole lot behind me as I walked back to Naiad.

"Girls, he's back!" came the cry and fifty faces appeared at the windows.

"Did you get *everything*?" one of the girls asked pointedly, she'd been the one to ask for certain products a man had no business buying on his own, if you know what I mean.

"Yep," I said, "How did you want me to get it in?"

"Door's open," Mary said, a glint of mischief in her eye as she told me this.

I rather believed I was about to be double-crossed...

I lowered the various supplies to the hall floor, about a dozen heavy plastic bags full of all manner of things they should have bought *before* starting a siege nobody was actually interested in as far as I could tell, and which nobody was enforcing.

Mary was at the top of the first floor landing with six others, and the corridors either side of the hall had another dozen or so, all carrying improvised, but thoroughly un-dangerous, weapons like pillows, swimming floats and ping-pong paddles.

"Well done, Male Oppressor," Mary said.

"Oh, we're not back to that again?"

"Always! Sisters forever!" she cried, which was greeted with whoops and cheers.

Oh no. They'd formed a pack. Not good. Mono-gendered groups tended to become cliquey and mean, and there were a *lot* of ladies under that roof.

"If you renege on a deal, then your group becomes known as people who don't keep their word, and you lose all credibility. What is your group, by the way?" I asked.

They all looked confused.

"Group?" someone asked.

"Oh for heaven's sake," I said, "Did you have any plan going into this, or were you just planning on having a week long party and were looking for an excuse?"

"The second one?" a girl offered from next to Mary, who slapped her own forehead in exasperation.

"Worst activists ever," I said, they bristled at that.

"We caught you, didn't we?" Mary asked.

"No, no you really didn't."

"Seize him, girls!"

"Can I put Tom in his room, first? He's not well, and I can't detox him again for a couple of days, his liver will take damage, and then I'd have to fix that...," I asked, "For humanity's sake?"

"Um, I guess," Mary said, "We don't want anyone to get

sick."

"Thank you, I'll be right back," I said, walking up the stairs, past the girls, who looked a little dumbstruck as I made my way past, watching as Tom floated behind me.

I deposited him in his room and went back down, where a girl apiece took an arm, adopting a threatening pose. One of them was shivering.

"Are you ready for your trial?" Mary asked with a grin.

"You feeling alright?" I asked the shivering girl, ignoring Mary's attempt at intimidation.

The girl nodded, swallowing in a way I recognised.

"No you're not, you're about to be sick," I said.

And you can guess what happened next. I caught most of it in a bowl of Shadow as she fell to her knees, groaning. The other girl let go, and I knelt next to the sick one, casting a modified Mage Sight spell I'd learned recently called Flesh Sight (which was a rather useful little diagnostic Spell).

"Fever," I said, "You've got a pretty bad case of food poisoning."

I floated the vomit into a nearby sink and flushed it, placing a hand to her head. She was young and quite plain looking, with nice green eyes and brown hair. Her figure was soft and attractively plump. She was shaking harder now.

"I can fix you, if you like?" I offered.

She shook her head.

"Oh, go on Penny," Mary said, "Let him take a look."

She held the girl's hand, and the others gathered around, worried looks on their faces, suddenly looking very young and scared.

"It's just food poisoning, everyone, no need to worry," I said, "She'll get better on her own in a few days, unless you want me to see what I can do?"

"Let him, Penny!" Mary said.

Penny groaned, puking into another Shadow bowl. When she was done, she nodded.

I got rid of the vomit again and knelt next to Penny.

"I'm going to pick you up now, is that okay?" I asked.

She nodded.

I used my Will to help and gathered her up into my arms.

"Her room?" I asked.

Mary led the way to the second floor, and I lowered Penny gently into her bed in a green and poster covered room. I pulled her duvet over her and she curled into a ball.

"What do you need?" Mary asked.

"Time," I said, looking Penny over.

Now that I was looking more deeply, I could see that it was actually a pretty bad infection. She wasn't too far off sepsis, actually.

"How long have you been sick?" I asked.

"Four days," Penny said, "it's only got worse in the last couple."

"That's because you have a tiny bit of chicken bone lodged in your stomach lining," I said after a long look. It was a shard, almost like a needle of bone, barely half a centimetre long but swimming in evil-looking bacteria.

I put my hands on her head and stomach, concentrating.

"Try and relax, this will take a while, and you may feel odd when I extract the bone, try not to move.

I grabbed the bone with Will and slowly pulled it away from her stomach lining. She gagged as it came out of her mouth and into a tissue. Penny and Mary both grimaced. I used a Flesh lattice to close the wound in her stomach and a more extensive purification spell to gather all the harmful bacteria back into her stomach, where I drained the Chemical Energy out of them, killing them instantly. She'd digest the remains eventually.

Next the fever, which would take care of itself in time, now that the bacteria were gone, but I could ease the symptoms for her. I cast a light painkiller spell on her, which would make things a bit easier until the fever was gone, which should be by morning.

"There," I said as Penny relaxed into her pillow, the spasms gone, and the pain in her head decreasing, "Drink plenty of water and call me in the morning."

"Oh, thank you, that's so much better," Penny said, already half asleep.

I gently patted her shoulder and shut down my Mage Sight, following Mary into the corridor, where the girls were waiting for news. Say what you like about the female pack, they did take care of their own. The male equivalent would leave the sick to puke in an alley and think it was hilarious.

"She's going to be alright," Mary reported. They all relaxed.

"Party!" said a pretty blonde girl, all bounce and cheer.

"Shh!" Mary said, "The doctor said bed rest."

"He's not a doctor," one of the others pointed out.

"No, a doctor wouldn't have spotted the chicken bone, and she'd be septic!" Mary pointed out.

"Chicken bone?" the blonde asked.

Mary brought it out and explained, one or two went a little green.

I took the opportunity to slip away and back to my room while they were chatting, a conversation which had quickly devolved into an indictment of the poultry industry (activists...).

I yawned, a little tired. Flesh-crafting required an obscene amount of concentration if you wanted to do it properly. I settled down on my bed, a book in hand, thinking to doze my evening away quietly.

Naturally that blasted girl wasn't going to let me.

Though at least she knocked.

"Come in," I said, sitting up.

"Thanks for that," Mary said.

"No need. What else was I going to do? Let her get sicker?"

She smiled, it was quite attractive on her...

You know, they may be right about my redhead thing.

"Still, we were a little hard on you, I hope you know that we're just doing a bit, here. You know? Fun? We don't mean anything hard by it."

"Wouldn't matter if you had. Still would have helped," I said truthfully, "Though I'd appreciate it if you kept that under wraps. Healing Magicians tend to become targets pretty fast, and I have enough problems."

It was a big issue, in fact. Healers were immensely valuable, and very difficult to come by. Add to that a large population of people afraid of cancers and infections and you have a recipe for disaster, with desperate people fighting over Healing Magicians, it didn't tend to end well. And most of them weren't like me, they couldn't really defend themselves.

"Of course, your secret's safe with us."

She subsided for a minute, "Um, you hungry? We have food," she said, "Betty's cooking."

"I wouldn't want to impose."

"Don't be silly," she said, grabbing my hand, "You're an honorary sister now!"

I thought of protesting, but I *was* hungry.

And as it turns out, Betty was kind of a genius in the kitchen.

And that's how I came by fifty overprotective denmothers.

Naturally they came to me with every ache, sprain and boo-boo you could imagine, and I had to fix them, not to mention all the... social diseases that idiots can catch if they're not careful. I had to master an entirely new set of spells to fix Agatha's herpes, which wasn't fun (I lost an entire weekend getting her through it).

I didn't get a minute to myself what with one thing or another, but I have to say that it was rather nice to be trusted and valued like that. I got to know a lot of them very well in the following weeks (a little *too* well in some cases). Tom thought I was some sort of genius. After all, a parade of women was walking into my room and walking out again, sometimes hours later, with smiles on their faces.

Mary, though, became something of a nag. The only other person who fretted that much over me was Tethys, not that Mary was quite on her level yet. She and the others *stuffed* me with food; it was getting a little ridiculous. And they even did their level best to enforce a bed time, which was worse.

And when they weren't doing *that*, they tried to make me go places I had no desire to go, just for example, two weeks after I'd fixed Penny's stomach, it was a Friday night, and Mary was wearing makeup and a set of tight clothes, which I was *not* sneaking peeks at...

"Oh, come on, Mathew, it'll be fun, I promise!" she said, tugging gently on my ear. This was her thing; whenever I was being (according to her) difficult, she tugged on an ear until I cooperated. Not too hard, but enough to be distracting.

"For you, it'll be fun. For a high level, and technically proficient, Sorcerer it'll be like watching two Neanderthals clubbing at each other with spongy bats."

"But we have tickets! And we want you to come!"

"I hate duels, Mary, loathe them, in fact," I said.

"I'll let you nitpick, all you want," she said in a tempting tone, "You can call them stupid all you like and tell me how."

"The last time I did that, you hit me," I reminded her, "and then Penny hit me, and Emily, and Sasha, and Temperance and Leticia..."

"Once, that happened," she pointed out.

"And then they told everyone else, who also hit me."

"Please?"

"No."

"I'll bring snacks."

"No."

"I'll have sex with you."

"Alright."

"What, really?"

"No."

She swatted my shoulder and let out a theatrical sniff.

"No, don't do that. Bad form, you swore you'd only do that once a week!" I said as her lower lip started trembling.

"I'm," sniff, "sorry," she said, her head hanging as she turned away, her shoulders shaking.

I sighed, "Oh, fine!"

"Good," she said, kissing my cheek to show there were no hard feelings, "We're off in half an hour, dress smart."

I grumbled and she smiled, leaving me to it.

See what I mean? It's not fair. Everywhere I go, women were bossing me around. I was one of the five most powerful Magicians on the face of the Earth, and I was that easily manipulated, it was getting ludicrous!

I didn't dress up, though. I managed that victory.

Mary led the way with Polly and Betty while I brought up the rear, yawning. I'd been anticipating a weekend at Blackhold; I'd rather become used to sleeping in a full bed, and I missed it. Alas, Mary and her brood had declared that I would be 'having fun' with them, so I was stuck at university.

Back at Windward, duelling was just another sport that Magicians could do. There was a team, but it wasn't huge, and it wasn't something I was into. After all, when you fought people who didn't bother with rules, rounds and niceties, it was a bad idea to get into the habit. Anyway, at Stonebridge University, it was a much bigger deal. The team had fifty members, ranging in power from low Wizards to mid-range Sorcerers. More than one world Champion had started right there, and it was well known for training Duellists.

Not Battle Mages, I should point out. Duellists.

They were concerned with putting on a show, making it look good for the Pureborn.

And in their way, what they did *was* essential. They demystified Magicians to the general public, made us something to be appreciated, embraced, rooted for. I'd been giving that quite some thought, of late. I knew that, generally speaking, Duellists were in it for the glory, the money and the adulation, but they'd done more for the acceptance of Magicians in wider society than any other group, the Archons included. I'd read that, worldwide, the Duelling industry had surpassed every other sport in viewing figures, with the top sportsmen able to command amounts in the million for every match, it was *that* big.

Anyway, duellists at universities were often snapped up by one of the major duelling leagues, which made these matches very important. That meant I couldn't mess with anyone without potentially wrecking a future, and even I wasn't that evil (most of the time).

The Duelling Ring was suitably impressive. And by that, I mean huge.

It's more like a miniature stadium. There was space in the stands for two thousand, with a large central space containing three separate, smaller duelling circles inside a larger one. The idea was to allow a tournament style arrangement, with three duels taking place at once, and then a larger final match at the end. It was surprisingly clean, and if not fragrant, at least not offensively smelly.

We showed our tickets at the doors and Mary lead the way up to the stands. We had seats up front, with a good view. It was half an hour until the first matches and the place was already two-thirds full. Mary put me firmly in the middle, between her and Polly, with Betty on the end.

"You ever duel, Matty?" Mary asked.

"Not like this," I said vaguely.

"Then how?" she asked, tugging my ear again to let me know that evasiveness would not be tolerated.

"Against people who wanted me dead, you happy?" I asked.

"Who would want to kill you? You're harmless. You're a Magic doctor, for heaven's sake!" Polly asked.

"I'm also a Shadow Mage, and other Magicians don't like us very much, I'm afraid."

"Why?" Betty asked.

"We tend to go bad. Use evil Magic. People have a right to be a bit wary."

"Have *you*?" Mary asked.

"Not yet, and not ever, with any luck."

"Then why would people hate you?" Polly pressed.

"It's like... having a venomous snake around. They want to make sure I won't bite, and it doesn't matter that I haven't *yet.*"

"That's sick. You Magicians are stupid," Betty said.

"Hey," I complained.

"You're one of the nicest guys I've ever met, so you've got the Ebola eyes-"

"Hey!" I protested again.

"-and those ugly scars-" Betty continued, no filter, that girl...

"-but just because you look dangerous doesn't *make* you dangerous. And you've never hurt anyone... have you?"

"Well...," I said, looking away, "nobody who didn't deserve it."

"That sounds like a story!" Mary said, "Tell us, tell us now!"

"Were you a bit of a troublemaker, then?" Polly asked.

"Ooh! Is that why you're doing medical Magic?" Betty asked, "To make up for your previous crimes?"

"Firstly, I was never charged. Secondly, it was self defence, apart from one or two minimal acts of spite, and three, I do Medical Magic because it seemed like the best use of my time," I said a little defensively.

"Hey, Matty, is this you?" Betty, who'd been frantically tapping at her phone, said, holding up a picture of me from my duel with Andromeda Caine, a nasty piece of work who went rogue with her whole Hunter Team and nearly got me killed.

"Nope," I said.

Crap, I thought Cathy had gotten rid of all the copies of that!

"You didn't even look at it," Mary said suspiciously.

"Sure I did," I replied, casting around for a topic change, "When is this thing starting?"

Mary started tugging on my ear again.

"Just what sort of a snake did we let into our garden?" she asked.

"A constrictor. All I want is to give you a hug."

They all laughed at that, and Mary nudged my ribs.

"I don't think you're dangerous at all," she said.

"I agree," Betty said, "nobody who cries during Bambi can be dangerous."

"There was something in my eye! I explained that!"

"You cried during Buffy, too, was there something in your eye then as well?" Polly asked.

"Yes," I said with a grumble, sinking in my seat.

The girls sniggered again.

They chatted, thankfully avoiding any further probes into my past while we waited. Mary talked around me, leaning on my shoulder, and I watched as the rest of the spectators filed in, which included a solid chunk of the various Magical students.

After a while, the lights went down, and the teams marched in. I have to say that they looked quite impressive. Our side wore Stonebridge's black and gold on their padded leathers, the other Cambridge's blue (which was actually a kind of light green; no, I don't know why they called it blue).

This match would kick off the year's inter-school tournament. Normally a big rival of ours, we wouldn't have expected to meet Cambridge until the finals or semi-finals, as they were one of the larger Magic Schools in the country. The big Magic schools were at the Universities of Stonebridge, Cambridge, Bristol (they were near Glastonbury, one of England's confluence points, it attracted all sorts of the lunatic /

elemental-druid fringe) and Winchester (same as Bristol, only with Stonehenge).

Most of the big universities had a team, but those four were the best, with Stonebridge on top; we generally attracted the Magicians from the older (and thus, generally more powerful) families, which gave us a stronger pool of talent to draw from.

The two squads for the night consisted of ten Magicians each. We'd likely tailored our squad to counter theirs.

The way those things worked was quite simple, really. There was an initial bout between team champions, which determined who selected a duellist first or second. Generally the winner chose second, so they could send their Water Mages against the opponent's Pyros and suchlike, providing the correct counters. Each duel was decided on best of three points, any magic touching a duellist's gauntlet shield scoring a point.

So that first duel was all important, and set the tone for the following matches, with each subsequent victory determining the selection order for the next round.

The Cambridge team was well turned out, shiny and tidy striding purposefully into the stadium. They were all young, strong-looking men and women, handsome or pretty. Most were powerful; their average strength was higher than ours, in fact.

It would be an interesting match.

# CHAPTER 14

And it was too. An impressive performance by both sides that kept everyone interested. I found it a bit... watery, if you know what I mean. When I fought, it was always with terrible consequences in mind if I should lose. That made it sharper, harder... deeper, in a way.

Watching those duellists was like watching kids *pretending* to fight. I have no doubt that they were doing their best, giving it their all as they understood it. But, in the end, it just rang hollow. They fought like they had all the time in the world, with none of the desperation I'd felt when hurling energy at another human being.

I suppose I resented that, a little.

Stonebridge's team won, handily, and our small group filtered out with the rest of the crowd, I was lost in thought, just following the girls as they led the way back to Naiad.

"What's eating you?" Mary asked, poking me again.

"Just thinking," I said, smiling at her. She really was a nice person, very sweet, even if she was a little overbearing at times.

"About?" she prodded again.

"The philosophy of combat as it pertains to Magic, Society and self-preservation."

She blinked.

"I was thinking about dinner," she replied, making me laugh. She did that a lot.

We were walking along a wooded pathway near the edge of the city, about twenty minutes walk away from the main campus. The stadium was one of the new builds, and so was quite a ways off the beaten path.

"And I was also thinking that it's been too long since you treated me to something tasty," she added.

"Us, too, if that makes a difference," Betty chimed in.

I shook my head, mentally resigning myself to a severe lightening of my wallet... at which point the first of the figures stepped into the path in front of us.

He was dressed all in black, with a hood concealing his face and a strip of black cloth across his mouth and nose.

He wasted no bloody time, I'll give him that, he simply lifted his sawn-off shotgun and pulled the trigger.

Had he come up from behind me, I'd have died, right there, right then, with two twelve-gauge slugs in my face. As it was, I *just* got a Will shield in the way to stop the projectiles cold.

At which point, I felt the fireball coming at my head, from right behind me. I shifted my Will Shield into a dome, which caught the second attack, causing a minor explosion that lit up the dark. The girls screamed. Betty looked like she was about to bolt, but Mary yanked her down (and out of the line of fire of two *more* of the figures, who hopped out of the bushes.

A pulse of rage seared through my mind. It was one thing to come after me; I more or less expected that. What I simply would *not* tolerate was people hurting my friends. And these girls *were* my friends. They'd wormed their way into my life, and the idea of anyone hurting them, even accidentally, made me utterly furious.

My first attack was a shadow tendril which pulped the gunner's left shoulder and sent him spinning head over heels to land in the bushes. The pain overwhelmed him almost immediately and he passed out before hitting the ground. The latest pair hurled a combination of lightning and ice bullets that flashed against my Will Shield and made me grunt as too much energy was drawn from my Well.

I would normally have simply surrounded myself with

Shadows, but I had the distinct feeling that if I did, the girls would panic, and likely try to run, which would be bad, to say the least. Whoever these people were, they were throwing magic around with no concern for bystanders, another point of contention, in fact.

So I took the extra second to conjure some proper shields, expanding them to surround the girls (which would weaken them a bit) before lashing out with my Shadows, formed into discreet tendrils. It was only the presence of my friends that prevented me making a *true* mess of those attackers. Even so, I still did some rather unpleasant things to them.

One of them managed to produce a fairly impressive shield; that was the Pyrokinetic. He did his best, but after casting Mage Sight, I saw that he was little more than a Wizard, and a young one, at that. An ant would have had better luck holding back a boulder. He went next.

I wrapped a Shadow around his chest, easily tearing through his shields, before squeezing just hard enough to break a few ribs. He screamed, and then he *howled* as I hurled him at the other two Magicians with hideous force. The Pyro broke six more bones in his back and shoulders, but the men he landed on fared far worse.

The Air Magician, the one who'd thrown the lightning, was in the middle of an attack when the Pyro's legs hit him hard in the gut. He lost control of his energy, which roared through his own body before flaring into his partner. The Ice Mage screamed as thousands of volts passed through his body, charring his skin and, rather horribly, bursting an eyeball, which couldn't have been good for him, and that was all in *addition* to the broken bones caused by sixty kilos of rapidly flying Fire Mage.

They ended up in a smoking, broken heap and I glared into the darkness around us, searching for another target. I saw an energy signature, further away in the park, I only caught a glimpse of it before it vanished through a Portal, but it looked... familiar.

"Are you alright?" I asked, kneeling next to my friends.

"Alright?! That was awesome!" Mary squealed, "You said you couldn't duel!"

"That wasn't a duel, it was a fight," I replied.

"Sure looked like a duel," Betty said, smiling broadly.

"It wasn't," I replied, pulling out my mobile.

"And why would these people come after you?" Mary asked, "Were we right? Are you atoning for a dark past?!"

Her voice was approaching a pitch only audible to dogs...

"Yes, I'm an immortal hit-man, on the run for killing the son of a dangerous Sorcerer, and now he's out for revenge."

"Really?!"

"No, you donut!"

She flicked my ear as I dialled Hopkins' number, but before I could get the third digit in, there was a great flare of energy and Portals opened up all around me, swallowing my attackers whole before snapping shut again. I didn't even have the chance to see what was on the other side.

"Well, that's just not fair," I complained.

I still called Hopkins, though. Someone needed to know what was going on, and it wasn't like I could just blurt out that I'd been ambushed in the vicinity of Cassandra, she'd move a Warden in with me, and I'd had enough of *that* to last a lifetime.

After that, and with nothing else for it, I walked the girls back to Naiad, though I kept my eyes open for any threat. By the time we got there, I was so keyed up that I nearly Cursed a pizza delivery man. The girls didn't seem too traumatised, I was glad to see; it had all simply been an extension of the evening's entertainment to them. I'd thought about informing them of the danger, but I couldn't bring myself to destroy their innocence about the world. Mary was such a bright and hopeful thing. She believed that good would always triumph over evil, and that the world was essentially a good place. I wasn't going to ruin that for her.

Since they were so absorbed in their talk, I took the chance to slip away and back to my room, where I fell into bed. I sighed unhappily. It seemed that no matter where I went, trouble came with me. They still hadn't managed to completely clear up the mess I'd made fighting Solomon. Hyde blood stained something vicious.

I slid off to sleep, but it wasn't long before a trio of bodies landed on me, and woke me right up again.

"What?!" I said, darting to a sitting position, my Shadows coiling from underneath my bed and desk before I realised who it was, "Do you three have any idea how dangerous it is to startle a Sorcerer?" I said before flopping back onto my pillow.

"Spill!" Mary said, shaking me.

"I'm trying to sleep!" I protested.

"And we're trying to get a good story, now tell us what we want to know. We have ways of making you talk," Betty said, trying to be threatening, but coming across as gassy, if anything.

I groaned and sat up, rubbing my eyes.

"What do you want to know?"

"Who are you, and why would people try to kill you?" Mary asked, an almost fanatical gleam in her eye.

I sighed. They wouldn't leave me be until they got their gossip.

So I spun them a (mostly true) story. I told them about how Shadowborn were viewed in the Magical world and how I'd been tipped to be the next great evil of our generation. I made sure that they knew I wasn't like that, though I may have glossed over the whole 'Black Magic is inescapable to Shadowborn' thing. I didn't want them to be scared of me, and it wasn't like I could tell them I was an Archon, those four were *horrific* gossips.

In the end, my story only seemed to make things worse. Mary was practically drooling.

"Persecuted and alone..." she began, eyes gleaming.

"Oh don't start. I am not alone, and I am rarely persecuted."

"So, you're really not a duellist?" Betty asked, disappointed.

"Nope, sorry."

"Then how come you beat them?" Polly asked, her eyes narrowing.

"Because that wasn't a duel. It was a fight. I'm an exceptional fighter," I replied, repeating myself from earlier; they didn't seem to understand the difference.

They grinned widely, not the reaction I was going for...

"So you *are* dangerous, then?" Mary asked.

"Which answer gets you to let me go back to sleep?" I asked plaintively.

"Very definitely a no. Nobody really dangerous whines this much," Betty said ruffling my hair like I was a poodle.

"Do you want to get Cursed? 'Cause that's how you get Cursed."

"So, how did you end up learning to fight? Was there a master, did he make you carry things?" Betty asked.

"Yes, his name was Miyagi and he called me Daniel-san. Ow! You know, girls are supposed to be the civilised gender!"

Mary sniggered, withdrawing her swatting hand for another go.

"You should try talking to these people, I'm sure you can explain that you're harmless," Polly offered, she was the disarmament activist of the group.

"I'm *not* harmless," I explained, "I am, by any definition, horrifically dangerous."

"Then maybe you could actually *become* harmless? Peace is always the right way!"

"No it isn't," Mary chimed in.

"Since when has war ever helped?!" Polly snapped back.

"Depends on who starts it," Betty interjected.

"Not to put too fine a point on it, but I was trying to

sleep..."

A hand was put over my mouth.

"And shall we discuss what happens when nations disarm? There will always be people who don't!"

"That is circular reasoning, and you know i-"

"Look, can you hens cluck elsewhere? I'm trying to sleep, here!" I said, finally shifting the hand.

Oh, bad move, three heads swivelled to track me, like turrets, the argument forgotten in the face of a common foe.

"Disrespecting the sisterhood are we?" Mary said dangerously.

"Getting a bit above ourselves, are we?" Betty added, her shoulders arching dangerously.

I called my Shadows and they dropped to the floor, squealing and giggling, thrashing about while attempting to escape the tickling lengths.

"Never trifle with a man who knows your ticklish spots," I said after they'd surrendered, looking distinctly dishevelled.

"What did *I* do?" Polly asked, having lost a shoe, "I barely said a word!"

"You had that same predatory look on your face," I said with a smirk.

"You must realise, this means war," Mary said with a pretty growl.

"You're bluffing," I said, "I'm the only one who knows where to get those pastries you're obsessed with."

Mary made a frustrated sound, and contented herself with dropping back onto my bed, and on top of my legs, too.

"You shouldn't be so mean to us," Mary said, with a hangdog look, "we're your friends."

The others clambered back up as well, eyes suddenly glistening, looking at the ground, toes scraping on the carpet.

"Wait, how did we get here? I had the moral high ground, I'm certain of it!"

"Well, it's gone now, so make your apologies, and maybe

we'll let you off with a scolding," Polly said, enjoying my confusion, apparently.

"But I didn't do anything..." I said, but that only seemed to cause three sets of lips to start trembling, "Alright, alright, I'm very sorry for... whatever I did."

"I suppose you could make it up to us tomorrow. Breakfast? At that place your friend Tom mentioned?" Mary said.

"Um, okay?" I replied.

"Good, then we forgive you!" she said, pecking me on the cheek. The others did, too, giggling as they left me in a flustered and confused heap.

To summarise, I'd just apologised for something I didn't do, to girls that weren't even upset, resulting in my paying for a huge breakfast that I didn't want.

How the hell did that happen?!

And those three, almost in spite of their impressive figures, could *eat*. And they loved Maccaby's, too. It also appeared that Tom had been blabbing about it, because it was two thirds full of students. Tethys was going to kill me if she ever found out that I was the reason.

So, naturally that was the day she turned up.

"Oh, God, these pancakes are better than sex!" Betty said, her eyes closed as she chewed.

"Then you're doing it wrong," I muttered, which Mary heard, snorted and insisted on repeating, which earned me two pinches and a swatted ear.

"Mathew Graves, what have you done to my diner?" Tethys said, laying her hands on my shoulders and leaning her chin on the top of my head, "And who are your friends?"

"Morning, Tethys," I said, "I thought we were meeting later for coffee?"

"Yes, but that bug I planted on your phone told me you were here, and I thought I'd join you. Why are there students everywhere?" she asked, her hands kneading gently at my shoulders.

"It's not my fault, I swear!"

And did she say that there was a bug on my phone?

"Do I have to extract the truth from you?" she asked, whispering in my ear.

"Mathew?" Mary asked, "Who's this?"

"Oh, sorry," I said, my brain coming back online, "Tethys, this is Mary, Polly and Betty, my house-mates. Ladies, this is Tethys, my friend, and partner."

"Partner?" Mary asked with a raised eyebrow.

"Business," Tethys said, "I'm the brains, he's the money."

"Money?" Betty asked.

I tilted my head up to glare, and she simply planted a kiss on my forehead and dropped into the booth next to me, her hand on my thigh under the table.

What followed was an exercise in torture as Tethys offered hints, broad and subtle, as to my nature, occupations, hobbies and sexual indiscretions, all of which the girls lapped up, loving a mystery like they did.

"Wait, you caught him with your girlfriend?" Betty asked, drawing a groan from me, "And you still work with him?"

"Please stop, Tethys, I live with these people," I begged.

"What's in it for me?" she asked, squeezing my thigh.

"At this point, anything you want!"

She grinned evilly and seemed to think it over.

"Nah, I'm having too much fun with your friends," she said, though her grip didn't waver, and it was wondering a bit high.

"Anyway, he can't help himself," Tethys said, "He's just a man, after all, and she's just a sweet, innocent little thing. How was she to resist his charms?"

"He has charms now?" Polly said with a giggle, "Since when?"

"Hah! They're onto you, they know I have no charms!" I said with confidence.

Wait...

They all laughed, at my expense again. See what I mean about women and packs?

"Well, it was wonderful meeting you three, but I must be off. I'll see you at home, later?" she said.

I nodded and Tethys kissed my cheek before walking out.

All three of them just sat, staring at me, for quite a while.

"What?" I asked.

# CHAPTER 15

"Well, thank you very much!" I said as I walked into Tethys' study later that day.

She laughed as I dropped into an armchair and then came to join me, sitting on my lap and putting her arms around my neck.

"No, this has worked in the past, but it's not going to work today, I'm very angry with... with...," she kissed my neck and cheek and my brain stopped working.

"I'm sorry, Love," she said softly, kissing and nibbling, "How can I ever make it up to you?"

"Tethys, that's not fair," I complained.

"Then I'm sorry for that too," she whispered, in no way convincing.

She finally pulled back after a few more kisses that left me unable to think properly.

"Now, what were you saying?" she asked sweetly.

"Something very important..."

"I'm sure," she said, nuzzling my neck again.

I turned towards her, our noses brushing against each other's.

"You are quite evil."

"As advertised."

She hugged me tight, grinning all the while.

"You know..." she began.

I gave her a raised eyebrow.

"What?" she protested, "I didn't even say anything yet!"

"That tone *always* means trouble."

"That's just mean."

"Then prove me wrong, what were you going to say?"

Her eye twitched, "Shut up."

I laughed and she rolled her eyes before joining in.

"What *were* you going to say?" I asked.

"No, you've ruined it. I had a whole bit where I was going to tell you that I've changed my mind, and that I fully intended to ravish you, you've spoiled it."

Now it was my turn to roll my eyes. She cuddled in closer to me.

"But, now that you mention it, that redheaded friend of yours looked tasty. Dibs."

"She's straight."

"So was Kandi."

"Hands to yourself."

"If you don't surrender the redhead, then I shall just have to find something else for these hands to do," she whispered, tracing her fingers along my jaw and neck.

"Too bad you already told me that this can't happen. I am immune to your charms, Tethys Smyth!" I said with a smile, "From now on, I'm just going to assume that anything naughty you do is to be resisted."

"I take it back."

"Too late. You've surrendered the war. Mathew wins."

"Wait just a minute! That is *not* what happened! I had you on your back, in the palm of my hand. You'd have gone there if I wanted, I win!"

"And now we're permanently platonic. I win," I countered with an evil smile.

"Oh no, don't you dare try to turn this around like that!" she said, darting up and waggling a finger.

I grinned widely and darted for the door. She pursued and grabbed my illusion around the chest, causing it to disintegrate.

"You little bastard, you come back here and I'll show you who won!" she shouted, darting around to see me climbing out the window. I tossed her a jaunty two-fingered salute and dropped, catching myself with my Will, lowering myself gently to the ground outside the front door.

She was already through after me, landing with a gentle flex of her legs before shooting off in pursuit.

"Come here," she whispered menacingly, her eyes black, her horns in evidence.

"Nope," I said, running away past the two Wardens on duty, both of whom looked confused more than anything else.

"You are mine, Magician, come here!" she ordered.

"Now, Tethys, what were we just talking about?" I said over my shoulder as I ran towards the library, that's generally where I'd find Kandi, my hope being that I could throw her at Tethys as a distraction.

"Don't care anymore."

I felt her call on her power and she blurred with speed, grabbing me with a squawk and throwing me over her shoulder. She started walking up the stairs.

"You're coming with me now," she said, "Feel free to struggle, it just makes it more fun."

"Lacy? Be a dear and see if you can find Kandi for me? Quick as you can," I said to the woman. The Warden darted away, and I turned my head back towards Tethys, "And this is far below the dignity of an Archon."

"You shouldn't have run. You knew I'd chase you," she said, her grip on my hindquarters tightening.

"No, I didn't, I thought we were past this!"

"Sorry," she said, not sounding like she meant it, at all.

She carried me to my room, kicking the door open before throwing me down on the bed. I sat up and was flattened back to the duvet as she jumped on me. She shoved my hands above my head and leaned down to sniff at my neck.

"You know I don't actually need these, right?" I asked, nudging my hands against her grip.

"Then stop me, if you can," she growled, biting my ear.

"Tethys," I said softly, injecting all the affection and love I had for the woman into that one word. She stopped, bringing her head up to look in my eyes. She frowned.

"Why'd you have to say it like that?" she asked, letting me go.

I cupped her face; she closed her eyes and leant into the touch.

"Because I do love you. And I'm not going to let you do anything you don't really want to do. And because you were quite right, I am yours. And above anything... like *this*, I am your friend, and sometimes that means doing the hard thing rather than the fun thing. I will never give you a reason to regret, that's my promise to you."

Tears trickled down her face and she collapsed onto me, her cheek on my chest.

"You ridiculous man," she said, wrapping her arms around me.

I stroked her hair and back as she laid there, holding her tightly to me as she composed herself.

"How are you like this?" she asked, "Nobody should be this strong. It's not fair on the rest of us."

"You know me better than that. You know I'm not."

"No, I know you *think* you're not. That's different," she said.

"I'm a big old coward, Tethys, as you well know. I'm not strong as much as I'm terrified of consequences. Which is good, it keeps me on the straight and narrow."

She sighed, looking up at me. She shook her head.

"Only you can make morality sound like a sin," she said, taking my hand and kissing it gently.

I sighed instead of arguing, and that was when Kandi turned up.

"What's up? I was summoned- Am I interrupting something?" she asked with a lascivious grin.

"Just get over here," Tethys said, "before I do something indiscreet."

Kandi bounced over and dropped down onto my other side, her arm around both of us, her hand helping mine stroke

Tethys' back.

"Dare I ask what you two are doing in here?" Kandi said.

"Best not," Tethys replied, "I don't come out of it looking too good."

"You always look good to me, baby," Kandi said, tickling Tethys' ear.

"Stop that, I'm determined to be upset, don't ruin it."

"Want I should do something degrading for you? Make you feel better?" Kandi offered in a high and tempting voice.

"Maybe later," Tethys said, "I'm rather comfortable just now."

"He does make a good pillow, doesn't he?" Kandi said.

"The best," Tethys said, snuggling in, "the very best."

"So, just throwing it out there, but we both like him, would there be any way that- OW!" Kandi said, rubbing the spot on her rump where Tethys had landed a stinging spank.

"Baby, that didn't discourage me," Kandi said with a shudder, "you're going to have to do it *much* harder than that..."

"Oh, good grief, that's my cue if ever there was one," I said, trying to slide out from under all that... everything.

They giggled, and Kandi squeezed some inappropriate things as I made my exit.

"Please don't wreck the bed, I'm planning on sleeping in it," I said.

"No promises," Tethys replied as she enveloped Kandi and kissed her hard.

Cassandra found me as I was making my way to the library.

"What's going on?" she asked, her hand in her jacket, no doubt resting on a weapon, "I hear things about Tethys flipping her lid, Kandi being called, what happened?"

"Oh, nothing much," I said, giving her a *very* watered down explanation as we walked.

"Oh, for heaven's sake, Mathew," she said as we dropped

onto my favourite sofa in the entertainment nook, "Can't you find a nice Sorceress and date like a normal person?"

"I refer you to my previous attempt at that," I said, meaning Jocelyn.

"Who loved you, and was willing to give you up to keep you safe, how's that so bad?"

"Can we please talk about *anything* else?"

"Such as?" she asked.

"How about the Demigoddess? That has to be more interesting."

"Than your misguided relationships with part-Demons that feed on sex?" she asked with a smirk, "No, not really."

I harrumphed and she chuckled.

"Things got complicated?" she asked, "Between you and Tethys and Kandi?"

"Enough to leave me in a state," I said, leaning back, "and rather confused."

"Well, we always knew the day would come where you'd get yourself all in a mess over that woman. Thank God she's decided to be sensible about the whole thing."

"Humph," I managed neutrally.

"I did tell you, didn't I?" she said, nudging my knee with hers.

"Yes, Mother," I replied with a glare.

"Think of it this way, you've always got me," she said, slapping my shoulder hard enough to make me yelp.

"What a wonderful compensation," I said dryly, rubbing the now tender spot.

She snorted, "Feel like some lunch?"

I nodded, smiling.

The Pixies showed up as I was finishing my meal, stealing my dessert while I wasn't looking (it's a miracle I ever managed to get anything down my neck with so many sticky fingers around the place...).

"You smell funny, what have you been doing?" Melody

asked after she was done gorging herself on cheesecake. She'd flitted over to my shoulder, looking for a place to nap her afternoon away.

"Nothing I can think of," I said, "maybe a new shampoo?"

"Nope," said Jewel, snuffling at my neck, which tickled, "this is something else... has the pretty monster been having at you again? It smells like that. We told her not to."

"Yes we did," Meadow said before belching adorably and draping herself over my arm for her post-lunch snooze, "we won't have her hurting our Shade."

"She'd never hurt me, silly," I said, stroking her back, which made her sigh happily.

"They all do," Jewel answered sadly from on top of my head, patting me gently.

"That's not true," I protested.

Though... no. Not true. Tethys never hurt me, well, not after she stopped trying to enslave or sell me, anyway.

"Name one," Melody challenged.

"Cassandra," I said, gesturing over at my Warden, who raised her sandwich in salute.

"Didn't she try to cut your head off with a sword?" Jewel asked.

"She only *threatened* to."

Cassandra rolled her eyes, "Never hearing the end of that," she muttered.

"Shall we go into the time you punched me?"

"You had that coming."

"What about all the *other* times you've beat me up?"

"You deserved those too!"

I didn't really have a good reply to that.

"It's okay, Mathew, we'll never hurt you," Melody said, hugging my neck.

"I know," I said with a smile.

Cassandra rolled her eyes and went back to her lunch.

A couple of hours went by, and I was dozing quietly in

front of the TV in the library when Kandi staggered in.

"Matty, little help? So much chafing," she wailed. I jolted awake, which roused the Pixies sleeping against my thigh, one of whom turned her face to glare at me while I apologised and went to help Kandi, who was limping and shaky.

"What happened?" I asked.

"What usually happens when you get her all riled up and throw me at her, I got carried away, and now I'm sore," she complained as I simply lifted her into my arms with my Will and carried her back to my sofa, gently laying her down.

"Let's take a look," I said with a sigh.

Hadleigh had taught me far better ways to diagnose and treat basic sprains and low-level damage. Flesh Sight let me really dig into each injury and understand exactly what was wrong, while more delicate healing spells let me piece the damaged tissues back together with minimal stress on the body. Comparing the way I used to handle healing with how I did it *now* was like comparing a jackhammer with a hammer and chisel. I couldn't believe how inefficient I'd been!

Having found the damage, which was concentrated in her large muscle groups and... private bits, I started working on it, taking each site in turn, touching gently to allow better transmission of energy into the deep tissues.

"Good grief, Kandi, you've got to take these things more slowly," I said, going to work, soothing the muscle sprains, rebuilding the chafed and blistered flesh and replenishing badly depleted protein stores.

"I know, I know, but it's hard in the moment, you know?" she said, sighing as her pains slowly vanished one by one.

It took about an hour to deal with her injuries. The Spellwork was more delicate, but it was also slower.

"You're getting better at that," she said after I was just about finished.

"Thank you, I aim to please," I said with a grin before frowning, "Hm, your hormones are a little off. And your adrenaline levels are spiking. Are you feeling alright?"

She coughed, "Um, Matty, where are your hands right now?"

"What?" and then I paid more attention, I'd left her 'private' injuries for last, you see, "Oh, sorry!"

"Not a problem," she said, kissing my cheek.

She settled against my shoulder, "So... now that you've fixed me up, care to break me again?"

"That sounded sexier in your head, didn't it?" I asked with a snigger.

"Yes, yes it did," she said, blushing heavily.

"Like to take it back?"

"Can I please? I think I can do better, something about cleaning me up and getting me dirty again, I'm working on it," she said.

I laughed and wrapped an arm around her, rubbing her side.

# CHAPTER 16

My weekend was punctuated by frequent texts from the mother hens, Mary most prolifically.

Kandi thought it was hilarious. Tethys simply glared, which made Cassandra smile. Kandi was even more inclined to spend time with me than usual (I think she was just looking for a buffer between her and her overly-amorous Succubus girlfriend). She did return a back-rub on Sunday, though, and that was just terrific, she eased out knots I didn't even know I'd had, and was scantily-clad enough to make the whole thing incredibly interesting.

But, in the end, it was back to school for me, which wasn't as much of a wrench as it had been, now that I had friends. Naturally, that came with its own set of drawbacks...

"You look terrible," Mary said as I walked through the front doors of Naiad Hall. She'd been waiting for me, which couldn't be a good sign.

"That's just the pick-me-up I needed, thanks Mary," I said, walking up the stairs so I could fetch my things for first lecture.

"I'm serious. Wherever you go at the weekend, they don't take care of you, I'm thinking you should stay here," she said, walking next to me.

"I have a life, you know."

"And we don't think that you should be spending so much time with that Tethys woman, she's obviously just using you," she said, ignoring me.

"Is that the Royal 'We'?" I asked indulgently.

"No, we all agreed, the whole Ladies' Council."

Now, it would be nice to think that Mary's concern was born out of some sort of attraction. After all, this was a girl that spent large portions of her day with me, even happily coming right into my room when I was in a state of undress. Right?

Wrong.

As far as I could tell, that girl thought of me as a half-wit little brother, someone to be protected from the dangers and pitfalls of the world. Between that little revelation and Tethys' recent running for the hills, my manly pride had taken a couple of hits.

"You know, some might consider University a place to, oh, I don't know... study? Instead of nosing into peoples' business arrangements? Just a thought," I said as I unlocked my door and headed into my room.

"And we also think you shouldn't leave your door locked, we like your DVD collection," she continued, "that one was the Royal We."

"Firstly, Tethys is family, and is quite possibly- no, certainly, the best friend I have, maybe the best one I ever had. But, to put your mind at rest, we are not involved in any sort of physical relationship. She's made it perfectly clear that's not on the cards. And secondly, the door stays locked, Kate has sticky fingers, and I don't mean that as a euphemism, her fingers are always covered in jam, and she smears."

"Oh," Mary said as she digested the information, "well, alright then."

"Just like that?" I asked, shoving the last of my things in a bag.

"Sure," she said, "You wouldn't lie to me."

"Would too, have so, and will likely do so again."

"Sure you did," she said, tugging my ear playfully as she walked me back down the stairs, "Did you eat this morning?"

I nodded, still a little full, actually.

"I don't believe you. You'll come to Marx for lunch? Good!"

"Do I even need to be around for these conversations?" I asked as we walked.

"Not really, but it helps preserve the illusion that you make life decisions," she said, patting my shoulder.

She walked me over to the Magic School, where Jocelyn was waiting, leaning against a column, her bodyguard unobtrusively watching from nearby. She looked over as I approached; her face lighting up in a smile.

She came over to me and threw her arms around my neck, hugging me tightly.

"Thank you," she whispered in my ear, "Thank you so much, Mathew."

"S'alright," I managed, patting her back, suddenly very aware of her pressed up against me. She wore heavier clothes, but still stylish and sleek, silks and high grade cottons, in black and forest green with platinum on her fingers and around her slender neck. I could still feel the wonderful shape of her, though, and I kept my hands to gentlemanly places only with effort.

"Ahem!" Mary coughed unsubtly to attract my attention.

Jocelyn pulled back, still beaming, "Who's your friend?"

"This is Mary, one of my housemates," I said, making introductions, "Mary this is Jocelyn, an old friend of mine."

They shook hands, but Mary's expression had turned distinctly calculating, and Jocelyn's slightly frosty as they looked at each other.

"Nice to meet you," Jocelyn said a little coolly.

"You too," Mary replied.

"All well at home?" I asked Jocelyn, aware that I had class in less than ten minutes.

"Very, thanks to you. I moved out!" Jocelyn said to me, practically bouncing, "I even have full control of the family trusts, I can't tell you how grateful I am to you, Mathew."

She put her hand on my arm, smiling widely, and I couldn't help but smile back. She'd used her gift wisely, clever girl.

"I owed you that much," I said quietly.

She smiled again, a more gentle, knowing thing. Mary was becoming agitated.

"You have class, Matty, you're going to be late," Mary said after another few minutes of this, "perhaps your... 'friend' would like to join us later for lunch?"

"I'd like that," Jocelyn said, turning her eyes back on Mary.

I couldn't imagine lunch together was the best idea, not if their introduction was any indication of what was coming. Naturally, before I had a chance to say a word, Mary had told Jocelyn where we were eating, pecked me on the cheek and marched off.

"I like her," Jocelyn said, smiling naughtily at me.

"The last person I liked as much as you like her got eaten by a Leviathan," I said dryly.

She smiled, kissed my cheek right on the spot Mary had, and walked off to her own class with a wave, leaving me confused and worried about what was going to happen at lunch...

Marx was a great little place towards the edge of the campus grounds. There had been some confusion about the name when it first opened up, with some rather heavily socialist students turning up thinking it was a communist cafe. They quickly discovered that it was actually named after *Groucho* Marx, not Karl, but the ambiance was so cheerful that they stayed anyway! The interior was brightly coloured, with framed pictures of the comedy greats on the walls, many of them signed, not all of them authentically. The waitresses were all cheerful, the proprietor was quick with a joke, and the food was a real treat.

And *all* of the mother hens were there. Well, not all of them, but enough that any private details Jocelyn let slip would never be forgotten. Jocelyn herself was already in situ when I showed up, along with Mary (naturally), Betty, Polly and Penny, the hardened core of the 'Council of Ladies', (a name I desperately wanted to snicker about, but didn't dare) as well as six more besides.

Nobody noticed as I came in and headed towards their table, they were engrossed in something Jocelyn was saying.

"What, Matty? Dangerous? Of course he is, he's a Shadowborn Sorcerer. He's just not dangerous to you or anyone who doesn't offer an immediate threat. And he's so old fashioned, you'd have to be packing the equivalent of a small atomic weapon before he'd even consider engaging a woman in a fight *at all*. He doesn't like it when people go after ladies, you see."

"Aww," was the almost universal response to this, making me blush.

"Oh, good grief, please stop telling them things," I said, coming up to the table.

Jocelyn turned and smiled, and the others looked evilly gleeful.

"You've already told them far too much, haven't you?"

Jocelyn's smile turned evil as well, "No, of course not, as if I would," she said completely deadpan. I couldn't help but smile back. Mary patted a chair between her and Jocelyn and I sat.

"So, Matty," Mary said in a tone of voice that just screamed at me to run, "Jocelyn tells us that your first kiss was with a Succubus? Care to expand on this delightful piece of information?"

I turned to glare at Jocelyn who just smiled back.

"That was really more an act of domination than anything else. I really count Jocelyn as my first kiss," I said with a flush, not really realising what I'd said until after I'd said it.

That 'Aww' sound again, which just made me want to hide.

Jocelyn was blushing, too. Mary looked a little miffed. Well, she brought it up, so she can lump it.

"That wouldn't be the same lady we met the other day,

would it?" Mary asked, "The one who lives with you?"

"Oh, Matty, you didn't move in with her, did you?" Jocelyn asked, aghast, and crestfallen, "That's so dangerous!"

"No it isn't, and anyway we aren't like that, and for heaven's sake, shush in front of the mother hens!"

"Wait, you're living with a Succubus, and you're not *with* her?" Jocelyn asked, her face crinkling in confusion.

"She's his 'business partner'," Mary said mischievously, placing as much innuendo into the term as she could.

I sighed, already resigned to humiliation. Thankfully Jocelyn was a very smart girl, and knew to take anything Mary said about me with a grain of salt.

It carried on like that while we ate. I thought my face was going to catch fire by the end of it.

Thankfully, the conversation eventually moved onto more normal things after the initial humiliation. Much to my horror, Mary and Jocelyn discovered a mutual love of horseback riding, shoes and the work of Justin Bieber. They were quoting the latter's songs and getting along like a house on fire before the end of the meal.

Jocelyn walked me back to the Magic building with Mary right beside me. They were still chatting, and now also holding hands, which was making me sweat.

"Thanks for lunch, Matty," Mary said.

"Thanks for making sure everyone forgot their wallets," I replied.

She grinned evilly and simultaneously kissed my cheek and tugged my ear. The girl was a lunatic. Not that Jocelyn was much better, giving me a full-contact hug and nuzzling my neck enough to raise goose bumps. They left together, waving cheerfully as they walked away, apparently deep in further conversation, which was even *more* disturbing.

I was seriously considering moving back to Blackhold; I wasn't going to get any peace!

When I finally got back to Naiad at the end of the day,

tired and eager for bed (Magical labs were demanding no matter how powerful you were), I found my path blocked by girls in black clothing.

There were three of them, tall and thin, not very healthy looking. All wore some form of leather and silver, almost like a uniform. The one in the middle was so highly pierced by the metal that I was concerned she'd clang if she sneezed. They looked a lot like those girls who'd accosted Tom, actually.

They were looking at me with distinct hunger in their eyes, and not in the fun way, either. Though they didn't do anything threatening as I walked up to them.

I sensed the faintest trace of Magic and cast Mage Sight. Yes, definitely like the girls who'd gone after Tom. After my first meeting with their sort, I did some research into what I'd seen in their Wells, and discovered that they weren't Magicians in the traditional sense; they were Witches.

I should probably explain about that, and why this lot were eyeing me up like Burglar (my dog) inspected an unguarded pork chop.

Witches were a little different than your standard Magician. They were almost exclusively female, and were rather the 'have-nots' of the Magical World. You see, they had Wells, just like a standard Magician, but they didn't fill up on their own, like mine did. No, a Witch had to consume things in order to get Magic, or draw the power out of those things in other ways. This happened naturally just by eating, drinking and breathing as there was at least a little Magic in everything, but that was a very slow process.

If they wanted *real* power, then generally that meant blood or bone, or even flesh. Now, they *could* get these things from animals, and that *did* provide power (more than plants and air, anyway) but you can probably guess where they'd be far more likely to get a good jolt.

That's right. Human beings; especially, other Magicians.

As far as I knew, the really nasty, cannibalistic Witches were all eradicated during the last Black Purge, as they fought for the *other* side (for fairly obvious reasons). But the ones that remained weren't above pinching a sip of Sorcerer's blood (or noble blood, hence their interest in Tom) when they had the opportunity.

"Good afternoon," I said politely.

The trio bowed, which was new. The one in the middle spoke.

"Good afternoon to you, sir. I've been sent by my Coven Mistress to invite you to our college for a brief meeting," she was very polite and sounded friendly, her expression open and smiling (if still a little predatory).

I thought about it for a moment, but anything that could put off the probe into my relationship with Jocelyn, which waiting for me inside Naiad, was a good thing. I decided to see what they wanted.

"Lead the way."

They bowed again and set off; guiding me towards the older parts of the campus, through the administrative heart and out the other side into a grassed area where some of the smaller sports clubs had pitches. I knew that the University's board of governors had been trying to poach that land for ages, but the clubs and the ancient colleges surrounding it had fought so hard that it simply wasn't worth the aggravation (you'd be amazed at the bureaucratic mess better than six *hundred* law students could make, and that was just *one* of the colleges).

At the far end of the pitch was a walled off Georgian mansion, surrounded by trees. It was built in a classic style of dark grey stone, the slate roof darker still. The main gate was as tall as the outer walls, made of hard wood and painted black. There was a small plaque on the left mounting which identified it as 'Pendle College'.

The name was a bit on the nose, but that was Witches for you, not the most subtle bunch. The Pendle Witches were tried in the 1600s for murdering ten people by Witchcraft. They hadn't done it; it was actually a Necromancer on a binge. The Pendle Witches weren't even real Witches, as far as I was aware. Witches may not have been especially powerful, but they were generally strong enough to avoid getting caught by an angry mob.

To my knowledge, only one *real* Magician was ever caught by a Witch-hunter, and that only because he was drunk at the time. Unfortunately, the idiot didn't sober up in time to avoid his hanging.

And *that* is why, as a rule, Magicians didn't take mind-altering chemicals. After all, the ability to hurl fire and shoot lightning from your eyes is greatly diminished when you're too trolleyed to even stand up.

The gates opened as we approached, swinging inwards to reveal an immaculately maintained garden, with extensive herb patches and an impressive rose bed surrounding the house. There was a gravel road leading to a broad driveway where six cars were parked next to the front doors, which were thoroughly warded. The whole house was pretty well protected, actually; not as well as Blackhold, or even Faust's mansion, but I was still quite impressed.

The girls led me in (and hadn't spoken a word the whole way, by the way), and right into a small reception room just off the hall. It was clean and bright, decorated to take advantage of sunlight. There were three women waiting for me, dressed much as my guides were.

They all stood to greet me.

"Good afternoon," the one in the middle said. She was older than the rest, perhaps in her early twenties. She wore black and silver as well, but hers was in the form of a rather tasteful business suit, the silver in a pendant and earrings, "I'm Lytta Jones, the Coven Mistress."

"Mathew Graves," I said, shaking her offered hand.

She introduced the two with her as Sylvia and Louisa, her assistants, but neither of them spoke during the meeting, simply staring at me the whole time, occasionally nibbling on a lip in a rather distracting fashion.

I was invited to sit and offered tea, which I accepted (I didn't really like it, but I wanted to be polite), making small talk about their house and garden until it arrived and the door was closed behind the departing server.

"So, what can I do for you, Ms. Jones?" I asked after sipping my tea.

"I believe you came upon a couple of my girls some weeks ago?" she said, meeting my eyes.

"I did. They were about to assault a friend of mine."

At this, she looked a little uncomfortable.

"I must apologise for that. I would have done so earlier, but it only came to my notice recently. I hope that you understand that youthful exuberance can get out of hand?"

"Of course. As long as they haven't done anything similar since, I consider the matter closed."

"No, you scared them straight, I assure you!" she said with a smile, "Which leads me to why I called you here."

She looked down for a moment, her fists clenched, like she was gathering herself for a high dive.

"You demonstrated that you are a Magician of means; strong, in other words. Research told us who you were, and what you were capable of. Simply, we need help, an ally, some sort of power we can call on."

"Why?" I asked.

She twitched a little, "Something has changed around here. Something's gotten... darker. My girls were friends with the Duellists for ages, a mutual cooperation and respect, even the occasional... donation," this last said with a lascivious smirk.

Blood wasn't the only way to absorb energy from a donor, just so you know. This was how Witches got a bit of a reputation back in the day...

"But now... now they've become cold, almost militant."

"When would you say this started?" I asked.

"About three weeks ago? Four maybe? They cut off all contact, stopped responding to our invitations. One of our number was rather close to a Duellist, she was hurt trying to get into their club. That's when we knew something was wrong."

"Did you report it?"

"To who? Who would take the word of a Witch for *anything*?"

Unfortunately, she had a point. When I'd asked Hopkins about them, she spoke with some fairly obvious contempt. Witches were not well regarded by Magicians, not that you could blame them. Witches were known to seduce my people just to get more access to power.

"What can I do?" I asked.

"Help us. Teach us. I know you're qualified to Level Ten."

"Nine, actually."

"Only because you were subject to the same sort of discrimination we suffer from every day!"

Oh, she was good, I had to give her that.

"Look, Ms. Jones, I'll do what I can, I'll teach you what I know, of course, but I must warn you that allying yourself with me can do more harm than good, I am *far* from well regarded by the Conclave, and they occasionally try to kill me."

"We know. We do have one or two sources. We're not asking for a military alliance, we're asking for a teacher, someone who can guide us, help us with Spells and acquiring reagents nobody will sell to our kind."

I nodded, thinking for a moment.

"Alright, I can do that. I presume you'll want me to keep this to myself?"

Oh, this was probably a bad idea...

"If you wouldn't mind. Also... if we did find ourselves under attack... could we call on you?"

I didn't need to think about that one.

"Of course."

We talked a little more after that, but it was largely

done. I agreed to come by on the next Wednesday, and then I took my leave, heading back to Naiad. I wondered how the hell I was going to explain *this* to everyone. I'd just agreed to be the Magical teacher and protector to a group of people known to sneak up on Magicians, like me, in the dead of night with needles in their hands.

There was going to be yelling... a lot of yelling.

I decided to put off telling people for a while (which I thought quite sensible), thinking I'd have a little time to come up with a good explanation before they found out.

That led me to the Tuesday before my meeting, when another of my persistent problems showed up to have another shot at giving me a heart attack.

I was sleeping soundly, probably snoring, when I was woken by a gentle pressure on my cheek. I awoke into darkness, which wasn't a problem for me, and I was easily able to make out Maggie's face inches from mine.

"Hello," she said softly.

I couldn't fully suppress a jolt of fear, bearing in mind that she'd broken my bones the last time we'd met.

"My arm and shoulder ached for a week, you sadist!" I said eventually.

She looked a little sheepish about that and muttered an apology before looking me right in the eye, and smiling.

"I've made a decision regarding you," she said.

"Please don't break any more of my bones."

"You gave me your surrender. You were mine to do with as I please, just as I was yours."

"And?" I asked, looking into her eyes.

"I've decided that I like you."

She sat on the seat next to my bed, looking down at me.

"I've also decided that you are just of no use to me as a lover, you'd break. But that doesn't mean I can't enjoy you."

"What did you have in mind?" I asked warily.

She smiled again, "Put some clothes on," she commanded.

I obeyed and she took me by the hand, leading me out into the night, her grip warm and firm, but not too tight. I might have resisted, but there was something different about her that night, something... vulnerable, something delicate which wasn't there before. It was almost like she'd been wearing a mask, showing me the face of a warrior, but now she'd set it aside, revealing the person underneath.

Something about *that* person made me want to follow her, to find out what she'd been hiding... and why.

I hadn't known what to expect, but I certainly hadn't anticipated her taking me to dinner at a little place down by the river. For a while, I was wary that she was going to do something nasty to me, but I quickly realised that she meant me no harm, not anymore.

Now that I had a chance to see her when she wasn't in 'warrior mode', and talk to her, I began to understand her a little. She was passionate about martial arts and shooting; she loved riding motorcycles and had a disturbing obsession with needlepoint, if you can believe that.

But under all that, it wasn't hard to see an intense loneliness, and an almost desperate desire to reach out to someone, anyone who might understand her, even if only a little. She asked me about my life, the normal, everyday things that I enjoyed, fastening onto every detail of the world I could provide her with. She never asked about my fights, or my enemies; she asked about my favourite colour, or my favourite movie; the little things you and I take for granted, but which she'd been deprived of by a life of service and battle.

She was so earnest, so shy and honest, that my heart went out to her, and I swore to myself that I would do my level best to be there for her, to give her a little of the normality that she so obviously craved.

After dinner, we took a long walk along the riverbank, enjoying a companionable silence as we looked up at the stars. She smiled in a sweet way, the tension gone from her stance as she walked with me. Eventually, she started to talk about herself, even if only a little, and in general, almost vague terms. I did my best to gently draw her out of her shell, and I think that I even succeeded, at least a little, but I knew that one night wasn't going to be enough to undo a life of hardness and loneliness.

However, this was one task I was willing to devote the time to. She had rather endeared herself to me with her simple enjoyment of the little things in life, and her shy desire to reach out to another human being. Why she'd chosen me, I was never really sure, but I wanted to reach back.

Eventually, we fetched up back at Naiad, and we sat on a bench outside the front doors, finishing a small box of chocolates I'd bought at one of the night markets.

"Solomon's back," I said, perhaps stupidly, "I thought you should know. In case... in case you felt you should be back with him."

"I know," she said with a smile, "he sent me here to pry your weaknesses from you. What are those, by the way?"

I *think* she was joking...

"Fried food and dangerous women," I replied with a matching grin. She thumped my side gently, like she was afraid my ribcage would crumple, which it might have.

"I like that you told me that," she said, "You could have kept the information to yourself in the hopes of keeping my loyalty."

"No, I couldn't."

She smiled again and went back to seeking the last of the caramels.

"I think you will be a very useful ally. Or maybe a pet, I haven't decided yet," she said a little gruffly. This was her preferred way of covering up her brief moments of emotion and vulnerability. With practice, I was getting better at cracking that shell of hers.

"Well, rub my belly, and we'll see how we feel afterwards," I offered.

She sniggered, which was cute, and she nudged me with her shoulder.

I coughed for a moment, trying to think of how best to phrase what I wanted to say. In the end, I just decided to say it, "There's a B-movie marathon in the multiplex off campus this Saturday. Would you be interested?"

Her face broke into one of the most genuine smiles I'd ever seen in my life. It was so earnest and grateful that I nearly cried on the spot. Naturally, she stuffed it away as quickly as it had appeared.

"I suppose I could make a *little* time for you. Assuming that you can get more of these," she said, popping what I was fairly certain was the last good chocolate into her mouth.

"Alright," I agreed.

"Saturday, then," she said with a firm nod before standing and walking away. It was too late, though, I'd seen her blush.

Something in me just went out to her. She seemed so desperate for a friend, but something was preventing her from just *looking* for one. I had no doubt that it was related to that dumb warrior code of hers. Can't date someone weaker than you, can't go to dinner with someone who can't toss you like a salad... but it wasn't like I was innocent in the 'dumb reasoning' department. I would just try and do my best to be there for her.

And, before you point it out, yes, I knew very well that befriending someone who'd both fought me *and* broken my bones in the recent past wasn't necessarily the best idea, but I just felt that she was worth the risk. I can't explain that well, it just felt... *right*, and that was good enough for me.

And you'd think *that* would be quite enough emotional stuff for a while, wouldn't you? But no... because I lived with *lunatics*, now.

I woke up to a horrific banging on my door, which was followed immediately by it being flung open and Betty darting to my side, shaking me all the way awake.

"Mathew, Mary's in trouble, please come, please, please!" she said, already half dragging me out of bed.

I had enough presence of mind to grab my dressing gown and wrap it around myself as I followed her down the corridor and up the stairs to the fourth floor, where there was quite a commotion around Mary's door.

"I don't care what you say, you're coming home now, and that's all there is to it!" said a deep male voice from inside the room.

"You aren't Dad, and you can't make me- Ow, let me go! You're hurting me!"

"Make a hole!" I barked, already angry at the sound of Mary's pain. The students obeyed, smacking into walls in their haste to get out of my way. Tom was there, a startled look crossing his face as he realised where the order had come from.

Mary's room was covered in posters, flyers and all sorts of girly memorabilia, her desk similarly in disarray with papers and books. The man grabbing her by the arm was wearing a navy blazer, covered in gold buttons, dark trousers and a cream shirt. His face was similar to Mary's, though naturally more masculine, but there was something in the eyes and chin that was definitely of her, a cousin perhaps? Or even a brother?

She wore a pink shirt and cotton shorts, obviously just having been asleep. The man had her by the arm, and she was in obvious pain.

"What's going on here?" I asked, my voice low and cold, the man turned to look, and was obviously surprised enough by what he saw that he instantly let her go in shock, and Mary pulled away to dart behind me, where Betty pulled her into a hug.

"Who the hell are you?" the man asked, recovering his calm and realising that he had a good six inches and fifty pounds on me (most of it muscle).

"Mary's friend," I replied quietly, "and someone who takes a dim view of people attacking young women in their rooms, particularly at this ungodly hour."

It was seven in the morning. I'd only gone to sleep about three hours earlier, and it had me in a bit of a mood.

"Get out of my way," he said in a menacing voice, and then to Mary, "And you come here, you're packing!"

"I'm going to ask *once* nicely, and then I'm going to take the hump; what are you doing here?"

"He's my brother. He thinks I'm a whore, and he's here to drag me home," Mary said.

"Am I wrong?! Look at you! Cavorting in your underwear, and with this... *creature* at your door, how can I not think that? Now get packed! We won't tolerate the shame any longer!"

Right, right, Mary told me that her family was rather... fanatical about certain things. They'd apparently mellowed with the current generation, but she'd mentioned that her brother was trying to revive the old 'hellfire and damnation' ways. Oh, it was far too early for me to have to remember things...

"Look, just calm down," I said, stepping forward, my hands out in a placating way, hoping to get this sorted without my having to make a mess.

Apparently that was enough provocation, because he slugged me in the face.

Hard enough that I flew back into the wall and smacked my head soundly enough to lose consciousness.

Yes, he knocked me out.

That's right, a bloody Pureborn knocked out an Archon. If anyone heard about this, I'd never live it down...

# CHAPTER 17

When I woke up, I was angry enough that Betty and Penny recoiled from the look on my face.

"Where?" I asked, my voice a rasp as I stood woozily.

"Out front," Betty said, her composure coming back quickly, "Kate's following."

Her phone buzzed and Betty looked.

"They're driving off!"

"Direction?" I asked.

Betty typed into her phone. Another buzz, "Ploughman's Street."

"What's the car look like?" I asked, opening the window.

"Red Ferrari."

I smiled nastily as I dropped out the window, my Shadows collecting me as Betty shrieked and darted to watch as I flew away.

"You little prick! You could have warned me!" she bellowed as I flew off.

It didn't take much to find that car. It had roared right into a rush-hour traffic jam and was currently lodged between a garbage truck and a bus. I slid to a stop above it, wrapped in a cocoon of Shadow.

Now, how to deal with this? Tear the car in half? Cast an oxidation spell that would turn the engine into a chunk of rust? I sighed as I realised that those were likely not the best ways to deal with the problem, and especially not with so many witnesses around.

So, I extended my Will and simply picked it up.

There were aggravated squawks from inside the car,

as the Ferrari (which probably cost more than most small houses) lifted gently off the ground and followed me sedately back to Naiad. I made sure to surround it with an Illusion, so we wouldn't be followed.

It didn't take long to get us back to the Hall, where I placed the vehicle gently in a parking spot outside the front doors (I made sure to drain all of the electrical energy from it so Mary's brother couldn't just drive off again). Mary jumped out of the car almost before it landed, throwing herself at me as I stepped from my Shadow Cocoon. I accepted the hug and patted her back.

"Are you alright?" I asked.

She nodded, her cheek on my shoulder. Her brother got out of his car, and he looked very unhappy, rage warring with fear as he glared at the pair of us. Rage won, and he took a menacing step forwards.

"Go on up. Your brother and I are going to have words," I said.

"Okay," she said, pecking my cheek before heading towards the door.

"No! She will not stay within a hundred miles of you, abomination!" the man shouted.

He took another step towards her and was suddenly flung back into the car hard enough to crack a window. His eyes widened as he looked at me, gulping audibly as he looked at the blood trickling from my rapidly swelling nostril.

I believed that it had *finally* dawned on him.

"Yes. You attacked a Sorcerer. Not your best idea, if you were willing to leave me alive. And even then, not a great idea, because I have opportunistic sadists on the payroll, and they would avenge me in a wide variety of very painful ways, but I digress."

He actually peed himself, which was a strong reaction, even for me. I can't say that it didn't amuse me, though.

"Alright, I will keep this simple," I said as I called my Shadows and set them to work behind him, casting a little

Muffling Spell so he wouldn't hear what I was doing, "you will go away. You will not come back unless she asks you to. I will be watching, and I'll know if you have."

"You can't just-"

"I'm still talking," I said acidly. He shut up.

"If you *should* come by again without Mary's permission, then you'll end up much like that lovely car of yours, and neither of us wants that."

Watching his expression go from quizzical to alarmed to horrified rather redeemed my day. He spun and let out a half-gurgled squeak of horror as he saw what had happened to his pride and joy. It wasn't so much a car anymore as it was a paperweight, a rough sphere of mangled metal and plastics, about a metre across, weighing in at about a ton and a half. The look on his face was priceless, and highly amusing to me.

He turned around, fury on his face to find me gone. Well, safely behind an Illusion, but as far as he was concerned, I was gone. He spun in place, terror and rage fighting it out once again, as he looked for me.

"Run, little piggy, run, run," I whispered from ten different directions, making him jump.

This time, terror won and he ran like the clappers, but not before tripping neatly over the remains of his car and falling flat into a puddle.

*It's the little things that keep you sane*, I decided, as I walked up the steps into my Halls, dropping my Illusion as I went, a broad and evil grin on my face.

The door flew open as I approached and I was dragged inside by about a dozen hands that then began checking me over none too gently, prodding and poking at the mangled nose and bleeding scalp (which I hadn't even noticed until Betty let out a squeak and presented a bloody palm).

"Hospital!" Penny said, already dragging me towards the door.

"He can fix himself, you twit, if we just give him a minute and maybe some air," Betty replied.

"Oh. Sorry, Matty," Penny said sheepishly, "Forgot."

"That was awesome!" Sasha said, "But aren't you worried he'll sue?"

She was a law student. Thoroughly overworked, but her heart was in the right place.

"Shouldn't think so. Doesn't know my name, and he'll be worried that I'll turn up and do the same thing to his face one day," I replied, gingerly touching my nose, which was almost certainly broken. That was going to take ages to fix, and I had early appointments to get to.

Terrific, I'd have to walk around with a broken nose for half the bloody day...

Mary made her way through the crowd, which parted to let her through. She stopped in front of me and reached up a tentative hand to touch my nose. I winced on contact and she flinched back.

"That arsehole!" she said, back to her old self, "But did you have to wreck that car? He may be a dick, but that was a work of art!"

"My humble apologies," I said dryly, "Next time, feel free to shop around for more delicate Magici-"

I didn't have a chance to finish. Mary grabbed me and pulled me into a huge hug, nuzzling in close to my neck, trembling a little.

"Thank you," she said before giving my ear a little tug and darting up the stairs, several girls in tow.

There was giggling and pointing and whispering, which quickly turned me an interesting shade of red. I almost ran up the stairs to my room, followed by the laughter, where I changed to start my day.

Initially, I'd been worried that the brother would come back, in spite of my warning, but I needn't have. If he'd somehow managed to get Mary home, her parents would have thrown a fit, and just sent her right back again. They didn't subscribe to any of that Old World nonsense. In the end, my intervention wasn't strictly necessary, other than to save

Mary a little inconvenience, but the hug she'd given me was rather worth the broken nose, in my opinion.

And, because of that, I actually made a breakthrough in my High Magic classes that day!

I mean, it was a very *disturbing* breakthrough, but still, I'd take what I could get.

I was starting to get better at the meditation, aided by a sort of mental-sharpening field that Professor Law maintained while we were practicing, but I was still having trouble perceiving Space Magic. The meditative state we'd been taught *was* helpful, and allowed for some quite impressive contemplation, even to the point of enabling one to think of several things at once. It was a very interesting experience, even if it did make me feel like an idiot once the field was shut down.

Frustration had made my mind wander off topic that day, and I found myself thinking about Mary, and that wonderful hug. That led me to a contemplation of her brother, and how he'd hurt her, which made me angry. I could feel my mind divide as it contemplated these two opposite concepts, like the thoughts were almost brushing against each other.

And then they sort of... caught and merged. It was an astonishing sensation, a messy combination of feelings; affection, interest and anger all combined in my mind, and something... changed. Something *clicked.*

And that's when I felt it.

Now, you'd think that in that sort of state, thinking about a dear friend and protecting her, would bring about one of the pleasant, or at least benign types of High Magic, Space, maybe or even Life.

Nope. I got Death.

And, by the way, it was *everywhere.*

And I do mean everywhere. In everything, every particle of air, every chemical reaction, every cell of our bodies, every part of every person and every thing in every building *everywhere.*

Intellectually, I knew that it wasn't Death *per se*, but Entropy, that force of decay and degradation that exists to keep the world balanced. It was a strangely scientific phenomenon...

But, in that moment, it felt like the world was dying right before my eyes, and I couldn't bear it.

I threw up.

Very, very hard.

It went *everywhere*, all over me, the floor and the Sorcerer sitting in front of me. I kept heaving until there was nothing but clear yuk flowing out of my mouth, and then I heaved some more. I groaned, and shut my eyes so I couldn't see it anymore, but naturally it wasn't that sort of sight, and I could still feel it all around me.

"Breathe, Graves, just breathe," Law said as the other students backed away from me and my mess.

Law was kneeling nearby, surreptitiously breathing through his mouth. But before he could say anything else the door slammed open and a voice like something from the grave spat at Law.

"What did you do to my brother?!" Bartholomew Killian, Lord Death rasped, looking thoroughly unhappy.

He wore black (what a surprise), a designer suit worth more than most cars, with a tasteful platinum tie clip and cufflinks. His signet ring was silver, with a black grinning skull on the upper face. He carried a cane that seemed to almost warp the world around it with Death Magic now that I could sense it properly. I wanted to throw up again.

"Lord, he was conducting his studies... and did you say brother?" Law asked, aghast.

"No, now be quiet!" Killian barked before turning towards me. Law recoiled in fear, and I couldn't blame him. Even Killian's *smiles* could be terrifying if you didn't know him. The other students had already vanished from the room, no doubt in a distinctly 'fleeing' way. And Law rapidly followed.

"Fill your mind, Kid," he said, grabbing my shoulder to prop me back up, "equations, favourite songs, clutter your imagination with anything and everything you can think of, except that thought which allowed you to See."

I did my best, breathing carefully, filling my mind with minutiae and details of nonsense, reciting Magical Formulae and constructs, listing every member of my Windward classes and their rankings. The impressions faded, the Sight dimmed, and I relaxed by degrees until I could breathe normally again. But it was still there, that Higher Sense, lodged in the back of my skull like a tick.

I shuddered.

"Wow, that was unpleasant," I said, fetching up against a seat.

He snorted.

"What do you mean by arsing about with High Magic without one of us supervising? You could have melted half the city!"

"What, really?" I asked, suddenly terrified.

"The way you were carrying on, maybe," he said, settling himself on a chair, "and why the hell did you start with Death? You're supposed to start with Space and work your way up *very* slowly!"

"Oh like I meant to!" I protested, "I was just following the sodding meditation instructions and wham, Death is all around me."

He chuckled again, "Yes, you can never do things the easy way, can you?"

We both smiled, and I took a moment to breathe.

"Thanks for coming. I was in rather a bad way," I said once my heart rate had returned to normal.

"Well of course I came, and right in the middle of a meeting, too, I might add, but you feel an Archon-level pulse of Death Magic, you turn up!"

"Still, thanks."

"You want to thank me? Drop this class, right now. They

have no idea what they're doing, not with you. It's like poking at a nuclear bomb with a slightly smaller nuclear bomb while blindfolded and wearing oven mitts."

"Lovely metaphor."

"And what happened to your face?"

"Would you believe I got sucker-punched by a Pure-born?" I said, rubbing my aching belly.

"You're kidding?"

I shook my head.

He froze for a long moment.

"Looks like a good hit," he said, almost nonchalantly. I should have taken that as a warning, but I was still a little groggy.

"Knocked me out," I reported.

That was the last straw. He burst out laughing, and then just didn't stop, the bastard.

"Oh, when I tell Jen, she will pee herself!" he said, still laughing his arse off.

"I bet you would tell her too, wouldn't you?" I said with a theatrical glare.

"And Lucille, oh my, what will *she* say?"

"Oh no, not Lucille, I'm begging you, she already gets in quite enough cheap shots as it is!"

"Oh, was he little? I'm picturing something five-foot two with a lisp and plastic shovel beating you something merciless," he said, pulling out his phone and tapping something in.

"No he wasn't, and he had the element of surprise!"

"Yes, the frightening young woman-"

"It was a big, strong guy, at least a head taller than me!"

"Little girl, pigtails, definitely a lisp," he continued, still tapping at his phone, "broke your nose and kicked you in the crotch because you stole her lollypop."

"I can't describe how much I hate you right now."

"And I'll bet she said 'And let that be a lethon to you, you big meanie'!" he said in a lisping voice.

"And this is why I don't tell you things!"

He continued laughing, but I was feeling better.

"Come on candy-thief," he said once he'd gotten control of himself (mostly), "Let's get you home before any other small children with kittens in their arms beat you up again."

I groaned as he helped me up and opened a Portal for us.

We emerged right into Blackhold's front hall. It didn't take long for a Warden to go looking for help (I didn't look especially well).

"Matty?!" Cassandra shouted, darting towards me before recoiling at what I assumed was a rather horrific smell (at least there was one benefit to the broken nose...), "What the hell happened to you?"

"He got beat up by a little girl," Killian said, completely straight-faced.

"That is not what... oh, never mind," I said as he let me go and Cassandra took my arm.

"A regular, human little girl," Killian continued as Demise came along and gave a brief nod to her former master.

She looked very intently at my face for a second before her expression hardened dramatically.

"Tell me who did this, my Lord, and his intestines will be at your feet by nightfall," she said.

"Please don't say intestines," I said, feeling queasy again.

"Would you prefer something in a brain? Perhaps I might provide a lung? Or a spleen, I hear they're all the rage these days," she continued with an evil smirk on her face.

"If there was any food left in me, you'd be wearing it right now," I said after I'd finished gagging.

"What else happened to you? A beating shouldn't have created this much vomit," Demise replied.

I glared and she took my other arm, helping me along on my shaky legs.

"He was trying to use High Magic under those ham-fisted twits at the University," Killian said to Cassandra, "naturally he ran face first into Death Magic and took too good a look behind the curtain."

"Shit," Demise said, taking a better grip on me, "How much did he see?"

"Everything, I should imagine," Killian said.

"Damn it. He's too fragile for that!" Demise said, "It's a miracle he's not a drooling wreck on the floor right now!"

"Hey!" I complained bitterly, "I'm standing right here, and remain relatively both compos mentis and readily hurt by that sort of implication."

Demise pulled my eyes open and peered in, one at a time. She placed her hand on my forehead and I felt a tingle of Magic that made me shiver.

"Hm," she said finally, "I really thought he'd be insane."

"I've seen the Black, Dee. Death isn't much to be afraid of after that," I said, my hand almost unconsciously moving towards her side where she'd been wounded by the Black. It hadn't been pretty.

She saw the gesture and captured the hand, squeezing it gently and offering me a little smile.

"Big daisy," she muttered.

"Seriously, it's starting to hurt my feelings a bit."

"Yes, mention feelings, that'll butch up your image," Cassandra said, which made Killian roar with laughter and make us all jump.

"Oh, sorry," he said, "It's just a little bit great that we have a First Shadow with a sense of humour, I think you may be the first one, actually."

"Oh, don't encourage him!" Cassandra barked, "If I hear one more egg pun over the breakfast table, I'll break my oath and throttle him, I swear!"

"You took an oath?" I asked, "Since when?"

"Really, little brother? Puns? The lowest form of whit?" Killian asked disgustedly.

"Egg-sactly right," I said, deadpan.

Cassandra emitted a faux-scream of frustration and

made to swat me before remembering the vomit and giving me the finger instead, all of which drew the attention from up above. Tethys had been attracted by the commotion and let out an enraged squawk as she took in my appearance, practically flying down the stairs.

"God, what the hell happened?!" she said, darting through the gathering crowd of witnesses to my humiliation.

"What I'm hearing is that he was beat up by a little Pureborn girl and then frightened himself into projectile vomiting, that about right, Lord Killian?" Cassandra asked innocently.

"That is *exactly* what happened," Killian said judiciously.

"People used to be afraid of me, what happened?" I asked in a grumble.

"You decided that your girly feelings couldn't stand spreading a little terror, and now nobody thinks you're dangerous," Killian said bluntly.

"I am so!" I protested, "I have laid out some creative and vicious punishments."

"Yes, your enemies tremble at the Sleep Spells you throw," Killian said, "no doubt they wet themselves at the thought of a good night's sleep."

He sniggered at the end there, not able to keep his face straight any more.

"I need a shower, and then some plotting time," I said, giving him an evil look which just made him grin wider, "And thanks for helping today."

"Any time," he said, looking at his phone.

I offered lunch, or even tea by way of a thank you, but he had appointments and left as quickly as he'd appeared. My Wardens and partner trailed me as I wobbled my way up the stairs towards my room. I think a few of them wanted to help, but were rather wary of the vomit, not that I could blame them there.

"I'm not going to keel over, you know."

"You're not looking at you right now," Tethys said with a snigger.

"I had a teeny altercation, and a slight stomach upset, that's it," I said as my legs started getting shakier still and Cassandra had to actively hold me up.

"An altercation with a little girl," Demise sniggered.

"It was a great big guy!" I complained.

"Sure it was, Love," Tethys said, patting a clean patch of shoulder

"It really was, though," I said in a small voice. Everyone laughed.

I grunted and walked through my bedroom door, Tethys in hot pursuit as the others went back about their business.

"Come on, tell your Tethys what happened," the Succubus purred as she followed me into the bathroom.

"Can I shower first?" I asked.

She sniggered and helped me undress, keeping the foul-smelling clothes at arm's length until she could shovel them into a hamper. I hopped in the shower and washed while telling Tethys what had happened. She laughed when I told her about my nose.

"That's not nice," I said as I hopped out and brushed my teeth before dressing in a fresh t-shirt and tracksuit bottoms.

"Oh, Love, it's just so very you," she said, planting a tiny kiss on my cheek (which was at least clean, if now throbbing from the lack of medical attention, exacerbated by all the throwing up), "sticking your head into something that has nothing to do with you on account of a girl."

I sighed and headed to my bed so I could lie down and give my injuries some attention. Tethys laid down with me and stroked my chest and head while I attended to it. It took a while, but I got the job done, and by then I was ready for a rest. I yawned and Tethys curled up around me, her arm over me.

"Tethys?" I asked in a small voice.

"Yeah, Matty?"

"I know it's an unreasonable request, but... promise me you won't die?"

I'd told her about the Death Sense thing, but I don't think she really understood. You couldn't unless you'd seen it with your own eyes. But she still understood enough to know that it scared me, and was willing to do whatever she could to comfort me.

"Of course, I won't, Love," she said, kissing my cheek very tenderly, "when the last star in the sky goes out, you and I will toast the end of everything from our little secure bunker and make like bunnies while we wait for the next big bang. How does that sound?"

"Thank you," I said, closing my eyes, exhausted and scared, but feeling better in her arms.

"Any time," she said, squeezing in tight.

# CHAPTER 18

I woke up to find Kandi playing with my phone and Tethys still comfortably wrapped around my chest, gently stroking Kandi's leg.

"What time is it?" I asked groggily.

"Just after five," Kandi answered, "Now, who is Mary? And why is she sending you dirty pictures?"

"What?" I asked, suddenly waking up.

Kandi turned the phone so I could see what had been a rather long text conversation I'd had no part of, but no sign of dirty pictures, thank God.

"Why are you trying to kill me?"

"You keep snuggling with my girlfriend," she said with a grin and a glare (a rather sexy combination on her).

"In my defence, I also snuggle with your girlfriend's girlfriend," I said returning the smile.

"Well, that's alright then," Kandi said sarcastically.

"Seems quite fair to me," Tethys said sleepily.

"It would, you hedonist!" Kandi said, reaching down to pull Tethys hand to her mouth so she could nibble gently on her girlfriend's fingers.

Tethys smiled and settled her head more comfortably on my shoulder.

"Oh, I really don't want to go out again tonight," I said with another yawn.

"Then don't," Tethys offered.

"I have to, I made an appointment, and I gave those Witches my word."

"What Witches?" said a dark, brooding voice from beyond the door, which I now noticed was slightly ajar.

"Um... did I say Witches? I meant-"

The door opened *very* slowly, creaking alarmingly to reveal Cassandra, her eyes *daring* me to lie to her.

"Um... so... here's the thing..." I started.

The eyes, already narrowed, narrowed further still.

I broke. Confessed the whole thing.

The poor woman was banging her head against the wall before I was half-way done.

"Absolutely *not*, understand?"

"It's only a small coven."

Her eye began to twitch. I swallowed convulsively. Kandi started giggling, thoroughly enjoying my discomfort. Tethys smothered her before she could draw the glare down upon *them* (sensible woman).

"So, just to clarify, you, a notorious idiot when it comes to women, have accepted an invitation, attached to a sob story, from a group of young, likely attractive, young Witches to... 'help them with their Magic'."

"That sounds about right. The idiot bit is a little harsh."

"Really, Matty? Is it *really* harsh?"

I looked away, muttering, "I believed Ms. Jones," I said after some thought, "she looked genuinely afraid of what was happening. If something happens to them, and I could have helped... I don't think I could live with that, Cassie."

Cassandra sat on a convenient chair, rubbing her eyes.

"Alright," she said, "Go, but you will take your phone, and you'll maintain an open line to me the whole time, understand?"

"Sounds fair."

"And if I hear so much as a *toe* go over the line, I'll make what they did at Salem seem like a friendly neighbourhood barbecue."

"You realise they didn't actually get any Witches at Salem, right?"

"Shut up, Graves."

"Yes Ma'am."

Cassandra took one more look in my eyes to make sure I was telling the truth, and then she left, apparently having forgotten whatever had brought her within eavesdropping distance of my bedroom door in the first place.

"So, these Witches..." Tethys purred in my ear.

"No."

"I didn't say anything yet!"

"I know. Still no."

"Give in, you know I'll get my way eventually," she whispered before gently pecking me on the neck.

"Kandi, that's your cue," I said, slithering away.

"No! Not again, I couldn't walk right for days after the last time! You got her going, you sort her out!" Kandi protested, darting for the door. I caught her with my Will and dropped her into Tethys' waiting arms while I collected my phone.

"Oh, you naughty girl, running from Tethys," my Succubus said, planting a line of kisses down Kandi's neck, "You know I'll always find you."

"Maybe a little gently, this time? Don't let her get carried away?" I suggested.

"I suppose," Tethys said with a long-suffering sigh. Kandi giggled and slid herself down into my former spot.

"Ooh, still warm," Kandi said before settling against her girlfriend while I closed the bedroom door discreetly behind me.

Miss Jenkins made me a light supper, which filled me up nicely, and I headed off to see the Witches. A less evolved man may have heard some music from 'The Wizard of Oz' in his head as he walked down their drive, but I didn't, no sir...

The house was brightly lit, with soft music coming from the upper floors. The front doors opened almost the second I knocked, revealing Ms. Jones, dressed in a set of baggy robes, her hair pulled into a loose tail.

"Ah, Mister Graves, thank you for coming!"

"Ms. Jones," I replied politely, shaking her hand.

She led me into the house, past some common areas full of women cheerfully chatting, studying or watching TV. There was no sign of cauldrons, no beakers containing preserved body parts... no eye-of-newt. It just seemed like a normal hall of residence, though a busy one.

I was a little disappointed. One expects certain things from the lair of a Witch.

"Are you always this full?" I asked.

"No. About a third of the Coven lives in other halls or off campus. We're banded together for safety right now, at least until we know what's going on."

"Sensible," I replied as she led me into a small study near the back of the house, where I could see a meticulously maintained herb garden. There had to be several hundred varieties of flower, herb, spice and fungus, all neatly laid out in beds, pots and heated greenhouses. It was an impressive space, and I said so.

She practically preened at the complement.

"Fifteen years of work went into that!" she said proudly, "I started it with two students and a handful of coriander seeds, and now look at it!"

"Is that Phoenix Bane?" I asked, having seen a particularly vile-looking purple flower, tucked into a corner of the greenhouse. Refined properly, it could rob a creature of its immortality. They were notoriously difficult to find; and thought to be impossible to cultivate. There were also a number of other *very* rare plants I knew in passing, some of them could be *very* dangerous, if handled improperly.

"Good eye!" Jones replied, "Yes, that took nine years to grow to its current state. We use it to make antidotes to the immortal conditions, Vampirism, Lycanthropy, things like that."

"Really?" That was actually quite amazing.

"Absolutely! I can even show you how. Though you

might have trouble getting some of these reagents."

That led to a discussion about potions that I won't bore you with. Potion making was yet another sub-skill of Crafting, and thus wasn't something I knew a lot about. Magic potions were hard to make, hard to store and uneven in effectiveness, but they had been known to be quite effective as curatives, and even for healing purposes, though that last one was often a bad idea. Healing potions tended to cause rampant, uncontrollable cell growth, which *could* repair damage, but could just as easily cause *horrific* tumours and lethal mutations.

Flesh Magic was the better way to go.

However, potion making could also lead to some interesting discoveries, assuming you could come up with the necessary volunteers to test your results. This was another reason Witches had a bad reputation; historically, they weren't too scrupulous about things like 'informed consent'.

These ones seemed nice, though.

"So, what do you need?" I asked, my mind packed full of new possibilities that would likely have to wait years for any sort of resolution.

"What all Witches want, power," she said bluntly, "Oh, don't worry, we don't want anyone's body parts. What we *need* is research materials. Texts, rare herbs, some hard to come by reagents. But especially the texts."

She had a list. A very long list.

"I haven't even heard of these books. I'd imagine the Archive has them, though."

"Of course. On Level five, where no Witch has ever been allowed."

"Fair enough," I said, knowing how prejudiced the Archive could be, "I can't get you in, and they won't sell a copy of anything below Level Four for security reasons. I'll have to see if I can get it from a private collector."

"We'll happily pay for anything you can get. Money's not the problem, it's the contacts. Nobody will sell to a Witch."

I grimaced at that. Magicians did like to talk about equality, and they *were* pretty good at that, generally speaking, but sometimes they could be a rather unpleasant lot.

"I will see what I can do."

"Thank you! One of the most valuable parts of that book is a formula for making a potion that will rapidly replenish someone's Magical powers, using simple reagents, just certain plants and flowers. With that, we can stand alongside other Magicians as equals."

That sounded fine to me, she just wanted the same chances as anyone else with a Well. Goodness knew I'd had my own problems with Magical Society, if there was something I could do to help these people make a better life for themselves, then I would.

"And with more power available, we'll need someone to train us in more advanced Magic. Most of our powers are devoted to infusing solutions and simple projections of energy. We want to do more!"

There was a flash of something like hunger in her eyes for a moment, but then it was gone. I dismissed it, thinking I must have imagined it. I was likely projecting my own desire for acceptance onto her.

"Well, your best bet will be the standard texts. They're designed to provide a comprehensive education."

"We don't want that simple crap! We want to *learn*. To understand *real* Magic."

"Then read the government books. That's how I learnt, and they provide the foundation you'll need."

She scowled, and again there was a flash of emotion that left as quickly as it came.

"Look, I know it's tempting to use short-cuts. Magic is good at providing them, after all, but if you *really* want to learn Magic, as you claim, then you should do it properly."

Her eye twitched for a moment, but she nodded.

"I'll bring the first five levels' worth for you next time.

"And the book from the list, as well, right?" she asked,

almost desperately. I wondered if I was getting through to her...

"If I can," I agreed, doing my best not to sigh.

"Good. Then we can talk more in a week or so?"

"Again, if I can. People don't necessarily like to sell to Shadowborn, either."

Not that they would be, they'd be selling to Tethys and her band of stealthy lackeys, but the Witch didn't need to know that. I may have been willing to help, but that didn't mean that I trusted her with my secrets.

"Good," she said, standing up.

"Would you like me to start with some basic instruction? I've largely memorised the texts I've read, and I could start passing that on to your people."

"Um... would you mind waiting until next time? If we have the formula, we can do this properly, but until we have an easy access to Magic, we need to hoard what we have, in case... well, in case, you understand?"

I did.

"Of course."

"I'll introduce you around, though."

And that was my evening. The Witches were a little stand-offish, not that you could blame them. Their experience with Magicians hadn't been great, and I hadn't been especially nice to the two I'd met...

They seemed a reasonable, peaceful lot; very tight-knit, very loyal to one another. The stronger ones stood in front of the weaker or smaller when I came in, instinctively protective. I could respect that.

I left feeling quite happy about my new contacts. The knowledge of potions and ingredients could be very useful to me some time down the road, and they'd promised to provide specifics later on, as well as the finished potions themselves and some rare plants when they could be spared.

I was a little worried about Jones. I just got an odd impression from her. Perhaps she was just tired of her lot, and that of her sisters, but she just seemed a little... I don't know, desperate, perhaps is the right word.

I hoped to be able to change that, in time.

It would actually be a few weeks before I could get what she wanted, and she refused my offers to come around and do some preliminary teaching in the meantime. I thought that was a shame, but it wasn't like I could push the issue.

When I finally arrived back at Naiad, I was lost in thought. That happened when I discovered a new branch of knowledge I wanted to play around with.

Jocelyn had to touch my arm to snap me out of my reverie.

"Hi!" I said smiling at her.

"Hi yourself! I was wondering if you were in a daze!"

"Sorry, just thinking. What brings you by?"

"I have tickets to the Brighton Chocolate Festival on Sunday," she said, actually blushing.

I smiled.

"Would you like to come with me?"

Beautiful girl, gigantic room full of chocolate...

"Absolutely!"

# CHAPTER 19

Even with everything that happened later, I still view that weekend as one of the best I'd ever had. Saturday was spent with Maggie, watching movies and arguing about the correct way to eat popcorn. I had quite a few female friends, most of the important people in my life, actually, but only with Cassandra did I feel that sort of... innocence, if that makes sense. There was such a complete lack of sexual tension, or any other sort, for that matter, that I could feel completely comfortable with her, talking freely with her about a thousand different things as we walked and ate between screenings.

She finally told me a little about herself, how she'd been raised in Greece, sent to schools all over the world, learning a dozen languages and twice as many ways of fighting. She spoke of how she'd met Solomon, how he'd recruited her into his Champions.

Even if the Champions had ended up a little evil, she'd done a lot of good in her time with them, fighting monsters on every continent, human and inhuman alike.

She was a hero in every way, and I admired the hell out of her. She was what Cassandra would have been, if she hadn't had such a hard start in life. Maggie was a much... gentler soul, in her way. She was softer inside, sweeter (when she wasn't armed). It made me feel protective of her, which was ridiculous, as Maggie could have bent me in half without breaking a sweat.

She'd started having doubts about Solomon in the last two years, though. He'd started taking jobs against people whose evil was far from certain. Bringing the big Vampire into their group had very nearly been the last straw for her, but she'd trusted him, believed in him, even when he started including Hyde mercenaries against the larger targets.

Even then, she couldn't leave, it wasn't her way. Her people attached themselves to causes or warriors; they gave their lives to them. She couldn't leave until I'd had given her an opening. And then she'd started to think back, to really examine what she'd been helping the Champions to do... and she didn't like what she'd become.

She'd tried to attach herself to me, in that same way, but found me quite inadequate to the task. That meant that, for perhaps the first time in her life, she'd found herself with a choice, and she'd decided that she wanted to see the other side of the world, the side she'd been fighting for, but had always been separate from; the side with chocolate and movies and friendships that didn't involve blood and death.

So, I suppose, in a way, she *did* attach herself to me. I'm all about that side of life. When I suggested that to her, she pushed me into a fountain, but she helped me out again. I took that as a win.

When we eventually came to the end of our day, she gave me a hug, and wouldn't let go for a long time before promising to pick something fun for next time, and vanishing. Again, without handing me a phone number.

The contrast between the simple friendship and pleasure of Maggie's company, and the innuendo and tension of the time I spent with Jocelyn, was quite jarring. But that was also a terrific day. We ate a light breakfast at the Compass Point Eater before making our way to the festival, where we stuffed ourselves to the point of immobility. And if you think that being stuffed and slightly bloated made that girl any less attractive, then you're dreaming.

We laughed and held hands as we wondered around, trying sweets and combinations from all over the world. It was... truly wonderful, a day-long date with a girl I never thought I'd be able to look at that way again.

It was so easy to slip back into old and comfortable ways with her, that simple back and forth that we'd had back before... well, before she'd saved my soul in the worst possible way.

As we walked from the festival, I found that I didn't want the date to end, and it seemed that neither did she, so we went for a walk along the waterfront and ended up sitting on the sand, with a shield around us to keep us warm.

We talked as we watched the sun set, and then we weren't talking anymore, just staring at one another. We kissed. It was sweet and wonderful, she still tasted like chocolate.

We spent the night right there, staring up at the stars, talking, laughing and kissing until we fell asleep under my shield, cuddled up together, more peaceful than I'd been in months.

We made our way back to the university the next day. Both of us were late for class, but neither of us cared even a little bit. We made arrangements to meet for lunch and had a lingering goodbye that left me very happy.

But not in a good state for learning, I doubt if I remembered a quarter of what I was taught that day.

The days that followed were... amazing.

Mary and Jocelyn, now firm friends, spent vast amounts of time together and there was frequent giggling and the occasional squeal when I came into view, which made me blush horrifically (which was the point). Spending time with those two was always fun, even if Mary did tend to... prevent the more amorous activity Jocelyn and I would have preferred to get up to.

I had dropped the High Magic class, as Killian had suggested. In its place, Hopkins had agreed (with what I'm fairly certain was *feigned* reluctance) to teach me properly. It had taken a while for her to clear her schedule, but we eventually met at Blackhold, first thing in the morning on the second Wednesday after my big date with Jocelyn.

After saying hello, we adjourned to the garden, the quietest and most peaceful place in the house, where she sat me down under my favourite oak tree.

"Before we start, could I have a word? I'd ask Tethys, but she'd only make a sex joke."

"Ah... this is about a girl," Hopkins said with a smirk.

"Jocelyn," I replied.

She frowned, "Go on."

I explained how we'd started to grow closer again, and then I asked the big question.

"Can I trust her?"

She leant back against the oak. Hopkins had been the one to arrange all that... Jocelyn-Des stuff. Something I was still a little mad at her over, by the way.

"She's loyal to the Archons, I suppose."

"That's not helpful."

"No, I suppose it's not. Look, I can't really answer this question for you, Matty. You'll have to decide for yourself if you can trust her with your heart. Listen to your instincts, what are they telling you?"

"That I suppose I can."

"Suppose? That's not good."

"I really like her. I loved her before, and I can see myself heading that way again, it's just..."

"If she betrayed you once, she could betray you again."

"She didn't betray me, though, did she?"

"Again, that's for you to decide."

"You're being very helpful today."

"It's what I do," she said with a smile, "But feelings like this don't come along every day, and Archons, especially, have trouble with these things as we generally out-live everyone we love."

I winced at that.

"Sorry. Just keep an open mind. She's a good girl, from a good family, she could be great for you. But be careful, many Magicians would find the idea of dating an Archon... difficult."

"How did you handle it?"

"Oh, I made all the classic mistakes. I tried not telling them, I tried being up-front... I've done a bit of everything. In the end, you have to find what works for you."

I sighed and she patted my arm.

"Don't worry, push comes to shove, she'll only live three hundred years, you can get out of it then."

"Damn it, Jen, too dark!"

She laughed and nudged me.

"You'll find someone. I did; I have three live-in boyfriends at my home right now, each one faithful and wonderful and a joy to me."

"Damn, Jen, you dog!"

"Right? And they're pretty, too."

"I don't think I'm grown up enough for that, yet."

She laughed, "Said no other man, ever."

I laughed with her.

"Thanks, Jen."

"Any time, little brother. Now shall we get started?"

"You said that in a manner that makes me fear for my sanity."

"Don't be such a baby! Now get settled, this is going to take a while. Don't worry if you don't get it right away, you're not supposed to."

Eight *hours* passed. I didn't think I'd made much progress, but Hopkins was pleased enough. She stayed for dinner, and hugged me before leaving. Tethys was at my side before the door was even closed properly.

"You smell magnificent," she said, sniffing heavily at my neck, "carnal shame with just a hint of crushing guilt, I love it when you smell like that."

I chuckled and turned to receive the hug. I felt better for

it, calmer.

"I am not feeling guilty."

Well, maybe I was feeling a bit bad about that 'outlive her' thing Hopkins had mentioned...

"Yes you are. And I detect the faint whiff of imminent consummation."

"There is no way you can smell that!"

"Come on," she said, ignoring me, "you can tell me all about it. I'm fairly certain I'm smelling more than one girl on you."

We settled in my library, in front of the fire, her legs on my lap and her head on my shoulder. I laid out what I'd been up to for her and she trembled, rubbing gently at my belly and chest while I massaged her feet. And I hadn't told her anything spicy at all. Goodness knows what she'd have done to me if I'd had dirt to share.

"The redhead. Of course," she said with a sigh, "How is a poor raven-haired supposed to compete?"

"You do just fine," I said, tickling her sides, making her laugh.

"And so do you. Not quite there yet, with the redhead, but you're managing."

"Ha, ha."

"And that Maggie girl! She likes you?"

"And I like her. I wish I could do more to help her into the world."

"You are. Believe me, you're good at that," she said softly, very meaningfully.

I hugged her a bit tighter.

"Does Jocelyn know I sleep in your bed?"

"It hasn't come up."

She chuckled, "Record it when it does, I want to hear how loud she screams."

"Not funny, Tethys."

"Yes it is!"

I frowned.

"Imagine the noise she'll make when I show her the pictures," Tethys whispered.

"What pictures?"

"Shh, just relax..."

I should have known better than to ask.

"You'll be alright. And I'm sure things will go better this time. Or maybe they won't. It doesn't really matter, anyway. You're mine in the end."

I laughed and held her close, feeling immeasurably better, and I didn't know why. Well, I did, but we're not going there.

"I'm not kidding," she said, nuzzling my neck happily.

"I know," I said softly, linking my fingers with hers, "and I pity any girl I bring home to meet you."

"Yes, just imagine all the dirty things I might do to the sweet and innocent girls that are your usual choices," she purred into my ear, making me shiver.

"You were perfectly civil to Cathy," I said.

"Please, like I could have done anything about that. That mess had to run its own course."

"That sounds suspiciously like you have plans to do things to my other relationships."

"Does it?" she asked a little too innocently.

I just smiled.

"All I can say is, thank God those Sidhe took themselves off, I had no idea how to get rid of a Spirit Bond," she said, which made me laugh again.

"I honestly don't know what I'd do without you," I said.

"Well, it's a good thing you'll never have to find out, then, isn't it? Now, tell me about these 'encounters' of yours. Spare no details, tell your Tethys, nice and slowly..."

# CHAPTER 20

After some hard thinking (which Tethys didn't help with), I decided that there was no point in fretting and getting miserable over things I couldn't change. I was going to enjoy my time with Jocelyn and Maggie, and the new friends I was making at University. I was actually quite surprised by how much I'd started to enjoy myself at that place. In my first days, I'd considered just leaving, but now it was like I was finally fitting in, and I loved that.

My anger hadn't gone, but it was ever so slowly starting to fade, to become part of the background, allowing me to just be *me*, apart from all the pain and fighting that came with being the First Shadow.

Alas, whenever I thought things like that, whenever I'd started to come towards some sort of catharsis, or peace, the Universe liked to come around and kick me hard in the arse for my trouble.

We slipped into November with my hardly noticing. I spent a lot of my time getting to know Jocelyn again, taking Maggie out on little trips and fending off the increasingly authoritarian dictates of Mary and the mother hens.

The fear of those in the Magic School had largely vanished once it became clear that I wasn't going to hurt anyone. Even Hadleigh seemed to have gotten used to me (a little, there was generally only one scream a fortnight).

Tethys finally managed to get a hold of those things the Witches had asked for and called me back to Blackhold on a wet Friday night.

I found her in her study with a heavy carrying case on

the floor next to her. She smiled and hugged me as I came in.

"Hi!" she said brightly, "I have that stuff you asked for, but... do you know what's in this book?"

She pulled it from the case and handed it to me.

"Journal of Patricia Krell, Witch," I read from the cover. It was a copy, neatly bound in modern materials, clean white paper and string. The original had likely been hand-written going by the title, but this version had been transcribed into a modern font, the diagrams copied neatly, or even scanned.

"There is some nasty stuff in there, Matty. That's the journal of a *Red* Witch."

"Red... as in?"

"You guessed it. Cannibal. A very *enthusiastic* cannibal going by some of the entries, or should that be entrees?"

I shuddered at that rather dark joke, "Does it contain the recipe Jones asked for?"

"It does," Tethys replied, flipping to the right page, "but it also contains Spells to rip living energy out of a human body for absorption by a Witch; poisons that kill in a variety of ways, potions that can dominate a mind... I don't think we should let this stuff out of our sight. Certainly not to people we don't know that well."

"Let's see."

I took a moment to leaf through the thing. I didn't get more than half way through the first chapter before my eyes went wide.

"Nope," I said, slamming it shut.

"Saw the recipe requiring the testicle of a virile Sorcerer, huh?"

"What?! No! I just saw the one requiring the liver of a newborn! There was a testicle one, too?!"

She sniggered, taking a sheet from her desk, "This is a photocopy of the potion recipe. If this is what she *really* wanted, then there shouldn't be a problem."

"You say that like you have doubts."

"Well, of course I do, but you shouldn't let that stop

you. I completely trust maybe three people, and they all live under this roof. Not that you're any better."

"Hey!"

"Come on, be honest. Me, Cassandra, Kandi, Demise, the other Archons. Do you trust anyone else?"

"My parents!"

"Oh, well struck, sir, you've really showed me," she replied dryly.

I glared at her and slid the recipe sheet into the case, which was full of little plastic bags containing all the strange materials Jones had asked for. Tethys had told me that the market value of these things was in the tens of thousands, which really made me hope that the Witches were good for the money.

It wasn't that my finances couldn't take the hit; it was just a bad precedent to set.

I said goodbye to Tethys, and used my Will to levitate the case so I could carry it with me through the Shadow Realm to the Witches' House.

It was quiet, no music this time, though the lights were on, as it was late in the day.

I knocked, and was taken through to see Jones.

"You're late! Do you have it?" she asked, her eyes darting to the clock on the wall beside me, which told me I was *maybe* two minutes late.

"I was able to get the recipe you asked for, yes," I said, handing her the case.

"What about the rest of the book?!" she practically snarled, snatching the case from me and quickly digging through it.

"My source was only able to get this one recipe. But I'm informed that the rest of the book was somewhat... unwholesome."

Rage crossed her eyes for a long moment, and I realised...

"You knew what else was in that book, didn't you?"

Her face went bright red, and she opened her mouth to say something-

BOOM!

An explosion. A big one, coming from the front of the house. It was large enough that the house shook, and several windows broke, I could hear the sound of falling glass, followed by screams.

I was running in an instant, Jones and her duplicity forgotten as I shoved my way through one door after another. I had shields in place before I'd left the first corridor and Mage Sight cast seconds later.

That let me See that we were in a spot of bother.

There were *twelve* Magicians out front, two of them Sorcerers, one with an affinity for Air, the other for Fire. The rest were Wizards, a mix of Primal (Lower) Magics, mostly Fire and Air, with a smattering of Water and Earth Magicians for variety. That was strange in itself. A group of Mages this size, and no High Mages? No Flesh Magicians, Telepaths or Ghostwalkers?

Not that I'd ever met the latter (thank God), but still, it was a very narrow sampling of talent, and that meant something important, if only my brain wasn't diverted by fear for the people behind me.

I barged through the front door and onto the driveway, skidding to a halt, Jones hot on my heels. The front gate had been blown off its hinges, there were molten fragments all over the driveway, still glowing.

I recognised the Aura of the Pyromancer who'd attacked me on the way back from the tournament duel. He was dressed as he had been then, and so were the others with him, all in black, faces covered. Why the hell were they attacking me there, of all places?

Were they attacking *me* at all? Maybe they were there for the Witches?

"Mathew watch out!" Maggie snapped.

Wait, *Maggie*?!

When... what... how?!

I spun to see my friend clutching Jones' wrist in an iron grip, a wrist attached to a hand holding a long, Enchanted *dagger*, glowing with Dispel constructs that would likely have shredded the weaker shields around my back before sinking right into my ribcage. There was also some form of bright-green, viscous substance on the blade; poison?

"What in the *hell*?" I managed.

"The Duellists are here to kill you, she tried to help," Maggie said simply before swatting the Witch like a bug. The smaller woman went flying head over heels (literally!) to land in the rose bushes (ouch) with a broken jaw, a broken nose, a fractured eye socket and a pretty serious concussion.

In other circumstances, I might have felt bad, but she had tried to kill me.

The other Witches, naturally, did not like this, and there sure were a lot of them all of a sudden. They started moving towards me, hands beginning to glow with their meagre powers. Thirty-plus of them might not be too much of a threat on their own, but when combined with the dozen Magicians on the other side...

Duellists, Maggie had said... after that *huge* clue, it wasn't difficult to figure out who the Magicians were. They were Stonebridge's duelling team (some of them, anyway). It was their powers that should have been the giveaway, I should have realised it earlier. High Magic and Telepathy couldn't be used in the ring, Flesh Magic didn't put on a good show, and Spirit Mages tended to be reclusive and highly antisocial. That left Earth, Air, Water and Fire... which was what I was seeing. Serves me right for not using Mage Sight during the Duels...

The Witches were still advancing; quick as a flash, no-*faster* than that, Maggie had a pistol in each hand, pointed at the Witches.

"Please, *please* give me a reason," she whispered. Her guns were black and blocky, automatic pistols with extended magazines. The way she could shoot, I had no doubt that she could kill everyone there with no trouble, and not even have to reload; Witches couldn't shield for toffee. They stepped back, hands up, energy dissipating.

There was a standoff for a second, with none of the sides willing to start a Magical battle, not now that their surprise attack was neutralised, but nor could anyone back down, things had progressed too far. I was about to say something to calm things down (or try, anyway); the Witches were a decent sort, who might be reasoned with, but Maggie decided to move things along herself.

"Come out! I can smell you two!" Maggie snapped, her voice blasting out into the night, loud enough that the air seemed to shake with a deep resonance that sent more than a few of the Witches running.

There was a dull chuckle from behind the Magicians.

"You always were the smart one, Maggie."

The Warlock; *Solomon's* Warlock.

That explained a few things.

My mouth twisted into a snarl as he appeared from behind some sort of Warped shield, which was why I hadn't been able to see him. Mage Sight worked well on just about everything, but if you twisted Space enough to create a pocket, and hid in it, you could conceal yourself from even that Spell.

And where *he* was to be found...

The grass behind us rustled and the girl appeared, the Lycanthrope. Her teeth were elongated into fangs and her fingers had sprouted bear-like claws.

At least that answered *that* question. Werebear.

"Oh, I've looked forward to this," the monster snarled, her, now yellow, eyes locking onto my friend.

"Everyone just calm down, we don't need to do this," I said, trying to be reasonable, as Maggie shifted one of her guns to the Were's head.

"Need?" the Warlock said, sneering at me, which thoroughly pissed me off (but then, everything about that kid pissed me off), "No, Shadowborn, we don't *need* to do this. We *want* to."

"Are you sure?" I asked lightly, "Because the last time we dealt with one another, your Master exploded and you had to be carried off by your girlfriend."

Which made all this a little peculiar. It wasn't like Solomon was stupid enough to underestimate me. If this pair of idiots was there, then he should have been as well, he wouldn't send them in alone (their 'armies' didn't count)...

But then it clicked, "He doesn't even know you're here, does he?"

The Warlock's eye started to twitch. He even started to sweat.

I could draw conclusions from that...

"Ha! Not only does he *not* know you're here, he also told you not to go near me, didn't he?"

The girl growled, but there was an undertone of nervousness to it. Another hit.

"Aw, bless you two walking clichés, you thought you'd impress the old man by taking *initiative*, didn't you?"

Half the Warlock's face was twitching now. I wondered if I'd accidentally given him a stroke, or something.

"Shut up!" Warlock snarled, as good as admitting I was right, stepping towards me, balls of Space Magic appearing in his hands.

"Let me see if I can guess the rest. The pair of you were sent to infiltrate these two groups, rile them up and set them working against me, maybe orchestrate the occasional attack or subterfuge, but you were supposed to keep it low-key, in preparation for a combined effort with your boss. Stop me if I'm going too fast."

"We'll kill you," he growled, his eyes lighting up with fire.

"And it might have worked, too," I said, ignoring the threat, "The hammer of the Duellists against the anvil of the Witches, distracting me long enough for your boss to swoop in and take my head... only now it won't work because the Warlock went early and blew the whole operation."

"He was well known for blowing things a little early, just ask the girl," Maggie added, a little cattily, which made me laugh again, and only seemed to enrage the young Warlock. He looked like he wanted to attack, but I'd likely planted some doubts in his head (which was the whole point).

That just left Jones to figure out. She was clearly a power-hungry loon. The question was whether she started working with Solomon's pair of imbeciles before or after she'd formed her alliance with me, not that it especially mattered. She was a clever one, I had to admit, she saw an opportunity to acquire some rare ingredients and she took it. I wondered if the Werebear was aware of her side-deal? Well, a problem for another day...

"First things, first, why don't we get rid of the peanut gallery?" I suggested, "Maggie, close your eyes and cover your ears."

She obeyed immediately and I cast Sensory Overload. Normally it was a directed Spell, with anyone behind the caster safe from the effects, but I was casting it all around us, and that would likely have knocked Maggie out, too.

Witches and Duellists dropped like stones, completely insensible, and would remain so for quite some time. Anybody with even the slightest experience of Battle Magic knew to layer their shields with sound and light elements. Aside from anything else, Laser Lances and Sonic Overpressure Spells were *astonishingly* dangerous, and capable of bypassing simple shields completely (and lethally), and that was without taking into account more subtle things like my Sensory Overload.

The Duellists fell like the Witches. Because they were only trained to perform, not to fight, they'd never been taught to create proper battle shields. And now they were on the ground... that made me smile.

Unfortunately, Warlock was different. He didn't know anything *except* Battle Magic, and he was just fine. His girlfriend, however...

Not only was she flat on her back and twitching like a landed fish, she had also soiled herself rather badly. Lycanthrope physiology was a little different to human standard, even in their unchanged form, so the frequencies affected them slightly differently (oh, what a shame...).

I nudged Maggie and she opened her eyes again.

"Nice," she said, taking in the dropped enemies. She turned to aim her guns at the Warlock, who was staring at me with incredulity all over his face, coupled with a growing fury.

"You should see your face," I said, a little smugly, happy to goad the idiot now that it was just him left, and I didn't have to worry about Spells in the back.

And that was all it took...

He screamed with rage and hurled his Space-attack right at me.

A quick Dispel caused it to explode less than ten feet from him, hurling the duellists near him all over the place and ripping several of his shield layers apart. Not to be out-done, Maggie started firing her guns. Though she remained within the shields I'd put around us both, she made sure to poke the muzzles of her weapons outside my defences before firing (which was good, the bullets were Dispel-Enchanted, and would probably have damaged my constructs on the way out).

Warlock's shields were quickly peeled away by bullet and Spell, but he recovered quickly, very quickly, I have to say. His form lit up with electricity and flickering flames that he quickly hurled at us. A vortex of spinning air met the attacks, dispersing the energy back into the air, where I stole it for myself, merged it into a Chaos Lance, along with some Force I'd been gathering, and sent it right back at him.

His few remaining shields bent under the strain, and then shattered, forcing him to dodge out of the way. I felt his body start to hum with Flesh Magic, and then he *moved*. And wow, was he *fast*! Whatever he'd done to himself, he moved with Vampire-like speed, all but vanishing and reappearing in front of me. He wasn't quite Demise-fast, much less Cassandra, but damn!

His hand struck my shields, and the release of kinetic energy tore half of them away in a single attack.

Alright, leaving aside the fact that Warlocks were heinous, nasty creatures that should be repeatedly beaten in a sensitive place... that was damned impressive. If he'd been fighting just about anyone else, he'd have won right there. It was only the fact that I vastly over-engineered my Shields that kept me alive.

He had obviously anticipated a swift victory, too, because when his attack hadn't taken my head off, he just stood there for a long second.

One second *too* long.

For an instant, our eyes locked, and I smiled, just a little. The boy's face slowly twisted into an expression of fear as his accelerated thinking allowed him to realise that he was now thoroughly, irretrievably screwed.

The night seemed to compress on him as my Shadows dropped onto his head. This was the problem with the 'speedy' ones. When moving at speed, they relied too much on all-out attack, to the exclusion of any defence at all, thinking that they could dodge everything they needed to. Demise and Cassandra were the same, I still hadn't managed to persuade them to change their ways *completely*, but Demise was making progress, at least.

Anyway, he hadn't restored his shields, none at all.

Idiot. I strangled him with my Shadows. I rarely had the chance to practice that. It was hard to come by volunteers willing to endure a little mild suffocation, and the ones that were, liked it too much (I'll give you three guesses...). The trick was to get enough pressure around the arteries and veins either side of the neck. Cassandra had showed me the physical version of this, something she called a 'choke-hold', which was *not* fun (you can probably guess how she'd demonstrated it), but the Magical version worked quite well.

He was out in seconds, dropping to the gravel in an insensible heap. Maggie looked down at him, a broad grin on her face.

"Oh, Solomon is going to be mad as hell," she said with a laugh.

"How did you know what was happening?" I asked her. She'd shown up at just the right time.

"I almost missed it," she said, a flash of fear crossing her features, "I'd been following Orion, that's the Warlock, by the way, and I'd seen him talking to people around here, building his little army; that's where I've been these last few days. A friend of mine let slip that he was up to something in Stonebridge, and that I should stay away."

"Naturally you did the opposite," I said fondly.

She smiled, "I was about to come tell you when I saw him come this way, and who should I see but you, heading into the Witches' House; very clever, by the way."

"Look, I've got enough tellings-off to deal with on that score without you giving me a hard time, too!" Cassandra was *never* going to let me forget about this...

"Oh I haven't even *begun* on this topic, we *will* be revisiting it," she said, her eyes narrowing in a very familiar way. Did all Demigods glare like that?

"Where was I? Oh, right. I saw them attack, and I was about to intervene by kicking Orion in the soft places when I saw the Witch come up to stab you, and you know the rest."

"You saved my life," I said, "Thank you."

She rolled her eyes and gently punched my shoulder, "Don't be so stupid next time! I mean, really, who trusts Witches?!"

"One bad egg..."

"They were all in on it, Mathew. They were ready to ambush you! Did any of them look doubtful? Confused?"

I harrumphed, but couldn't argue with her.

"That's right. Now, you gather the wood, I'll get the petrol. We'll burn us some Witches!"

I gave her a look. She held her scary eyes for maybe a second before she burst out laughing.

"Fine, no burning, but can I stab them a little?"

"No."

"Shoot them? I promise only flesh wounds?"

"Still no."

She pouted, rather adorably, actually.

"Can I at least kick the Warlock in the balls?"

"Have at it... Gah! I thought you were joking!"

"I never joke about testicular football."

Oh, that looked like it *hurt*, or would have, if Orion were conscious.

I shook my head and pulled out my phone.

"What did you do this time?" Hopkins asked after picking up the phone, without even giving me the chance to speak!

I rolled my eyes; Maggie smirked, but kept her eye on the slumbering idiots.

"Remember I mentioned Witches?" I began.

Her sigh could have sand-blasted my floors clean.

Long story short, I stayed long enough for a couple of Hopkins' highly trained leg-breakers to arrive, and then I left as quickly as I could. Hopkins said she'd take care of it, but that I'd have to make a statement. Thankfully, that was all someone else's problem.

I did pause on my way out to take back my box of rare materials... as well as a few other things, as I was in the area.

The Phoenix Bane would look lovely in my garden, for example.

As would the Dragon's Eye, the Bellatrix Claw and the Lucian Fuge. It was only fair. New policy; try to kill me, I take your stuff.

Maggie decided to come back to Blackhold with me, her hand in mine for the whole journey back.

"Thank you," I said to her as we approached the front

doors.

"You're welcome. But you're one of mine, now, I couldn't do anything else."

I smiled at my friend and invited her in. She smiled, and I opened the door...

To reveal an unbearably smug looking Cassandra standing in the front hall with her arms crossed and an *unholy* smirk on her face.

"Goddess, I've never seen a human being shrink that fast!" Maggie said as I cringed away from the look, which only got worse as my Warden realised that I understood what was about to happen.

I tried to distract her with Maggie, but all that meant was, that when the hammer finally fell, there were two sets of hands wielding it.

And you'd think that would be the end of it, wouldn't you?

No.

First Killian came. He turned up to have a good go at me for nearly letting both Witches *and* Duellists get the drop on me. He found that all quite hilarious, especially on top of my getting knocked out by a Pureborn, which led me neatly to Palmyra, who showed up ten minutes later and spent the next thirty laughing her adorable arse off at my expense.

Having been informed of this, Kron wasn't far behind and ensured that I received a good talking to for being an idiot several times over, and all this *after* she made Killian repeat his version of how I was knocked out (including the lisp, which was mortifying).

Finally, Hopkins arrived, after having sorted out the mess I'd made with the SCA, the University and Jones' superior, the county's Coven Mother, who was not happy at what her protégé had been up to. She, at least, would not be a further problem (or so I thought...).

The rest of the Coven was largely given a pass, on my

recommendation; they hadn't been responsible for the actions of their Mistress. The Duellists had been suspended, briefly, but I was willing to let it lie at that (they were just dumb kids, and they hadn't actually managed to do anything except wreck a gate). Orion and Greta (the Werebear) had been arrested and sent to an SCA Processing Station somewhere in Stonebridge, I didn't much care, as long as they couldn't bother me. I hoped they ended up at the Farm with all the other monsters.

Suffice to say, after having to deal with *that* much bureaucracy while the rest of us were enjoying an impromptu dinner, she was not in a good mood when she finally dropped into a spare seat at the table.

That didn't stop her from getting in the swing of things, though. I introduced her to Maggie, who was rather a hit with my fellow Archons. Killian looked half-entranced by her, in fact. She seemed to fit in with my extended family like a glove. She and Cassandra had immediately bonded through their mutual appreciation of my continuing idiocy.

Eventually, she slipped away, but not before hugging me, and promising to come back soon.

She told me she was going looking for Solomon, to make sure that he couldn't get up to any more mischief, and I begged her not to confront him alone. She promised that she wouldn't, but I couldn't say that I really believed her.

She was a Demigod, though, she'd be alright.

It was actually quite a wonderful night. Even Kron was laughing towards the end, relaxed in ways I'd never seen before. Relaxed Kron was scary, though. Even her laugh was terrifying.

# CHAPTER 21

With the Warlock and the Werebear neutralised, I felt quite light and even relaxed over the next few days. I felt so relaxed, so optimistic, that I made a *big* mistake.

Things had been proceeding very well with Jocelyn, to the point where we were starting to get *very* close again. I felt that it wouldn't be fair to her for the relationship proceed to any more intimate places without her knowing who I really was, and what she was getting into.

So I decided to invite her to dinner...

At Blackhold.

Yes, I know that was a mistake *now*. At the time, it seemed like a perfectly natural thing to do.

Now, you'd think that the biggest danger to my budding relationship would be Tethys, wouldn't you? After all, she liked redheads almost as much as I did (see Kandi), and she was well known for taking a perverse delight in playing with me.

But no, Tethys wouldn't do that to me, not in any direct sort of way. Say what you like about my Succubus, she was utterly faithful to me, and wouldn't even *chance* hurting me that way, particularly not with Jocelyn, who, let's face it, sort of had form.

Nope, tonight's problem was all *me*.

I collected her from outside her halls of residence at just gone nine, and we took a cab to Blackhold, with her being rather amorous the whole way, and in such a manner that the cabbie was becoming distracted and irritated. She was dressed very nicely, in a dark green dress, a matching bow in her hair.

I was still smiling as we walked up the drive, but we were barely half way to the front door, when Jocelyn froze, nearly tripping me.

"Matty," she croaked, "This is Blackhold!"

Oh... damn. How the hell didn't I think this one through? Of course Jocelyn would know what the place was, she'd been brought up in this world (and only a few streets over), there's no way she couldn't have known...

Stupid, stupid, stupid!

"Um..." was the best I could come up with as my carefully laid plans started unravelling.

And here was the real problem. Jocelyn was clever; very clever. She figured it out *very* quickly. And then she went really pale.

"No!" she said, backing away from me, "No, Matty! Please tell me it's not true!"

She started crying.

"Jocelyn..." I started.

"Why didn't you tell me?" she hissed, "Why'd you let me fall for you?!"

"Jocelyn, please, just give me a minute to explain, I was going to tell you everything. Tonight, in fact."

"I can't, Matty, I just can't! Do you know what you've done? What you've *exposed* me to?!"

"What? Exposed? I don't understand."

"Of course you don't! You get women to fall for you, and then you leave them in heaps!" she said, turning on her heel, "Don't call me, don't text, I never want to see you again!"

"Please, Jocelyn, just let me explain!" I said, now thoroughly upset and confused. Why the hell was she reacting like *this*? It wasn't that bad, surely?

I tried to go after her, and she simply slapped me, hard enough that I felt tears in my eyes, and saw sparks. And then she was gone before I could catch up again.

I stood there for a long time, in the dark and the cold, staring at the gate she'd walked through on her way out of my life.

Cassandra appeared at my side after a while.

"I was... at the door," she said, taking my hand.

"I take it you heard most of that?" I said sadly.

"Hard not to; sorry," she said squeezing my fingers.

"That fell apart so fast!"

She put an arm around my shoulders.

"You want my opinion?" she asked.

"Always."

"You know I'm an Empath?"

I nodded.

"Well, she was *terrified*. Down to the bone, utterly and completely, pee-herself terrified."

I frowned, "Of me?"

"Empath, not Telepath. All I know is that something scared her so badly that she nearly threw up on you just now."

"She covered it well," I said, massaging my stinging cheek.

"She seems like she's good at *that*, if nothing else."

I nodded slowly.

"And-" Cassandra started, but she stopped.

"What?" I asked.

"Nothing."

"Cassie..."

"You love her... again?"

I nodded.

"Then don't ask me to tell you. Just let it lie."

"Seriously? You expect me not to ask after you dangle something like *that*?"

She smiled, but it was sad.

"I didn't sense love from her."

I didn't get it.

"Huh?"

She scowled, "Don't make me repeat it."

"What... what *did* you feel?" I asked softly.

"Satisfaction... avarice... maybe a little... distaste; before she figured out who you were, and then just the terror."

"Distaste?!"

"Emotions aren't fixed Matty, she could have been thinking about the shrubbery."

"You don't believe that, or you wouldn't have mentioned it!"

She turned away from me.

"I told you to let it lie."

"Knowing I wouldn't!"

"Shut up, Graves."

I sighed and she took my hand again.

"Sorry," she said.

"So am I."

I wasn't going to leave it at that, no way in hell. Empathy was not an exact branch of Magic, not by a long shot. Cassandra could be wrong.

She *had* to be wrong. I knew Jocelyn. I'd looked in her eyes, I'd seen the love there.

Hadn't I?

Cassandra tried to feed me, but I'd lost my appetite. The meal didn't go to waste, though. She ate the whole thing by herself while I was up in my room feeling sorry for myself. That was where Tethys found me.

Cassandra had filled her in.

"All part of my plan," she whispered after dropping into bed with me.

I chuckled, though a bit darkly, "Weren't you just telling me to get a girlfriend?"

"No, I told you to go have sex, different thing entirely," she said, pinching my nose.

"You are a terrible influence."

She snorted and kissed my cheek affectionately.

"And yet, here you stay," she said with that smile I like so much on her face.

"Nowhere else I'd rather be," I said, closing my eyes.

"Me either, Love," she whispered, almost too quiet for me to hear.

Three days of texts and increasingly desperate phone messages to Jocelyn got me nowhere. She didn't reply, and she didn't go to class, it was like she'd dropped off the face of the Earth which left me feeling crappy enough, but then Mary got involved.

"What did you do to her?" she asked, barging into my room while I was busy brooding, "She hasn't answered any of my texts in two days!"

"What makes you think it was my fault?!"

I mean, it *was,* but she didn't have to *assume* that!

"You're the boy, it's always your fault!"

I sighed and slumped against the wall.

"Something *did* happen, didn't it?" she asked, kneeling next to me.

I nodded.

"Is she... is she coming back?"

"I'm trying, but... it doesn't look like it."

"What did you do?" this time it was less of an accusation.

"I tried to be honest with her."

She recoiled, "You *cheated* on her?!"

"What? No! Where did you get *that*?!"

"Sorry, when a boy says he's 'going to be honest', that's normally the thing."

"What sorts of boys have you been dealing with?"

"The bad ones, apparently."

I snorted and she leant against me.

"What were you going to tell her?"

"Nothing important."

"Of course not. Girls generally run screaming from 'not important'."

"You don't know she was screaming. Or running."

"Spill it."

For the life of me, I don't know why I did, but I told her. Maybe it was just to see if Jocelyn's reaction was the norm.

If anything, Mary looked confused.

"So... you're royalty?" she asked.

"No, not as such, just... in a position of authority, if you like."

"And this is different to what you were before?"

"It's a matter of perception. As I am, I'm just a Shadow-born Sorcerer, an outcast to Magical Society, a potential danger. As First Shadow, I have sovereign immunity just about everywhere, carte blanche to deal with any threat as I see fit and allies that could make what happened to Hiroshima look like a gentle suntan. I am horrifying as the former and terrifying as the latter."

"But she wasn't scared of you until she found out that you were her head of state. Doesn't that worry you?"

"Why would it worry me?"

"Well, think about it, why would she be happy with Mathew, the Shadow-wotsit, and yet afraid of Mathew, the *authority figure*? Attached to *government*, protected by scary people?"

I frowned. I hadn't thought of it that way. Neither had Cassandra, for that matter.

"You don't think..."

"I don't know," she replied, "All I know is that if I loved someone, then having them tell me who they were wouldn't send me running from them unless what they told me was an active *threat* to me."

"That's a very dark thought, Mary."

She shrugged, "I can be dark."

"You're currently wearing a Bambi t-shirt."

She covered it up with her hands, smiling at me.

"And you... you don't feel any different?" I asked.

"No, why would I? This Magician stuff isn't that important to me, and it's not like you're a different person today than you were yesterday."

I smiled and hugged her, which made her laugh.

"You are such a baby!" she said, tickling my ribs, "You really thought I'd do a Jocelyn, didn't you?!"

"Maybe a little."

"Idiot. For assuming the worst of me, there will have to be compensation."

"Here we go..."

"Naturally, it must start with ice cream, that's a given, and none of the cheap stuff, either. Next we will meander into a movie night, and I'll pick what's on..."

That was just the start. She described things that would make any man with normal interests cringe, but it just made me like her more. She really didn't care about my Magic, not a bit. She only liked *me.*

There are just some people that you meet... you click with them in a way that makes you feel like they've always been a part of your life. Mary was one of those people for me, and I knew that she would precious to me for the rest of my life.

Our conversation didn't stop me trying to get back in touch with Jocelyn, though. I so wanted to see her. But without any luck, I just had to get on with learning, and hope that I'd get my chance. At least, on the learning side of things, I was able to start making a little progress...

"No, no, no, focus on the *energy*, you twit!" Hopkins said as my latest attempt to create a Portal failed dismally.

I said a *little* progress.

"You know, name-calling is just not an effective teaching method."

"Poor baby," she said with an evil smile.

I should state, in her defence, that there wasn't an impatient bone in her body. This was just Hopkins being Hopkins. I knew she was kidding, and would gladly sit with me until the sun went out if she thought it would help.

And she *had* been helping.

I was now able to sense Space Magic, which wasn't easy, because it wasn't really there. The idea was immensely complicated, and an accurate explanation required an understanding of Quantum Physics, so we'll just skate past that.

Simply put, Space Magic was all tied up with Vacuum energy, which sort of linked all points in the universe. By manipulating this energy, a Magician could call a Portal or alter the placement of objects, play games with gravity or even create micro-singularities. It was possible to cast a Portal spell without being able to work completely with the element, but Hopkins was teaching me properly, so that I'd understand how it all worked.

We were out on Blackhold's grounds, this time, so as to give us both plenty of Space (see what I did there?). She had a Portal of her own up and running so I could see what was necessary, and it was helpful, but it was also hurting my head trying to manipulate Space when it was already being warped right next to me. And Space-sense itself was a bloody pain; I frequently had vertigo while using it, and I'd thrown up twice in the last four hours.

Naturally I got no sympathy (but more than a few laughs).

"It's all about knowing where you are and where you want to be," she repeated.

"With my sense of direction?"

She snorted and knelt behind me, her hands on my shoulders.

"Relax, you tense up and you'll end up in Siberia, and we know you can't handle the cold. Or the heat. Or anything remotely uncomfortable, you're like a little girl in many ways," she said, making me laugh.

"I'm writing all these barbs down, you know. Revenge slithers its way towards you," I said in as threatening a manner as I could manage.

"Ooh, I'm so scared," she said, tickling my ear, "Now concentrate."

I did as I was told, and very slowly, the air started to shimmer, and then warp. It flared and flickered, turning bright purple before brightening into a light blue oval...

Through which a soaking wet, thoroughly naked, Kandi tumbled with a screech as she fell into my lap along with an entire bath's worth of soapy water.

I was flattened, and Hopkins barely avoided the deluge, howling with laughter, as the Portal closed with a pop. Kandi and I tried to disentangle ourselves, while I apologised profusely.

"Matty, what the hell? If you wanted to see me naked, all you had to do was ask!" she said, now laughing as I covered her up in Shadows.

Naturally Hopkins was still rolling around on the grass, near to wetting herself as far as I could tell.

"Oh, just wait 'till I tell Lucille! His first successful Portal, and he drops a naked redhead in his lap! Don't need Freud to interpret that one!" and then back to her guffaws.

"Sorry, Kandi," I said sheepishly.

"How did this happen, exactly?" she asked, her Shadow-covered arms crossed.

"Well, I was thinking about where I was, and where I wanted to be, and then I wondered what you were up to, because I was looking forward to playing chess tonight, and then I remembered you said you were taking a bath about now-ish, and then there *may* have been a stray thought about where I'd actually want to go, and... well, Magic took care of the rest," I said, rubbing the back of my head, going bright red.

"Your train of thought meanders through quite a few strange stations, doesn't it, Sweetie?" she said, stroking my cheek, grinning all the while.

"I'm working on that, I promise."

She snorted and wrapped me up in a hug, kissing my cheek.

"Next time, just knock on the door, you know that tub's big enough for two," she whispered before turning on her heel and walking back towards the house. I put some extra energy into the constructs covering her so they'd last a while away from me.

I grinned like an idiot and turned towards my teacher, who was still lying on the ground, grinning and emitting the occasional chuckle.

"The next time *you* mess up, I'm going to laugh, and then you'll be sorry, you big hyena," I said, dropping to the grass next to her. I cast a little spell that drew the water out of my clothes.

She laughed and patted my thigh, "God, I love teaching you, Matty. None of my other students made me laugh," she said, and I knew she meant it.

"You do have to admit, when I screw up, I do it in style," I said, lying back.

"That you do, little brother."

We laid like that for a while, and I yawned, starting to doze.

"Oh no you don't!" she said, startling me, "Start again, from the top, and try not to drop any naked women in your lap this time."

"Maybe I like dropping naked women in my lap," I said straight-faced.

She rolled her eyes and swatted my ear.

"Concentrate!"

That was how I spent my Wednesdays. I loved it, truth be told; and I'd missed Hopkins. She and I liked to 'debate' things. We called it that because if we told people we sat around for hours nitpicking each other, they'd say we were insane. We'd spend the mornings practicing, and then afternoons arguing about it in increasingly vague and tangential ways until an early supper time, at which point we'd stuff down food while continuing the fight, and the rest of the household looked on in horror.

Then there was more practice, which, as you saw, was actually getting me a bit better. The actual mechanism for creating a Portal was fairly simple; it was just navigation that was a problem.

Days went by. Jocelyn still hadn't returned my attempts to contact her, leaving me feeling a little blue. At least I hadn't heard anything about Solomon in a while. I even allowed myself to hope that he wouldn't come back at all.

I should have known better.

On a Thursday towards the end of November, I was walking back to Naiad with Mary and a group of her girls, when my phone rang.

"Hello?" I said, still chuckling at a joke Mary had told.

"Mathew, you need to come home, someone took Kandi," Cassandra said.

For the record, never moved so fast in my entire life.

I didn't bother with Shadow Walking, I simply called my Shadows and flew home, my heart hammering in my chest, fury warring with terror as I streaked over Stonebridge's rooftops, close and fast enough to tear roof tiles away in my slipstream. There would be a lot of annoyed people the next time it rained.

I almost failed to decelerate in time and nearly ploughed into my lawn. As it was I got fairly serious whiplash, which would take me ages to fix later. I sprinted for the door, and was met by Cassandra.

"Where's Tethys?" I asked. If anyone could tell me who to burn, it would be her.

"She went after her," Cassandra said, "That was... half an hour ago. We haven't heard from her since."

"Who?" I asked, my voice becoming very low and very cold as I stopped being able to contain my temper and my fear.

"Thornsby, Kandi's father. Tethys tracked her phone to his building."

"Why?" I asked.

"As far as I know, they managed to take a controlling interest in his company this time yesterday. It would appear that they underestimated his willingness to go to any lengths to address his grievances."

"Where's the building?" I asked as quietly as I could, my hands now shaking, the room darkening as my Shadows responded to my fury.

"Matty, I don't think that-"

"WHERE?!" my voice resonated through the Shadows, coming out ugly and horrible.

The house shook, Cassandra took a step back.

"God, I'm sorry," I said, suddenly ashamed of myself, looking away.

Cassandra pulled me into a hug, and I trembled, fear making my legs weak.

"It's going to be alright, Matty, we'll get them back."

I nodded and pulled away.

"Where are they?" I asked, more calmly this time, "And where's Kandi's Warden, is she alright?"

"Demise found her, she's banged up, but she's okay. They just left her in an alley, the bastards. She never saw it coming."

"So, where are they?" I asked again.

"Are you calm?" she asked, looking me in the eye.

I nodded, lying.

"One-seventy Warmington Plaza. Thornsby International Securities," she said.

That might be a problem. They'd told me in passing that 'International Securities' was business-code for 'Mercenaries'. In theory, they shouldn't have been allowed firearms, not in the UK, but enough money could buy you a lot of leeway with the right people.

Not that this mattered much to me. I was still going.

"Follow along with a team. I may need backup in a few minutes. If they're not out by..." I looked at my watch, "twelve, come in and don't stop until you get to them. I am not a priority in that case, understand?"

"Absolutely not."

"Glad we had this conversation," I said dryly, pulling out

my phone and tapping the address in.

I didn't have time to argue with her. I went to my usual bathroom and opened a Gateway.

It took only a few minutes to find the building. In the real world, it was a thirty-storey silver monstrosity on the outskirts of Stonebridge, where there was a small commercial high-rise district. It was one of those art-deco horrors that had a lop-sided pointy top, I'd have hated it even if my two favourite people weren't being held there against their will.

I had to stop for a moment and *force* myself to be calm. Every fibre of my being wanted to tear that building to the ground and visit every unspeakable thing I knew onto the inhabitants. I can honestly say that, in that moment, I'd never been closer to the darkness that I feared so much, and it was only my desperate need to keep Tethys and Kandi alive that prevented me from falling to it.

I forced that part of me away, but the best I could do was mute it a little, just enough to come up with a coherent plan, to take it slowly, gather the information I needed. I opened my mind to the Shadows, and I started hearing voices through their counterparts in the Newtonian World.

*Come on. One of you say something...*

There!

A laugh, Tethys'.

I brought myself to the relevant Shadow.

"That's right, keep laughing, bitch," a man's voice growled.

"Oh, I will. You have no idea who you're dealing with, it's actually rather hilarious," she said as if she were sitting in her study, not a prisoner in a mercenary stronghold. It helped to calm me.

A little.

I opened a tiny Gate in a shadow behind a potted plant, just in time to see the man slap my Tethys hard in the face.

He nearly, oh so nearly, died then and there.

"Leave her alone!" Kandi screamed.

The room was wide and expensively furnished. Tethys and Kandi were tied to chairs, the former was bound by silver chains that worked in much the same way as Spelleaters, only for non-human powers. They looked a little banged up, but not too badly, thank God; Tethys was bleeding from her lip and Kandi had a black eye.

"Shut up," the man said, turning to glare at Kandi.

He was one of five Mercenaries, all armed, all carrying Spelleaters. They were sneering or leering at my friends, which didn't improve my mood. They were dressed like soldiers, in body armour and urban camouflage, complete with helmets, goggles and gloves. They wore complete sets of webbing, festooned with equipment, pistols holstered at their hips, knives pinned to their chests for an easy draw. Their long-arms were slung on their backs, a collection of rifles and shotguns, all of which looked well maintained. They looked fit and healthy, packed with muscles, or lithe and graceful; these were not slouches.

And they were clearly expecting me.

Tethys started laughing again.

"You know," said the man who'd struck her, "the boss says we can keep you when we're done with all this hostage crap. You put on a good show, maybe we'll let you keep those good looks for a while."

The others smirked or grinned at that. One or two licked their lips.

Tethys laughed even harder, "Oh, you poor, poor man," she said, her voice sweet like honey, "You really shouldn't have said that."

"Yeah?" he said, grabbing her hair, "And why's that?"

"Well, it's my employer, you see. He likes to think he's an enlightened sort, women's rights and all that. But secretly, he's very old-fashioned, thinks women should be taken care of. It's all a little backward-thinking, really, but very sweet. The problem, as far as you're concerned, is that he can't abide people doing women a mischief, and if there's one thing you probably shouldn't have said where he could hear you, it's something like *that*."

"Good thing he can't hear me then. Maybe I'll start early, tell the boss you tried to escape," he said, drawing a long, shiny knife.

"That's the thing, precious," Tethys said, her voice a deep, sensual whisper, "my Love is already here. And unless I've missed my mark, he's angrier than I've ever known him. If I were you, I'd jump out the window now. It'll be much quicker than anything *he'll* do to you."

A bluff? Or could she sense me through my Gate?

Not that it mattered, I couldn't pass up a cue like that.

The man smiled and moved his knife towards Tethys' chest. Naturally, he didn't get it very far.

I hadn't just been sitting around, twiddling my thumbs. While I'd been watching, I'd also been drawing in heat through my Gate, lots of it. That's why I hadn't acted. I didn't want any of them to die.

That would be far too easy for these pigs.

My Shadows exploded through a rapidly expanded Gate, burning with all that heat I'd drawn in. The first hit sheared the knife-wielder's arm off half way between elbow and shoulder, the heat cauterising the stump, stopping the blood-flow. He screamed. I liked it.

I stepped out of my Gate, now large enough for the task. I called my Will and yanked their Spelleaters away one by one, putting Shadows between them and the girls as they opened up with their guns.

"I told you," Tethys said acidly to the screaming man on the carpet next to her.

"Kandi, close your eyes, you don't want to see this," I said as I stepped towards the second man. He was tall, looked young and strong; my Mage Sight detected the faintest trace of Kandi's blood on his knuckles.

Here's something you might not know; if there's one

person you don't want to get mad with you, it's a skilled Flesh Mage, and, not to blow my own trumpet, but I was very, very skilled, especially after all that time in Hadleigh's class. I'd actually been giving this some thought, only idly until that moment, but with what I knew, I could do some rather monstrous things to a human body. I could cast a spell that would cause complete, instant, metabolic shutdown (otherwise known as *death*), another that could leave a human being in searing pain for the rest of his life, another that would cause skin to slough off in seconds, leaving a person a raw mass of exposed musculature... a dozen others came to mind, each more horrific than the last.

But those weren't what I was after here. Those things were too quick, too easy for *these* people.

They were going to hurt Kandi and my Tethys.

Death was too easy for them because Tethys was right. I'd *never* been this angry before.

I took the second man's sight; seared his eyes out of his skull with shards of burning darkness. He dropped his weapon and screamed. The third started convulsing as his muscle mass dropped to a quarter of what it had started at, and all the while his bones were growing too brittle to carry his body weight. His legs snapped and he crumpled, in too much pain to make a sound. The fourth's tongue grew rapidly in his mouth, becoming four inches long, then five, then *more*. In seconds, it had expanded like a balloon, breaking his jaw before snapping off his teeth. He fell to the ground, clutching at his face, wailing a muffled sound. The last, I sent my Shadows for, taking his legs and his gun hand before he could do anything more than pass out from the pain.

The first, the animal that had handled Tethys... he tried to raise a gun with his remaining hand. If he'd pointed it at me, then perhaps he might have gotten off rather more lightly... but he pointed it at Tethys, and that made me... angry. Spikes of Shadow erupted from under his sleeves, flensing the skin from his bones before curving down, for his legs and hips. Each spike was burning hot and punctured him a dozen times, back on forth, through muscle, flesh and bone, searing each wound closed until he was left in an insensible, mewling heap, his legs ruined, his one hand a stretch of singed meat.

The room filled with screaming and terror, some of them had soiled themselves. The one I'd blinded was tearing at the remains of his eyes, weeping and begging. In the end I took a certain amount of pity on them, and I knocked them all out before sweeping them into a heap in the corner with my Shadows. The room was suddenly quiet, but I could feel minds approaching from all around us, drawn by the awful noise.

There was one door, and I blocked it with solidified Shadows before going to Tethys's side. I used my Will to tear those nasty shackles away as I dropped to my knees next to her, looking her over for damage. She smiled at me and threw her arms around my neck before I was half done, holding me tightly.

"Never do that again," I whispered, "You scared the *hell* out of me."

"I wasn't scared," she replied, "I knew you were coming, Love. I do feel a little stupid for letting these Neanderthals get the drop on me, though."

"Can I look yet?" Kandi asked, her eyes had been shut tight the whole time.

"Sure," I said, letting Tethys go so I could attend to her.

I unlocked Kandi's cuffs with a wave of my hand. Tethys and I both hugged her tightly, and she burst out crying. I rubbed her back and she buried her face in my shoulder.

"God, I'm sorry," she sobbed, "I'm being such a girl!"

"We'll give you a pass this time," Tethys said, stroking Kandi's hair as I attended to the redhead's scrapes and bruises. The swelling quickly went down and the cuts healed cleanly as we held her.

"Okay," I said, "let's get you two back home so I can have a chat with the boss around here."

"Oh, you have to let us come!" Kandi said, "It's personal

now."

"Kandi, you... you don't want to see what's about to happen to him," I said.

"I've been waiting twenty years for him to get what's coming to him, Matty," Kandi said, steel in her voice, "I wouldn't miss it."

I looked to Tethys for support, but she just shrugged.

"You two stay behind me at all times, understand me?" I said.

They nodded.

I released the Shadows around the door, and a pair of men fell into the room, off balance and stumbling, another dozen right behind them. I cast Sensory Overload, it would have taken too long to relieve them of their Spelleaters one by one. Wow, they sure had a *lot* of those; they were expensive, six figures each as a matter of fact.

The men dropped to the ground. I made sure that there were no more coming, and went to relieve them of their Amulets, which was much easier when they were unconscious (the Spelleaters ran on Living Energy, but shut off when the user was unconscious, a safety measure to prevent injury). I handed the amulets off to Tethys, who grinned and stuffed them in a pocket (no need to break them, they were a valuable resource, and the company technically belonged to me, now. Not that I'd be running it, or anything).

With the immediate threat over, I used my Mage Sight to look for Kandi's father. I found him in an office five floors up (the top floor, actually), and there were a *lot* of armed men between him and us. If even a fraction had Spelleaters, then we could quickly get bogged down in what was practically a maze of stairwells, corridors and offices, which would put Tethys and Kandi in danger.

That meant we couldn't use the traditional route, and I couldn't risk taking two people through the Shadow Realm (it simply wasn't good for the sanity of non-Shadowborn).

I took a good look around, shifting my Mage Sight so

that I could see into the walls, taking in the construction; specifically, the reinforcement points. I smiled. The place was very well built, with the load spread carefully and evenly. A few holes shouldn't cause too much of a problem (or the place to collapse), as long as I didn't go through any of the major load-bearing sections. I called my Shadows (now no longer burning), and slammed a whole bunch of coils into the ceiling. Kandi squeaked as concrete shattered and chunks hit the floor. A hole quickly appeared, and my Shadows poured through it to slam into the ceiling above. I sent them up further and further, tearing through all five floors.

I beckoned the ladies closer and wrapped all of us in Shadows, pulling us up, smashing the holes wider as we went.

"You don't really do subtle, do you, Love?" Tethys said with a giggle as I gently lowered us onto the correct floor.

"Not in the right mood for subtle," I said with a small smile, leading the way forwards again.

Three more men and women came at me, and they fell as well. I didn't even bother disarming those. Even more of the mercenaries were coming up stairs and in lifts as news of what I'd done spread, but they'd be too late.

I got us close to the CEO's office and turned to seal off the approaching corridors with solid shadows, enough energy making them physical objects that wouldn't be affected by Spelleaters. It cost me a lot of power, but the barriers would allow us to have our... conversation with Mr Thornsby uninterrupted.

I smashed his office door off its hinges and made sure that it smacked heavily into the guards in the room. The splintered wood dropped three of the four, and the last one opened fire into the mass of Shadows beyond the door, screaming horribly in his terror. He ran out of bullets and I opened my Shadows to cast Sensory Overload again in a tight beam, sending him to the ground.

I walked into the office to see Thornsby sitting in a huge, red, leather chair, behind an equally colossal desk. His expression was smug and very confident. His office was big, even for someone in his position, with an impressive view; his furniture old and very expensive. There were shelves and display cabinets full of weapons, some of which were gold-plated, *all* of which I was fairly certain were illegal in the UK (much like just about everything else his people were carrying). The carpet was thick and rich, the walls painted in neutral tones, it was actually quite elegant (tacky golden weapons aside).

"Lord Graves, how good to see you again," Thornsby said evenly, like he hadn't a care in the world.

"You seem remarkably calm for a man in a room with a very angry Sorcerer," I said, moving forward slowly.

"You won't hurt me, Carol would never forgive you," he said, grinning evilly.

"Very bad bet, old boy," I said, gesturing at him.

Shadows surged and he was yanked from behind his desk, wrapped neck to toe in darkness, holding him fast.

"You can't do this! I'm a public figure, the SCA will skin you alive!" he shouted, his voice trembling now.

Tethys snorted.

"Mister Thornsby," I said softly, ignoring his threat, the tone of my voice making him go very pale, "I've been giving some thought as to what would happen when we met."

I strolled casually towards him, taking my time, "And you're quite right, I don't want to leave Carol with any particularly dark memories of you."

His winning smile came back, though it was a little nervous, this time.

"That's why I have something far *worse* planned than simply killing you."

I touched his forehead.

I was at work for half an hour, setting blocks in place, implanting commands and wards, altering his physiology. When I was done, and the last piece fell into place, Thornsby opened his eyes and simply burst into tears, wailing fit to wake the dead.

I released my Shadows and he fell to the floor, curling up into a ball. I turned to the women.

"We can go now," I said cheerfully, moving towards a nearby window.

"What did you do?" Kandi asked, looking confused, "He's just... crying."

"Do you really want to know? It's not very nice. I think it might change the way you look at me," I said.

Kandi smiled warmly at me, cupping my cheek with one delicate hand.

"Nothing could do that, Matty. Tell me," she said.

"Did you know he had a dicky ticker?" I asked.

She shook her head.

"Well, he did, bad, too. And if that hadn't gotten him, the rampant liver cirrhosis would have. I fixed them both. He'll live another forty, fifty years."

"And?" Kandi asked, "That can't be it, surely?"

"Wait for it," Tethys said huskily, biting her lip.

"Well, I figured since I'd given him so much, it was only fair to exact a *little* payment, so I took something in return. Nothing much, I'm sure he won't miss it..."

"Matty, we have talked about gloating," Tethys scolded, smirking and ruining the effect.

"You said it was sexy!"

"It's less so when you're standing in an enemy stronghold with Mercenaries trying to break in and do unspeakable things to your hindquarters!" she countered.

"Fine, fine," I harrumphed, "I took his happiness. He'll never know joy, satisfaction or even simply comfort for the rest of his *long* life. And I made sure he'd never be able to kill himself. His life will be nothing but sadness and hopelessness for as long as he lives, and it's going to be a while."

Tethys shuddered and pressed herself up against me, nuzzling hard at my neck, "Oh, you are delightfully, creatively *evil*, Matty. I'd never have thought of something so simply... sadistic."

"He took you, had you hurt, had Kandi hurt. He's deserved something... *special*," I said, holding her tightly.

"Let him go," Kandi whispered.

I just stood there for a long second.

"What?" I asked.

"Don't leave him like that, Matty, I can't bear it, please?" she said.

Tethys scowled, but said nothing.

"Sure, Kandi, whatever you want," I said, a little annoyed (that piece of creative justice had taken a lot of work!). But I understood, and Kandi was crying, tears streaking down her face, I couldn't have that. I went over to her father and released him from my Enchantments. He groaned in relief, his eyes red and puffy as he looked up at his daughter.

"Thank you!" he said, tears rolling down his own face, "Thank you so much, Carol."

My little redhead kicked him square in the face and broke his nose.

"If you ever come near me or Mum or my sisters again, I'll let him come back, do you understand me?!" she shouted.

He nodded, his hands clenched over his bleeding nose.

"I'm keeping your company. Be out by tomorrow morning," she finished.

He nodded again, quite vigorously, his eyes darting between me and his daughter. She glared at him one more time and then came over to me.

"Okay, we can go now," she said.

I smiled and used my Will to pull a window inwards, the pane shattering over the carpet as I led them over to the edge.

"You are a special girl, Kandi," I said, taking her hand, "and a far better person than I could ever hope to be. You amaze me every day, you know that?"

She went bright red and there were tears in her eyes

again.

"Never change, Carol Thornsby," I said.

She smiled and I wrapped all three of us up in Shadows before dropping us out the window and lowering us to the plaza below, where Cassandra was waiting with two cars and three Wardens. We landed and they darted over, weapons pointed up at the building behind us.

"Mission accomplished?" Cassandra asked with a smile, checking me over.

I nodded, tired and in need of a nap.

"Anyone alive in there- Matty, duck!" she shouted, no-*screamed*!

I barely obeyed in time to save my life.

I was still too late.

# CHAPTER 22

Solomon had simply dropped out of the sky. I never had a chance to see him coming. By the time I sensed his Black Magic, it was too late. But for Cassandra's warning, I'd have died, cut in half by his sword.

As it was, I took a hit, a bad one.

The tip of the blade sliced me open from the top of my left shoulder to my right hip, about half an inch deep, not *too* bad in and of itself.

But that sword was leaking Black Magic, and... well, it got into the wound. I slammed into the bonnet of the car, but I felt no pain, the wound was already closing, the Black responding to my need instinctively, already a part of me. I felt it at the edge of my perception, flowing around my body. I shivered; it was a rush, warm and comforting.

I don't know why I'd thought it would be cold... it wasn't.

I felt Solomon advancing on Cassandra, and my Warden was putting up one hell of a fight, firing off everything she had, Magic and bullets. Tethys had taken Kandi and dived for cover, sensible girl; the other Wardens were firing on the half-breed, too.

It wouldn't help. He was stronger than all of them combined, and he was calling more of the Black. I turned and saw him raise his hand.

He tossed a sickly ball of Black Magic at Cassandra, my friend, my guardian, and someone I considered a big sister, and I knew that, right here, right now was the moment I made a choice. *The* choice, as a matter of fact.

In theory, I could spend my strength and get the Black already inside me out, it hadn't spread too far, and it hadn't reached my Well yet. I could do that, and maybe save myself.

But if I did that, if I shoved the Black out, then I wouldn't be able to stop that ball heading for Cassandra. It was too late for Will, and I didn't have the focus, anyway, it was almost at her, moving faster than the eye could follow. But I could stop it.

Save myself or save Cassandra... It wasn't really a choice.

I reached for Solomon's Spell. It didn't even resist me. That Spell was of the Black, and the Black was *mine.*

I raised my hand and the Spell simply stopped six inches from Cassandra's face.

It felt so... right. It wasn't pleasure, it wasn't a drug. It was simply a feeling of... coming home, of completeness. The dark power of creation, right there in my control. I sent it back to Solomon and a tiny voice inside me roared in joy as his face stretched in panic. He threw up a frantic shield, and the ball slid right through, shattering it and hitting him in the shoulder.

He screamed. An awful, *awful* sound, as the skin and bone warped and mutated. The flesh bubbled and exploded as the bone shot out, growing long and sharp, a whole new Grotesque limb with a blade-like appendage on the end that started stabbing his face and chest.

His expression contorted in horror as he grabbed at the new arm with his one good one, desperately trying to keep it from his eyes. He screamed in pain as his new limb grew fingers of razor-sharp bone and started tearing at his desperately grasping hand.

I smiled at my work, and felt immediate horror at my own enjoyment.

Cassandra reloaded and threw out a Chemical Burst that burned the flesh of his legs down to the bone while she opened fire again, each bullet finding its mark in his flesh now that his concentration had been disrupted.

He threw up his hand to protect his face from the shots, but that forced him to release his new appendage, and it attacked again, tearing ever larger chunks of flesh from his head and neck. He panicked, and his wings exploded from his back, pulling him into the air and away, pursued by Magic and gunfire.

I could have stopped him, taken him down, but I was too busy fighting my own battle.

The Black in me was getting stronger, I could feel it, I was *feeding* it from my Well. In a matter of moments, the flow would be two way, and I'd be done.

Cassandra was turning towards me, horror in her eyes and grief in her soul.

"Cassie, shoot me!" I shouted.

"What?" she said, her mouth opening in shock.

"In the leg! Do it now, we have to drain the Black before it gets in my Well. Shoot me, and keep firing until I stop regenerating. Now, Cassie, please, for God's sake! I can't hold it much longer!"

I was desperate, and I could feel it, oozing towards my core, my heart and my soul. I was fighting it, but I was also beckoning it, drawing it in. I craved it, wanted it, loved it already.

"Now, Warden!" I shouted.

"God forgive me," she whispered.

She fired.

Pain blossomed from my knee and I fell with a scream of agony.

"Damn it, Cassie, I said *leg*, not *knee*! Do you have any idea how much that's going to ache?!"

The Black surged and rebuilt the damage. Cassandra fired again, this time into the meat of my thigh, the muscle exploded, blood went everywhere. Still the Black came and repaired me.

She fired again and again. Thankfully, I passed out after the fourth shot, but I knew it was working. The Black was being drained, pulling back from my Well. I heard Tethys scream my name towards the end there, but, either way, they'd be safe.

I wouldn't be able to hurt them.

To my immense surprise, I woke up.

And immediately wished I hadn't.

The Black was gone, but the *need* for it wasn't. I shook hard, already sweating as I came back to consciousness. Everything below the waist *ached*, which was only to be expected.

I was in my room at Blackhold; it was dark and should have been pleasantly warm, but all I could feel was a deep chill. Palmyra was there, sitting next to me, holding my hand, Hopkins, too.

"Easy, little brother," Palmyra said, her eyes filled with affection and distress, "You were very brave, and you're alright, now."

I swallowed, my teeth chattering.

"Why am I so cold?" I asked, pulling a blanket around myself.

"You're in withdrawal," Hopkins said simply.

She pulled a spare blanket off the sideboard and put it over my legs.

"I am so very, very proud of you, Mathew," she said, a tear in her eye, "You came back. You pushed it out of you, and you came back to us."

I tried for a smile, "I wish I could claim credit for that, but Cassandra was the one who saved me. Damn, but it's like the worst craving, ever..."

"I know. And if you try, you can probably get it back, too. Is that what you want?"

I breathed in a shuddering breath and shook my head.

"N-n-no," I managed.

She put an arm around my shoulder and squeezed. Palmyra surreptitiously cuffed a tear away.

"You alright?" I asked Palmyra.

"I'm fine," she replied, "We just couldn't know for sure who would wake up. Kron was sure you'd still have it in you."

"No, it's gone," I said, feeling the craving, the gaping hole in my soul, "definitely gone. But I presume you've been checking? You'd know that."

"Sure, but it's different when you're awake. If you'd been... changed, we wouldn't necessarily be able to tell with a dormant mind."

"Well, feel free to check, if you like," I suggested.

Palmyra rolled her eyes and placed a cool palm on my forehead. I felt the tingle of Magic as she looked into me. Her face brightened into a smile after an ugly pause.

"You're fine," she said with a sigh.

"You don't have to sound so surprised."

"Sorry, it's just that this hasn't happened before, not to anyone stronger than a low level Wizard," Palmyra said.

"I got lucky," I said, "very, *very* lucky."

"Yes... Can you tell us what happened?" Hopkins asked, "We've spoken to your people, but I'd like to hear your perspective."

I laid it out for them, told them what had happened from after I'd been told Kandi had been taken.

"That sounds remarkably coincidental, doesn't it?" Hopkins said, tapping her lip.

I nodded. Solomon had turned up at *exactly* the right moment to catch me off-guard. That stunk of foreknowledge.

"After I got his infiltrators, Solomon needed some other way to wear me down, so he probably went looking for my enemies. I'm surprised he picked Thornsby of all people, but that did provide him with the kind of bait that would guarantee my being in a certain place at a certain time," I said, "And it worked, too. I was tired and slow, and I got hit from behind."

"You're always tired and slow," Palmyra said faux-sympathetically.

"If I could stand up, I'd get you for that," I said, bending over my stomach, which was cramping, "God, what's happening?"

"It's like chemical withdrawal," Palmyra said, "You had the Black flooding though your system, it rebuilt you a few times. Being without it is going to hurt."

"Terrific," I said, breathing the cramp away, "How long? How bad?"

"Days until the worst of the symptoms are gone, which would be anxiety, insomnia, stomach cramps, fever, and just generally feeling like puke. It'll get worse for the next three to four days before it tapers off and you'll finish with a couple of weeks where you feel like low-level crap, like a bad flu that won't end. After that, it's just an incessant craving for the rest of your life."

"Oh, you paint such a rosy picture," I said dryly. The sweating was already getting bad. I had to shed the blanket, which just made me shiver again.

Palmyra patted my shoulder, "It's going to be harder for you. That description is based on a Wizard-level Shadowborn. It's worse depending on how much Black was used and the strength of the user. You're so screwed."

"Oh thank you very much!"

"Hey, you played with the Black...." Palmyra said.

"I did not play with it! It got stabbed into my back!"

"Sure it did," Palmyra said, giving a theatrical wink. Hopkins sniggered.

I muttered darkly under my breath as another withdrawal symptom made its presence known, and I sprinted for the lavatory. I'll spare you the gruesome details, but suffice to say it wasn't pleasant, and by the time I'd staggered back to bed, I felt like I'd been wrung out by an enraged gorilla and left to dry in a blender.

I toppled into bed and Palmyra touched my cheek. I felt Magic and the pains eased a little.

"I can't do too much, Matty. If I interfere, it could mess up your own system's detox, and we don't want that."

"S'okay," I said, "There are drugs."

"Ah, Pureborn medicine," Palmyra said with a sneer, "why don't you just get a bucket of leeches and have yourself bled while you're at it?"

"Doing both would be redundant, seeing as both treatments remove blood from the body," I said.

"Well, look at Mister Smartypants, thinks he knows more than the Lifeweaver?"

"First, that's *Lord* Smartypants to you... and yes."

Palmyra laughed and pulled a blanket around my curled up body.

"You laugh now, I get this every week," Hopkins said.

"I missed debate night those first few weeks," I said, "there's nobody fun to argue with in that wretched school."

Hopkins smiled and dropped herself into one of my more comfortable armchairs.

"How much did you spend making this place as comfortable as humanly possible?" Hopkins asked, putting her feet up on a stool.

"I try not to ask Tethys those questions. It makes me feel guilty."

"So... a lot?" she persisted.

"More than a lot. But worth every penny, you've seen my library."

"Love that room so much!" Palmyra said, "It's nerd heaven in there. Have you seen the graphic novel section?"

"Seen it, felt great shame over my brother's hobbies, blocked it out of my mind," Hopkins said with a grimace.

"So that wasn't his signed copy of 'The Dark Knight Returns' on your coffee table?" Palmyra said slyly.

"I've been looking for that!" I complained.

We chatted for a while, but I got the distinct impression that I was being watched, like I might expire at any moment. So I decided to go for a little walk (while I still could, and all).

"Don't leave the house," Hopkins said, "We don't want you catching a cold."

"I'm a grown man, you know," I said, walking out the

door.

"And wrap up warm!" Hopkins said.

I walked slowly towards Tethys' study, trying to ignore the stomach problems, swallowing a little hard. The sweating was back, too...

I raised my hand to knock on her door.

She opened the door and pulled me clear off the floor and into her arms.

"Oh, I'm so glad to see you!" she said, putting me down so she could hug me more conventionally (and thoroughly).

"I would have been there when you woke up, but your sisters threw me out. They... they weren't sure you'd be you. You *are* you, right?"

I gave her a look and a raised eyebrow.

She smiled and pulled me into another crushing hug.

"Naturally," she said, "like anything could change you."

She looked me up and down, "You don't look well," she said.

"You know how I was *never* supposed to use Black Magic, and *everyone* told me it wasn't good for me?"

"Vaguely," she said with a smile, pulling me gently into her study and settling me down on the sofa.

"Well, it turns out they were right, who'd have thought?" I said, returning her smile

"Isn't it a pain when other people are right?" she said, leaning her head on my shoulder, her nose twitching, "I'm not smelling nice things, Matty."

"Sorry. And from what Lucille tells me, I'm not going to get more fragrant for a while."

"We'll survive; but you're going to be alright?"

"Of course. I'm always alright."

"You always say that, and then some other terrible thing happens to you."

"And then I'm always alright."

She shook her head.

"How's Kandi?" I asked.

"Better, if a little blue. I'll do some naughty things to her later, she'll perk right up. She's a little conflicted about stopping what you did to her father. Why'd you let her, by the way?"

"Her Father, her choice. And I didn't take *all* my modifications out."

She laughed again, "You sly monster, you! I knew you'd done something crafty, I could feel it in my water!"

"It's just a tiny Asimov, he won't even notice it's there... unless he tries to kill someone, or hurt someone, or looks at you funny, or Kandi, or her mother, or a whole bunch of other... best not to dwell."

She chuckled happily, leaning against me.

"How's Cassie?" I asked.

"Well... there we may have a tiny problem..."

Cassandra wasn't doing well.

I found her face down in her bathtub (empty, thank God), several bottles of whiskey (also empty) strewn around her bathroom. She was snoring heavily and drooling onto her bundled-up suit jacket. I shook my head and lowered myself to the ground next to her tub.

I looked her over, and she was still rather hammered. I cleared the alcohol out of her system and used my Will (which hurt, by the way. Any Magic hurt) to carry her to her bed. I laid her down, and smoothed out the pulled muscles while I waited for her to wake up.

She groaned as she awoke, her hands going to her head.

She opened her eyes and quickly went pale, freezing as she saw at me, her hand going instinctively to her holster.

"Still me," I said with a smile, "You can ask Lucille, if you like."

She closed her eyes, and tears started trickling down her cheeks. I moved over and took her hand, but she shook me off.

"No!" she said, "You were exposed, and it's my fault. You

should be corrupted. You should be stained!"

"I'm not," I soothed, "I'm fine."

"You used the Black!" she almost shouted, "Nothing's going to be alright again! And it's because of me! I wasn't fast enough or good enough, and now you're a monster!"

"I am bloody not!"

"Yes, you-"

"Listen!" I barked, and she actually shut up. I tried not to enjoy the first time that had *ever* happened, "Even if I was stained, even if I was using the Black, which I'm *not*, I'm the one who decides who I am, *what* I am. I am no monster because I say so. Monsters don't love, they don't grieve and they don't care. I do. Now kindly stop this masochistic crap, because even if I'd gone dark, I'd have considered it a price well worth paying, because you aren't just my Warden, you're my friend, my family! And, so help me God, if you try to pin this mess on yourself I will kick your arse. Well, I'll try and you'll defenestrate me, but the principle stands."

She stared at me while I talked. She stared for a long time afterwards.

She nodded once, definitively.

"I'm going to talk to your sister," she said.

I nodded.

"Could you help me up, first?" I asked, "I feel like crap, and I'm not sure I can do it on my own, and using Magic hurts."

She sighed, but she smiled.

"You really are a weed," she said, hefting me under the arm and lifting me to my feet, where I swayed, dizzy.

"Want me to help you back to bed?" she said in a long-suffering way, a little more relaxed.

"Would you?"

"Sure. Stupid Shadowborn."

That made me feel better.

She had to catch me a couple of times as she walked me back to my room, but we made it without my face-planting.

"Did you do something to me while I was out?" she

asked, "I feel far better than I should."

"Sorted the nine muscle sprains you'd accumulated from spending the night in the bathtub and detoxed your bloodstream."

"That's a bit presumptuous, don't you think?" she snapped.

"Sorry, I just wanted to help."

She coughed and looked a bit guilty.

"No, I'm sorry. You know Black Magic's a bit of a hot button for me, and I'll try not to snarl at you, I know you don't mean any harm," she said, and then she stopped walking for a moment, "I know you'd never hurt me."

That last said in a rather profound manner. She still looked miserable, though. It didn't take a genius to realise why.

"It was a trap," I said, "You couldn't have done any better than you did, we were set up."

"What?" she said.

"Hopkins and Palmyra can tell you properly, but it looks like Solomon's been playing silly buggers."

"I'm reserving judgement."

"Yes, you wouldn't want to miss out on any self-flagellation, that would be crazy."

"You want me to drop you? 'Cause I will," she said with a glare, but I saw the edge of her smile.

"Seriously, Cassie," I said as we got to my door, she stopped, and I put my hand on her shoulder; she didn't flinch this time, "if I don't blame you, why the hell do you blame yourself?"

"The same reason you carry all *your* guilt around, I guess. We both think we should be better."

"Nobody can be their best being ambushed! And for what it's worth, you did a damn sight better than I could have hoped to."

"Well of course I did, you're just a man, after all," she said with a smile, "We can't expect too much."

I jabbed her ribs with my fingertips and she jolted with a very girly squeak before turning to glare and then laughing at me. She punched my shoulder and I wasn't ready, and she had to grab me before I fell over.

"Come on, let's get you back into bed and we'll see what your sisters say."

What followed was a long and involved conversation, which I didn't get much of; I was too busy in the bathroom again. I knew that they were discussing me, Cassandra desperately seeking confirmation of what I'd told her, and my sisters doing their best to provide it.

I eventually dropped onto the bed in a shivering heap that Cassandra kept staring at. I think she was getting worried.

"Has he eaten yet?" she whispered to Palmyra during a brief break in their talk, thinking I didn't, or couldn't, hear.

"He's already thrown up twice, let his stomach settle first. He might be able to eat something tonight," Palmyra replied.

"What day is it, by the way?" I asked, sitting up and immediately regretting it.

"Saturday," Hopkins answered.

"I missed a whole day of school?" I asked, "Oh, and I was supposed to meet Mary yesterday night, she's going to be pissed."

"Kandi already called her, she said she'd come visit you tomorrow, if you're up for it?" Hopkins said.

"Oh, she's going to make my life hell," I complained, "the last time I got a *paper-cut,* she didn't stop nagging for three hours, two of them *after* I'd fixed it right in front of her."

"Yes, can't have that, that's really Kandi's thing," Cassandra said.

I glared and collapsed, sinking into sleep before I'd noticed.

I woke up with Pixies staring worriedly down at my

face. Jewel was crying.

"What's wrong?" I asked them, touching their faces gently with my (now slightly shaking) fingertips.

"You're hurt," Melody said, her eyes shining.

"I'm just a little sick, Melody, I'll get better."

"We don't want you to die," Jewel said with a sob.

"No we don't!" Meadow said.

They fell on my chest and I held them as they cried.

"I'm going to be alright, girls, I promise. I'm just a little bit ill."

"You're sure?" Meadow said.

"I am."

"Promise us again?" Jewel said.

"I promise. But I won't look good for a few days. After that I'll start to recover and everything will be fine again."

Jewel sniffled and I stroked her back.

From there, I wasn't left alone, and I did get steadily worse.

Kandi came in just after seven that night, I didn't even notice, I was shaking so hard, focussing on not throwing up. She placed a cool hand on my cheek.

"Hi," I managed, turning to smile at her.

The Pixies were curled up on my sofa, next to a flickering fire, sleeping well enough. The TV was on low, showing something boring and gentle. The little Fairies were my designated watchers, self-appointed, I believed.

"How are you feeling?" Kandi asked.

"A little better, now. Are you okay? I know you had a rough go of it, and I'm sorry I've been too out of it to help."

"Don't be dense," she said, lying down next to me, "What can I do? I'll do anything if it will help you."

"Anything, eh?" I said, giving her a leer and then ruining it when a stomach cramp made me wince, which made her snort and swat my shoulder. She kissed my cheek very softly.

"There aren't a lot of people in my life who are willing to do for me what you are, Matty," she said, holding my hand,

"I wanted you to know how much that means to me. I haven't had much reason to trust men before you. I never thought that any of you were more than walking wallets, flash some cleavage, get money. But you... you're different."

"You still flashed me."

"Please, I got much further in my jammies than I ever did in a thong!"

"That's because even your jammies are cut *very* low."

"That, and you're just that little bit weird."

"Can't disagree with you there. At least I'm the good kind of weird... most of the time."

She laughed and rolled onto my chest.

"Your sister says you're probably going to be out for a while," she said, "So I'm going to get you back up and running. It's my new hobby!"

"Oh, not again! The last time, your physical therapy was worse than the poisoning!"

"Do I have to start tickling you again?" she said menacingly.

"With my dicky guts, I wouldn't recommend it."

She laughed and snuggled in closer.

"Don't worry, Matty, we'll get you better," she said gently.

"I know," I said, squeezing her arm.

Ah, if only it were that easy...

# CHAPTER 23

I was actually starting to feel a little better the next day (if only a little); the symptoms seemed to come in waves, and I was at the (slightly) nicer end of one, but naturally the Universe couldn't have that, oh no.

And of course, things went horrifically wrong at the worst possible time, while Mary was visiting.

She and I were sitting in my room watching TV. Mary had already been through it like a small hurricane, tidying everything, forcing soup down me, and otherwise brightening up the place.

"You do realise that Shadowborn thrive in the *dark*, right?" I asked after she'd opened the curtain and turned my headache up to eleven on account of the bright sunshine.

"You need sunshine and vitamins, now shush and absorb your medicine," she said with a grin.

I was about to reply when I heard the scream.

A man's scream; long and loud and horrible.

Mary tensed.

So did I.

Mira appeared.

She was the avatar of the Grimoire, the store of every Black Magic spell and technique ever devised. She looked like an amalgam of all the women who bossed me around, all those I cared about. Her body was Tethys, along with her bone structure, there was a little Hopkins in the nose, some Cassandra in the lips, Kandi's freckles and Crystal's hair. Her eyes were mine and she wore Gabrielle's clothes. The whole ensemble was rather attractive, actually.

Since I'd brought her home, she'd taken over the management of the house's defences. They were now ridiculously powerful, and nigh impenetrable.

"Master, I think you should come, there's an army at the gates, and they've already taken shots at Cassandra, I had to kill some of them."

Crap, see what I mean?

"Kill?" I said, suddenly very alert and moving shakily towards the doors.

"You told me to follow the Captain's orders," she said, "and that's what I did. They had your butler. I had no choice if I was to prevent them holding him hostage."

"Bloody hell. Who are they?" I asked.

"Unclear. Battle Mages, certainly. They've invaded the grounds and are approaching the front door. Definitely foreign, likely mercenaries as I don't think they know who you are. Nobody local would have been so foolish," she said, her face creasing in a snarl, "I have to go, the Captain is calling me. She's going to kill them, Mathew, and I have absolutely no compunctions helping her do it. They're here to murder you. That will not be permitted."

"Please be careful, they may not be guilty of anything more than following orders."

She nodded and vanished.

I picked up my phone. No signal, probably jammed, should have known.

This could have been anyone, I had too many enemies... but one in particular sprung to mind. One who had form for using patsies and proxies. I really was going to have to deal with him, soon.

"What should I do?" Mary asked.

"Stay here, you are perfectly safe. The house will protect you. I give you my word," I said, standing up.

And then I fell back down again. Too shaky, my Magic too hard to use. This wasn't going to end well. I needed *help*. But what could anyone here do? Except kill the bastards...

I couldn't stop it except by giving myself up, and I wasn't willing to die, I wasn't a martyr.

"You know, a little Black Magic would clear this whole mess up."

"Oh, please not now," I said with a groan as I finally noticed that Time had stopped again.

Gabrielle... right on bloody cue.

She placed a hand gently on my shoulder, tracing up to my neck with her fingertips.

"It would be so easy," she said, "the Angel's already abandoned you. You use it *once*, and you're out as far as they're concerned. All that's left is me. And Us."

"Gabby, please," I said, unable to keep the quiver out of my voice, "I'm begging you, please don't do this now."

"Why?" she asked, perching next to me on the bed, "This is exactly the right time. Your Will is as weak as it's ever been. Your Magic is as far from you as it's going to get. This may well be the only real chance I get to convince you of the right path."

"You owe me. Don't do this, please?" I begged.

She kissed my cheek, then my lips. She released her glamour and let me see her true form as she slid onto my lap and wrapped her arms and legs around me; I felt her tail snake itself around my leg.

"You get me," she whispered, "Use the Black, and you get me. That's the deal, that's always been the deal. Become who you were supposed to be. Who you *want* to be, and I'll show you joy like you've never imagined."

"You don't even *like* me, Gabby. Do you really expect me to believe that you'd be happy with that?"

"Are you *really* sure about that, Mathew? And besides, I fail to see how that matters. This is about what *you* deserve."

"Oh, Gabby," I said, cupping her cheek, looking into those dark red eyes of hers, "it's the only thing that matters."

"It wouldn't, if you'd just take what's yours," she whispered, her lips close to mine, "then, perhaps, I might like you a little bit better."

"I don't want to be that man, Gabrielle. Even if Rose and her lot don't want anything to do with me, it doesn't matter. I get to choose what kind of man I am. And I hope that I can be a good one. I don't doubt that one day I'll use it again, I can feel it, scratching at the back of my mind. But until then, I intend to be the person my parents raised, the one that looks after his family."

She smiled at me and licked her lips.

"So you *are* taking my deal, now we're just negotiating a time frame?"

She ran her lips and tongue along my neck and chin.

"Nice try," I said, pushing against her. Unfortunately, my arms had all the strength of a soggy noodle.

"I'm getting to you," she whispered, "I can feel it. And not just in your soul."

She thrust her hips against mine, just enough to make her point.

"I have to go, and I am just of no use in that department, right now, as you well know," I said, "any sort of vigorous movement and I'll throw up."

"If you'd just use the Black..."

"I have enough left in me to banish you," I threatened.

"No you don't," she said, kissing me again and again, "and you'd miss me if you did."

"I know," I said with a sigh.

"So weak... so pliable... I love it," she said, gently pushing me onto my back.

"I'm in the middle of a crisis," I said weakly.

"And?"

"And I have things to do... oh."

She pulled my t-shirt up and kissed my chest, licking and biting. It felt amazing. Sexy and tender all at once. This wasn't good. In that state, the attentions of a pureblood Succubus might kill me. Enslave me, certainly.

I relaxed. Gabrielle moaned in the thrill of the hunt, the

impending victory.

In that moment, in that crisis, Professor Porter was the hero. If not for her teachings, I'd have been lost. But because of her class, and all the practice, I was able to put up a Mental Shield, not a big one, but strong enough. Her power was cut off from me, and I sighed as my soul was once again safe from harm.

Naturally, she noticed.

"Damn you," she said without heat, still nuzzling.

"If it helps at all, you're still thoroughly getting to me," I said with a smile.

"Why can't you just let me win one? Just once? Is that too much to ask?"

"When you winning means my enslavement? Afraid so."

My hands had been in some rather delicate places by this point (heat of the moment); she took them and pressed them down above my head.

"Now tell me, my dear," she purred, "can you fight me up here-"

She kissed my forehead.

"-*and* down here?"

Another little thrust of her hips, the clothes between us feeling rather inadequate to the task of protecting my modesty at that moment.

I swallowed. She noticed.

"That's what I thought."

Her lips came for mine again... and suddenly she was yanked off me, a slim, pale arm around her neck.

"How *dare* you?!" Rose rasped into the Demon's ear.

"Oh thank God," I said.

"I'll pass that on," Rose said wryly, and I blushed as I realised the other meaning of my comment, and then her expression was icy again as she contemplated the Demon, "I have never been more angry at you!"

She tossed Gabrielle like she was a bag of potatoes, and she landed heavily on the floor next to the bed, her eyes wide.

She was actually afraid.

"And how could you tell him that I'd abandoned him?!"

There was suddenly a glowing sword in the angel's hand as she advanced, her form shimmering with power.

"I was only following my orders!" Gabrielle said, putting her hands up, "How do you think I was able to stop Time?!"

Rose stopped, the blade glowing brighter.

"*He* helped you do this?" Rose asked acidly.

"I wouldn't have hurt him. I couldn't have. And I didn't want to," Gabrielle said softly, "I never want to, don't you understand?"

Rose looked at her, her glare softening. Her sword vanished.

"If you come near him again before he's finished recovering, I *will* banish you. Once he is of sound mind, you may tempt him all you wish, that will be his choice. But you will not take advantage of his good nature as long as I'm alive, do you understand me?"

Gabrielle nodded. She looked at me.

"So close, my dear," she whispered, a smile on her lips, and then she was gone.

Rose came over, a look of intense worry on her face as she touched my cheek.

"Oh, Mathew, what did you do?" she said, sitting next to me, "You weren't ready for this."

"It wasn't by choice."

"The wound wasn't, the rest was," she said.

She took my hand and leaned her cheek on it, "I can't decide whether to be angry at you or proud of you. It's maddening; you do this to me *a lot*."

"I'm sorry," I said, feeling dreadful again. Gabrielle had taken a lot out of me, and I was aching and shaky.

"Oh, that's alright. At least I'm never bored."

She turned her head, her pretty nose darted up.

"You smell nice today- oh! Not again!" she said, darting up and standing back.

"What?" I asked, and then it twigged, "Oh no... please tell me that she didn't give me another dose of those bloody pheromones!"

She bit her lip, looking me over, her hands bunching into fists as she started sweating, "Looks like it. And this one's a little heavier than last time."

"Can you block it again?"

"I guess I'll have to," she said, but she just stood there.

"Are you alright?"

"It's really strong. She did it on purpose, the bitch. I'll never block it all."

"Hold your nose," I suggested.

"It's not just chemical," she said, coming forward at last. She placed a hand on my forehead and I felt a tingle of something vaguely Magical.

She sighed and suddenly her nose was against my neck.

"Oh, it's so tempting," she whispered.

"Aren't you really more anti-temptation?"

"I'm complicated," she said. She held me, and it banished pains and aches. It made me feel like me again. She kissed my cheek and slowly pulled away.

"I really am very proud of you, Mathew Graves," she said and then she was gone as well.

Time resumed.

Mary started.

"Weren't you just over there?" Mary asked, gesturing at the other end of the bed.

"Nope," I said, dragging myself up, the respite of Rose's presence already fading.

So, just to clarify, I was low on Willpower, my Magic was hard to use, more like wading through a swamp than sliding along a river; there was an army at my gates, Cassandra had used my Grimoire to kill some of them, and there was nobody to come help me.

Sometimes, it just didn't pay to do good deeds...

I staggered through my bedroom door, my Shadows just barely propping me up as I walked. Even using *them* was a strain, like trying to squeeze the last drop of toothpaste out of a tube.

I made my way down the stairs to the front doors, and saw a small war being waged.

Lacy and Connie were holding the pillars, firing blocky, black rifles at a dozen Battle Mages closing in on us. They were really strong, Sorcerers all, and that was *very* odd. Magicians of that calibre were rare enough, and they didn't generally work together. Sick as I was, I didn't stand a chance against so many. Hell, at full power, I would probably still have been screwed.

Four Magicians were out in front of the others, acting almost like a skirmish line for a larger group behind; the latter were gathered together, where they could pool their defences. I spotted two corpses off to the left, the grass around them scorched, their necks badly broken. I shuddered. Mira was not to be trifled with.

And the book had been right, they didn't look local. Of the twelve Magicians, eight were of African descent, two were Middle Eastern, and two were Asian. But it wasn't the colour of their skin that marked them out; Stonebridge was quite a cosmopolitan city, after all, and so was the Magical community. It was their *dress* that gave them away. The Africans wore the robes popular in their territories, brightly coloured with beads of precious metals and gems sown into the hems and cuffs, the Asians wore armoured leather, heavily Enchanted and chased with gold, the Middle Eastern men were covered in silver plate that shimmered with power.

They *had* to be Mercenaries, and very well paid ones, at that. Otherwise they never would have attacked a Magician in his own home, his Place of Power. Hell, even with their numbers, they had to be at least a *little* insane... unless they weren't told what they were up against (although, even if they had been given the broad strokes, the true extent of my defences was a closely-guarded secret, in preparation for days like this one).

Cassandra was inside the door, firing as well, for all the good it did against that much Sorcerous defence. I heard automatic fire coming from the upper floors, the rest of my Wardens, no doubt. The enemy skirmishers were firing off spells by the dozen, mostly bolts of lightning and shards of razor-sharp ice. But they were just the distraction, something to focus the attention of my Wardens while the group at the rear prepared the real strike.

Before I could warn anyone, a big lance of power, empowered by the entire rear group, smashed into the column shielding Lacy, causing it to shatter, the house's defences overwhelmed; her own shields *just* saving her from a messy death.

As it turned out, I may as well have stayed in bed. I'd arrived *just* too late to do a damned thing- except watch as Cassandra lost her temper.

"Alright, enough is enough, we've given them as many chances as we can," my Warden Commander snarled, "Mira, take them!"

"With pleasure," a silky voice said from the air.

There was a single, terrible pulse of energy, and six men simply *exploded* into fountains of gore. Blood and shards of bone, scraps of clothing, splinters of staves and staffs went *everywhere*. I saw the top half of a skull ricochet off one of the remaining Magicians' shield and impale another right through the neck, it was *horrifying*.

I grabbed a nearby vase (full of Tethys' favourite roses, by the way) and vomited heavily into it. That was bloody awful!

But it was over, they were running like hell, what few of them were left.

"Mira!" Cassandra said, "What the hell? I meant put them to sleep or something!"

"You were unspecific; I used my initiative. And I doubt they'll be back after *that*," Mira said.

"I didn't mean murder!" Cassandra protested.

"I'm just following your orders, it's not my fault if I got a lethal impression out of you, you should have been clearer," Mira answered.

"Well, I guess it's not *so* bad," Cassandra said, a touch sheepishly, "and it's not like it was anyone we're fond of."

I might have chuckled, if not for the fact that my lawn had been painted in a wonderful new colour called *'Hint of Lower Intestine'*...

Before I had a chance to reply, the familiar voice of Jeremy Braak boomed from beyond the main gates (the last person I expected to hear, let me tell you. The implications of him being involved in this mess were rather terrifying...).

"Mathew Graves! You have murdered agents of the SCA about their lawful business. Come forth and answer, or we shall cut you down with the full force of our power!"

The SCA?

Mira just killed *nine* SCA Agents?

Oh... bother.

I knew they couldn't *really* be SCA, but if someone had established the legal fiction... that could be very, *very* bad.

# CHAPTER 24

"Well, crap," I said, making my way to the front door.

"Matty..." Cassandra said, jumping at the sound of my voice, "I'm so sorry."

"Don't even start. You did your job. They invaded our home, and they didn't identify themselves," I said confidently, "They didn't, right?"

"Of course not!"

This was very bad. We needed a plan, some way of getting official help, someone who could stop this before it got worse. If Braak was involved, that likely meant Faust, and *that* likely meant some sort of Conclave involvement (which would explain the SCA declaration); that turned the complication factor up to eleven.

"Where's Demise?" I asked, not spotting her. She might be fast enough, and powerful enough, to sneak out the back and-

Suddenly there were screams from outside my walls, and Death Magic started to flow.

"Never mind," I said.

Braak turned, raising a gun to fire at something on the other side of the wall, where I couldn't see. There was a flash, a burst of energy, and suddenly he was flying through the air, tossed by an astonishingly well placed bolt of Space Magic. He tore into my lawn face-first, and slid to a halt with a whole bunch of broken bones and a much less pretty face.

And then Hopkins was there, along with Killian. I felt Kron bringing up the rear with Palmyra and about a dozen of their Wardens. Demise was front and centre, walking with

Hopkins, her black rod in hand, shimmering with Entropy as she glared around her, looking for threats.

Bless that little lunatic Warden of mine, she went for help!

And my cavalry was *terrifying*. They each had prisoners in tow, including a couple of the Sorcerers who'd run, now blubbering as Killian dragged them behind him with his Will. I walked out to meet them.

"Magnificent timing," I said, extending my hand, which Killian took in a crushing grip before pulling me into a one-armed hug.

"We don't like it when the lesser powers pick on our brother," he said, his voice filled with ice and steel. He stuck a thumb over his shoulder at the prisoners, "Can we borrow your dungeon?"

"Sorry, I don't have a dungeon-" I started to say.

"Yes we do," Tethys said, having emerged from her bolt hole (she had strict orders in the event of a crisis), "but most of it's not really equipped for actual... prisoners."

She pulled me into a hug and kissed my cheek before taking a sniff. At which point I remembered my little problem...

"Oh, my, you smell terrific," she said.

"I got musked again, maybe maintain a discreet distance for the next few days?"

"Un-bloody-likely," she said, suddenly very hard up against me, her hands everywhere.

"Oh God, I did not leave my lunch meeting to watch this... and is that a new cologne?" Palmyra said, also suddenly a little close.

"I was dosed by a Succubus again, would everyone calm down?" I begged.

"Oh, not again," Palmyra said, but she didn't back away.

"And how are you not smelling the vomit I just used to destroy your roses in the front hall?" I asked Tethys, who now had her nose in my ear.

"I'm working around it."

"Jen, could you take her for a sec?" I asked my sister, who was also staring.

"Hm?" she managed, biting her lip.

"Oh, not you too?"

"What? Of course not," she said, blushing horribly, "Don't be such a pervert."

She used her Will to pull Tethys away and suspend her in mid-air.

"Hey! That's not fair, who knows when I'll get an excuse like Succubus-musk again!" Tethys protested, her legs kicking out.

"You have the most interesting friends," Palmyra said with a snigger.

"Good grief," Kron said, her hand over her eyes, rubbing at the bridge of her nose.

"Jillian? Would you get Kandi for me?" I asked the Warden in question, who darted away.

"Just for curiosity's sake, what's wrong with the dungeon?" Killian asked.

Tethys chuckled evilly by way of an answer. I was suddenly rather worried.

Kandi was found, and I had her take Tethys indoors, while I hid behind an Illusion, after which Cassandra took us to a set of stairs leading down into the ground.

"How did I not know about this?" I asked as we started downwards.

The stairs had been carpeted, and the walls were brightly lit by brand new fixtures, all hidden behind a non-descript wooden door.

"We thought you did. Or that was the impression Tethys gave when she... appropriated it."

"Oh. So I probably don't *want* to know?" I asked.

"I shouldn't think so. There's a room down here with your name on the door," she said.

"That's not reassuring."

"I mentioned it to Tethys and she showed me the inside, there's nothing for you to be worried about. I'm scarred for life, but it's nothing sinister."

At the bottom of the stairs was a short corridor, with heavy wooden doors either side, except for the two rooms at the far end, which were heavily barred, each containing a hard wooden shelf, a nasty-looking stainless steel lavatory-sink hybrid and some manacles attached to the ceiling by chains.

"They'll have to go in there until you're ready to deal with them," Cassandra said, "the other cells aren't... well, they're not... that is to say..."

"They're too... specialised for our immediate needs?" I suggested, coming up with a fairly good idea of what Tethys would have done to a *dungeon*.

"Yes. That, we'll go with that," Cassandra said with a shudder.

"That bad?"

"Depends on your point of view, I suppose," she said.

"My God in heaven," Hopkins said from one of the doors, "I'm certain getting in that thing can't be good for you."

I went over and peeked.

I shouldn't have. It was a mess of straps and chains and fur... and some *things* on a shelf that I couldn't identify and had no wish to know the purpose of.

"Well, better than an actual dungeon, I suppose," I said, contemplating what looked very much like a saddle.

"Depends on what *that* thing is for," Hopkins said, pointing at what looked like a series of electrodes attached to a set of leather underpants.

"Hey, stay out of there, you!" Kandi said, bounding down the stairs and shoving the door shut, "You want in there, you make an appointment!"

"When all this is over, we are going to have a long talk about what constitutes the dignity of an Archon," Kron said, glaring at Kandi, who darted behind my back to cower (sensible girl).

"Matty, why do you smell so nice?" Kandi asked.

Bugger...

Alright, so there were a few messes to clean up...

My staff got the muck on the lawn cleaned up quickly enough, and Killian called in the *real* SCA to get rid of the bodies. That was the *easy* part. The parts involving prying secrets from people pretending to work for my government... that was going to be ugly, and I was in no fit state for it.

So, as soon as I was confident that they had everything they needed, I returned to my room. I needed to lie down, throw up and check on Mary (not necessarily in that order). I found my housemate playing cards with Tethys, who in turn had to be restrained before she could do some unseemly things to me. The odd thing was that she... she wasn't doing it right, if that makes sense. It was like she was trying too hard. And I remembered that she only became amorous *after* I'd told her about the musk... but that was a problem for later.

Demise Portalled Mary back to Naiad Hall, and she promised to visit again in a couple of days, which was rather decent of her, bearing in mind how well *that* visit had gone.

The interrogations, I was told, were not pleasant.

Mostly they involved Kron drilling into the minds of the invaders, and being none too gentle about it, either.

I wasn't there. It was a combination of cowardice and the simple fact that as soon as I got back to bed, and the adrenaline wore off, I was struck by a wave of stomach cramps and nausea sufficient to keep me quite supine for a while. And from there it got worse, much worse. As Sunday progressed, the aches in my muscles and head became shooting, then stabbing, pains, and I didn't have the Magic to numb it away.

Hopkins came in about dinner time to find me sweating and shaking, my head on fire and my muscles aching like hell. The Pixies had been in and out, and Cassandra hadn't been far away since the battle had ended. She'd even helped me into the bathroom, which was so far above and beyond the call of duty, she deserved a medal.

Cassandra had also decided that it was up to her to keep Tethys, Kandi and Demise away. The musk, plus my condition, would not make for a pleasant encounter. Cassandra was immune, though, as she didn't think of me in any sort of non-platonic way, not even a little, thank goodness (and neither did Mary, I noticed; she thought I smelt nice, but felt no other urges... damn it).

"Well, things aren't looking good," Hopkins said as she sat on the bed next to me.

"Huh?" I managed articulately.

"You seem to be rather in the crap, no doubt about it."

"So what else is new?"

"What's *new* is that now you've managed to piss off so many people that they've started working together."

I sat up (somehow) and rubbed my eyes.

"Come again?" I said.

"Some of this is conjecture, but it looks like Solomon has been watching you, and he's also been following you around, picking up the pieces you dropped. Braak and his SCA credentials, Thornsby and his mercenaries, the Witches, the Duellists, that professor that loathes you, Faust and his contacts.... At least *there* you came up lucky, Jocelyn mostly took those and ran for the hills when she found out who you were."

"So she's safe? She's alright?"

Hopkins smiled, "Yes, she's fine. But I think she's not too keen on you at the moment, and... and it looks like she was a plant... for Aiden Foltre."

"Foltre? The Primus, Foltre?" I asked, "What did I do to him?! And Jocelyn was a what?!"

He was the Magical equivalent of the Prime Minister. He was not a *big* fan of mine, true, but this was ridiculous.

She sighed and took my hand, "I have no doubt that she had real feelings for you, in her own way, but she is a Faust, Mathew. She's ambitious. What we're getting, is that her grandfather spoke to the Primus, and then Foltre spoke to her. I'm confident that she didn't know that she was ultimately working for her grandfather, she was just reporting on you to what she thought was her own government."

I didn't know what to say.

"Was it all a lie?" I asked softly.

"I don't know. She may have been recruited *after* she started seeing you. There's no way to know without asking her, and no way to guarantee the truth without... taking steps. Is that what you want?"

I sighed, and shook my head.

She carried on.

"We aren't sure about this part, but we think that when she found out who you *really* were, who she was spying on, she panicked and told Foltre where he could stick it before running for the first flight out of the country. We think that this attack was a last ditch effort to get you to reverse what you did to Faust before the girl's knowledge of who you are becomes public, and you become untouchable."

"That's complete madness!"

"Yes. And they worked with Solomon to get you while you were weakest, using his knowledge of your comings and goings to set up the perfect raid. They just didn't know about Demise and your book, thank God."

I didn't know what to say. Jocelyn... *again*?! Solomon making alliances with my enemies? The government wanting me captured...

"And where was Solomon during the attack?" I asked, trying to focus, and not spiral.

"Waiting for them to drag you out, we presume. Kron found traces of him on the roof opposite. He'd have swooped in while you were disabled; at least, that's what we think. They wanted you alive; he wants you dead, in the worst way."

"I can't believe Jocelyn..." I started, but couldn't finish. Just the thought was exhausting.

"Try not to be too hard on her. She tried to do the right

thing."

"The right thing would have been to warn me!"

"And risk pissing you off with another betrayal? She's a smart girl. Only a fool gets involved in one of *our* fights."

"So you think she knew something like this was coming?"

"Not that we could prove it without a probe or a truth stone, but... probably. Like I said, she's a smart girl," Hopkins said.

I sighed and rubbed my eyes, "Naturally."

"The Fausts have always been pragmatists, Mathew. She'd have learned that at her parents' and grandparents' knees since she was old enough to crawl. Alas, the current Lord Faust seems to have forgotten the lesson."

"Anyone else I should know about?" I asked.

"Oh yes. And this is why we're all rather hopping mad. The Primus isn't just a silent partner and a rubber stamp, he's in it right up to his neck," she said, her eyes going cold, "We're formulating a strategy now, but it doesn't look good for the bastard. The problem will be proving that he knew he was authorising an attack on the First Shadow, and not just Mathew Graves, Shadowborn Sorcerer... who, I'm sorry to say, is almost fair game as far as the world's concerned. We'll probably need Jocelyn for that."

"This has all the makings of a rather huge mess, Jen," I said.

"We can't let this stand, Matty. We will not allow it, we can't. It's one thing for Braak to try on some deniable crap for his other boss. It's quite another for a Primus to put his weight behind fielding an army against an Archon. There *must* be a reckoning."

"Even if it means a civil war?"

She laughed.

"Oh, you're sweet," she said, patting my thigh, "If they went up against *one* of us, they'd lose. All five? It's not even a competition. You think you've seen our power on display, but you haven't, really. Each of us can call on whole *armies*, Mathew. You will too, one day; hell, you could *now* if you put your mind to it. We do our best to be gentle, like you, but when we play for keeps, the world trembles."

I sighed, too sick to argue, and not really sure I wanted to.

"So what happens next?" I asked.

"Find Solomon, chop him up into tiny pieces, do it slowly, repeat as needed with the other conspirators."

"Try not to mangle Thornsby, Kandi wouldn't get over it."

"Acceptable, but he needs to do some time for what he's done."

"Fine with me."

"And Faust should go back to the Farm."

"Feel free to throw away the key."

"One more thing," she said, and now she was serious, very serious, "The time when you can pretend to be just another Shadowborn has come to an end, Mathew. I hate to say this, especially to you, but if you had simply revealed yourself, this would likely never have been an issue, and the fact that you kept your real nature a secret likely made everything much harder for everyone, you especially."

I rubbed my eyes, just wanting to collapse and go back to sleep.

"Nobody messes with the Archons, Mathew. It is universally known what happens to the people that do. Because of your hiding, people have deniability, excuses lined up, a whole mess of things they can do or say to get them clear of retribution.

"I have no doubt that Foltre and Braak will have any number of excuses lined up, though goodness knows how they're planning to justify attacking Blackhold, which is *known* to be the First Shadow's residence, but I'm sure they'll come up with something. You see the problem?"

I did, unfortunately.

"I just wanted... oh, I don't know anymore," I said, dropping back to the bed, thoroughly unhappy, "Tell whoever you think necessary, I won't make a fuss."

"And from now on I want you to take a Warden with you wherever you go. We have them for a reason, Mathew, and it's time you accepted their necessity. Going solo may have been an option when you were relatively anonymous. It's not anymore, alright?"

"No, but I'll do it anyway because you'll just nag if I don't."

"Quite right, you're learning."

She hopped onto the bed proper and rested her back against the headboard.

"How are you feeling?" she asked, more softly, resting her hand on my shoulder.

"Been better," I said tiredly, patting the hand.

"Here's something that will cheer you up, I heard Palmyra ask Tethys if she could come back once in a while and use your dungeon," Hopkins said.

"Oh God! Why would you tell me that?" I said, grimacing, "That's an image I can't scrub out of my head!"

"It does look fun in there. I might come by once in a while myself," she continued.

"Gaah!" I bellowed throwing my head under a pillow.

She linked her mind with mine, so I couldn't escape.

*Did you see those electro-shorts? I bet you'd look good in those...*

She tried to pull the pillow away, her thoughts becoming increasingly graphic as she tried to embarrass me to death. Finally she settled to tickling me until I gave up the pillow, at which point she laughed.

"You're a monster!" I said as she tweaked my nose.

# CHAPTER 25

Sunday rolled over into Monday morning... no, afternoon. Just after two, in fact. Damn, I was groggy...

I woke up with the Pixies playing tag around the room, their darting forms relaxed and obviously enjoying themselves. Cassandra was sleeping next to me, a really big, heavily enchanted stick in hand.

I felt absolutely dreadful.

I curled myself up into a ball and tried not to cry, it was that bad. I had a high fever, muscle cramps, and I was dizzy enough to need to close my eyes.

"Matty?" Cassandra said, waking up when I moved, "How're you feeling?"

"Okay."

"Liar."

I heard squelching sounds and then a cool, wet flannel was pressed to my forehead.

"Oh, thank you," I said with a sigh.

"Don't mention it."

I heard rustling and plastic crinkling.

"Pills. Muscle relaxants, anti-histamines, anti-emetics, a couple of others. Take them."

"Twist my arm," I said, extending my hand. She dropped quite a few pills into my palm and then a small bottle of water. I downed the lot and rested my head back onto my pillow.

"You should start feeling better soon," she said.

I sighed and tried to relax.

"How's everyone?" I asked.

"Not bad. On high alert in case Solomon tries something else."

"I think he's probably learned his lesson."

She chuckled, "That was delightfully gory, wasn't it?"

"Delightfully?"

"Well, interestingly."

"And you say *I'm* evil?"

"Oh, you are, I'm just a product of the environment *you* created, Lord Shadow."

I glared, but she just smirked.

I relaxed, letting the pills start to work, and they did *wonders*. Where had they been this whole time?

Maggie called me while I was dozing, which I appreciated. She'd missed the attack by minutes, her contacts failing her for once. She'd followed Solomon as best she could, but had lost him at the edge of the Old Quarter.

I enjoyed talking to her, she made me feel better. She said she'd be by later on to cheer me up, and I said that I was looking forward to it, smiling for a while after she'd hung up.

By the time the conversation was done, I was starting to feel a little more perky. My various symptoms had decreased enough that I felt like a little walk around the place, to get some fresh air, if nothing else (my bedroom was not the most fragrant of places by that point).

I took a stroll around the grounds, wrapped up against the winter chill, until I ended up at the central garden, where I lowered myself to the ground under my oak tree. Cassandra kept close by and settled herself on the bench opposite.

"What keeps you going through this?" she asked, her eyes on me very intently, "I know you could get the Black back if you wanted. So why are you fighting so hard?"

I chuckled and leaned my head against the warm bark.

"I think, at this point, it's simple bone-headed stubbornness," I admitted, "There are too many people insisting that I'm going to go dark, and I'm simply too contrary to let them be *right*."

She looked at me for a long moment, and then she burst

out laughing.

"Oh, I actually believe that! That would be just the most appropriate motivation for you."

"I'm trying not to take the peals of girlish laughter personally, but it's getting hard!"

She grinned widely at me and shook her head.

"Sorry, it's just sometimes I forget just how very... *you*, you are," she said, her tone very affectionate.

"Thanks... I think?"

"It's just... I've met a lot of Shadowborn, and Black Magicians. The last one was a woman named Uria, about fifteen years ago. I was with her when she turned. She was strong, very nearly a Sorcerer, smart, headstrong. When she first used the Black, I cried. I watched, and it was over *nothing*!"

She barked out the last word and stood, agitated as she paced back and forth. Any mention of Black Magic, and she got all riled up.

"She was sleeping with some idiot in the City, and I was having lunch with her when she found out that he was cheating on her. We saw him across the road with the other woman, a chance encounter, utterly idiotic and unlucky. But she saw, and she flipped right there. I never had a chance to stop her, I was so surprised. She was the most gentle creature I'd ever met, I once saw her jump at one of her *own* Shadows. But in an *instant*, Uria turned, using the Black like she'd been born with it.

"She lashed out, and the other woman exploded into this... fountain of black ooze that ate the man she loved and a hundred square feet of pavement besides. And then she just stood there, laughing for about five minutes while I sat there like a lemon, too shocked to move."

She stopped pacing and came over to me, kneeling in front of me.

"But you, you ridiculous little man... you used the Black, and the first thing you did was save my life, in an admittedly gruesome way, really, *really*, gruesome, by the way, but you didn't kill, and the second thing you did was to have me shoot you," she said with a smile, "I'm not scared of you anymore, Mathew. If I'm honest, I always was, a little. But if you did ever start using the Black, I'm not sure it would be the end of the world."

I snorted, "Don't you, of all people, give me permission!"

She smacked my arm and dropped next to me.

"This really is a beautiful place," Cassandra said after a while, "the last time I was here, before you, it wasn't beautiful. Nothing about this house was. There was no laughter here, no joy. It wasn't a place you could relax, or live, or feel safe. No First Shadow before you was... well, *you*, simply put. I have no idea what made you like this, but you are all wrong! It's almost as if the powers went to the wrong brothers. Desmond is harsh and cold, the very thing a Light Magician shouldn't be, and you're the opposite, smart, compassionate, *gentle* in a way Shadowborn shouldn't be, and First Shadows *never* are. I mean, don't get me wrong, I know you're also a cunning little bastard with a vindictive streak a mile wide, but you're good people. I wanted you know that I knew that."

"Thanks Cassie," I said with a smile, "That means a lot."

She squeezed my arm again and leaned back against the tree.

We were there for a while, chatting a little, but otherwise just relaxing.

Kandi came running in about half an hour later, barefoot, wearing a t-shirt and shorts.

"Oh, thank God!" she said, darting for me, "You've got to do something! If I spend any more time with her, she's going to break something!"

"What?" I asked as she dropped to the ground and pulled me forward so she could crouch behind my back, which in no way hid her, by the way.

"Tethys! She won't leave me alone!" Kandi said, which made Cassandra smirk.

"I'm coming precious," said a silken voice from around the edge the doorway, "I can smell you, there's no escaping me."

I shivered, Tethys did more for me with her voice than a lot of women could do with their whole bodies.

Kandi emitted a little whimper and buried her head in my shoulder.

"Help me, Matty, I'm *so* chafed and sore," she said, wrapping her arms around my chest, "and you still smell amazing, by the way."

Tethys walked around the door, wearing a silk dressing gown, red and sumptuous, revealing long lines of perfect flesh that I had a sudden urge to kiss...

I shook my head to clear it. Now was *not* the time for that...

"So, my pet, you seek the protection of the Magician, clever. But he can't save you now, he's still too weak. But, I suppose I might be willing to accept a trade. He is, after all, the sacrificial type," Tethys said, sidling closer, her walk very slow and rolling, drawing attention to all the right things, her eyes suddenly very intently on mine.

"He'll take the deal!" Kandi said before darting away and letting me fall back against the tree with a thump.

Tethys smiled and continued towards me.

"Easy you," Cassandra said, lifting her club so Tethys could see it.

"Please, I'm harmless," Tethys said, smiling sweetly at my Warden, "I just want a cuddle."

"A cuddle?" Cassandra said with a raised eyebrow.

"I was trying to be discreet, have you no subtlety?" Tethys said.

She stopped close to me and extended her hand, which I lifted mine to. We entwined our fingers, and it felt good, my heartbeat picking up.

"See?" Tethys said, "He wants to come play with me."

"Of course he does," Cassandra said, "he's a male, and he's

been dosed by Succubus musk. But he's also sick as a parrot and in horrific withdrawal. So maintain a discreet distance or I'll introduce you to Morticia."

She patted the club.

"You named your bat?" I asked.

Cassandra stuck out her tongue.

"Would you like to come with me, Matty?" Tethys said, ignoring the threat.

I brought her knuckles to my lips and brushed a kiss over them. She smiled at me.

"Don't trust yourself to speak, eh?" she said, grinning ever more widely.

I shook my head, nuzzling at her hand.

Tethys licked her lips and sat next to me despite Cassandra's warning. She leaned her head on my shoulder and pressed her side against mine.

I freed my hand and put the arm around her. It was immensely... comforting, funnily enough. I fell asleep almost immediately.

I woke up with the smell of chicken soup wafting its gentle way up my nostrils, my head in Tethys' lap. Kandi was carrying a small tray, from which that wonderful smell was coming. Cassandra was back on the bench watching me with amused confusion.

"Hi," I said with a stretch, sitting up reluctantly.

"Soup!" Kandi said, putting the tray down across my lap on its little feet, "Miss Jenkins says it's the best cure-all ever devised by man."

"Thank you, Kandi," I said, taking a spoonful and finding it fantastic, soothing and filling, with little bits of perfectly moist chicken, mushrooms, carrots and noodles.

Tethys smiled at Kandi and the little redhead beat a hasty retreat, a blush colouring her cheeks.

"How are you?" Tethys asked as I ate.

"Good," I said, "those pills helped, thank you."

"I should get a medal, by the way," she replied, "You can't just fall asleep on me like that in your state! That's like a limping gazelle snoozing next to a hungry lion."

"I know, just think about all the *other* platonic things I'm going to be able get away with now," I whispered in her ear.

She shivered; but then she realised what I'd said and pouted adorably.

"When you're better, I'm making you pay for that," she said menacingly.

I smiled at her and she smiled back, and then her brow scrunched in confusion.

"What?" I asked.

"Why am I not jumping you?" she asked, "I can still smell the musk, it should be making me crazy, but I'm sitting here with you, and I'm just... happy. I'm just my regular horny."

I went so red that both she and Cassandra laughed.

"It's nice that I can still do that to you, Love," Tethys said, kissing my cheek.

I shook my head and concentrated on my soup.

"Maybe you just exhausted yourself on Kandi?" I offered.

"Doubt it," Tethys said, "And between you and me, I'm not getting as much... satisfaction as I used to. It's like Kandi's being watered down, and it's taking more to get the job done."

"Tethys, I just can't know that!" I said, blushing again.

She chuckled, "Want I should tell you exactly which of the things she does that work best?" she asked, very slowly.

I shivered again and turned to look at her, my dearest friend. I smiled, and she smiled back. I cupped her cheek gently and leant my forehead against hers.

"Hey, stop it," she mumbled, "I'm trying to be dirty over here!"

Cassandra snorted, "And the Succubus calls me dumb."

"What was that?" Tethys asked sweetly, but in a tone that promised revenge in the near future.

"Love, you gerbil," Cassandra said with a grin, "It makes you immune to the musk. How do you not know that? When you love the musk-ee more than you're attracted to them, it overrules the Magic. And it has to be a *lot* more, just F.Y.I.."

Tethys looked dumbfounded for a second, and then she turned to glare at me.

"Not a word," she said, waggling a finger at me in a threatening manner.

I couldn't help but smile, moved more than I can say.

She rolled her eyes and looked away, but I saw her face colour a little.

"And as for Kandi, the reason you're not getting as much out of *that* is because neither of you are giving it your all anymore," Cassandra said, "Can't imagine why that is..."

My Warden was looking increasingly smug. I didn't get it and decided to finish my soup instead of puzzling things out. My brain wasn't up to fighting speed yet.

"That any good?" Tethys asked, nodding at my bowl. I offered her a spoonful and she smiled as she tasted, "Not bad. Not very bulky, though. How many nutrients can there possibly be in chicken soup?"

"It's enough that he can eat something without returning it, don't nag," Cassandra said.

"I do *not* nag!" Tethys bristled.

"What happened the last time he fell over in the garden?" Cassandra asked.

"Nothing, I don't know what you're talking about," Tethys said, looking away sheepishly.

"You fussed over the tiniest little graze I've ever seen for an *hour*. He's a very talented Flesh Magician, could likely fix his own broken *neck* and you panicked over one of his boo-boos," Cassandra said, that evil look back on her face.

"Hey, that hurt, and you know I have no pain threshold," I said.

"You just liked the pretty lady touching your leg, let's not try and pretend victimhood," Cassandra replied.

I muttered and went back to my soup.

"I certainly didn't *mind*," I whispered. Tethys smiled.

"You never do, you pent up little pervert," she whispered back, nudging my side.

"Isn't pervert a little harsh?" I asked.

"Nope," Tethys said.

I sighed.

"When you're better, we'll discuss it," she purred into my ear.

"Oh this is just getting ridiculous," Cassandra said, making Tethys pull back.

"You are such a mood-killer!" Tethys hissed.

"That's rather my job until the musk wears off," Cassandra said.

"And I'm immune!" Tethys replied.

"But no less a Succubus," Cassandra pointed out, "and he's fragile at the moment."

Tethys sighed theatrically.

"Was there no other word you could have used?" I asked.

"I'm sorry, I'm sorry," Cassandra said, "*she's* fragile at the moment."

I gave her my best glare... while the pair of them laughed.

I'll spare you the details of the rest of my convalescence, suffice to say that it was bad, and it took me a good two weeks to recover completely. I was able to go back to school after the first week was over, but Demise came with me. She was used to sleeping in with me due to that monitoring-mess last year.

Mary came into my room at Naiad without knocking exactly *once*.

Demise had a sword at her throat faster than I could blink. I still didn't know where she was hiding that thing...

God, the screaming... then the swearing, the tears, the guilt-trip...

I had to buy *so* much ice cream. I literally emptied three shops of Häagen Dazs, and she still wouldn't let me off the hook until I'd sat through three seasons of Gossip Girl (and I thought getting stabbed hurt...).

Demise, naturally, took it all stoically, but I think she was taking notes as to how Mary was controlling me for later use, which was worrying.

"So, all I need to do is tug on your ear and you'll do what I tell you?" she asked mischievously.

It was another Monday morning, eleven days since I'd used the Black. I was over the worst, and just fighting off the last of the flu-like symptoms. My Magic was back up and running, and I was feeling much improved. I'd moved back into Naiad Hall on Saturday night, and spent Sunday getting fussed over by Mary and the flock.

"Probably."

"Is it some sort of fetish? Would I like it?" she asked very evenly.

I gave her an evil look, but she just smiled at me.

We were walking across the square in front of Naiad, heading for my first class of the day (my professors had been very understanding about my absence, thanks mostly to Tethys' writing skills). As we got closer to the Magic building, a distinct silence had started to descend. I barely noticed, but Demise seemed to be a little on edge.

"Something wrong?" I asked as we walked through the front doors.

"People are staring at you. I don't like it."

"A threat?" I asked.

"I don't think so, just attention."

"Any of it female?" I asked, though it was an automatic response. I was still rather stuck on Jocelyn, though I couldn't tell you why. Stupid hormones.

She rolled her eyes and swatted my shoulder, "Coming here has done nothing good for your sense of propriety," she replied.

I chuckled, stuffing some notes back into my bag, "Nor

has it really done much for my love life, so excuse me for a little desperation."

"No, this I cannot do."

I sighed and made my way along the necessary corridor.

"It's changed a lot since my day," Demise said.

"Really? You never told me you came here."

She smiled, "This was back when there was still a 'St Margaret's College for Gifted Ladies', meaning 'girls with Magic'. This was in the days before Suffrage, mind you, quite a few days before, in fact. So, it was an all-girls school, and getting in was tricky. But it was a good time for me; I made friends and learned my craft. My Mistress was an excellent teacher; she's still around, does the same job over in the U.S. somewhere."

"I have trouble picturing you as a student," I said with a smile, "I always rather thought you'd been hatched fully grown with a sword in your hand."

"Thank you; that's the image I was going for."

I pulled the door of the classroom open, and there was a deathly hush as I walked to my usual seat, followed by an almost palpable tension in the air. Demise moved to the back of the room, where she could watch and be ready for any threat.

Hadleigh came in, took one look at me... and burst into tears.

Different than her usual reaction, but certainly *not* better. She darted over and dropped to her knees next to my seat, her hands clenched into fists in front of her chest.

"My Lord, I can only beg your forgiveness!"

Crap. Looks like Hopkins wasn't kidding about telling people about me, and damn if word hadn't spread *quickly*! That explained the looks I'd been getting...

"Um, what for?" I asked, utterly mortified.

"For how I treated you! For my prejudice and my thoughts! I am so sorry, if only I'd known! Please, please forgive me?!"

More crying, I was horribly embarrassed.

"Professor," I finally managed, kneeling next to her and putting my hands around hers, she stopped crying, ending in a croaking sob, "You have nothing to fear from me, you do know that?"

Her lips trembled, I'm not sure she believed me.

"You are a good person, and yours is a most honourable profession. You were scared and you were still willing to teach me. Why do you think that I would have *anything* against such a person?" I said, gently squeezing her trembling hands.

She emitted one more tremendous sob, and I smiled at her as she nodded.

"You mean that, Sir?"

"I can't afford to hold anything against you, Ma'am," I said with a grin, "If you fail me, I'll never get my Level Ten Certificate."

She choked for a second and then she laughed.

I helped her up and she took a shuddering breath. I patted her shoulder and she went back to the front of the class, where she arranged her notes carefully, and started the lecture as if nothing had happened.

It was certainly a more relaxed affair after that; there was no longer an aura of barely-suppressed terror coming from Hadleigh, and that lightened the atmosphere immeasurably. It was astonishing, really; show someone a Shadowborn Sorcerer, and they'll run. Shadowborn Archon? Maybe this might be a good thing, after all?

"That was... very kind, Mathew," Demise said as we sat down for a sandwich after the morning lectures, "I know what she put you through, the prejudice and the fear. You could have handled that differently."

"No I couldn't," I said with a smile.

Demise returned it, "No, I don't suppose you could, you big girl."

I snorted and went back to my meal.

The attention explained, Demise relaxed a little, but

remained vigilant, eyes darting to every movement, hands never far from her weapons.

Not that it helped when the *real* threat materialised.

It was Tuesday morning, that same week, and we were walking towards my Telepathy lecture. I was whistling, quite cheerful, in fact, feeling like the world was becoming a brighter place.

We were coming from breakfast at a nearby cafe, making our way into a small garden square bound by three halls of residence and a small gymnasium. It was very quiet, especially for the time of morning.

Demise noticed the problem well before I did, and put a hand on my shoulder before we were a quarter of the way across the grass.

"Hm?" I said.

"Something's not right," she said, backing us away. I frowned and put up my Shields; so did she. I cast Mage Sight and scowled.

There were four alleys leading into the square, one behind us, one in front, one either side. The three ahead of us were now blocked by some rather impressive Spellwork, a combination of Illusion and Mental Suggestion Magic, designed to keep people away from this place. I felt it as another Illusion dropped onto the alley behind us, and I spun, Shadows gathering around my feet.

Was it Solomon? Had he finally finished screwing around?

After a thought like *that* (and the terror that came with it), I almost relaxed when the first of the Witches appeared, coming through the various alleys to surround us. There were thirty-two of them, with Jones front and centre, straight ahead. They were armed, this time, with a collection of staves and wands made of wood and bone. They looked... determined, and *hungry*.

"Witches," I said to Demise, who nodded, drawing her

stave, which transformed into a long-bladed sword, shimmering with Entropy.

And not just Witches, either. A Muffling Spell descended on the whole square, designed to keep what was happening within from being heard outside. There was no Witch alive that could maintain that *and* the Illusions, and I could feel them both being controlled by one practitioner (which annoyed me. Using Illusion Magic to mess with people was *my* thing!).

It didn't take long for my newest headache to materialise, either. He appeared from the alley opposite us, walking sedately, like he was out for a morning stroll. He smiled as he slid up next to Jones, his flinty eyes locked onto me, a smug expression all over his face.

"You," I hissed, angry and feeling trapped (not a good combination for rational thought).

"Yes me," Professor Aldwich said, that sneer on his face growing wider, more satisfied, "Shall we resume that discussion on courtesy now, 'My Lord'?"

# CHAPTER 26

Thanks to Demise, it was now impossible to ambush us, which essentially meant that the end of this was a foregone conclusion. The problem was that, for the most part, these were *kids*. Stupid, ignorant kids who almost certainly didn't understand what kind of horror they were walking into. But they were also Magicians, and that made them dangerous, even in their limited way. If we started fighting, then I couldn't think how we were going to get out of this without Demise killing a *lot* of them.

An *awful* lot of them. Demise's training hadn't included a lot of non-lethal tactics, and I wasn't going to hamstring her by ordering her to go against her nature; that might get her killed.

"What do you want?" I asked, figuring I should keep them talking as long as I could, hoping that a solution would present itself.

"Oh, it's not what I want, is it, Ladies?" he said.

The women looked smug, a couple licked their lips. I really was feeling the idiot. I'd been warned about the Witches, *repeatedly*. I shouldn't have assumed that they were completely neutralised. And now, here they were, eyeing me up like Cassandra stared at a plate of cupcakes.

It didn't take a genius to figure out how they'd been roped into this. You can just imagine what sort of a boost they'd get from drinking even a *little* of my blood. If they tried Demise's they'd likely melt from the inside (Death Mage and all), but mine was worth its weight in gold to them, now that I'd been outed as an Archon (assuming that there weren't any residual bits of the Black floating around in there, which would be even worse for them than Death Magic).

This *couldn't* be allowed to go that far. I had to get through to them, remind them of who they were. They weren't Red Witches, and they would not become so, not if I could possibly help it.

Because they'd die if they did. Red Witches were *not* tolerated in a civilised society.

"Alright, what do the ladies want?" I asked, calmly and softly, like I hadn't a care in the world. It was important to keep everyone cool (especially Demise!).

"You, little Archon," said Jones, "Every last drop of you."

She was particularly striking that morning, with a certain predatory grace to her movements that hadn't been there before. She wore black, neck to ankle; skirt and bustier over heavy under-covers made of soft leathers and silk.

"And then?" I asked.

She looked confused for a second, like she hadn't been expecting my reply, which was rather the point of it.

"And then you'll be dead?" she said, still sounding confused.

"I mean, and then what for *you*. Once you've shared my life's blood around thirty or so women, making them all murderers, then what? What's the power for?" I asked.

"What does that matter? Once we have your power, we can do what we want! We'll be a force to be reckoned with," she said, a dark smile crossing her face.

"So, it's just power that you're after? You have no goals? No idea what you want to do with it? Power is the end?" I said, letting confusion cross my features. Behind me, Demise was tense, her sword ready, her Magic on the cusp of action. I needed to defuse this before she became agitated enough to start swinging.

"Power is all," Jones hissed.

I smiled sadly at her.

"Does it keep you warm?" I asked.

At that, she looked even more confused, and so did the others.

"What?"

"I can see your aura. You're no murderer, not yet. You've got a lot of death on you, but it's all animal, nothing human. Taking a sentient life leaves you cold, empty; *stained.* Do you think that the power you gain from my life will keep you warm after *that*? Do any of you?" I said, looking around the square now.

"Don't listen to him!" Aldwich barked, "He gets in your head!"

"Power is a means," I said, ignoring him.

"Spoken like someone who *has* it!" Jones snapped, trying to regain control of the conversation. The other Witches were starting to think about what they were doing. With any luck, that's all it would take to stop a bloodbath.

"All power!" I replied, "Political, physical, oratory, charismatic, Magical. All of it is simply a means to an *end.* Power without purpose is nothing but self indulgence. The things that are *really* worth having can't be gotten with power. Of *any* sort."

I was looking around me. Many of them were listening, but they were on a knife's edge, one bad word away from violence.

"Power *doesn't* keep you warm at night. It can't hold your hand when you're hurt, or nurse you back to health when you're sick. It can't care for you when you're old," I let my voice soften, "Power only loves power, and you can't take it with you when you die. Trying leaves your life even more empty at the end than it was at the beginning."

A few of them were looking doubtful, even Aldwich, even Jones.

"When the end comes, we all have to pay the debts we incur in this life. Murder in the pursuit of power comes with a *terrible* price. And it means that you've given up on all those things that truly make life worth living. Power cost me the best thing in my life. I'd give it all up for one more day with her," I said, realising that it wasn't entirely a lie, "Don't be like me. Go home, find someone you care for, and who'll care for you. Live well and die happy, surrounded by hope, not lonely ambition."

They were quiet for a long minute, some obviously thinking, others confused.

"We can just go?" one of the ones from that first night (Patty, I think) asked, "You won't chase us?"

"I didn't before, did I?" I pointed out.

She nodded, and took her friend by the wrist, backing towards a gate which stood in front of an alley.

"Stay where you are!" Jones barked again.

Patty looked back at me.

"Nobody will stop you leaving. I give you my word as Lord of the Deep," I said, my voice firm, the tone hard enough to make Jones swallow.

Patty and her friend left, and then more and more of them too, until only Jones and about half a dozen remained, along with Aldwich.

"I'll make them pay," Jones said, glaring at me.

"No you won't," I said, my voice cold; she stepped back, readying her Magic, fear banishing the self-satisfaction from her expression, "Those girls, each and every one, are under *my* protection. The protection of the First Shadow, do you understand what that means? Do you know what happens to *you* if you hurt them?"

"Screw you!" she shouted.

And just like that, it started.

It didn't last long.

Demise had just been waiting for an excuse.

I'm just thankful that she had a strong sense of justice and fairness.

She killed Aldwich, though. There was nothing I could do to stop that. He had blood on his hands, and he'd wanted very much to add mine to it. I'd seen him gather electricity for a nasty strike, and Demise would have, too.

She made it quick, though.

Her Magic flowed, and her reflexes were boosted to superhuman levels. The only other people I knew who could move as fast as Demise were Cassandra and Kron. She lashed out exactly *once* with her sword as she passed by Aldwich.

His neck vanished in a cloud of Death Magic, and his head rolled neatly to a stop next to Jones, even as she was raising her hands and speaking the words to a spell (lazy, you didn't need Magic words, there was no such thing, they were only memory and concentration aids, and those were for amateurs).

She stopped immediately, her face filling with terror as my Warden walked slowly towards her, blade outstretched.

"Stand down in the name of the First Shadow," Demise said, pointing the tip of her sword right at Jones' neck, her voice cool and steady, "You are all under arrest, get down on the ground or lethal force will be used."

All but Jones dropped immediately.

"I won't surrender!" she shouted, but her voice was shaking.

"Don't be stupid, girl! The Lord Shadow could have killed you a hundred times over, and so could I. Now get down before any other stupid thing happens!"

Jones obeyed, but her eyes almost pulsed with hatred as she did so.

I sighed as I pulled out my phone.

"Can't even take you for a walk from A to B without you starting a small war," Demise muttered.

"How was this *my* fault?!"

"It's always your fault somehow," she replied, giving me a glare.

I called Hopkins, who called the SCA, who sent Braak of all people. He had the good grace to look sheepish, at least.

"Hello," he said as he walked into the square.

"They sent the traitor?" Demise asked, her voice quiet, almost a whisper as she looked him over.

"Or possibly a patsy, depending on who you ask," I replied.

Demise looked him in the eye. Braak swallowed loudly.

"Don't give me cause to notice you again, turncoat," she snarled.

Braak nodded vigorously and pulled out a notebook.

I lowered my defences, thinking that we were probably safe, and then we gave him our statements. After which, there was the discussion of what was to happen to the Witches.

"I want to take them in for questioning," Braak said, "They did attack an Archon after all."

"I don't think that'll be necessary."

"What?" Demise, Braak and Jones all said at once.

"I think that the young lady and I can come to an understanding," I said, calling my Will.

Jones was pulled up to her feet and she squeaked. I stepped up to her.

"Do you understand that the rest of the Coven is now protected?" I asked, sliding a Mental probe into her mind so I could make sure she was being honest.

"I do," she said.

She was telling the truth.

"Do you intend to do any of them harm?"

She shook her head, again no deception.

I nodded.

"Good," I said, "I meant what I said, it wasn't a trick. Please, remember my advice, before it's too late. Listening to people like Aldwich can only end badly."

She didn't react, just stared at me, rage, hate and disgust flitting over her features. I shrugged and turned my back on her.

*Big* mistake.

It turned out that she had a little knife in her sleeve, three inches long and razor-sharp. In a single move, she cut my throat. Before I even had the chance to scream, she'd clamped her lips to my neck and drank down a good mouthful before Demise could act, darting up to us and punching her hard in the face.

Jones' nose broke, and she flew back, revealing the slice in my neck, which had gone right through both my jugular and carotid. My blood sprayed into the air, and the other Witches suddenly leapt towards me, overcome by blood-lust, and out of their minds from hunger. I dropped to my knees, my vision already blurring from the trauma.

Two of them dropped to the ground and started lapping my blood off the grass while the others went for my neck, their eyes wide and ravenous. That was *not* a good sign, losing control like that was indicative of some *very* dark practices.

There was no time for anything subtle. I called my Shadows and sent them flailing at my attackers. That would hopefully buy me the time to cast the quick triage spell which would keep me alive.

Jones, glutted on my blood, her Well full of my power, called electricity from the air and threw a bolt of Lightning at my Shadows. The light it released tore a hole through my constructs and let a small surge of energy strike my chest hard enough to char my shirt and the flesh underneath. The pain affected my concentration and I almost lost my preparations for the Triage Spell.

I sent more power into my Shadows and got back to work, finally casting the Triage Spell just as Jones threw another pair of Lightning Bolts. My reinforced Shadows took the first hit, and I put up Will in time to absorb the second. She snarled in frustration and pulled back her arm, calling a much larger attack this time. Energy started to gather, but before she could cast it, Demise slammed into her like a battering ram.

Death Magic flared, and my Warden punched a fist right *through* Jones' chest and out the other side while she brought up her sword and stabbed the Witch straight through the head. A single twist and a pull, and the woman flew apart, the edges of her wounds turning to dust as Demise flung the bits away.

I might have thrown up again, but I was busy gasping for air, feeling very lightheaded. I cast a stimulant spell to keep my mind sharp while I started weaving the Flesh Lattice that would close the wound in my neck. I had no attention to spare for anything else, but it wasn't like I was necessary.

Demise and Braak charged right into the Witches, laying about them with weapon and Spell. I had no idea how the pair managed to avoid killing the girls, because they were *vicious*. I saw teeth fly, limbs bend at horrific angles, joints get dislocated and skin bubble from the sudden, acidic introduction of chemical energy. It was ugly, but at least it was over quickly, leaving the Witches in an insensible, mangled heap, but *alive*.

I lowered my Shadows as the last of the screams stopped and Demise came over.

"Christ!" she said, inspecting the damage. She pulled out her phone and started dialling.

"Lady Hopkins; it's Demise, there's been an incident."

Oh dear. Hopkins had been snarky enough on the phone when I'd called her a few minutes ago. She was going to yell...

I couldn't hear Hopkins' side, but Demise said:

"He's hurt, but coping, Ma'am. I would have called Blackhold for help, but I'm the only Portal-trained Magician we have, and I dare not leave him."

"Braak, Ma'am, and we know he can't be trusted," Demise said, glaring at the SCA agent, who was securing the Witches with Spelleater Manacles.

"Thank you, Ma'am," Demise finished.

She turned to me and stood next to me, her eyes everywhere.

"How's it going?" she asked.

"Not too badly," I answered, "the wound's simple, but it's full of germs, I don't think her knife was very clean."

"You lost a lot of blood, how's your thinking?"

"Fuzzy but functional," I said, concentrating.

A Portal opened before I was half way done, and Hopkins came out of it, followed by Cassandra, Jillian, and six of Hopkins' own cadre of personal soldiers. They were professionally trained, one and all, tough and competent. They were normally a cheerful, tight-knit bunch, but today they looked seriously miffed. They wore black tactical gear that you might find in a military assault force and carried various automatic weapons as well as staffs, wands and swords. They looked imposing, to say the least.

And there was Cassandra and Jillian, in suits, their weapons concealed, very understated. I know which group I'd prefer to have at my back.

Hopkins initially started moving towards me, but saw that I was in the middle of healing myself and stood off, moving towards Demise instead, Cassandra hot on her heels.

"What happened?" Hopkins asked.

I barely heard what they were saying, and didn't really remember it until later. Demise explained what had happened, and Hopkins' face went white with fury. Cassandra started eyeing up the remaining Witches with a rather evil eye. I finished casting the spell that would stitch me back together, and I felt a tingle as it went to work. The wound on my neck started to close, itching all the while.

"I still don't know how he did it," Demise added softly, "He actually managed to talk most of them down! Two dozen Witches who'd been promised Archon blood, and he talked them into just... leaving, it should have been impossible!"

"Our Mathew always did have a silver tongue," Hopkins replied with a smile, "Just pray you never get into an argument with him, he'll twist you around so badly you'll end up taking his side somehow. I hate it when he does that..."

Demise snorted.

My wound slowly pulled itself closed, and I cast a little Spell to stimulate blood cell production. I also needed fluids, so I pulled water from the air and drank it greedily, it helped.

"I just can't leave you alone, can I?" Cassandra asked when she was sure I was finished and that she wouldn't be interrupting anything important.

"It seems not," I said with a smile, "all I can say is thank God, Demise was here, I'd be dead otherwise. Very dead. And eaten, probably."

"See? I told you that having Wardens around is good for you, didn't I?"

"Yes," I grumbled.

"So...?" she said, nudging my side.

"You were right."

"And...?"

"Really?" I asked with a wince.

She nodded, smiling evilly.

"And I was wrong," I continued.

"There we go," she said, patting my back.

I grumbled and she laughed. Hopkins came over.

"Really, Matty, Witches? Again?"

"It wasn't my fault, I swear!" I protested.

"This is starting to get ridiculous, Mathew!" Hopkins said, "Can't you go five minutes without something trying to kill you?!"

"I thought I'd successfully talked her down! How was I to know she was a raving lunatic?"

"Here's a clue: *She was a Witch!*" Hopkins almost shouted.

"They're not all bad."

"Oh yes, thanks a bunch for *that*, by the way. *Twenty-five* witches now under your protection, and thus, ours? That's just bloody terrific. Do you know what 'under your protection' means? It means they can claim sanctuary whenever they want! They can come to your *house*."

"Oh, what an unfortunate turn of events. I was, after all, definitely going to turn away a bunch of kids that asked for my help, and now I can't, oh bother," I said dryly.

"I will beat you to death with your own shoes one day, Mathew Graves, I swear to God!" she barked, but then she dropped to the ground and pulled me into a hug, "Stupid boy."

"You're starting to confuse the crap out of me," I said, returning the hug.

She thumped my back, but gently(-ish) and pulled away.

"Stop getting hurt!" she said, "I can't handle the stress! Any more of this and I'm going to have to start seeing a Healer for my blood pressure!"

"I'm fine. A little patch job and I'm ready to go."

"Yeah, right back to bed, if I'm any judge," Cassandra muttered.

"Well excuse me for being a little tuckered out!" I said, glaring at her.

Cassandra rolled her eyes, so did Hopkins.

"How do you manage this day-in, day-out?" Hopkins asked, "He's such a weed!"

"Hey!" I complained.

"Mostly I ignore it," Cassandra replied, "That's the main reason I let him move the Succubus in. She likes that he's weedy, takes the pressure off me."

"This is starting to get a little hurtful."

"Poor little fella'," Cassandra said, patting my head like I was an errant puppy.

"I'll sulk," I threatened.

They sniggered like there weren't two corpses nearby; I guess they were used to that sort of thing.

"Why is Braak walking around, by the way?" I asked.

"He was following orders from the Primus," Hopkins said, turning a glare on the agent, "He gets a slap on the wrist. No doubt when Kraab gets back from wherever he is, there'll be more of a reckoning, but at the moment, we're stuck with him, unfortunately."

I sighed and tried not to grumble.

"You head off to class, now," Hopkins said, "try to keep

a normal schedule going until this breaks. There's likely to be fallout, though. Aldwich was a respected man."

"I'm going to get blamed for this, aren't I?" I asked, resigned.

"It's you, so... probably," Hopkins said.

"Crap."

"And you may wish to do something about the blood on your shirt?" Hopkins suggested evenly, "don't want to scare the villagers and all?"

I looked down at the mess and winced, "You may have a point."

# CHAPTER 27

After that start to the day, I would have expected the rest of it to have been rather a horror show as I relived the deaths over and over, but Porter rather took my mind off it.

I walked into her classroom, Cassandra in tow this time, and saw my professor's face break out into a mischievous smile. She stood and came over to me.

"Your highness," she said with a smirk as she gave a clumsy curtsey.

"Oh, ha, ha!" I said.

She snorted and smacked my shoulder hard enough to bruise, "That's from Vanessa, she says you're a dick for not telling her, and now she feels like an idiot for not spotting it. She says she'll administer proper retribution later."

"That sounds unpleasant," I said warily.

"You'd better believe it!" Porter replied, "The last time a boy pissed her off this much, she married him!"

I must have looked confused, because she started to explain.

"It was on a dare, the boy in question got her mad, a wager was made, it ended badly, and let's leave it at that."

"Do we have to? That sounds like good dirt to me!" I said with a grin.

"Get to your cushion, or does his majesty need a red carpet these days?" she asked sweetly.

I muttered mutinously, but did as I was told.

"I *love* her," Cassandra whispered in my ear after introducing herself to Porter and having a quiet word while I sat down.

"Me too, she's a great teacher," I said warmly.

"I was thinking more along the lines that she makes you her bitch."

"The other Archons have nice Wardens," I said acidly.

"That's enough of your back talk!" she said with a faux-growl.

"Yes, Ma'am," I replied, which made her snort.

The lesson got underway; this time it was all about practicing mental manipulations with a view to healing mental trauma.

Generally those classes had been about defence, but now were moving towards treatment. This part of the module covered repairing damage done to a person's mind; from excising painful memories to healing mental scars. I had already been pretty good at both, but the methods Porter been teaching had been elegant and refined, not to mention far simpler.

I loved learning that stuff.

Now, as you might imagine, finding volunteers to let unqualified Magicians poke around inside their heads wasn't easy. So Porter had a workaround.

Each of us was given a blue crystal about the size and shape of a human brain, into which Porter had implanted a basic mental structure that we had to examine and probe to find the damage, which we then had to repair. It was an impressive construct, and I enjoyed using it. It was almost like the real thing.

I was at that for the majority of the day, followed by shielding practice for the last two hours of the afternoon. Porter had produced some challenging defences that had nearly gotten the better of me. I chatted with her for a while afterwards, smiling most of the time.

Thanks to her, I hadn't had the spare attention to think about Jones and Aldwich, for which I would always be grateful.

At the end of the day I went home to Blackhold. I felt the need for security that night.

Tethys met me at the front door (obviously informed by Demise about what had happened) and shook her head before taking me by the hand to her study so I could explain myself.

She sat me down on a sofa, an antique originally from the Palace at Versailles. Sitting on it made me *very* uncomfortable for fear of breaking something both steeped in history *and* worth six figures. Naturally, this just made it more fun for her, and she draped her legs over my lap before laying her head on my shoulder.

I told her what had happened. She just listened, holding me a bit tighter when I described the deaths, which weren't sitting well with me, now that I was forced to think about them. I knew that it was likely them or me, but... I still felt awful.

She was quiet for a time after I was done.

"Demise told me about how you talked to the Witches," she said softly, "did you mean what you said?"

It was a loaded question.

"I did... once," I said, turning to look at her, "Cathy was my first real love. I would have given anything to stay with her... right up until the moment she broke my heart into tiny pieces just in time for several nights of fever-induced night terrors which featured her, prominently, as a result. I didn't lie to the Witches so much as I recounted a previous version of myself. One that doesn't matter anymore."

"That simple? Demise said you sounded pretty sincere."

"Maybe I was, just not about Cathy, and maybe not for a while. Decades, did you say?" I said with a smirk, looking at her.

She actually blushed, "You're a very odd Magician, Graves," she said before planting a very tender kiss on my cheek, "You really don't give a crap about power, do you?"

"Why would I?" I asked with a naughty grin, "I'm an Archon."

She laughed and leant her head against mine.

"Cheeky bastard," she said. She kissed my cheek over and over before settling back against my shoulder.

We sat like that for a while, but I couldn't completely relax.

"The sofa's still scaring you isn't it?" she said with a giggle.

"It's just so fragile!"

She smiled and stood, holding out her hand, "Nap before dinner?" she offered.

"With pleasure," I said, taking it and letting her draw me to my feet.

I showered, changed into tracksuit bottoms and t-shirt, and crawled into bed with my Succubus, which sounds strange, I know, and was a million times stranger when you think that all we ever did was sleep with one another (no, really, I swear!). But I didn't sleep better with anyone else.

We generally slept on our sides, facing one another, arms and legs entwined, our chests and thighs close, usually touching. Even so, I never felt any tension. It's always peaceful and wonderful. Right, in fact.

Yep, if I ever do manage to keep a girlfriend, she was probably going to have some problems with that...

And that doesn't even take into account Kandi, who was wrapped around my other side when I woke up. Yes, no way I was ever going to be able to explain my situation, not *well*, anyway.

And... I wasn't sure I cared about that anymore. If there was one thing that seemed to be a constant for me, it was that romantic relationships crashed and burned. But my friendships... they lasted (the important ones, anyway).

The landline buzzed with the intercom tone, which likely meant dinner, but I was warm, and Kandi was moving in a rather interesting way, so I cast a Muffling Spell on the wretched thing. But I was too late, Tethys was awake.

"Nice try, Mathew, but I'm feeding you back up if it's the last thing I do," Tethys said, turning those eyes of hers on me as she reached behind her for the phone.

"Hello?" she said, still staring at me, "Thank you Miss Jenkins, he'll be down presently."

She smiled, replacing the phone, "Now, are you going to be good, or must I employ my wiles upon you?"

"Knowing how I feel about your wiles, will that really encourage the right behaviour?"

She glared, and while I was distracted, staring into those lovely eyes of hers, she got her hands under the covers and tickled me until I fell out of the bed, which woke me up quite thoroughly. I tried to hold it against her, but her smile prevented that.

Dinner was fun and relaxed, and I started to decompress after my day. I eventually found myself back where I'd started the evening, sandwiched between Tethys and Kandi. They made sure that the last thing I was likely to think about was death and blood.

It was in much the same condition that Hopkins found me the next morning, having shown up for our tutorial. I'd normally have been waiting for her in my library or in the garden, but I'd forgotten to set my alarm the night before.

"My, my, what have we here?" Hopkins said in a rather over-satisfied tone, waking me up.

"Wha?" I managed, my bleary eyes opening to see her smirking from the foot of my bed, dressed in jeans and a t-shirt.

"What ever would your mother think?" she said, shaking her head as she gestured at my bed.

I looked around and blushed as I discovered both Tethys and Kandi in states of almost complete undress, draped on top of my chest, my arms around both and my legs tangled with theirs.

"I'd point out that I'm fully dressed," I said, attempting

to salvage some of my dignity.

"Doesn't count, look where their hands are!" Hopkins said, her grin growing wider.

Finally I did notice, and... well, I was losing the moral high ground.

"Can I meet you downstairs?" I asked levelly.

"Of course, I wouldn't want to interfere with your morning... intimacies," she said with a leer.

I called my Will and three spare pillows pursued her laughter out the bedroom door.

I tried to shift myself, but two warm bodies wrapped themselves around me just that little bit tighter.

"Ten more minutes," Kandi muttered sleepily.

"At least," Tethys agreed, burying her head deeper into the crook of my neck.

"If I don't get up now, Hopkins will sulk for the rest of the day, and you'll have to explain to her why," I said, through I was having *real* trouble mustering up the will to move.

Kandi ran the tip of her nose along my earlobe and I shivered. This was followed by a trio of little kisses down my neck before a nuzzling of my cheek.

"Kandi, that's just not fair," I protested weakly.

"Comfy pillow," she said patting my chest, "shush, comfy pillow."

Tethys snorted, and right up against my neck, which produced all sorts of interesting sensations.

"I need to go," I said.

Tethys slid further over, so that she and Kandi were covering even more of me. I wasn't going anywhere. Okay, I could work with that...

It took a minute to craft the spell, quite a few minutes, actually. But finally, I was able to cast a remote viewing construct and wrap an Illusion of myself around it before guiding the combination to the kitchen, where Hopkins was eating toast.

She took one look at my projection and burst out laughing.

"Alright, so they won't let me out of bed, get it *all* out of your system."

She stopped for a second... and then just continued laughing.

"Oh, that is priceless!" she said, yanking out her phone, "I'm telling Lucille, she'll *love* this."

"Jen, don't you dare!" I said, darting forward before I remembered that I wasn't *actually* there, and couldn't do a damn thing.

"And... send!" she said evilly.

"Nooo!"

"Yep, you let your Succubus boss you around, you must suffer."

"But... why Lucille? Doesn't she torture me enough?"

"What's this about Matty being more whipped than Indiana Jones' secretary?" Palmyra said, darting through a Portal and making me jump (sort of).

"Seriously? How little do you have to do that you can come and mock me this quickly?" I asked.

"I thought you said he was trapped under a Succubus?" Palmyra said with a glare at Hopkins.

"I know, isn't it terrible how she lies?" I asked.

"Look again," Hopkins said.

Palmyra looked at my Illusion, and her face broke out in a wide grin.

"Oh, that's lovely," Palmyra said, smiling evilly, "just... lovely. The Archon of the Deep, can't get away from two girls."

"If I were here, I'd get you," I grumbled, but before I could elaborate, I felt something...

Something rather intimate.

"Oh good grief! Got to go! Be right back," I said, and released the Spells.

I found both Tethys and Kandi atop me, their lips and hands in some places which you don't need to know about, my t-shirt pulled up to my neck and Tethys fingers on the drawstring of my bottoms.

"I'm back, I'm back! Damn, I can't turn my back on you two for a second!"

"You should have come back sooner, don't want to stop now," Kandi said, tickling my chest. I shivered and tried to capture her fingers, but Tethys caught one of my hands, and trapped it between her knees, and the other was under Kandi's hindquarters.

"I'll soon teach you to leave your body unattended within reach of a Succubus, Love," Tethys whispered in my ear before biting down gently on the lobe, "did you really think I wouldn't notice you were absent?"

More lips, more teeth, more warm skin. But then Kandi shifted, and I was able to get my hand free and to her ribs, which I tickled. She squealed and leapt for my arm, pinning it down and squeezing it between her thighs.

I called my Shadows, but Tethys saw them coming, pulled my head around and planted one on me. They vanished as quickly as they appeared, my focus completely gone. Tethys pulled back only after a while, her eyes dazzling as she looked down at me.

"Your resistance fails, Love," she purred.

I laughed and smiled warmly at her again, and she immediately clapped her hands over her eyes.

"Oh no, not again," she said, "You're not getting me with that trick a second time!"

"What's the trick?" Kandi asked, "Something dirty?"

"The opposite!" Tethys said, "He gave me this look, and just killed the mood completely! And then he used his wicked words, and I couldn't do anything, don't look at his eyes!"

"Aw, I think it's really sweet," Kandi said, kissing my cheek, "Oh! I get it now! He's cute-ing his way out of naughtiness! That's... well actually a bit brilliant, but hey!"

She swatted at my chest and I turned my smile on her, which she returned.

"Tethys, I think he's doing it to me," Kandi said, her eyes

on mine as we smiled at each other. She relaxed a little, and I got my hand free so I could cup her cheek. She kissed my palm, and held my fingers.

"He got you, didn't he?" Tethys said.

"Little bit," Kandi said.

I grinned at Kandi and gestured at Tethys' sides. Kandi smirked back and held up three fingers, then two, then one... then we went for her ribs and feet.

Tethys shrieked and dropped to the bed, Kandi quickly jumping on top of her.

"Oh, you wicked pair!" Tethys yelped before slithering around Kandi's grip, and twisting to pin the redhead down in her place. She fastened her lips to Kandi's neck and kissed her mercilessly as the girl giggled and squealed happily.

I used the opportunity to throw an Illusion around myself and sneak out the door, grabbing a jumper and my slippers on the way.

"I'll teach you to form an alliance with the Magician," I heard Tethys whisper right before I heard some rather... intimate sounds that need not concern us here.

"Ooh," Kandi moaned, "I'm not sure I'm learning my lesson, perhaps you could try again?"

I covered my ears, none of my business. I wished it *were*... but it wasn't.

I returned to the kitchen to find my sisters still chuckling (and raiding my biscuit cupboard).

"All... *finished* up there?" Palmyra asked with a smirk.

"You know what, you live with a Succubus and let's see how well established your morning routine gets," I replied.

Palmyra stuck out her tongue, which made her look ten years younger (and she maybe looked five minutes older than me to begin with).

"Such witty repartee, do you do town hall meetings?" I asked.

"I'll cry," Palmyra said with a theatrical sniff.

Damn it. I couldn't beat that...

"Why do I never win one?" I asked with a sigh.

"That 'whipped' thing darts back to mind," Hopkins muttered.

"Have some pity, I haven't had breakfast yet," I said (alright, whined).

"Aww, poor baby," Palmyra said evilly.

"There are Shadows under your clothes, you know," I said as menacingly as I could.

"You meant that to sound threatening, right?" Palmyra asked, "Because it came out more as a proposition."

I went bright red and muttered as I went rooting around for cereal.

"It's nice that he still blushes, you'd think living with the Succubus would have broken him of that," Palmyra said in a stage-whisper.

"I'm begging you, now..."

# CHAPTER 28

Naturally Wednesday was a wash. My sisters started trying to teach me, but when one wasn't mocking me, the other would take up the slack and I learned nothing. It was a fun day, though. It was a shame that it had to end, but I had a 'date' with Maggie that evening. We were going to the opening of a new wing in the Waystone Museum of the Arts.

Cassandra and I had taken a taxi as close as we could, but the traffic that night was bad, so we got out to walk the rest of the way. I was in a good mood after my day, happy to be seeing Maggie, and glad that the threats to my person seemed to be diminishing.

We were walking across a moderately sized park, just to the east of the museum. It was just after nine, and the area was empty and quiet, lit only by a couple of street lights often hidden by trees or bushes. It had started to rain, and I put up a Will shield to keep us dry.

Cassandra's phone rang and she picked up, nudging my arm to slow me down.

"What?!" she snapped, "When?!"

She had my attention now, her posture was rigid and worried. Cassandra didn't generally look like that without a *very* good reason.

"You'd better find them, and you'd better find them *now,* or so help me-" she said, still on the phone.

"Yes."

"No, we haven't seen them. Keep me updated."

She hung up, scowling.

"Dare I ask?"

"The Warlock escaped. He took the Werebear with him."

"How in the *hell* did that happen?!"

"He gnawed off his own thumbs to get out of the manacles, waited until they came to get him for a meeting with his lawyer, and then... you can guess what happened."

"His own *thumbs*?! Why didn't he just break them, like a normal person?!"

"Because we ordered them kept tight. Breaking his thumbs wouldn't have done it."

"Jesus," I said with a grimace, "When was this?"

"Day before yesterday."

"And we're only hearing about it now?!"

"Bureaucracy," Cassandra commented with a shrug, "We should probably go home."

"I don't think we need go that far. Those two are still relatively... relatively..."

My speech slowed to a halt as I felt it, just off to my left. Getting closer.

Black Magic. I was certain of it.

Solomon?

"Something's wrong," I said.

Cassandra instantly armed herself, aiming where I was looking.

I relaxed a little when Maggie appeared from an alley in that direction, moving towards us. That was odd, because we were supposed to meet her at the museum, but maybe she'd heard about the jailbreak, too, and wanted to make sure we were okay?

In any event, I had to get her out of the line of fire, as whatever Black Magic was about, it was coming from the same direction she was.

"Maggie, we've got trouble, I can feel Black Magic coming this... way?"

Oh no...

The night lit up with lightning, illuminating the park

for a long moment, showing me the parts of Maggie that had been hidden in the dark. I hadn't been linked to my Shadows, so I hadn't *seen*.

Maggie wore heavy black motorcycle leathers, pitted and torn as if by battle. She was carrying weapons, but many of them were broken or nicked. Her skin was corpse-pale, her eyes black from side to side.

I cast Mage Sight, but I didn't really need to. I was already crying because I knew what had happened.

Maggie was dead, and I knew exactly who had killed her.

Because she was a Revenant.

There were two types, the ones made by Death Magic, and the ones made by the Black. The Death kind, the less dangerous kind, were souls trapped in their own bodies, often willingly in order to avoid a final death.

The other kind... the Black kind, were much, much worse. The body was reanimated and completely repaired; the animating force of the Soul was then replaced by a twisted Black-Magic mimic. The Revenant retained the body's memories, most of the powers they had in life and their intellect. But they also come back *hungry*, hungry for flesh and thirsty for blood, above all for the target of the raising. I'd imagine it was me. The last time I'd seen this spell cast it reanimated everyone Jennifer Hopkins had ever loved and lost, including my predecessor. This casting appeared to be a bit more selective.

My eyes were streaming with tears and my chest compacted with grief. I honestly didn't know what to say, what to do. Maggie had been one of the sweetest, gentlest people I'd come to know. I had started to love her simple kindness and her inherent goodness; the innocent way she looked at the world.

And now... and now she was just *gone*.

Cassandra was still standing next to me; she had her guns out and ready, but not pointed at Maggie, she was Cassandra's friend, too.

"Matty, what's going on?" Cassandra asked.

"She's a Revenant," I managed. The Maggie-thing smiled, revealing teeth that were stained with something dark, shreds of flesh lodged between them.

"Revenant?!" Cassandra said, "Oh, God, no..."

"Go get help, Cassie. And I think it would be best if you stayed out of the line of fire, this one's going to be *bad*."

"I'll not just leave you," she said, tears in her own eyes, now.

"This is Archons' work," I said, raising my shields, "Trust me?"

She nodded and backed away slowly, her guns trained on Maggie, who was staring right at me and only me. Finally my Warden was away, hopefully to call Demise and Hopkins for help.

"Alone at last," Maggie said, sounding just as she always had, but twisted; cold and vicious.

I just stared, I didn't know what to say.

Sending Cassandra away was dumb. It was the safest course for my friend, but the one person who should *not* face a Black Revenant is someone who loved them. I'd cared for Maggie, very deeply, and now I didn't know what to do, because the true danger of the Black Revenant wasn't the enhanced strength, the regeneration, or the Black Magic; no.

It was the *hope*. The awful hope that you can reach the person inside the monster.

I *knew* that. I'd spent hours convincing Tethys of that very thing when she'd been faced with her great love just like this.

But when I was faced with it myself, all I could think of was helping her, bringing her back. I was an Archon, surely there was something I could do?

"Nothing to say, pet?" Maggie asked.

More tears streamed down my face.

"I'm sorry," I managed.

"You should be. I'm only dead because of you. If I'd never met you, I'd still be alive."

Every word lanced into my heart, a shard of agony. Because she was right.

And yet it didn't matter, not really.

Because if we'd never met, she and her then-master would have mutilated Crystal and the rest of the girls at the Red Carpet, not to mention all the innocent people in that casino. I'd done the best I could, I knew that, and I couldn't have done anything differently, for to do so would have been to sacrifice my people.

So why did I feel like it was my fault?

"And to think that I loved you," she said, "Such a small man, what would you be without all that power?"

"Not to toot my own horn, but a genius. I've been tested," I said, trying to project confidence and cool. I was just buying time. I needed help, *lots* of help. I wasn't even gathering energy; I was too shattered by grief. It was all I could do to *talk* to her without weeping like a child.

"And what's that worth to a coward?" she asked. Tears were flowing down her cheeks as well. She took a step towards me. I took a corresponding one back. I knew those tears were false, but seeing them still hurt.

It's not Maggie, it's not Maggie, it's not Maggie...

"Enough that I've lived this long without ending up in prison, or the graveyard... yet," I managed.

Her eyes darted dangerously at me, her lips forming a sneer.

She laughed, an ugly, gurgling sound. I could smell rot on her breath, even from steps away.

"In another life, we would have made such a team," she said with a smirk.

I nodded.

"In this one I loved you very much," I replied, "and for what little of the real you may be left, I'll make sure that Solomon pays dearly for what he's done."

"Oh, I wouldn't worry, once I'm done with you, I'll be returning for him. He has little or no idea what he's doing. He created me for a purpose without thinking about what would happen when I was done. What do you suppose a heart tastes like?"

The tangent was so jarring, I was shocked into silence.

"I think *yours* will taste bad; withered, nasty. I think that your heart is shrivelled and broken, and I think that seeing me like this was the last straw. I think you're already dead, Mathew Graves. I think that your body just needs someone to give it a little push."

She slowly drew a broken sword from a scabbard and then, before I could even try to stop her, she jumped for me, hard. She swung, and the blade slashed through... my *Illusion's* neck, dispersing it.

She chuckled again.

"Fool me once, shame on you..." she said, drawing a gun.

She fired and the bullet smacked into my shields, which an Illusion had been hiding. I was very surprised; how had she found me so quickly?!

When she came again, I was ready, and though it broke my heart, I threw a Shadow Lance.

Which she *parried* like it was nothing!

It hit the grass and exploded. She rushed me again, but I called my Shadows and they threw me into the air, high above her. Even under attack, I couldn't bring myself to fight properly. I was holding back, having trouble bringing my strength to bear. That first Lance had been small, a fraction of what I was capable of.

I lashed out with a Shadow, and she darted out of the way, so *fast*. I expanded it into a cloud, and she was smothered in darkness, but she didn't need air, and she was apparently quite able to see where I was, as she looked right at me, high above her, and out of reach. She threw her sword and it bounced off my shield. She drew another gun and opened up on me with both of her firearms.

I breathed, trying to calm down. She was no real threat to me. My shields were up and strong, my Shadows were now in place, and the bullets weren't Enchanted. I had time, time to think, time to plan...

Or so I thought.

She screamed.

It was different this time.

Uglier, nastier, and laced with something... terrible.

It lanced through my soul, bypassing every defence I had, and my Magic failed on the spot. Everything from my Shields, to my Shadows, Mage Sight... it all lost energy, and I dropped out of the sky like a stone.

I screamed as I fell, and she leapt into the air, catching me in a vice-like grip as we soared through up and onto the roof of one of the buildings bordering the park. She slammed me down, smashing the slate with my body. I felt my shoulder break, and then her head was at my chest. She bit down hard and tore a chunk of my shirt and jumper away with her teeth.

She roared in triumph as she darted down again, straight at my unprotected flesh. I somehow got my good arm in the way, which was somewhat protected by the sleeves of a thick blazer and jumper, but I still felt *teeth* through the layers of cloth.

And when her head pulled back, there was a golf ball-sized chunk of meat missing from my arm.

I screamed horribly; and tried to call Magic, but she grabbed my wrist and bit down again, my blood smearing around her lips and chin as she tore at my flesh. My world dissolved in white-hot pain, agony searing me as another chunk of me was ripped away.

And then she did it again... and again.

She was eating me *alive*.

I thrashed against her, desperate and screaming, my mind on the verge of breakdown from the pain and the desperation that came from knowing that I was about to die a horrible death... and that I couldn't do anything to save myself.

Almost frantically, I tried to call my Magic again, but another bite stopped me from forming a Spell. Even my Shadows were just out of reach, my brain still half-scrambled by her scream. I felt myself start to go into shock, and I cried out, desperate and afraid, pulling every ounce of focus I could muster into a Magical scream for help, sent right down the fragmented link to my Shadows.

I didn't really know what I was doing, it was all instinct and fear...

But something heard me anyway.

It started as a subsonic roar, one I'd felt before, but barely recognised in the state I was in. Maggie noticed it as well, and she halted her feeding long enough to look around her, searching for the source. The roar became a shriek, and the sky above us split open, revealing a gaping tear in reality, through to the Shadow Realm. Dozens of Elementals spilled out, each one resonating with my fear, each one terrified...

And angry, so *very* angry.

They looked like a mix of aquatic creatures, some like eels with flippers, some like sharks, but these were the relatively small ones, no longer than a wolf, some as big as a pony. Behind them swam something else, something different. Something bigger... much bigger.

The Leviathan.

If I had to describe him, I would say that he looked like a great Sea Dragon, made of Shadows, with two pairs of fins like a whale and long spines along his back. Huge and powerful, he could turn a city to rubble given the provocation.

And he was *pissed.*

Maggie, or the Maggie-thing, never stood a chance. The first ten little ones hit her as she turned to face them. They repaid her in kind for what she'd done to me, their fangs tearing chunks out of her arms and face as they flashed by. She turned and lashed out, but missed them all. And lost a hand for her troubles; something about the same size and shape as a crocodile bit it off.

Desperately, I called my Will. To my surprise, I felt it respond, and I blasted her off me before casting a painkiller spell. I groaned as it took effect, and the agony dulled to an ache. I cast a hasty Triage Spell, and made the mistake of looking at my arm.

I found it hard to hold onto my dinner as I saw at the ragged and horrible wound. I could see white bone through the torn mess of red meat. Blood was still spurting from damaged blood vessels, but it slowed to a halt as the Triage Spell took effect. Suffice to say, the damage was bad. Parts of the major veins and arteries had been ripped away completely, along with the nerves; my hand was numb below the wound. There would be no fixing *that* quickly.

But that wasn't the problem at that moment, because Maggie was back.

She swatted a couple of the elementals away and leapt back onto the roof, shreds of my flesh dangling from the side of her mouth as she came for me. I got a shield up and she bounced off, smacking into a chimney, which collapsed.

There were screams from surrounding streets as brick and slate crashed to the ground. The sounds were quickly drowned out by the hunting cries of Shadow Elementals as they swung around and back for my would-be murderer.

The Leviathan swung by, but its jaws closed on nothing as Maggie was elsewhere and coming back for me. He was too slow to catch her, and using his breath attack would smash the buildings under us and any people in them (thank God he was intelligent enough to realise that and sentient enough to understand the implications).

I couldn't run, my legs were weak and shaking. My brain was working fine, but my body was useless what with broken bones and what amounted to mutilation.

I really thought I was about to die.

But then I felt my Elementals' tense as Magic flowed into the area, and not just a little; *whopping* amounts of power. Suddenly, they were gone, back into the Shadows as the night was rent by lightning, and not from the rainclouds above my head this time. Great forks of it smashed into Maggie's chest as she leapt for me, infinite hunger in her eyes and my blood on her lips.

Her chest exploded and she was flung back, thrown to the ground, but already her wounds were closing, and she was up on her feet. Revenants were hard to destroy; generally you needed to take the head *and* destroy the heart; only one won't do it.

I added my Shadows to the attack, and made them sharp, they took an arm, but I needn't have bothered, because suddenly Kron was there, blink and you would have missed her.

She was wearing armour, bright and shining with power, her form flickering with electricity. She held a golden hammer in her hand and brought it up with blinding speed. That first strike knocked Maggie's head off like a golf ball, the sheer force of the impact making it explode in gore. Another strike and the Revenant's chest imploded, a black mess blasting out the back of her, heart and all.

The body ignited, fire flowing from the hammer. A gesture from Lady Time, and a pulse of flame followed the head as well, rendering Maggie's remains down to ash, harmless once again.

Just like that it was over, and Kron was standing at my side on the mangled roof, her weapon hooked onto her belt.

A word to the wise: *never* piss off Lady Time, just some sound advice for you. She made me look like one of the Pixies, which should give you an indication of how powerful and dangerous she was.

She knelt next me, her eyes compassionate.

I didn't know exactly how long she'd been around, but she was well over a thousand years old, though she didn't look much beyond her mid-twenties. It was her eyes that gave her character and gravitas. Strom-cloud grey and piercing, they stared right into the heart of you. We often butted heads, but

I'd never felt safer than I did right then as she leaned over me and smiled reassuringly.

"It's alright, Graves. You're safe now," she said.

I believed her. I relaxed, sending my gratitude into the Shadows.

*We serve the One,* the Leviathan whispered back, his consciousness already flowing deeper into the Shadow Realm along with the others. And then he was gone, though I could still feel some of the smaller ones waiting nearby, in case I needed them.

I sagged, exhausted. Kron took a quick look to make sure I wasn't going to bleed out, and then helped me to stand, making sure to grab the unbroken shoulder. She opened a Portal, and I saw my lawn. I sighed as I staggered through, weaving my way towards the door, assisted by Kron's steady hand. My legs gave out on the front doorstep, and I fell to my knees, shock setting in again, no doubt.

Jillian and Bethany were on guard duty and darted forwards. I yelped when Jillian touched my broken shoulder, the spike of pain cutting through my numbing Spell. Bethany took one look at the mess that was my right forearm and recoiled, going a bit green.

It looked even worse in the light. A lot of the dorsal muscle was just gone, leaving a wide, ragged hole, eight inches long and three wide. My arm bones were clearly visible (if somewhat stained red), complete with tooth marks and chips. That was some nightmare fodder right there; the human brain is not built to easily process the sight of its own bones...

Into this bedlam came Kandi, who took one look at my arm and barely managed to turn her head away from me... which meant that she vomited onto Bethany instead. The poor Warden got more than a little in her mouth and, already on the cusp after seeing my arm, hurled as well...

It was chaos, and the smell was simply awful, cutting through my trauma and shock, like a demonic version of the beckoning scent fingers that come from a Walt Disney pie. The stench invaded my senses, and, with that, my stomach finally lost its battle with nausea, and added a *third* heap to the floor.

Needless to say, nobody covered themselves with glory, but most of us did manage to get covered in vomit.

"Oh bloody hell," Kron said, guiding me around the mess and into the hall, where Demise and Tethys had just reached the bottom of the stairs. She cast a series of Spells that threw the vomit off everyone (bless her) as she helped me walk.

"What happe- what's wrong with your arm?!" Tethys almost shrieked, darting to my side.

"Slight accident," I managed to mumble.

"Has Vallaincourt returned yet?" Kron asked.

"No," Demise reported, her tone clipped and professional even as her eyes were on my wound.

I was having trouble remaining upright. I'd cast the Spell that would increase my blood cell production, but I was feeling dizzy and ill (Again! I'd just gotten rid of those symptoms...).

"Ensure she's on her way," Kron ordered, "and fetch me his chef."

"His *chef*?" Tethys asked, standing very close, but afraid to touch me in case she hurt me.

"He'll need to replace large amounts of tissue, that means protein, that means *meat*," Kron said, and then to me, much more gently, "This way, Graves."

She led me into my garden and carefully lowered me to the ground against my tree. Miss Jenkins came in at the run seconds later and Kron took her to one side. Tethys knelt down next to me, tears in her eyes.

"Hey, it's fine," I said, smiling at her, "This kind of thing happens all the time."

She choked on a laugh and grabbed my thigh. I think she wanted to take a hand, but one was next to a grizzly mess and the other attached to a broken shoulder...

"What happened?" she asked.

I told her, and her eyes narrowed in fury.

"That man needs to die *horribly*, Mathew," she said once I'd finished, "I've had enough!"

"Me too," I said.

My mind was getting a bit clearer, so I decided to start working on my wounds. The shoulder, at least, was relatively easy to repair, so that was where I started. A few simple Spells slowly drew the jagged edges of my clavicle back into place, while another pair reattached the ball joint to its humerus. When they were in position, a final Spell started fusing everything back together. It was itchy as hell, but at least it wasn't painful (not with the overpowered Numbing Spell I had in place!).

That was the easy part. I then started crafting the Flesh Lattice that would re-grow my musculature and nerves. It wasn't going to be fun.

"Hold off on that, Graves," Kron said, "Palmyra's on the way, we caught her at a busy moment."

I nodded and took Tethys' hand with my now (mostly-working) spare. She squeezed, perhaps a little hard, her eyes on the mess.

"I know, right?" I said to her, "You see idiots in zombie movies and you never believe it can happen to you."

Tethys laughed and sobbed all at once, leaning her head against mine.

"Stop making me laugh, this is *not* the time!" she said, grabbing on to my shirt.

"Sorry, but I can't help it if I'm *handy* in a crisis," I said, waggling my mutilated limb.

She trembled, and I felt tears on my neck.

"I can't have you dying on me, Mathew," she whispered.

"I'm not going *anywhere*."

"But *you're* the one that gets murdered, Mathew," she said with another choke, waving at Kron, "They get to choose when they die, you get set on."

"I'm still here," I said, "They look out for me; you keep

me safe and happy. This was an aberration."

"Which seems to happen a lot lately!"

"It's the same root problem," I replied, "One which I will deal with as soon as Lucille's fixed my arm up."

And speaking of the Lifeweaver...

"Alright, what seems to be the proble- oh God, that's disgusting!" Palmyra said as she came into the garden.

"Thanks Lucille, way to settle the patient," I said testily.

"I was talking about your face," she said with a nasty smirk.

Tethys burst out laughing and even Kron cracked a smile.

"You know, I have centuries to come up with ways to get you back for things like this," I said with a glare. Palmyra just smirked back.

Miss Jenkins came in with two glasses, one full of pink gloop and the other with water.

She kept her eyes fixed rigidly above my head and away from the wound as she set the tray down next to me.

"Thank you, Miss Jenkins," I said.

"You will be alright, Sir?" she asked, swallowing hard.

"I'm in good hands," I said cheerfully.

She nodded and backed out with haste.

"Drink the pink one," Palmyra said, "and hold your nose, it won't taste too good."

I freed my hand from Tethys and picked up the glass, "What is it?"

"Don't ask," Palmyra said with a grimace.

I took a breath and downed it. The aftertaste was *horrific*, like raw eggs, milk and uncooked mincemeat, which I later found out was *exactly* what was in there...

Palmyra sat next to me and got to work. She did a much quicker and more elegant job than I could have managed, and the wound quickly covered with skin before starting to fill out. It was warm and tingly, but not unpleasant.

The look on Palmyra's face was a little worrying,

though.

"What is it?" I asked, as I started drinking the water.

"Nothing," she said.

I poked her side and she jumped, "Just tell me."

She scowled, "Fine, you want to know? You should already be dead. Revenants' bites are poisoned; you should have died on the roof."

Tethys looked like she was going to be sick.

"This means something bad, doesn't it?" I asked.

"It means that the Black's in you," Palmyra replied, "And because you are who you are, it means that the Black can't kill you any more than a Shadow could."

"But I haven't been using it!" I protested, "I swear."

"I know you haven't, dummy, but this likely means that if you ever *do*, then a detox won't help again. It's in you now and even the slightest use will mean that it's there *forever*. Even a minor exposure could do it at this point."

"But I'm not bad yet, right?"

She smiled at me, "No, you daisy. You're just more susceptible now, that's all."

"Well, then why the grimace and the need to scare the crap out of me?!"

"Don't be such a doily," she said, swatting my shoulder, but she seemed relaxed again.

"You do these things just to see how I'll react, don't you?" I said with realisation.

"Yup, the girlier the response, the less I worry. Currently you're still firmly at 'Shirley Temple', as girly as you were the first day I met you."

I called a few Shadows and administered a quartet of pinches to her bottom, which made her squeal and spin before turning back to glare at me.

"Oh, bad move, Graves," she said, her eyes narrowing, "Now it's *very* on!"

"Bring it, Hippie Chick," I said with a matching glare, but we were both struggling not to grin.

"Oh, you wanna go?" she said, "We'll go!"

"Oh, I'll go... just as soon as you've finished fixing my arm."

"Yeah, I'll fix it so I can shove it up my arse!"

"You want to try that one again?" I whispered, nearly losing it.

"Your! I meant 'your'. Stupid language! You know what I was getting at, you pervert!" she glowered, going bright red.

"Why do people keep calling me that?" I asked.

"The Succubus, the Nymphs, the Princesses, the frequently naked Pixies," Palmyra said immediately before taking a breath.

"Alright, alright, for heaven's sake!" I said, going red myself.

"The Redheads, the Vampires, the other Succubus, the Elves you think we don't know about, the Blonde Pureborn, the Half-Werewolf, the Pureblood Succubus..." Palmyra continued.

"I have done nothing untoward with most of those!"

"Most?" Palmyra said with an impish look, "Which ones are you willing to confirm? Jen and I have a running bet."

"How do you two have nothing better to do?"

She laughed and patted my newly healed arm, "All better," she said.

"Oh, thank you," I said, clenching and unclenching my fist, "Again!"

She grinned and helped me up, Tethys right next to me.

"Now, who do I speak to about booking a dungeon?" she asked innocently.

# CHAPTER 29

After Palmyra and Kron had left, with my thanks (and grovelling it was too), Cassandra finally arrived back at Blackhold and hugged me tightly enough to nearly throttle me. Kandi had apologised profusely for her weak stomach, and I had to hug the guilt out of her, something Tethys helped with (enthusiastically).

I held my tongue and my smile until everyone was out of sight, and I was finally alone.

They didn't need to see me cry.

I broke down in my bathroom, crying for Maggie, who'd died because of a monster, and because I'd gotten involved in her life. I was there for a long time, grieving for her. I was all she'd had, really, her only friend in the world; the only one who would really grieve for her, and that made it even worse.

I could only imagine what her last minutes of life were like, but the way her clothes and weapons had been damaged when I'd fought her Revenant, she hadn't gone peacefully. She'd fought, to the death as it turned out.

And I hadn't been there to help her.

I think that's what hurt most of all; what might have been if only I could have helped her, if only I'd been able to persuade her to call me when she needed help...

But now it was too late, and she was gone forever. I'd never see her sweet smile again, never argue with her about movies or show her a new pastry.

I didn't know if I'd ever be able to forgive myself for that. I knew, on an intellectual level, that it wasn't really my fault, that only Solomon was to blame for what had happened, but that didn't stop me from hurting, from blaming myself.

And from missing her terribly.

I kept my grief to myself. My people were already worried enough without adding my moping to the list of things to watch out for, but I doubted that I was entirely successful hiding it, especially where Tethys and Cassandra were concerned.

It was decided that I should remain at Blackhold for a while, likely until Solomon had been tracked down and dealt with, and I couldn't muster up a protest. I was perfectly happy to stay with the people I valued the most, where I could be ready to pounce if that bastard ever came back.

And it was good for me, too. Between Tethys, Kandi, Demise and Cassandra, I was never alone for long enough to dwell and spiral, each distracting me in their own way, something I appreciated more than I can say.

Tethys, especially, wouldn't let me out of her sight; I think that seeing me half eaten had shaken her a bit.

The days passed slowly, and the grief... remained, but became easier to manage. Spending time with my friends was a great comfort. They kept me going, kept me laughing and thinking.

A few days after the attack, Tethys and I were lying under the oak tree, reading. I had chosen an old novel; Tethys had her Financial Times (I think she picked it more to gloat than anything else, going by the grin on her face).

She sighed after a while and put it down, before turning to look at me.

"You know that I love you, right, Mathew?" she said, taking my spare hand.

I put down my book and turned to her.

"Of course. You know I feel the same about you?"

She nodded.

"And you know that I would never leave you? You know I'm not Cathy, right?" she asked, her voice vulnerable.

I smiled warmly at her.

"You know, it hadn't even occurred to me for a moment?" I said, pulling her knuckles to my lips, "Which is selfish and presumptuous, I know. But I never considered the possibility that you'd leave. Sorry."

She smiled back at me, a tear in her eye, "Good," she said. She leaned up and kissed me, just a little thing, but it held a hell of a lot of meaning.

She was no Cathy. She was stronger, and a far truer friend. We were different in a lot of ways, our outlooks on so many things. But deep down, where it really mattered, we were very similar. When we found someone we cared for, we didn't let go. We went to the end for them. She was my partner, my dearest friend, and even if she wasn't ready for more than that, it was enough just to have her in my life.

And having her redhead around didn't hurt.

"Hey!" Kandi said, stomping into the garden, "The least you two can do is not do *that* where I can see you, you know it confuses me something vicious!"

Tethys pulled back and beckoned, "Sorry, Honey, come here, we'll make it up to you."

"You'd better," she muttered.

She came over and draped herself over our laps, her head in the crook of my arm and her legs where Tethys could stroke them. I ran my fingers through Kandi's hair and she sighed happily.

"I love this," she said, "the three of us, like this."

"Us, too, Honey," Tethys said, smiling at me. I squeezed Kandi's shoulder gently to show my agreement. She turned to smile at me.

It was wonderfully peaceful and relaxing; I felt very at home in that moment. The nastiness of the world outside just faded away.

"Are you the older one, Matty?" Kandi asked, "Of you and your brother, I mean?"

"Nope, ten minutes younger," I said, "and he never let me forget it, either."

"It's funny, you always seemed like the big brother type to me," Kandi said.

"No, but I tried to be a good brother," I said, with a sigh, "I wish I could have done better by him."

"Funny you should mention that, because I was having a chat with Jen the last time she was here," Tethys said, "Would you like to know what the other Archons think about you and your brother?"

"I can't imagine they're happy thoughts."

She snorted.

"There are a lot of theories about how Archons are made, how they're chosen. For each one, the power seeks out a certain type. Time chooses someone careful and clinical, Life chooses someone compassionate and gentle, for example," she said.

I paid close attention.

"But that would mean that who we are is determined before we're even born," I pointed out.

"Well, they're not sure about *that*. The consensus, according to Jen, is that the power of the Archons enhances certain *potential* personality traits in the growing Magician. They can't enhance what's not there, which is why the powers have to go to someone with those predispositions. Which leads us to you and Desmond. Historically, First Shadows have always cold and self-serving; bullies, for want of a better term, sound like someone you know?"

I frowned.

"So, you're saying... you're saying *Des* was supposed to be the First Shadow?" I said.

"They think so," Tethys said.

"So, all of this, everything I've done, it was never supposed to happen? I'm supposed to be the one rotting at the Farm?"

I felt awful. Des was supposed to be here, not me? He was supposed to be sane and well? I was supposed to be the mess?

"It doesn't work like that, Mathew, and besides, I know you better than that. If you'd set out kill your brother, you'd never have been caught."

"How reassuring," I said dryly.

Also *true*, but we're not dwelling on *that* idea.

"Hopkins thinks that you were always supposed to be a Sorcerer, but you were supposed to be a *Life* Magician, at least that's what Kron and Palmyra think. Des was going to be a Wizard, but he was supposed to be a Death affinity. But then the process which chooses an Archon came down on you two, but somehow, instead of it going to Des, it went to you, and because twinned Magicians are always opposites, he got Light."

I felt a little sick.

I was supposed to be someone else entirely. Maybe even a better person; one that wasn't desperate for Black Magic and a danger to himself and others.

"Why didn't they tell me?" I asked, miserably.

Tethys turned to look at me, sudden worry in her eyes.

"You can't think that this is a bad thing?" she said, "Think, Matty! Think of Des facing the things you have; what decisions would a person like *that* have made? Would those Pixies be alive? Would I? Would this house be anything other than a place of horror and misery? Would Cassandra be here? Where would Demise be?"

Well... she had a point.

"I'm sorry," I said, patting her arm, "I was just thinking on 'what-ifs', that's all."

"I think you'd have made a good Life Mage, Mathew," Tethys said, "but I can't imagine anyone else in this house. Compassion is a great and *rare* thing, and we should all be very grateful that it's you, not Desmond. First Shadows are known to be the Archons' enforcers. They are generally loyal to the others, but nobody else. To other people they're brutish and monstrous; something to be feared. Des would have been a *catastrophe*, he went bad at a *whiff* of the Black, for heaven's sake, and here you are fighting it with every fibre of your being. Do you really think that this is an accident?"

"I don't understand, you said that Hopkins thought it was," I said.

"That's what *she* thinks. I think it has something to do with," she covered Kandi's ears, "our feathered friends."

"I highly doubt that," I said, "I am nobody's choice for this sort of power."

"Maybe it was the lesser of two evils?" Tethys replied impishly.

"Oh thank you very much!"

She laughed and then leant her head against mine, "Seriously, though, there are five Archons in all the world, and at a time when terrible things are happening, and all manner of awful decisions need to be made, I highly doubt that the choice of a compassionate man for this responsibility was an accident," she said, "I believe in you, Mathew Graves. I only wish you weren't so hard on yourself. Of course, if you weren't beating yourself up over things you had no control over, you wouldn't be you... so I'll just try to live with it."

I smiled at her.

"Thanks," I said, maybe feeling a bit better.

Tethys had that effect.

"I'd imagine the others think a lot about what might have been," I suggested.

"I'd imagine something more along the lines of thanking God that they have *you* to deal with and not your crazy brother," Kandi chimed in.

I tweaked her nose and she subsided.

"I know that all of this can be hard on you, Mathew," Tethys said, "but if you could go back to the moment when this happened, knowing what you'd become and knowing that your burden that would be placed on your brother instead, would you change it?"

"No," I said, looking at her right in the eyes.

*And you know why.*

She smiled; she understood and leaned over to kiss me.

"Yeah, that's right, now undo the bra," Kandi whispered.

We both looked down at her and the little redhead grinned mischievously.

"I wonder what that meeting would have been like," Kandi said, her voice growing deeper, just a little bit husky "Life Magician Mathew and Tethys."

Tethys shivered at the thought.

"Ooh, Kandi, don't put thoughts like that in my head, you're the one who'll have to deal with them later," Tethys purred, her hands a little more busy on Kandi's legs.

"I can just picture it now," Kandi continued, "young Mathew, brimming over with youthful innocence and good intentions, he descends into the Purple Pussycat for some benign cause, a girl perhaps, someone who needs help, you know his usual goody-two-shoes bit. He comes into your office, and there you are sitting at your desk... No, no! He catches you 'in flagrante' like he did the first time."

Kandi paused as Tethys hands migrated up her leg a little further.

"Go on," Tethys whispered, her eyes closed, licking her lips.

"Must she?" I asked.

Tethys leaned against me and put her arm around me. She slid her palm over my mouth and her nose hard up against my neck.

"Go on," she repeated huskily.

"Well, this time, honest, open, empathetic Mathew just stands there watching, his young hormones raging as he sees what you're doing to those beautiful young dancers. Maybe one of them has red hair."

Alright, even I had to admit that Kandi told a good story, it was her tone more than anything else...

"Dumbfounded, rooted to the spot, what can he do, *but* watch? And then you look up and you see him standing there. And you think, what have we here? How did he get past Molly? And so young, with such interesting eyes. What could he want? And then you decide that it doesn't matter, and you're standing next to him.

"Now, *our* Mathew's as paranoid as a midget nun at a penguin-shoot, but this other Mathew... oh no, he's as trusting as a newborn and when you tell him that you're there to help, he believes you, and even though you haven't dressed, he trusts you and follows you into the back. You tell him that the girl he's looking for is fine, and that she's been fed and given a place to sleep. He thinks you're beautiful, so he trusts you even more, he's already half in love with you."

Tethys let out a little whimper and nipped my ear, which made me shiver. Kandi looked at her and grinned like the Cheshire cat before settling back in her spot.

"You take him by the hand into that big bedroom of yours, he asks where the girl is and *that's* when you pounce. He resists at first, but you're insistent and his Magic is no use against you. He can feel your desire through his Empathy, and soon it becomes his own, and he surrenders to you completely."

Tethys emitted a moan, and then she was in motion, and Kandi squeaked as she was pulled onto Tethys' shoulder.

"We'll see you later, Mathew. Kandi's going to be busy for a while," Tethys said.

She turned, and Kandi grinned at me, waving as she was carried off.

"Now, Honey," Tethys said as they walked around the corner, "what do you suppose *that* Mathew would be wearing? I'm picturing some sort of monk's habit."

"Ooh! We have one of those," I heard Kandi say, which made me snigger.

Those two would be the death of me, but oh, what a nice way to go...

"You three get weirder every time I see you together," Cassandra said from off to my left, startling me.

"How much of that did you hear?"

"Enough to know that you are in *so* much trouble," Cassandra said with a grin.

"How's that?"

"That Succubus is getting more and more attached to you as time goes on, and the girl isn't far behind."

"And?"

"Oh nothing, just don't say I didn't warn you," she said, walking off.

"You didn't actually warn me!" I protested as she vanished.

Her laugh was my only reply.

# CHAPTER 30

I was home for ten days after the Revenant attack without any sign of Solomon, and no attempts on the house. I spent a lot of the time relaxing, sleeping and eating, getting my health and weight back up.

But I hadn't been idle.

The first thing I'd done, on the night Maggie died, was to have Tethys start looking for the Warlock and his girlfriend. I knew that searching for Solomon was almost certainly a lost cause. His Black Magic, combined with his Celestial nature, meant that he didn't need easy things to track like food, a place to sleep or a car. But those two *did.* They had expenses, they had to live somewhere warm, they had to eat; they had to get around, pay bills...

And that's how Tethys found them.

She had been cultivating a number of law enforcement contacts lately, and one of them worked in the Stonebridge Police's Fraud Department. All we needed was the little weasel's birth name (Orion Paris), and they could hunt him down, though it took quite some time.

They had been tracked to an address in one of the more swept up parts of Stonebridge, a twenty-storey hotel of glass and chrome, where the smallest room would set you back five hundred pounds a night. They were holed up in one of the better suites on the eighteenth floor.

I kicked in the door... well, I tried, hurt my leg and fell on my arse before sending a Shadow to do the job, hoping nobody had seen me.

The main room was full of comfortable and expensive furniture, all in light pink and gold. I immediately sensed the Black Magic in the room and adjusted my defences accordingly. There wasn't enough to indicate the presence of Solomon himself, but he'd definitely been there, and recently.

I found *her* in the smaller bedroom.

Solomon had peeled her open and left the room coated with her remains. What little of the paintwork I could see told me that the room had once been white and green, but there wasn't much of that colour left. I turned away having great trouble controlling my stomach.

That was bad enough.

What he'd done to Orion was far, far worse.

The room was similarly coated with viscera, but, lying on the bed, was Orion's head, heart and lungs...

And he was still alive. He was staring horribly at the world around him, his mouth opened in a silent scream. I could feel Black Magic flowing through his remains, keeping his parts alive... and alert.

"You..." he gasped, revolting me. I could actually see his voice box shake as he spoke.

"What happened?" I asked, trying to conceal my disgust.

"The Master... he didn't approve of our failures."

"What failures?"

"Couldn't find what he was looking for, couldn't keep the Revenant from escaping. He had plans for her. Please... please, kill me?"

"Don't you want revenge, first?" I asked, "Don't you want him to pay?"

"Y-y-yes!"

"Then tell me where he is."

"He's still hunting Vampires. He's looking for someone, he never told me who. That's where he's been when he's not planning to kill *you*. It's something to do with the Hyde, but that's all I know."

That was no lead at all. There were Vampires *everywhere* in groups large and small. My next port of call would be Price, maybe she'd be able to predict where the bastard was going.

That just left the poor creature lying in front of me.

I made a decision and pulled out my phone.

"Hi Matty!" Palmyra said brightly, "How's my favourite pincushion?"

"Hi Lucille. Uh... can you come to the Watson Hotel? Room 1812?"

"Sure... why?"

"I have a... patient for you. I don't know if he can be helped, but if anyone can..."

"I'll be right there," she said, all lightness gone from her tone. I hung up.

"I have someone coming," I said to what was left of Orion, "she'll do what she can."

"Just kill me, I don't want to live like this!"

"What happened to Maggie?" I asked him, mostly to keep his mind off his... condition, but also because I wanted to know.

"Why does that matter?" he snapped.

"It might help me get Solomon."

That might not have worked if he wasn't half mad from his treatment, but he answered. I was, after all, his only hope for release from his pain.

"If you say so. I called her, told her that I wanted to talk, to help against the Master. When she arrived we triggered a gas bomb. Cyanide. She survived it, somehow. We had to fight her; it took both of us to bring her down. She broke half of Greta's bones, even half dead from poison, but in the end, we managed to hold her down long enough for me to cut her throat."

It felt like my heart had stopped. I hadn't expected... this. Sure, he may have been a brute and a bully, but I'd never thought that he...

I trembled in rage and grief.

"*You* killed her?" I rasped.

His eyes went wide, then. He'd realised his mistake.

"I-I-"

I pulled my phone out again, walking away.

"Yes, I'm coming!" Lucille snapped.

"Never mind, Lucille, sorry," I said, not looking back, "False alarm."

Orion's agonised wail followed me out the door, which I used Magic to seal behind me, leaving him to his pain, his madness and his loneliness.

He deserved no less.

I went home. Nobody seemed to mind that I'd left Orion like that. Maggie had been well liked, and Orion's fate was thought to be well deserved. I'll say this for Solomon, he may be a monster that needed putting down in the worst possible way, but he knew how to punish people. I could take a leaf or two from his book when I finally caught up with him.

I contacted Price about what I'd learned and she promised to come up with some ideas for me, and she was true to her word. Over the next week, Price fed me reports about attacks on five small Vampire Covens in Paris, Madrid, Florence, Milan and Rennes. At each one, the attack was carried out by a man matching Solomon's description, right down to the black wings. Nobody knew what he was looking for because... well, nobody who'd been close enough to hear the conversations had survived.

These victims were all attached to one of the larger Vampire Houses, which was naturally hopping mad that their people were being picked off. Price later discovered that this was only the tail end of a recent spate of attacks from all over Europe and western Russia. The secretive Houses hadn't shared this information, naturally, so nobody knew they were all facing the same problem until Price told them so (and for a hefty fee, I might add).

Opinions about where he'd strike next were many and varied, but the consensus appeared to be that he was zeroing in on something in and around Paris, where there was the largest concentration of Vampires in Europe.

And he *did* attack there, slaughtering everyone in a safe house near the Pont Neuf on the Ile de la Cite. I was informed that there were six very old vampires there for a meeting when he struck.

After that, he just... stopped.

Tethys figured that he must have gotten what he was looking for, but there was no way to confirm that. So we just kept waiting.

We figured that he'd come looking for me eventually, and we were even putting together a few tentative plans to hang me out as false-bait. But never, in our worst predictions, did we think that the bastard would attack somewhere he'd already failed to take, much less a place where I could be expected to show up at all but instantly, and in force... like the Red Carpet.

More fool us.

It was a Saturday, now well into November, when the package came for me.

I'd just finished my breakfast, and was full and happy, looking forward to a lazy day with Tethys, who was planning a movie marathon.

One of the valets placed a box in front of me. It was wrapped in brown paper, tied up with white string. I opened it, not really paying attention. That changed quickly.

It was full of hair.

Tiny locks of it, each one held together with spots of dried blood. Dozens of them.

I knew their energy signatures, one in particular.

Crystal.

There was a note.

*Where it all began.*
*Midnight.*

*Alone.*

*Or I send you their eyes next time.*

It wasn't even ten in the morning, yet!

There was no way I was waiting that long.

I didn't even think, I just opened a Gate and jumped into the Shadow Realm. I was at the Red Carpet in seconds, and it was all I could do not to go rushing right into the trap Solomon almost certainly had ready for me. He had to expect me to come running; there was no other reason for him to send that package *fourteen* hours before he'd told me to arrive.

So I forced myself to be calm as I walked through the Shadow corridors of the Red Carpet, listening carefully. It was as quiet as a tomb, until I heard the whimpers.

They were coming from down below, in the basement levels.

There were several large storage areas down there; one was full of wooden boxes, stacked neatly next to a row of freezers, no luck there. The next one along... that's where I found the casino's customers.

They were all dead, about a hundred of them, and they hadn't died quickly. There were men and women of all ages, most in suits and dresses, all had been well turned out and dressed for a good time. There was blood everywhere, torn flesh and shattered bone, staring eyes and faces frozen in the agony of their death throes.

I saw all this through a small Gate and shuddered, barely holding in my now over-large breakfast. I moved on, towards the source of the sounds.

The girls were all alive, but they'd been restrained with silver, and each had a small cut that hadn't healed (probably to provide the blood for my lure). They were a collection of Vampires, Shapeshifters, Ghouls and Weres of various stripe; the silver would be hurting the latter most. They were dressed for work, that, combined with the clothes of the customers told me that they must have been taken some time last night. About two thirds were in lingerie of some sort, some of it barely qualifying as enough for a handkerchief, much less underwear. The rest wore elegant dresses or business suits. They were largely unharmed as far as I could tell, apart from the cuts, but most could regenerate all but the most terrible wounds.

The room was bare concrete, with a few storage crates and plastic sheets against one wall. The girls were up against the far wall to the door, huddled together, heads bowed, some crying. Price was in the centre of them, head held high, a look of fury on her face.

I was about to exit the Shadow Realm so I could free them when I sensed... *something* in there with them. I stopped and looked very carefully, searching the room with both my eyes and my Mage Sight...

There!

Whatever it was, it was oozing along the ceiling. It was about the size of a pony, a mass of thick tentacles and oily black flesh. It had no eyes, or mouths that I could see, but its underside was hidden from me. I had no doubt that if I entered the room, that thing would drop on my friends, and I was fairly sure that Solomon wouldn't have left something guarding them if it couldn't kill them all with the slightest provocation.

Bearing in mind Solomon's predilections, it almost had to be a Demon, which was a problem; Demons were not to be underestimated. Its movements were smooth and almost graceful, leaving an oily residue as it moved around a broad circle, like a dog leashed to a post in a garden. I could feel its mind, and it was a dreadful, slimy thing, full of hunger and malice; but it was also simple, animalistic. I might be able to interfere with it. That was the easiest way to deal with the problem, and safest for the girls.

But it was a risk to touch something of the Pit, the deep Black, with my mind...

I did it, anyway.

But not before I arranged a little insurance. I took a few minutes to craft what you might describe as a Magical Emissions Sink. Mage senses worked by detecting the residual Magic let off by a Spell. Some people were more sensitive than others, but most Magical beings had some ability to detect such things. I had to assume that, wherever Solomon was, he was in detection range of this room, so I had to make sure that anything I did would go unnoticed, at least until I could get the ladies away.

I cast the Sink, formed a Mental Probe and lanced it straight into the Demon's tiny mind all in the space of a second. Finding its movement centres was difficult as they were spread out and hard to lock on to. It fought me *very* hard, but my practice with Porter paid off, and I quickly made progress.

The Demon wanted to go for Price, but I managed to interfere with it enough to lock it in place while I tore through what the monster had in place of mental architecture. The design of its brain and neurons was very redundant, with many clusters of tentacles controlled by a smaller brain, each of which I had to disable to stop it attacking one of the girls.

It was smart enough to know that it was under attack, and that it was losing. I felt it gather itself to scream for help, to summon its Master, and I *barely* stopped it. I thanked God for the piece of luck that had me attacking its mind. If I'd tried attacking it externally, it would certainly have gotten a warning off.

I attacked all the harder, throwing out neural shredders that tore its mind apart, millions of delicate mental strands were obliterated and smashed, and it didn't last long after that.

Finally, it died, its essence returning to the Pit, the body turning to ash and dust. I let out a breath; that could have gone very badly...

I stepped out of the Shadow Realm and into the room, which was dimly lit. The ladies made as if to scream, but they were smart, and quick. They recognised me and settled down, more than one sagging in relief as I came across to Price. I used my Will to snap her bonds, and then moved on to the next while she started peeling the silver away from the others. Tethys's sister Karina smiled at me as I passed and I returned the expression.

"Where's Crystal?" I whispered to Price.

"He has her elsewhere," she whispered back, "insurance, he said. To make sure we wouldn't try anything. He mentioned the penthouse, but that may have been a lie, or a bluff."

I had to admit, it was a clever plan. Use Price and her girls as bait, making sure they wouldn't try to escape by taking one of their own; lure me in to rescue them, at which point a Demon would drop on my head and start eating me, which would in turn alert him in time to come finish me off.

Very neat, very crafty.

Wow, did I get lucky!

And it would have worked, too, if I hadn't become more sensitive to the Black. If he'd done this even a few weeks ago, before my exposure, I wouldn't have felt the creature before entering the room, at which point it would have been too late.

It took us a few minutes to free everyone, and they huddled together as I turned to Price.

"I'm going to open a Portal back to my place," I said, "Get everyone through as quickly as you can, I'm still new at it."

"Won't *he* feel it?" Price asked, her voice trembling a little as she spoke of the man who'd imprisoned her in her own home.

"I'm shielding this room. It'll work for a little while yet. Do you understand what you need to do?"

She nodded, and I concentrated hard; praying that I didn't screw it up.

A patch of air shimmered and then brightened before opening like an eye to reveal my front lawn.

"Go!" I rasped, my concentration wavering as my emotions started getting the better of me. After all, the last time someone I cared about ended up in Solomon's hands, I'd had to fight their *corpse*.

The ladies didn't need to be told twice and ran, two by two, straight through. Price was last and cupped my cheek.

"Don't be too long, Mathew Graves," she said.

I nodded and she darted through. I let the Portal close and opened a new Gate into the Shadow Realm. I wasted no time heading up to the top floor. Lie or not, the penthouse suited Solomon's ego, and it was the natural place to start.

As soon as I'd reached the Shadow counterpart of the top floor, I heard sobbing through a Shadow and headed towards the source.

"What could you possibly want?!" I heard Crystal scream, pain running through her voice.

I had to stop myself rushing in there, but I *knew* that this would end badly if I did things stupidly.

Solomon chuckled nastily.

"Nothing you can give me, I'm afraid," he said, evenly, like he was discussing the weather, not torturing an innocent girl, "The only thing you can give me is some amusement. You might provide a nice distraction for the Shadowborn when he arrives, but I doubt it'll come to that. It shouldn't be too much longer now. The package should be there in a little while."

Thank God for over-eager postmen, I was early!

I opened a small Gate and looked at what I was dealing with.

Crystal was tied to a chair, again with silver. She was stripped to the waist, and covered with deep cuts. She was still bleeding freely from her face and chest.

I felt fury, and then a horrible hatred, and all of it at that creature standing next to her.

Solomon wore a suit of baroque black armour, made of heavy metal plates that covered him from neck to toe, leaving his head bare. It hugged his form, perfectly made for him, articulated around his joints to allow easy movement. He stood with a blade in his hand, covered in her blood.

I had to say that he looked the worse for wear since

the last time I'd seen him. His skin, one bright with life was now pale and sickly, sunken at the cheeks. His eyes were dark and hooded, glinting with sadism and madness. His lips were blue, like he hadn't been breathing, his teeth yellow, lined with black, like they were rotting in his mouth. His face was covered in black veins, where his poisonous Magic was corrupting his very flesh.

The Black... it just wasn't good for you. It was corrosive to the body, the mind and the soul. It brought out the very worst in the people that used it, and Solomon was a sadistic, murderous bastard *before* he'd made his literal deal with the devil (who I was going to kick firmly in his cosmically powerful *balls* one day, but I digress).

Crystal was crying, obviously in pain. I started casting, unwilling to waste another second. I wasn't going for a quick win; I just needed two things to work. The first was a Spell called Alexandria's Hope. I crafted it carefully, knowing that it was crucial to how this would turn out. I had to let him cut Crystal again while I was doing it, but finally I was ready, and the cast was perfect! The Spell latched onto him and melded with his aura in an instant.

He felt it and turned towards me.

Then I threw *pure* Magic at him.

At his shoulder, to be precise.

Mage Sight had allowed me to see the residue of my earlier Black Magic attack. He'd cut the Grotesque arm away, as you might expect, but the root of it was still there. A little raw Magic was more than enough to wake it up, especially *my* raw Magic (make of that what you will; I was far from happy about it, even if I was willing to take advantage of it).

He screamed as a brand new limb tore its way clear of his shoulder armour, the plates ripped clear of the leather strapping to fly across the room. The limb formed as before, but bigger, thicker, and more muscular, black veins protruding from the pale flesh. It was a complete hand this time, and it closed around his face in a single, terrible movement that tore through flesh and crushed bone.

Such was the way of Black Magic; if you didn't dispose of it properly, it came back stronger until you did, almost like an infection.

I enlarged my Gate and stepped through it, lashing out with my Shadows while he was distracted (and bleeding). Barbed tendrils, as hard as diamond, slipped between the plates of his abdominal armour and stabbed into his chest, slamming him back and through the window behind him. He fell hard, but his wings extended before he could hit the ground (damn it), flapping hard to get him moving away from me. He smashed into trees, and then into buildings as he fought both against the Grotesque limb and gravity, gradually dragging himself back into the air, almost flailing as he drove himself faster and faster.

I only waited long enough to make sure that he wasn't coming back before I darted to Crystal's side. I used my Will to pull her restraints off before kneeling next to her and pulling her into a hug. She sobbed hard as she sagged against me.

"Oh," she managed, wrapping her arms around my neck, "oh, Matty, Matty. You came! You came for me."

"Of course I did," I said, holding her tight, not caring about getting blood on me, which now that I thought about it, was still oozing. What the hell was on that weapon?

"Are you hungry?" I asked, "You need to feed?"

"No, that's okay," she said, but her pupils were dilated, her fangs were showing, and she was licking her lips.

I shook my head and focussed on a little Extraction Spell, holding out my hand. A sphere of blood appeared and expanded to about four inches across. Crystal's head darted forward and she sucked greedily, drinking it all down.

Her wounds closed, but not all the way, and they were black around the edges, red and inflamed, which was worrying. Vampires didn't get infections. So, I repeated my spell and she drank again, her wounds closing fully this time.

"Mm, that's nice," she purred, "You do know how to

treat a girl, Mathew Graves."

I held her cheeks and looked in her eyes.

"I'm sorry I wasn't here sooner."

"You did just fine, as far as I'm concerned!" she said, dragging my lips to hers, she planted a deep kiss on me, and I tasted a little of my own blood on them, "I'm alive, I'm fine, and I got to drink a little of the good stuff. Everything's coming up Crystal!"

I chuckled and hugged her again, kissing her cheek.

"Affectionate today, aren't we?" she whispered in my ear, rubbing my back with her hands.

"I thought I'd be too late."

"But you weren't. And that pussy was nothing. I've had worse spankings off your Kandi."

I laughed at that but couldn't bring myself to let her go.

"Matty, if you hold me any tighter, there's a risk of me popping out of these panties," she said.

"Sorry," I said, finally pulling back.

"Oh, I wasn't complaining," she said impishly, "I just wanted my hands free to properly apprecia- oh, are the others okay, by the way?!"

"They're fine, I found them first; they told me where you were. They're at my place now."

I stood and offered my hand. She took it and stood up before slipping on a silk robe she pulled from a nearby cupboard. I focussed again, and after a few moments a Portal appeared. I led the way through.

She nodded approvingly.

"Finally figured that out, huh?" she said, pecking my cheek fondly.

"It took a lot of work," I said proudly, "Quite a few... mistakes."

"After this is over, you can tell me all about it. I should warn you, it's is going to be a very, *very* long and intensive... chat," she said in a husky voice.

I shivered and the Portal collapsed behind us with a pop

and a flare that smacked a tiny bolt of electricity into my behind, which made me yelp and jump.

"Ow!" I said, rubbing my bottom, "See what happens when you distract the Magician?"

"Aw, poor baby, want I should kiss it better?" she asked, stroking my arm.

"A little bit, actually," I said with a grin.

She giggled, and was about to reply when...

"Mathew Graves!" Cassandra barked from the front door. I winced.

"Ooh, you're in trouble!" Crystal said, hiding behind me.

"Why are there fifty Vampires and their hangers-on in my house?!" my Warden shouted, "And what were you doing out without an escort?"

"Crystal, would you go in? I think I'll need to have a word with my friend."

"Don't let her spank you, that's my job," she said, nosing my cheek as she walked past, her bottom rather eye-catching in that robe...

"Graves!"

"Sorry!" I said, turning my eyes and my brain back to the situation.

"What happened?" Cassandra asked.

I told her everything.

She didn't like it.

She didn't like what I'd have to do next any better.

"No, Mathew, I forbid it!" she said.

"I have to, Cassie. I'm finishing this now, while he's hurt and distracted. Just trust me, alright?"

"You haven't come out too well against this man, Mathew, what makes you think this time will be any better?"

I smiled grimly, "This time, *I'm* coming for *him*."

"How do you even know where he is?" she asked, her scowl wavering.

My grin became wider.

Alexandria's Hope was invented by a Greek Sorcerer in 230 BC. He was a bit of a sailor, but, like myself, a terrible navigator, so he created a Spell that he could bind to a person or location, that would forever allow him to know where it was, almost like a compass tied to his Aura, pointing him in that direction. His first casting had been on the Pharos of Alexandria, the great lighthouse, hence the name.

For my purposes, I'd wired it into Solomon's very Aura, and in such a way that it would take a rather powerful Magician quite some time to get it out. Until they did, I'd always know what direction he was in, and a general idea of the distance. According to the compass on my phone, he was North-North-East of me. I felt him to be about ten miles distant and getting further away, moving at a pretty fair clip, too.

Before Cassandra had the chance to talk me out of it, I wrapped myself in Shadows and darted into the air, rocketing after him. I made sure to get further up, so I could attack from above. I had no intention of being gentle this time. I was going to hit him with everything I had.

I increased my speed and quickly started to gain on him. He was well out of Stonebridge now, deep in the countryside, passing over sleepy hamlets and small market towns. I increased my height a little more and cast Mage Sight.

There he was!

A mile ahead and getting closer. He was trailing black blood from a brand new gaping wound in his shoulder, where he'd managed to rip the arm away again. His flight path was erratic and weaving, I assumed that he was in pain, and was pleased.

I threw my Shadow Lance from thirty feet away, and the bugger was still fast enough to evade the worst of it! It should have hit him centre mass, and caused his chest to explode, but instead it clipped a wing and tore off a chunk.

He still screamed and fell out of the sky, plummeting straight down, barely producing enough lift to avoid ploughing into the ground.

He hit the top of a hill, tearing a furrow in the soft earth as he skidded to a halt. I landed, Shields in place, and resumed my attack, tendrils of Shadow darting out, sharp and barbed. He screamed in pain as I tore off an arm and half his untouched wing, but then he had a shield up, and his sneer was back in place soon after.

I started gathering energy, Space mostly, as he conjured his black sword out of thin air, into his remaining hand, and leapt for me. He ran straight into my Shadows and slowed to a halt before I tossed him back, Shields and all. He landed on his feet and threw his sword at my face. I don't know how he knew where I was, but the sword was right on target, and only a hasty Will Shield stopped my head from getting bisected, as it passed right through my Shadows.

I saw him gather energy for a Portal, he was trying to escape!

Thankfully my own Spell was ready and I released it.

It was something else Hopkins had taught me. I may not be the best Portal maker ever, but I could mess them up just fine. The Portal Jammer scattered any Space Energy that tried to coalesce into a Portal, with a radius of about a mile, he wouldn't be escaping. If he was fazed, he gave no indication. He just smiled nastily and came back at me, his body reeking even more of Black Magic as his wounds healed, though the one in his shoulder remained open and weeping.

That was actually an interesting point. A wound made by Black Magic that couldn't be repaired by the Black... Was that a testament to the Black's ability to injure, or my greater affinity for it? Probably not a question I would enjoy the answer to.

He tore into my Shadows, and smacked straight into another Will Shield, where he took a face full of Force, which blasted his own Shields to bits, forcing him to retreat, but they were back up again in an instant, and he resumed his attack.

He was stronger this time.

It seemed that every time I came across him, he was more powerful. His shields regenerated faster, his Black Magic reserves were deeper, and his wounds were healing at an even more rapid rate; his arm was already half re-grown; his wings were already back to normal... I wondered why he even bothered to run away from me!

I was surprised that he wasn't using Black Magic as a ranged attack this time, though. It had been a big problem during our first battle; perhaps he was simply too angry? Too distracted? Either way, I wasn't complaining!

He blurred and the sword was back in his hand; then he was driving back at me, cutting through my defences one by one.

I was continually gathering energy, but I was very concerned. His defences seemed to be getting more resistant to my every attack the more I used them. I tried a Chaos Ball, and it barely made a dent. A flurry of Shadow Lances hardly slowed him down, nothing even got *close* to his skin anymore.

And I was getting tired. My energy supply wasn't infinite, and I'd already used quite a bit of it during the rescue and pursuit, whereas Solomon showed no signs of slowing down. If I didn't find a way to end this quickly... well, you can guess what would happen.

I cast a Dispel Cannon, and that worked for a while. His Shields came apart, and I managed to slide some Heat through, which charred him from neck to groin, causing his armour to smoke.

He just laughed as the damage repaired itself.

There was *one* thing I could do...

His body was full of it, after all, that's why he able to regenerate and bring up new Shields so quickly.

The Black.

I could feel it, it was all right there. I could end this with an instant of effort. The Black in his body was so concentrated, so potent, that with his shields in place, there was little else

I could do; he had just evolved too far since our first battle. What would he be like in a month, a year?

What if he didn't *stop* getting stronger?

Time stopped.

"Quite the conundrum you find yourself in, Darling," Gabrielle said from behind me.

I turned and tried not to roll my eyes. They were both there, Rose looked concerned, Gabrielle excited. They were unchanged from our last encounter; I could have seen them ten minutes ago.

"Really, do tell," I said.

"Glad you asked," the Succubus said evilly, "You find yourself opposing an all but unbeatable enemy, and the only way to defeat him is to let go of your precious principles and use the Magic that you fear so greatly, but therein lies an even greater problem. If you *do* manage to use the Black to kill him, well then... he's dead. And you're the one who killed him. You will have taken a life with Black Magic. It's hard to come back from that."

She grinned, Rose just stared at me, very intently, watching for something.

"But, if you *don't*, then he goes free and he comes back for you, and everyone you love. He'll torture them to death one by one until he finally decides to deal with you. So, my lovely Magician, what's it going to be? Death or damnation?"

I couldn't help but chuckle.

"Something funny?" Gabrielle asked, her eyes narrowing.

"You should have advised him to move quicker."

"Really?" Gabrielle asked, crossing her arms, looking rather annoyed, "And why's that?"

"Because he gave me three months to think this all through, to obsess, plot, plan and figure. Not a great idea, Gabby," I said with a smirk.

"What are you talking about?" she asked. Rose was

standing just a little straighter.

"You told me yourself," I said, "'Resurrection isn't one of the powers my side offers'. There's only one way you could have sent him back up here. He's a Demon."

Gabrielle stomped her foot and scowled at Rose, who was beaming at me.

"And that means that if I smash him, he just goes down to the Pit, he doesn't die, I'm not a murderer. But, thinking that I'm going to be and committing the act anyway produces much the same stain on the soul. It's actually rather neat, I have to give that to you."

Gabrielle swore. A lot, seriously I'd never heard so much profanity in one place, "I told him not to dick around with you, but would he listen? Oh no, there had to be an intricate plan, we couldn't just slip a little Black Magic into your bacon, it had to be *clever*!"

"Wait, what's that about my bacon?"

Rose chuckled.

"No! Wait a second," Gabrielle said, spinning back to me, "I still win! You can't beat him without the Black!"

"You know, that was *very* nearly true," I said, "but, bless you two, you've given me just enough time to think, and I do believe that I have another solution."

"You are *really* starting to annoy me," Gabrielle said with a glare.

I looked her in her red eyes and smiled at her.

"No I'm not," I said softly.

She growled low in her throat and took a step towards me.

"I am going to hurt you," she said throatily, her eyes dancing with anger and what looked disturbingly like arousal, "I'm going to make you *beg*..."

"Of that, I have no doubt," I replied, "but right now, I have something rather pressing, so, if you wouldn't mind?"

"This isn't over, Darling," she said, her fangs suddenly very long and *very* sharp...

"I know."

She vanished.

Rose smiled and clapped.

"So when did you figure it all out?" she asked, coming over to stand next to me.

I grinned.

"Oh, it took me far longer than I'm happy to admit. I've been distracted lately."

She laughed and hugged me tightly.

"You wonderful man! But she's going to be very angry with you for a while. You really have a terrible habit of gloating. Pride's a sin, you know!"

I chuckled, "Let her be angry, I owe her a lot. Unknowingly or not, she helped save my soul."

I was fairly certain she'd done it deliberately, though. Gabrielle was nobody's fool, and she'd been dropping hints both broad and subtle about what Solomon had become. Not only had she saved me, she'd meant to. The rest... that was just theatre, but necessary. I doubted that Neil would be happy if it ever came out that she'd done all this on purpose.

Unless it was all some elaborate double or triple bluff that was supposed to lull me into a sense of false security... ugh, too complicated.

"Oh, can I tell her you said that? The look on her face will be just priceless!" Rose said.

"Have at it."

"Do you really have a plan for dealing with him?" Rose asked, nodding at Solomon.

"If you can confirm that I won't be actually killing him?"

"You know I can't do that," she said, but she smiled.

I'd known for some time that Solomon wasn't a Cherub anymore, or a Fallen one, for that matter, but that was all I was really sure of. His Aura had been packed with conflicting energies, which left me in some doubt over what I was *really* dealing with. But, thanks to my Liaisons, and what they *weren't* saying, I was finally able to act with confidence (not that I wouldn't have destroyed him, one way or another, after what had happened to Maggie. At least now I was able to do it without staining myself irretrievably).

"I guess I'll have to take the chance then," I said, looking deep into my mind, for High Magic.

For Death.

"I'll be off, Matty," she said, kissing my cheek gently, "see you soon."

"Oh, Rose, before you go, I have to ask. Maggie... did she... is she... *home*, now?"

That sounded stupid, even to me.

"You know I can't tell you that, Mathew."

"I know, I just thought I'd ask."

"I can tell you that she was a sweet soul," she said pointedly, "kind and generous... *good*, understand?"

I smiled at her, "Thanks for everything Rose. And you really did give me the time I needed."

She held me, her head under my chin, and then she stepped back and vanished.

Time resumed.

I was ready.

Solomon leaped back into the attack. I strengthened my shields and focussed even harder. The Sight snapped on, and once again, Death was all around me.

But not in Solomon, which was actually reassuring. No Death means no Entropy, no Entropy means no Life. He wasn't alive, and thus, I couldn't kill him. I could only send him back home, where hopefully Neil will have an Imp waiting with a particularly sharp (and barbed) pitchfork.

I drew Entropy in by the bucket-load.

Now, you'd think that by drawing in Death, things around you would die, but it's the opposite. Without any Entropy around, the world burst into bloom and growth. The grass instantly grew and became greener, the air moved a little quicker. Little daisies bloomed.

That wasn't a problem for plants, which were relatively simple things, although the daisies would likely die in the cold now, and I felt like a bit of a dick about that. But you shouldn't do anything like that to a complex creature, or what you got was *everything* growing out of control. That's how you got things like tumours, for example.

Anyway, my Aura was now full of Entropy. That *did* feel cold, and awful.

But damn if it wasn't effective.

I focussed it into a beam, and he wasn't ready for it. His shield bowed and shattered. The energy tore straight into his torso and cut him neatly in two below the stomach.

He screamed as he fell, his eyes filled with pure agony and awful hatred as smacked into the ground, facing upwards, thrashing against the pain of Death eating him from below. I emerged from my Shadows so I could look down at him with my own eyes, rather than with Magic. I wanted to savour this moment.

He bucked and clawed at the terrible wound. It was grey and rotting, bubbling where Entropy and Black Magic were battling it out. I knew which would eventually win, but I had a little time.

"Oh how I wish I could make this hurt more," I said, sending further beams of Entropy to snip off the last of his wings and his other arm. He screamed over and over, and I did my best to fix it in my memory.

I wanted to hurt him, to make him pay for Maggie, for the Witches, the Duellists, and bloody Aldwich... but I dared not take too much time. He might recover, and I couldn't risk him becoming immune to Entropy, as well.

"Screw you, just do it!" he screamed; at long last, he was in too much pain to call his own power. Speaking from experience, there's very little that hurt more than Death Magic.

I glared down at him one last time.

"Well, if you insist," I said, my voice utterly unrecognisable, cold and dark.

I conjured a little ball of pure Magic, and dropped it carefully into his mangled shoulder. Like some horrific Jack-in-the-box, that Grotesque limb returned, and this time he didn't have Magic or even limbs capable of stopping it. The arm was now thicker than his thigh had been, with seven fingers, each tipper by a razor-sharp talon.

It reached for his head, and Solomon started screaming again.

I watched as Solomon was banished, and it took about fifteen *excruciating* minutes, but finally, once his face was ruin, and he'd stopped screaming, the limb reached down and tore out the Demon's heart. He collapsed into dust, leaving the ugly limb and its dreadful roots of blood vessels and veins behind (still writhing and twitching) for me to put a final end to with the last of my Entropy.

I watched as the dust blew away, the fresh air taking the stench of him with it until the last traces were gone, and I could relax at last. I felt the sun on my face and took a deep breath, finally dropping my shields.

Bloody hell, that wasn't fun...

But it *was* over.

"That was cold, little brother," Killian said, making me jump.

"Jesus Christ!" I bellowed, "Why does everyone feel the bollocking need to try and make me shit myself?!"

I turned towards him and he barked out a laugh.

"Sorry," he said, walking over to pat my shoulder, "That was some impressive work. Controlled. I felt it three counties over!"

"Thanks," I said, "And he's not dead, just to clarify."

"I know a banishing when I see one, Kid. I was referring to the torture as 'cold'. And the whole 'ripped apart by his own evil hand while unable to help himself' thing. Speaking as someone who saw the Inquisition at its height... that was lovely."

"He... he did some bad things to a friend of mine. If I

could have been assured that he wouldn't get away, I'd have made it last a lot longer."

"I know what happened," he said, sadly, "I'm sorry about the girl."

I nodded, "So am I, it was such a bloody waste."

"It always is," he said quietly, "Come on, let's get out of this field and Portal you home. Goodness knows what's happening back there."

# CHAPTER 31

It was bedlam.

The last time I'd packed the Vampires into the house, at least the staff had been given a little warning. This time there was a mad scramble of women who needed clothes, feeding (which presented its own problems) and shelter from the sun (not urgent, but necessary).

Killian and I arrived about the same time as an ambulance from the James Sutcliff hospital, which was quickly (and to my relief) revealed to be full of coolers (three guesses what was in them).

We walked in to find my staff darting about, their hands full of sheets and clothes. A jeep (one of mine) pulled up not long afterwards, and suddenly there were shopping bags being collected by a quartet of women, who smiled and hugged me on the way past to the East Wing, which was where they'd stayed the last time.

Tethys appeared from somewhere and threw herself into my arms.

"Again with the Vampires, Mathew?" she said, squeezing me tightly to her.

"I felt the need for a little attention this evening," I said.

Tethys chuckled, "Fifty-eight supernatural women and my sister... aren't we ambitious," she said, kissing my cheek playfully.

Killian snorted and waved as he walked past us towards the drawing room. Shortly afterwards, there were giggles and squeals. Apparently Lord Death was a bit of a fixture at the Red Carpet...

I held Tethys to me and she rubbed my back gently.

"Was it bad?" she asked.

"In the hotel, yes. I'm not sure about the fight."

"There was a fight? And you obviously won. Is he gone?"

"Back to the Pit, and it takes a while for anything banished there to get strong enough to be sent back. But I doubt he's getting out again. He made a deal with Neil after all."

"You want to talk about it?" she asked gently.

"I do."

"Okay, come on, Miss Jenkins has soup," she said, leading me to the kitchen.

Miss Jenkins was looking a little frazzled, but she ladled out a full bowl of something beefy for me and brought out a couple of freshly baked rolls. I thanked her and she smiled, returning to the meat she was preparing for the guests that ate solid foods.

I told Tethys what had happened and she smiled with satisfaction, dipping a spare spoon in my bowl from time to time.

"Good bloody riddance!" she said, "And very good work, Matty."

"I try," I said tiredly.

"Crystal's been asking about you, by the way," she continued, turning her eyes on me, "She's fond of you."

"I'm fond of her, too."

"They're all rather attached to you," she said, her smile widening further still, "imagine what would happen if I let them catch you sleeping."

I glared and she bit her lip.

"Stop it, I know that look," I said.

"What look's that?" she said, stroking my fingers.

"A very naughty look, indeed."

"You like the look, don't deny it," she said, lifting my fingers to her mouth and nibbling gently.

"You know I do."

"Do you have any idea what Kandi goes through when

you put this look on my face?"

I snorted, and she just smiled at me.

We sat there for a bit, just comfortable with one another.

She shoved her chair over and I put my arm around her. I kissed the side of her head and she leaned against me.

"So, you wouldn't let me keep them all last time, but how would you feel about a dozen or so? I'm willing to negotiate, but I won't go lower than eight, and I'm willing to share."

I groaned, which only made her laugh.

And that was more or less that.

Status quo restored.

Well...

Maybe not completely.

Crystal was waiting for me in my room.

Naturally I didn't notice. It was late that day. I'd spoken to Price, made sure her people were alright. She'd told me Crystal was resting, she just hadn't mentioned *where*. Tethys and Kandi had gone into the East Wing after dinner and hadn't been seen since. Karina had been her usual subtle self and groped me something vicious while pretending to hug me hello, but that was par for the course.

I'd showered and dressed for bed, tired and desperate for sleep. I only knew Crystal was there when her arms and legs went around me, and I... well there's no dignified way to say it. I squealed like a little girl and fell out of my bed with a thump.

Crystal laughed and I sat myself up on my banged bottom.

"That's not nice," I said with a glare as I stood back up.

She darted to me and wrapped her hands in my shirt, my bed sheets covering her chest as she pulled me into a kiss. Her arms went around my neck and she was up against me, warm and soft. She dragged me down onto the bed and under the covers where she held me very tightly, kissing and nibbling gently. She pulled back, her hands on my face as she smiled at me, the look full of affection.

I smiled back.

That was the start of a wonderful relationship. I have no idea what arrangements Tethys made with her, or with Price, but when the others reclaimed the Red Carpet, Crystal stayed with me. I was grateful for that; I'd been dreading the departure (particularly bearing in mind her profession). Apparently she was now working for Tethys, which both made me happy and very wary (in a good way). Tethys' sexual practical jokes were not for the faint of heart. She'd once arranged for seventeen male strippers to turn up at my evil grandmother's dinner party for her local MP. They took video, the look on her face keeps me grinning to this day...

But I digress.

I'd been forced to move back into Blackhold (literally. I'd turned up at Naiad Hall and found my stuff gone, replaced by a note from Cassandra telling me that all my things were back home and that was where they were staying for the foreseeable. Demise was with me at the time and thought it was hilarious).

Naturally that wasn't going to deter Mary, who simply declared that she and the other mother hens would come visit... and then never left. They've lived in the East Wing since then, don't ask me how that happened, but Miss Jenkins loved them, and had been mothering them every chance she got.

Tethys finally tracked Jocelyn to a small chateau in the Pyrenees, nestled in a valley that was *packed* with anti-Scrying Wards and Magical defences. If she'd been using purely Magical means, she'd never have succeeded. Jocelyn had beaten every search method Tethys' tame Magicians had at their disposal, but she still had to eat, and she still had to pay staff to look after her property, manage her finances and make sure she wasn't about to be prosecuted for spying on an Archon.

All of that required communications, and Tethys' mundane snoops finally sniffed her out after more than two weeks of electronic monitoring and painstaking searches through phone company records.

When Tethys actually explained to me the work that had been done, I authorised a sizable bonus for her people on the spot, it was *that* impressive.

Anyway, Kron dropped in to have a little chat with her, which eventually led to The Primus being dragged from the Conclave building by his ear, and then to the Farm for a six month sentence. It wasn't what I'd have given him, but politics demanded that we be reasonable. We didn't want a revolution and, besides, being ejected from power, never to return, was a wonderful punishment for such an ambitious man.

So things actually started to get to a new, better, normal, and I was happy for once.

But there was still the small matter of the Demon I'd annoyed...

Normally when Gabrielle woke me up, it involved a kiss and something akin to a very naughty cuddle.

This time she dragged me out of bed and threw me to the ground. Before I could wake up, she'd straddled my chest and was glaring down at me, her nails digging slightly into my skin.

"I *saved your soul*?!" she almost shrieked, full Demon now, not a trace of Illusion, "I'm a laughing stock because of you!"

"You'll have to forgive me, what's going on?" I asked, still half-asleep.

"What's going on is that I'm going to bloody kill you!" she hissed.

I raised an eyebrow.

"What?!" she said, her nails, no, bloody *claws*, dug in a little deeper, "What now?!"

"If you meant me harm, you wouldn't be here now. Mira wouldn't have let you in."

"Can't you stop being a know-it-all for one bloody

minute?!"

"What I *know* is that when your lot offer a temptation, you leave an 'out', an alternative. I'm guessing that's part of the rules?"

She glared, but nodded.

"Well, you told me the out, and you *meant* to. You helped me, and it *wasn't* an accident. I can't repay that debt, but if you ever need me, all you have to do is ask."

"How can you know these things?! It's not right."

"I know monsters, Gabby, and I know intelligence. You may be a Demon, but you're no monster. And you're too smart to make mistakes like that. I won't insult you by asking why; just know that I'm very grateful."

She scowled down at me, but her eyes softened, just a little.

"Do you remember when you came for me? When I was in that circle?" she asked, leaning down a bit.

I nodded, I was hardly likely to forget. She'd been taken by essence harvesters, drained nearly to banishment. I'd fed her back up to health, with a kiss. Nowhere near as romantic as it sounds, she could have killed me.

"Kiss me like that now," she said, smirking, "and I'll consider us even."

"No musk this time," I insisted.

She grinned, "Alright, just this once."

We kissed, and I didn't shield. She fed and made happy sounds for a long time until finally she pulled back, a satisfied look on her face, leaving me rather randy and a little tired.

"One more step towards my side of the road, Mathew," she said, pecking my lips once more.

I cupped her face with my hands and smiled.

"Very scary, Gabby," I said.

She turned away from me, but then stopped, snapping her fingers.

"I almost forgot. Message from Head Office. My father says thanks for returning his property in a timely manner, and far ahead of schedule. He would like to assure you that Solomon will be... well taken care of for the foreseeable future."

"That's reassuring."

She smiled, it was a very dark thing, "It should be. He failed to live up to his end of the bargain. Head Office doesn't like that."

"And his end of the bargain would be?"

As if I didn't know. He was there to infect me with the Black, and he nearly managed, too. I doubted that he'd known what the plan was. He was only supposed to hit me with the stuff, enough that I couldn't expel it in time.

Rather than reply, she just smiled, and then she was gone, without Crystal ever having heard a thing. She stirred as I got back into bed.

"Mm, Matty, you smell nice," she purred, half asleep.

Oh bollocks. Damn it, Gabby!

## Afterword

Thanks for reading *Heart's Darkness*! I hope that it was worth the wait, and that you enjoyed it. I would like to say a huge thank you to all my readers for sticking with me, and for all your emails and posts of support, they have been a real gift to me.

Heart's Darkness is a transitional book, where Mathew begins his journey from student to master, growing into his role as the First Shadow. The next book will begin 'The Descent Sequence', which this novel (and the one before) has (hopefully) set up. I leave you to guess what that title means, and what the books that follow will be like!

I can't say when Book 6 will be out, but it won't be a colossal wait (we aren't talking years, don't worry!). In the meantime, thanks again for reading!

If you enjoyed the book, and you have some spare time, I would greatly appreciate a review, and any comments or questions can be sent to me directly at hdaroberts@gmail.com, or to my Facebook Page, where I will be posting updates in the future.

Made in the USA
Monee, IL
02 April 2023

31118239R00256